The Looters

HAROLD ROBBINS
AND JUNIUS PODRUG

The
LOOTERS

A TOM DOHERTY ASSOCIATES BOOK
NEW YORK

THE LOOTERS

A Forge Book
Published by Tom Doherty Associates, LLC
175 Fifth Avenue
New York, NY 10010

www.tor-forge.com

Forge® is a registered trademark of Tom Doherty Associates, LLC.

Library of Congress Cataloging-in-Publication Data
Robbins, Harold, 1916–1997.
    The looters / Harold Robbins and Junius Podrug.—1st hardcover ed.
      p. cm.
    "A Forge Book"—T.p. verso.
    ISBN-13: 978-0-7653-1370-6
    ISBN-10: 0-7653-1370-7
    1. Antiques—Fiction. 2. Museums—Fiction. 3. Art thefts—Fiction. I. Podrug, Junius.
II. Title.
PS3568.O224D48 2006
813'.54—dc22

2007018766

First Edition: September 2007

Printed in the United States of America

0 9 8 7 6 5 4 3 2 1

Acknowledgments

I want to thank Hildegard Krische, Ginger Bevard, Madison Myers Keller, Bob Gleason, Eric Raab, Elizabeth Winick, Jonathon Lyons, and Barbara Wild for their assistance in putting together this book project.

❖

Harold Robbins

left behind a rich heritage of novel ideas

and works in progress when he passed away in 1997.

Harold Robbins's estate and his editor worked with

a carefully selected writer to organize and complete

Harold Robbins's ideas to create this novel,

inspired by his storytelling brilliance,

in a manner faithful to

the Robbins style.

❖

1

❖

Oh, how the mighty have fallen. I railed against the depressing thought, but it punched back. I had had it all, but now I was on the run from killers and the police, stuck in traffic as the Jersey-bound lanes of the George Washington Bridge turned into a parking lot. My gutless rental car was boxed in between a tanker truck that blew lung-blackening smoke back at me, a dangerously shaky, overloaded car carrier on one side and a Bekins moving van on the other. Another behemoth was behind me, but all I could make out was a grille the size of a wall with a silver bulldog glaring down.

Earlier I saw that the Bekins van had a California license plate. Jesus . . . what I would give to crawl into the back of that van and snuggle between mattresses as it headed for the West Coast—or anywhere but here.

Behind me was Manhattan, my penthouse with a park view and a lifestyle I might never see again. A thirtysomething woman with ambition and drive, I had ten good career years out of grad school with a master's in art history. Avoiding the safety net of academia, I had jumped with both feet into the cutthroat world where the superrich pay tens of millions for "priceless" art and antiquities.

❖

What a wake-up call that was about human nature for a girl from backwater Ohio. That writer who said the rich were different didn't go far enough—the superrich were way different, far out. They lived in a rarified atmosphere of privilege but often were bored and eager for stimulation. And for reinforcement of their own accomplishments. It's hard to keep your ego swollen when you've never had to do anything but eat, breathe, shit, and sleep.

Buying something that no one else could possess was a way for them to flex muscles. The rarer, the more desirable. That turned the world of art into a playground—and battleground—for billionaires, an atmosphere even more ruthless than that surrounding owning a champion racehorse or a sports team. Money and ego have turned the quest for art into a ruthless business in which the superrich battled to possess the rarest and most beautiful objets d'art on earth. Prices paid were stratospheric. The hundred-million-dollar mark for a painting by an artist most people would not recognize the name of had long since been surpassed.

When billionaire greed and egos collide, anything goes, at any price. And where mere money won't do the job, drugs, sex, and murder are used.

Yes, I saw some things a woman shouldn't see. Maybe I even did a few things a woman shouldn't do. Hard lessons. The Greeks thought highly of the concept of *pathos-mathos*—gaining wisdom through suffering. I wish to hell I'd gained insights with a little less damage to my life. If I only knew then what I knew now . . .

I sighed and melted down a little more in the seat. I was tired, beat, soul-weary. *Madison, you really know how to enjoy yourself.*

Madison Dupre. That's my name. My friends call me Maddy. But right now I had some openings on my list of friends.

LOST IN THOUGHT, GAZING blankly as traffic moved, I got a blast from the bulldog truck's horn behind me and almost jumped out of the seat. I pressed the gas, sending the cheap little import surging a few dozen feet before I had to hit the brakes again to keep from rear-ending the tanker truck in front of me. Tight-jawed, I dropped my chin to my chest and told myself to stay calm. The grating horn had scorched my frayed nerves and made my heart jackhammer.

I was usually a calm person, but I hated traffic, hated big trucks, and hated to be stuck in traffic with big trucks, breathing in their stinking fumes . . . when I desperately had to flee the city. My life was on the line and I was getting more agitated as the traffic slugged along.

I checked my rearview mirror as that monster rig closed in again until I could only see the massive front grille. If I were in my expensive sports car, I would have flipped him the bird despite constant reminders to myself not to antagonize anyone because road rage created roadkill. *Deal with it.* But being hemmed in gave me the sick feeling in my stomach that I was in a prison cell. I had already briefly experienced a jail cell at the federal detention center, and that was enough for a lifetime.

I turned on the radio to hear traffic reports on the threes.

"Forty-five-minute delay for the GW out to Jersey."

I banged my hands on the steering wheel. I already knew it—hell, I was stuck in it—but hearing it made it worse. It took away hope.

Okay, think positive. Forty-five minutes wasn't so bad. It could be worse. The bridge could be closed even longer for an accident, bridge maintenance, someone being murdered . . .

The sick feeling in my stomach started again. They wouldn't try anything in front of hundreds of witnesses. I was sure of that. But not that sure. Only one thing was for certain: If they were behind me, they were stuck, too.

Get ahold of yourself, girl. My nerves were on edge, and crawling in this stop-and-go traffic didn't help the situation; it just fueled my frustration and paranoia.

I thought about my predicament as I sat in the stalled traffic. My life was in ruins, the police were looking for me, and on the seat beside me was something "priceless" that someone wanted very badly, enough to kill for it. And here I was stuck in traffic on the world's busiest bridge.

I had left my $85,000 XK Jaguar parked in a monthly garage, my $10,000-a-month penthouse, my designer wardrobe, and everything else I'd worked for back in the city to run from imminent danger. I hadn't taken my Jag because I figured I'd be less noticeable in a rental car. They probably also knew where the car was garaged. At least that was my theory.

The traffic started moving. I started to zip out of my lane and in front of the moving van, but my economy rental car didn't have enough horses. Another car zipped into the coveted space.

❖

My mind went back to my problems. How could I have gotten myself in such a mess? I was basically an honest person, never involved in any trouble before. Now I'd gotten myself into trouble with a capital *T.* I had made a deal with the devil and he was coming to collect when I had only wanted to right a wrong.

Naïve, that's what I'd been. I thought ten years of big city and bright lights had made me as tough as the crowd I ran with, but the small town in me came percolating out when I saw greed that couldn't be satisfied with less than murder.

Another opportunity to change lanes arose and I pressed hard on the gas pedal. My Jag would have compressed me back into the seat with g-force, but this car had the surge of a tortoise. The brakes of the car carrier made a horrible rusty squeal as the big rig rattled and shuddered to a stop behind me. At least the driver didn't lay on the horn.

I rolled down the window a few inches and stuck my hand out to wave "thanks for letting me in." When I checked my side-view mirror I saw his hand come out with his prominent third finger extended in my direction.

I didn't seem to be able to please anyone.

Off the GW Bridge and on my way through Newark, I was exhausted and tried of traffic and trucks. I needed to get off the road for a while, get some rest, clear my head, and figure a way out of the mess. Only early evening, but I was too mentally drained to keep the car going.

A motel sign in the distance advertised "easy access" and "cheap hourly rates." Hourly rates? Perfect. It didn't take much imagination to figure out what that meant. Nobody would think to look for me at an "adult" motel.

The motel was close to the freeway exit. It looked pretty much like what could be expected from the neon sign—two stories of tacky pink caked on like too much powder on a whore.

I took one look at the place and shook my head. *Oh yes, how the mighty have fallen. . . .*

I was beginning to sound like a broken record even to myself.

Walking into the lobby confirmed that the motel was a sleazy dive for paid quickies, but I figured that a place that accommodated prostitutes and rented porn movies wouldn't be the kind of place to look for someone who lived in the Museum Mile area with a view of Central Park.

After I paid for the room, ignoring the lecherous look from the clerk and the hint that I should "tip him" if I planned to use my room for "business purposes," I walked past a condom machine, up the wood steps, and down the outside corridor to my room. I had the last room on the end, the one closest to the freeway. No surprise that the room reeked of cigarettes and store-bought sex. Both were popular vices.

I had asked for a second-floor room, as I always did after reading that it was a safer bet than a ground-floor motel room for a woman traveling alone. After I double-locked the door and wedged a chair under the door handle, I checked the big front sliding glass window. Unlatched, of course. I locked it.

The bedspread smelled as if it hadn't had sex washed off in a while, so I took it off and put my long coat on top of the bedsheets to lie on it. The sheets were the one thing in the room that got periodically washed, but I still didn't plan to use them; the room was rented by the hour, but that didn't mean the maids changed the bedsheets by the hour.

For a long time I half-sat, half-lay on the bed and stared up at brown water stains on the cottage cheese ceiling, thinking how capricious life was. One minute everything in your life is fine, and the next minute you're roadkill. Life just wasn't fair sometimes. Bad things are supposed to happen to bad people, not good people. And I was not a bad person. At least, not *that* bad.

I closed my eyes but couldn't fall asleep—I had company. The sounds of their real and faked lust came through the common wall: the excited grunts of a john and the false cries of a whore. Naturally, the walls were paper thin.

The sound effects got more intense and their bed rocked against the wall with a frantic rhythm: *Grunt-bang-moan . . . grunt-bang-moan.* The woman's moans sounded as sincere as a sermon in a whorehouse.

Please, God, make them climax. I resisted the impulse to pound on the wall and yell to the woman, *Goddammit, fake your orgasm and get it over with.*

My body was shaking, but it wasn't due to the vibration from the

❖

trucks that rumbled by or my neighbors' frenetic fury. I had really screwed up my life . . . or, more accurately, someone else had screwed it up for me. I had just been a willing victim.

Flickering flashes from the tacky neon motel sign in the parking lot passed through the dirty window and dusty sheers to give life to the mask on the dresser across the room.

As I stared at the mask I sensed it was staring back. The golden death mask of a Babylon queen from three thousand years ago, it was a valuable museum piece—over $50 million valuable.

After the greatest warrior-queen of antiquity died, the mask was prepared by taking a mold of her face. Over the centuries, it had gained repute as a harbinger of misfortune to the possessor. Strangely, that drove up its value.

People attached value to evil: The Hope Diamond rests in the Smithsonian not only for its size but also because of the bad luck—and death—it brought to its possessors. Hell, Hollywood made a cottage industry out of avenging mummies after archaeologist Howard Carter broke into King Tut's tomb in the 1920s and eleven people connected with the project had died of unnatural causes within a period of five years.

The vibrant mask staring at me from the dresser also carried a legacy of murder and lust across the millenniums. I had grown to hate it.

I wasn't sure how long I gazed at the cursed mask before I finally closed my eyes. But my sleep was interrupted by a nightmare.

I dreamed I was asleep on an iron cot in the corner of a large room that had cold, bare gray concrete walls. My cell phone started to ring, and I fumbled around on the cot trying to find the little phone in the layers of brown Army blankets. A man suddenly appeared beside me in the darkness. I didn't recognize him.

He bent down and said in a whisper, "You shouldn't be in here alone."

The irritating cell phone kept ringing. Why couldn't I find it?

Finally, my brain registered that my cell phone was actually ringing in the room. I sat up. Coming out of a deep sleep with a sense of dread, I looked around for the stranger, but I was alone. The dream seemed so real.

I got up and checked the door and the window.

My cell phone started ringing again. I followed the sound to my handbag on the table. As I fumbled with the handbag, the phone fell on the floor and bounced under the bed. I got down on my hand and knees in the dark to retrieve it. By the time I got the phone in hand and flipped it open, the ringing had stopped and the faceplate registered 1 Missed Call.

I hesitated to check my voice mail, wondering if this was a trick to trace my location. Curiosity got the better of me. I went ahead and accessed it. The message was simple. A man's voice said, "Maddy, it's me. I'll catch you later."

I recognized the voice. It raised the short hairs on my soul.

I hit the repeat key to listen to it again—and again.

I couldn't understand how he had called me.

He was dead.

2

❖

A month earlier

I looked at myself in a full-length mirror and smiled. Dressed in my $3,000 black Versace dress and $580 Domenico Vacca suede-and-crystal dress sandals that I had purchased especially for the occasion, I looked damn good. I had even splurged and bought a drop-down diamond pendant from Tiffany to match the tiny diamond earrings I already owned.

I had stepped into the pink marble and brass "Ladies' Room" at Rutgers, the auction house, to check my outfit after the taxi ride over. I was about to make the biggest purchase of my career, a buy so big that it would be in the news tonight and tomorrow. And I wanted to look like success when the cameras started rolling.

"Good luck, Maddy." I saluted my image and headed back inside, many thoughts colliding in my mind. One was that for a single thirty-four-year-old woman living alone in New York I had a pretty good life.

My most exciting personal possession wasn't expensive clothes or jewelry but my black American Express card. No one back home would have recognized it as a status symbol, but in New York and L.A., where people were sophisticated, servers in restaurants and bartenders knew exactly what it was: a badge that identified you as *Somebody*.

American Express gave out the cards by invitation only. I'd set out

❖

with a vengeance to get mine. I'd heard you had to charge a minimum of $150,000 a year to keep it, so I charged everything I could on it, even gas and groceries.

Oh yes, I knew it was shallow and superficial and materialistic to get revved up about the color of a credit card, but we all have our ego into something, don't we? That invitation from American Express represented my version of a ribbon for best cake at the fair.

To get that card and everything it represented took a long, hard decade from the day I left a small town in Middle America. My parents had both been born and raised in the same town where I was brought up. My mother and father were what snobs on the East and West coast called Flyover People because the snobs flew over them hopping from coast to coast. Climbing high in the snooty, cutthroat world of museum art and antiquities, I worked and lived on Museum Mile, a haughty Upper East Side neighborhood in Manhattan surrounded by Old Money and dot-com tycoons. A not-too-shabby accomplishment for a girl who came from a small town in Ohio and who lacked the requisite pedigrees in family, money, and Ivy League education.

Along the way a relationship up to the point of an engagement ring fell victim when I refused to move to D.C. after my investment banker fiancé accepted a promotion and transfer there. I cried at the time and sometimes I lie awake at night and think about him, imagining his warm body beside mine, but if I had to do it again, I would. He made a decision that put his career before me, and I put mine ahead of him.

Acquiring a position as curator for one of the richest museums in the world had been achieved with a lot of hard work, none of it on my back. Plenty of women were willing to put out to advance their careers, but I wasn't one of them. Sure, I'd cut a few corners—it was that kind of business. When a rare piece of art or collectible came on the market, it was war-to-the-knife, no-holds-barred, as collectors, dealers, and curators fought to possess it.

My employer was J. Hiram Piedmont III, the scion of the family and chairman of the Piedmont Museum of Mesopotamian Art, a small but prestigious museum on Fifth Avenue near the Met with a very impressive antiquities collection.

I personally didn't have that much contact with Hiram himself, but I knew a lot about him: He usually got what he wanted no matter what

❖

the cost, socialized with the superelite, drove only the finest cars, owned a yacht on each coast, a private plane, mansions in world-class venues, had his own personal curator who furnished his homes with art and a personal tailor-valet who made his wardrobe. His kids went to a summer camp designed to help them cope in a world in which they were . . . well, different. In other words, he was superrich.

Hiram the Third was also very generous about rewarding the museum's curators as long as they brought in the results that gave him the publicity and prestige he desired. The job came with a generous expense account, along with a generous salary . . . and a revolving door for those who failed.

Before I was hired by Eric Vanderhof, the museum's director, who ran the daily operations of the museum, I had been an assistant curator for the Egyptian antiquities at the Metropolitan Museum of Art. The Met's collection was world-class. But the work bored the hell out of me. Rubbing elbows with the great works of history never failed to thrill me, but the job itself was boring because I was just a tiny cog in a very big organization.

I had had little control when it came to the conception and development of exhibitions. The Met kept artifacts in boring glass boxes and display cases in rooms lacking atmosphere and charm. I argued that people wanted an adventure when they visited the museum, to experience it as if "they were actually there." It would leave a more lasting impression if the museum had an educational story about an exhibit that captured the adventure with authentic items and stories.

I was on the verge of leaving my job at the Met for an offer to be the personal curator for a top Hollywood director, traveling around the world chasing pieces for a collection being built as an investment, when I found out from a friend of a friend about the opening at the Piedmont Museum. Hiram's pockets were much deeper than the movie director's, and it gave me a chance to build a world-renowned collection. Luckily for me I had made a good impression with Eric and I had an excellent résumé.

With my generous salary I was able to leave my cramped apartment and rent a penthouse walking distance from the Piedmont. I gave my old car to charity and parked a new XK Jaguar in a garage. I also updated my wardrobe. I had some decent clothes, which I gave to charity, because I needed to dress with more class now. I started shopping at designer boutiques and higher-end stores. I considered my wardrobe an invest-ment, so I didn't feel guilty.

My passion was handbags and shoes. I had at least a hundred pairs of shoes and dozens of handbags. I had my eye on a Yves Saint Laurent white crocodile bag but decided I couldn't afford the $18,990 price. It seemed a little too extravagant to pay for one bag. Unless I got the big bonus I expected if everything went right today.

One of my neighbors, a poor little rich girl, was studying for a mas-ter's in luxury marketing, a growing field of expertise in a world as afflu-ent as ours. She gave me advice on how to dress for success.

Since most of my salary went for rent, clothes, accessories, food, and paying off my student loans and credit card debts, I didn't have much in my savings account. My theory was if you couldn't take it with you, you might as well enjoy it now. And I did, because tomorrow looked like it was going to be even better.

I had held the title of curator for over a year now. Besides caring for the objects belonging to the museum, performing research to identify the history of the objects in our collection, and creating and managing ex-hibits, I was also responsible for recommending acquisitions for the mu-seum. Basically, my job was not only to oversee the museum's collection but also to add to it. In four years the museum had gone through three curators because a centerpiece hadn't been found yet.

I was determined not to fail. The secret was to stay lean and hun-gry for pieces, keep a constant eye on the market, and fight hard and even dirty for pieces if that's what the competition did. But that "re-volving door" had been gnawing at me for the past several months. I had acquired some unique antiquities for the Piedmont, but I only re-cently found the pièce de résistance. I planned to bid on it at tonight's auction.

I SMELLED MONEY IN the air the minute I walked into the auction room.

So many designer labels were present, Armani, Chanel, Ferragamo, Wang, Zegna, Hermès, Versace, Cavalli, Gucci, Lauren, Prada, Magli, to name a few, it looked like a fashion show at a high-end boutique. Tiffany's, Winston's, Bvlgari, Cartier, were on wrists, necks, and not a few ankles. With a little imagination, you could hear diamond-studded Rolexes

❖

tick-tick-ticking. A few "underdressed" people were sprinkled among the haute couture.

The emotional and sometimes intense drama that took place in a tightly packed auction room full of elegantly dressed people, flashing their jewelry, ready to pay absurd prices to possess something that no one else had, was exhilarating. Texas hold'em poker players duel for hours over stakes of hundreds of thousands or even a million. At a high-end art auction, people have bid a hundred million dollars at the flick of a paddle.

An auction was a battlefield, a world-class chess match, and a group therapy session all at the same time. Friendships were forgotten, any weakness exploited. The highest bid was not always the winning bid . . . paying too much for a piece was worse than failing to be the high bidder.

All of them were here tonight . . . Old Money, New Money, Other People's Money . . . even Laundered Money. Everyone knew Mexican and Colombian drug lords were cleaning ill-gotten gains in the free-swinging art market.

With art, it didn't matter who you were: If you had money, you could play. And as in a game of Monopoly, the more money you had, the more you could buy. An amazing number of people played the art market much like others played the stock market. There are 8 million millionaires in this world, and a bunch of them buy art not just to hang up but also to hang on to as an investment. Often it wasn't money at issue but ego. When ego was the motivation for the buy, I treaded lightly, because things could really get nasty. The most blood I'd ever seen on an auction room floor, metaphorically speaking, was bidding between a couple involved in a divorce. The family law judge had ordered them to auction off their art collection because they couldn't agree on dividing the property. When the bidding between them got ridiculous over an antique chair, the husband suddenly rushed forward, grabbed the chair, broke it in half, and threw half at the wife.

I always wondered what happened to their children and pets.

Everyone has their own need for acquiring possessions. The rich want to increase their wealth; the passionate want to own beautiful things; the egotistical want to impress people; the greedy . . . well, they were just greedy.

Money had the power to make dreams come true—but as Humphrey Bogart said in *The Maltese Falcon* about the statue that spawned murder

❖

among those who desired it, the piece of art itself was the stuff that dreams were made of.

The stuff that dreams were made of . . . that's how I felt about the works of antiquity, that golden era of the empires of Greece, Rome, Babylon, Persia, India, China, and many other regions before the Middle Ages. Marble statues, vases, carvings in stone . . . all of them excited me. When I touched a piece or held it in my hands, it wasn't just an inanimate object to me but a magic talisman that caused my imagination to flow, to think about the artist or craftsman who had created it: A man or woman had taken shapeless marble or stone or clay and worked it into an image that caused oohs and aahs two or three millenniums later.

Maybe I'm a little far-out, but I believe that when we create an object some essence of our human spirit passes from our hands to our creation.

In college, while others went for jobs at McDonald's and Starbucks, I applied at museums. The positions amounted to nothing more than standing around watching other visitors and answering their questions, but it brought me close to what I loved. To get experience by actually handling pieces, I volunteered to work for free with the curator staff at the Met who set up the displays. That pro bono time was my ticket to a job there after I graduated.

As I WENT PAST the salesroom registration desk, the last bidder was picking up her paddle. Serious bidders had to register at the desk to receive their three-digit-numbered bidding paddles, but the process of clearing them to make deep-pocket bids had begun days earlier by verifying ability to pay. Some were here just for the fun of it and to watch other people spend millions of dollars.

My paddle number was 120. I would follow the commands of Hiram when I bid on the piece I was there to buy. The purchase was anticipated to be a big one, the most ever paid for a Babylonian piece, and Hiram wanted to be in command of the amount he was willing to pay. I let him think he had control, but I had been working on him since the piece came on the market two weeks ago.

I scanned the room. Several buyers who I knew would be bidding on tonight's lots, the auction term used for pieces being sold, were in the room.

❖

As I sat in one of the back rows, I figured there were at least two hundred people in a room that could easily accommodate twice that many.

Rutgers was one of the premier auction houses in New York, perhaps *the* premier house. Christie's and Sotheby's had offerings in a wide range of genres and price ranges. Rutgers specialized in antiquities. The CEO liked to brag that if it wasn't in existence before the barbarians raped Rome, it wouldn't be auctioned off at Rutgers.

Their business plan fit me perfectly.

Hiram wanted to have the museum's collection cover the whole Mediterranean art scene. That covered a lot of territory, including Greek, Roman, and Egyptian, the triumvirate of Western antiquities. Because the Piedmont Museum came into the acquisitions arena later in the game, though well-heeled, I convinced him to focus on pieces from the ancient Middle East—Babylonian, Chaldean, Assyrian, and the like. Those areas had more new pieces hitting the market than the triumvirate countries. Rutgers, a place that I had intimate connection with, was the auction house where many of these pieces were sold to the public.

I didn't realize until after I sat down that one of my knees was shaking slightly. A nervous habit of mine. But I had a lot to be nervous about as I thought about the purchase I was about to make tonight.

Since the museum opened four years ago, a hunt had been on to find the perfect antiquity that would be the centerpiece of the Piedmont's collection. Not only did it have to be unique, one of a kind, but it also had to be eye grabbing, a museum piece that would generate publicity from the media and covetous envy from the other museums and collectors.

The relic I threw down the gauntlet on was a piece connected to an Assyrian queen who had made an indelible mark on the history of war and lust.

Most people had probably never heard of Assyria or, if it sounded familiar, didn't remember where it was located, though they'd heard of Babylon, its most famous city—the location of the Tower of Babel and one of the wonders of the ancient world, the Hanging Gardens of Babylon. I wasn't surprised about the ignorance of most people about geography—how many of us could have identified Iraq or Afghanistan on a world atlas before the War on Terrorism had begun?

Going back several thousand years, Assyria was truly one of the greatest Middle Eastern empires. It rose to power around the same epoch that Egypt of the mighty pharaohs was declining. Much of the empire was located in Mesopotamia, the region we now call Iraq. Babylon itself was in its day the art and cultural center of Western civilization.

The antiquity I was bidding on tonight was a golden death mask of history's first great warrior-queen: Sammu-ramat. The Greeks called her Semiramis, and that was the name she went under in the worlds of art and literature.

The story of this ninth century B.C. Assyrian beauty was a fascinating tale of war, lust, and romance. My research revealed that her relationship with her kingly husband was the basis for a central theme of romantic fiction popular right up to our present time, the *roman d'aventure:* tales of faithful lovers who are forced apart and are reunited only after numerous adventures.

On the darker side of art was her notorious ability to incite more than the rape of empires: The mask carried a curse that passed to people who possessed it over the past three thousand years. *What nonsense,* I thought. But the legend of a curse made the value soar.

3

❖

As I waited impatiently for the bidding to start, people were still strag-
gling into the room at the last minute, some with bidding paddles, some
without.

The auctioneer, Neal Nathan, had just arrived, making his way to
the rostrum. He carried his precious black book with him. Neal would be
checking prices in the book as the auction went on because it showed the
"reserves," the minimum prices the sellers had set. The prices were written in code so only the auctioneer would know the secret amounts. It also
spelled out bids made by people who were not able to, or preferred not to,
attend the auction.

Two assistants sat next to the podium, ready to handle phone bids.
On the back wall was the currency conversion board for those bids placed
with foreign currency.

I knew that my lot would not be first on the block. Auctions were
choreographed like Russian ballets, every moment rehearsed for weeks,
sometimes months, in advance. While the order of offerings was cus-
tomized for every sale, typically the star of the show was presented for
bid about halfway through the event.

The catalog for tonight's auction listed 150 lots. A bidder's valuable tool, the catalog listed each numbered lot for sale, the description and ownership information, and the anticipated bid value.

I wore hands-free cell phone gear. A three-way conference call would take place between Hiram, who would make the final decision, Eric, who would offer his opinion, and myself, who would no doubt be blamed if anything went wrong. I would place my hand across my mouth to keep my lips from being read—it wouldn't be the first time a bidder had a lip-reader at an auction to discover an opponent's position.

I didn't know exactly how high Hiram would go, but I had a pretty good idea because I had been nudging him closer and closer to the figure I guessed it would take to get the piece. He wouldn't tell me, and I didn't expect him to. It was his money, even if he never personally earned a cent of it. I would have to wait and listen, picking up clues from nuances in his words and tone. Obviously, there was a point where he would not go a penny higher.

So far, the most expensive piece for the museum had come in at $10 million. That wasn't chump change, but it was a small fraction of what some works had gone for in the past. Somewhere beyond the initial authority he gave me was an amount above which he wouldn't go. I doubted if he had the exact figure in mind himself. Even if he did, auctions were akin to horse races—in the heat of the moment, the horse can be whipped to go those extra lengths.

Hiram would also be influenced by what I reported about the mood of the room as the bids were made.

My current authority was to let someone else open and stay in the bidding to $30 million. Hiram was hoping to get the piece for that amount. I knew he wouldn't. In a market where some paintings had brought in over a hundred million dollars, a masterpiece of antiquity could easily bring in more than $30 million. The Semiramis was certainly not the *Mona Lisa* or *Venus de Milo,* but it was unique . . . and it had a history. Buyers loved pieces with a history.

I figured the Semiramis would go for $45 to $50 million. Part of its attraction was its legacy of ill-fated love . . . and, of course, love's close kin: jealousy and murder. What would romantic tragedy be if passions didn't flare to the point of murder? Jealous rage had been fueling literature for eons and was the mainstay of Hollywood.

❖

I had an inside source for coming up with the $45 to $50 million estimate—Neal Nathan was my lover.

I don't want to leave the wrong impression about our relationship. It wasn't just business. The international trade in art and antiquities was a tough business. While it wasn't unusual to mix business with pleasure, I drew the line at sleeping with someone *just* to enhance my career.

I will admit that on a couple of occasions I had arranged "dates" for visiting out-of-town art dealers whom I wanted an inside track with, but I wasn't alone at doing that. Nor was it unheard of even for auction houses and museums to pamper their potential clients and donors with sexual favors. The idea repulsed me at first. I felt like a pimp. But then I found out that I wouldn't have to do the actual procuring. Eric told me to ask my apartment building doorman.

"They do that kind of stuff all the time. Just slip him a few bucks. He'll take care of the whole thing," Eric said.

He was right. When I mentioned to George, my doorman, that I had a couple of "visiting firemen" who needed a date, he acted like it was just a routine request that came up every day.

"No problem. Give me the name and hotel. I'll take care of it." The hundred bucks I slipped into his hand helped, too.

Okay, people could say I turned a blind eye to providing sex for a couple of out-of-towners, but there are worst things that happen than two people hooking up. A lot worse.

As for my intimate connection to Rutgers, I actually liked Neal. I wouldn't have had sexual relations with him otherwise. I'd sooner go back to telling tourists that the Egyptian exhibit was on the first floor of the Met before I'd lie down on the couch to further my career.

Romantically, I was going through a quandary. After my fiancé left to further his career in the nation's capital, I fell passionately in love with a man who I thought was Mr. Perfect and considered spending the rest of my life with but who turned out to be Jerk of the Century. I caught Mr. Jerk in bed fucking my best friend. The fact that my best friend was a guy added insult to injury. Pretty tough on a girl's self-image when she can't compete with another guy. I got rid of both of them.

After experiencing the heartbreak of true love of an undeserving bastard, I wasn't ready to jump back into a relationship. The psychobabble guide to true love and happiness in which I invested $24.95 said that sex was just titillation and that true love was a state of the heart that didn't require erections or orgasms. Sure. That was a nice thought, but I needed a little titillation once in a while to keep my soul—and my bones—oiled.

My friend Dillon, who married a rich oral surgeon, claimed that the best relationships were for love-and-money. I hadn't found that combination yet. But right now I had the best of both worlds. I was dating a much younger stud, once my personal trainer, who was someone I could work up a sweat with when I wanted to, and dating Neal, who was rich, cultured, and whom I enjoyed spending an evening of dinner and conversation with, even though I had to fake my orgasms with him. Add a vibrator for nights alone and what more could a girl ask for?

Neal tapped his wood gavel to bring the crowd to order.

I half-listened to him as he auctioned off the early lots. When a second century B.C. Hellenistic vase that I had already turned thumbs down on came up for bid, Hiram's voice came over my earpiece.

"Why aren't we bidding on that piece?"

Eric and I had already discussed the piece and agreed we would not bid, but as usual, when the boss questioned anything, Eric remained silent and let me take the heat. Did I mention that Eric was a weasel?

I covered my mouth and whispered, "I heard it has dirt on it."

"Dirt" meant there was a question in the chain of ownership. I started using the expression after Italian police put people on trial for buying antiquities that had been smuggled out of Italy. The police claimed that the items were not purchased from a legitimate collection but had been dug out of the ground by tomb robbers, a fairly common occurrence in antiquity-rich countries such as Italy.

The items excavated at night from antiquity sites and smuggled across borders would have a "provenance" by the time they were placed on sale or the auction block. A provenance was a certification of origin, literally the item's chain of ownership or history. Dealers and owners who sold antiquities and other works of art had to provide that evidence to prove that the piece was legally on the market.

It wasn't as hard as one might imagine to prove the chain of ownership of an antiquity, especially if it came through the typical route for the trade—illegally digging up an item that had been buried for thousands of years. Once the piece was in the hands of an unscrupulous

❖

dealer, usually in New York or London, the two main stages for selling stolen antiquities, a phony paper chain of ownership was created.

What made this type of illicit trade so easy for criminals was having no recorded history of the piece. Since it wasn't stolen from a place that had a record of it, like a museum or art gallery, prior to being dug up by the tomb robber, no one had seen the piece since its burial a couple thousand years ago.

Italy, of course, was one of those countries with so much "ancient history" that even excavations for new construction often uncovered ancient sites. Many other Mediterranean regions rich in undiscovered sites—especially Greece, Turkey, Egypt, and Israel and the Middle East in general—also fell victim to people who became aware of a potential site in their backyard or around the corner and sneaked out at night with a shovel. These tomb robbers inadvertently end up destroying priceless pieces as they probe with metal bars and dig with picks and shovels, cheating the entire nation out of their cultural heritage.

Some of these countries have thought of offering substantial rewards for discovering such sites but don't because it would only start a gold rush stampede.

In the case of the controversy between the antiquities buyers and the Italian authorities, the claim was made that several Italians had come across the antiquity site and surreptitiously dug up the pieces. Years later, when their homes were raided, the police discovered photographs of the items. It was impossible for the tomb raiders to claim that they had acquired the pieces legitimately because they took the photographs with dirt still on the dug-up pieces. . . .

I had questioned the provenance of the Hellenistic vase because of a bulletin I received that mentioned Turkish police had busted workers who had come across an antiquity site while digging an agricultural ditch in a rural area. Turkey was a rich source of antiquities because much of its coastline figured prominently in ancient Greek history. The men had confessed. *Wouldn't we all to the Turkish police?* I thought.

The vase that Neal was auctioning fit the description in the bulletin. Of course, its provenance showed it had been in the collection of a German family for a hundred years.

Eric, in fact, had argued that we should bid on the vase. "It's worth at least three million and it'll sell for half that because of the questions."

❖

Neal told me that the reserve on it was $700,000.

A reserve was usually about 80 percent of the lowest estimate. The reserve was supersecret, known only to the seller and the auctioneer. Neal revealed the reserve amount during pillow talk. After sex, while he was still basking in the masculine glory of my faked orgasm, he liked to "talk shop," boasting about how he could manipulate items being auctioned. I didn't sleep with him for insider information. I sincerely liked Neal and his titillating conversations.

It went without saying that if I wanted to acquire a large number of pieces for a new museum, I had to grab what was offered. But being eager didn't mean I would knowingly buy an antiquity that entered the market through the back door. With the word on the street that the piece was under investigation, you could bet that someone from the Turkish Department of Antiquities would come snooping around soon after the sale.

Besides, the vase didn't fit our collection. If it had, I would have bid on it. It did have a provenance attached. And I wasn't a police officer— my job wasn't to investigate whether the provenance was a fraud. Not unless there was something about it that was inherently suspicious. When it came to provenances, if I had acquired pieces in the past from the dealer and a degree of trust existed, I usually took the dealer's word that the paperwork was legit.

Neal had few bids for the Hellenistic vase even though it was a lovely piece. Not that anyone would know by his facial expression—auctioneers had to be good actors. And Neal knew how to work the audience. He was capable of making people give away more of their money than they had planned. When Neal didn't meet his reserve price, he showed no fear. He just moved right along.

He had a high bid of $690,000 with the reserve at $700,000. There had only been three bids. The room was going cold and he needed an extra $10,000 to meet the seller's reserve. With whispers that the piece had dirt on it, if he didn't meet the reserve, Rutgers would sell it privately to avoid the public exposure and they would never see a commission off of it.

If the piece went by auction, the auction house earned both a "seller's commission" and "buyer's premium," with the lion's share coming from the buyer.

In other words, the house got money from both ends.

I did a quick calculation in my head as to what the auction house would earn if the piece sold for its $700,000 reserve: On that amount, the seller would pay a commission of $35,000 and the buyer would pay a "premium" to the auction house of about $100,000, for a total of $135,000 going to Rutgers.

At this point Neal had a choice: He could "buy-in" the vase—auctioning parlance for failing to sell an item—and return the vase to the seller because it didn't meet the reserve. Or he could accept the $690,000 high bid. If he accepted that bid, Rutgers would have to pay the seller the $10,000 shortfall on meeting the reserve. But even after paying the shortfall to the seller, the auction house would make about $120,000 on the sale.

Having seen Neal in action many times, I knew exactly what he would do: take the high bid.

"It went cheap," Eric said. "We could have bought it for a few dollars more."

I just made a listening response. *Weasel.*

My father had a piece of advice for me when I got my first job: When the boss is right, he's right; when the boss is wrong, he's right. I didn't think much of the advice at the time, but since I've had to zip my lip to stupid statements from bosses over the years, I've realized it was sage advice.

I was saved from having to alibi to Hiram, falling on the sword to save Eric, by our lot coming up, the piece I was bidding on.

"What do you read with Hamad?" Hiram asked.

Ahmad ibn Hamad was a Saudi billionaire. I never really understood the source of his wealth, only that he was immensely wealthy. Someone told me ibn Hamad made his fortune selling bottled water, and that didn't sound too far-fetched for a country that I imagined to be a desert floating on a sea of oil.

He wore sunglasses for the indoor evening auction, probably because he didn't want other bidders reading his body language. He saw me looking at him and gave me a smile and nod. I returned his smile and nod, secretly wishing he'd drop dead. He'd come off on me once, at a gallery, intimating that I would find an evening in bed with him a trip to paradise. I told him to save it for his camels. It was a rude remark on my part, but he hadn't approached me as a man interested in a woman but as a superior willing to share his loins with an underling for a short time.

I hate guys who think their cock is an amusement park and every woman who rides it is going to get the thrill of a roller coaster.

"He's wearing sunglasses," I whispered into the mike draped down from my ear. "He wouldn't hide behind them if he didn't plan to bluff. He's interested, but I've heard he lost a bundle when the Russian government seized a chemical factory he owned. I don't think he's buying to collect. The piece has a connection to the Muslim world even if it pre-dates Islam. I'm reasonably certain he plans to resell it to Saudi royalty at a profit."

"What about the Getty?"

That was our other serious competition. The J. Paul Getty Museum was the most richly endowed cultural institution on the planet. All reaped from oil. They could write a check for anything they wanted.

"I believe ibn Hamad will stick longer than the Getty. Getty's own preference runs toward Renaissance and Baroque paintings and French furniture. Their collection of Roman and Greek antiquities is smaller. Their interest in the Babylonian piece is for its rarity. They'd want to trade it off someday for pieces that enhance their main collections."

As any good curator would do, I had had someone staked out in front of Rutgers with a camera to record people coming and going in order to track who was really serious . . . and really counted. Only the Saudi and the Getty would be serious bidders. Unless some dot-com billionaire with bushels of Internet IPO dollars made a call-in bid.

I had tried to get Neal to do a little pillow talk about who would be making telephone bids, but he had been more reticent than usual when we got together two days ago.

"Ladies and Gentlemen, Rutgers is pleased to offer you the next lot for bid."

The attention in the room was intense. All eyes went to the mask that was brought in.

"Almost three thousand years old, the Mask of Semiramis is a great prize of Babylonian art. Just as the *Mona Lisa* defines the Renaissance painting and *Venus de Milo* defines the Hellenistic sculpture, this queen's golden mask defines the ancient world of Babylon, when it was the richest and most powerful nation on earth."

❖

He looked at the audience and let the words sink in for a moment before he continued.

"Because of its value, we'll start the bidding at ten million dollars and mark it up by increments of one million thereafter."

The increment bidding was up to the auctioneer. Standard increments were usually 10 percent, but Neal could also change them if he saw the need. "Who will give me the opening bid?"

Two minutes and forty-eight seconds later, the bidding had reached $50 million. I had Hiram's permission to push the envelope a littler further.

When Neal asked for a bid for $55 million, sure that this was a defining moment in my life I raised my paddle. There was a hush in the room. My heart was beating fast. I felt like the whole world was watching me.

"I have a bid of fifty-five million in the back. Do I have another bid?"

Neal's eyes scanned the other two competitors in the room who had been placing bids. No more bids were signaled.

"Last chance . . . selling for fifty-five million dollars . . ."

Elated but calm, as the house was millions of dollars richer in auction fees, Neal slammed his gavel down on the podium and made it the final hammer price.

"Sold to paddle one-twenty for fifty-five million dollars."

THE CRADLE OF CIVILIZATION

In archeological circles, Iraq is known as the "cradle of civilization," with a record of culture going back more than 7,000 years. William R. Polk, the founder of the Center for Middle Eastern Studies at the University of Chicago, says, "It was there, in what the Greeks called Mesopotamia, that life as we know it began: there people first began to speculate on philosophy and religion, developed concepts of international trade, made ideas of beauty into tangible forms, and above all developed the skill of writing."

—Chalmers Johnson, "The Smash of Civilizations"

4

❖

Village of al-Jubab, Iraq, 1958

Abdullah ibn Hussein watched as his father argued with other men of the village. Abdullah was twelve years old. His name meant "Abdullah, son of Hussein," and his father was the headman, the sheikh, of the village.

The small village was about fifty miles south of Baghdad, near the Euphrates River, a waterway that made possible some of the great empires of the ancient world. The ruins of Babylon, the queen city of Mesopotamia, a cradle of Western Civilization, lay nearby.

The people of the village had once been a nomadic tribe of Bedouins, and though some of the tribe still roamed with herds of goats and camels part of the year, most had settled permanently after the Turks were driven out after the First World War. They were proud of their Bedouin heritage and resented being labeled fellahs, a word describing small farmers and laborers.

Abdullah and his father were watering camels at the river when the men from their village approached. When he saw the five men, Abdullah's father went to meet them but told him to stay at the water with the camels. As the headman, his father wore the loose-fitting outer cotton garment called a djellaba, while the other men wore long shirts and pants.

❖

He heard his father say to the men, "Salaam aleikum." Peace be with you. The men did not return the courtesy and show respect with a reply of, "Aleikum salaam." Also with you.

Abdullah had never seen anyone in the village fail to show respect to his father. To show disrespect to the sheikh was a deadly insult to people brought up in a close-knit, socially rigid society.

Angry words and gestures that frightened Abdullah erupted almost immediately. He knew why the men had come: A week ago the men had "found" a treasure, a relic of ancient Babylon, the city called Atlal Babil in Arabic and Bab-ilim, the "Gate of God," in Old Babylonian. In Hebrew, it was Babel—the city of the Tower.

The men had probed with an iron rod a mound near a section of wall at the ruins and felt something solid underneath. Digging down with pick and shovel, they uncovered a mask embedded in an ancient stone altar. Scratching the mask and seeing gold, they broke the surrounding altar to free the mask.

"Tomb robbers," his father had called them. "In minutes, they destroyed an ancient altar and crushed underfoot vases and clay figurines that have survived wars and the wrath of the elements for three millenniums. All because of their stupidity."

His father understood their motive.

The five were not professional tomb robbers but simple men who hungered for a better life. They and their families had little more than the clothes on their backs and a few possessions in their mud huts. Their only income came from picking dates from the trees near the river and herding communal goats and camels. The amount of money they would divide between them from a Baghdad antiques dealer buying the mask was small, no more than a month's wages for a city worker. But to these men who had so little of material value, a few coins in their pockets were a fortune.

When Hussein took the mask from them and turned it over to the authorities, he made blood enemies of the men.

"They are destroying our history," Hussein told his son after he had notified the National Museum of Antiquities of Baghdad of the find. "Our poverty does not entitle us to become thieves and destroy our history. The Iraqi people have a proud history going back thousands of years. We have been the crossroads of the great religions and cultures of half of the world."

He shook his finger at Abdullah. "An antiquity is not a treasure to be

❖

stolen and sold. It is a piece of our history that belongs to all the people of Iraq. Foreigners have already stolen much of our history. We must salvage what remains for our people."

An excited museum curator who came to collect the mask explained it to him.

"Your people have found the death mask of Sammu-ramat, the great warrior-queen of Assyria."

"What is a death mask?" Abdullah asked.

"A cast made of a person's face after death. The find is especially important because Sammu-ramat is believed to have built Babylon as her capital."

"And the Gardens," Abdullah's father added.

"Yes. She had the Hanging Gardens of Babylon created as a wedding present for her son's new wife. The Gardens are one of the Seven Wonders of the Ancient World."

Abdullah's father knew some legends about the queen. "Sammu-ramat brought bad luck to everyone but herself."

The curator nodded in agreement. "She was the mistress of a general. When the king saw her great beauty, he fell in love with her and had the general killed. Forced to commit suicide, it's said. But this woman had a lust for men besides her husband. When the king found out she was bedding her guards, she killed him and took over the throne. After she became queen, she took a different man to bed every night, having each killed the next day so another could take his place that night."

AT THE RIVER, ABDULLAH tried to ignore the men's shouting and concentrate on watering the camels. A very thirsty camel could hold up to a hundred quarts of water, but sometimes they had to be coaxed to drink. As he walked between the animals, stroking and scolding them, a wind suddenly arose and he tensed.

Two winds were the bane of Iraq: the Shamal from the north and the poisonous Simoon wind that shrieked out of the southern deserts. The Shamal was predictable, a hot, dry wind coming from the north during the summer months. The Simoon struck without warning. "Like a scorpion," his father said. Hot and oppressive, it seared across the deserts and plains, sometimes appearing as a whirlwind of dust.

❖

The dreaded Simoon was the wind that rose now as Abdullah worked with the camels. The beasts brayed and nervously stamped their hooves as the hot blaze suddenly struck.

An ill omen, Abdullah thought. The Simoom was the scourge of the desert people, from Saudi Arabia's Empty Quarter to Syria's Plain of Akkar. It could blind cities, turn sand as hot as lava, and bury caravans.

Abdullah swung around when he heard his name uttered out loud. The shout wasn't a call to him but an accusation yelled at his father.

He had warned his son that others would be disgruntled because he had arranged for Abdullah to work at the museum in Baghdad, a reward for turning over the mask. But it wasn't a monetary reward: Abdullah would share a small room with other boys at the museum and earn his keep by sweeping and cleaning.

The job, however, came with an unspoken opportunity. "You are a smart boy. You'll learn many things at the museum. Someday others will sweep the floors for you," his father expressed to him.

The real crux of the dispute was the other men's suspicions that Abdullah's father had not only arranged a better life for his son but had also been secretly rewarded with gold by the museum. Abdullah knew the only reward his father had asked for was a radio that could be used to call al-Hillah, the nearest large town, in case of emergency. The radio would benefit the whole village, not just Abdullah's father.

He suddenly turned his back on the men to return to his camels at the river.

Abdullah shouted when he saw a man draw the knife from beneath his robe. As his father spun around, the man sprang at him. A second man drew a blade, then another, all of them hacking and chopping at Abdullah's father.

"Father!" Abdullah screamed, running toward the melee. His father was barely able to stand up. He gasped and began to fall.

Abdullah ran into him, grabbing him around the waist, but the older man was too heavy for him. His father slipped to the ground, leaving a trail of blood down the front of Abdullah's shirt.

Abdullah tearfully shrieked at the five village men whom he had known since his birth.

"Murderers! Thieves!"

❖

5

❖

Baghdad, 2003

"Murderers! Thieves!" Abdullah ibn Hussein muttered as he staggered down a street on his way to the Iraqi museum.

Forty-five years had passed since he had uttered that accusation at five men along the Euphrates River near Babylon. Now another life-and-death crisis had erupted over antiquities.

Life is a circle, he thought, *at least the parts of it we don't want to meet again.* Confronting the pillagers of history had brought him full circle from the day his father had died in his arms.

Abdullah's dream as a child was to visit the great museum in Baghdad and see the cultural treasures his father talked about so often. The museum had been closed to the public for several years, so Abdullah was thrilled when his father told him that he would be working there. But his trip to the museum had been on the heels of tragedy. He had left the village of his birth soon after his father had been killed and had never returned.

As Abdullah's father had predicted, sweeping floors at the museum would change Abdullah's life. He had stayed with the museum and worked his way up to become a curator for the museum. The large facility had a number of curators. His special task was to supervise the public displays and arrange exhibits of Babylonian art.

❖

The museum actually started out as one room in a government building in Baghdad on the east bank of the Tigris River in 1923. Eventually it moved to a bigger building in the same district at the foot of the al-Shuhada Bridge and became the National Museum of Antiquities.

The museum's first director, Gertrude Bell, the famous British adventurer, explorer, and archaeologist, remained in charge until her death in 1926.

Bell had left Britain on the Orient Express in the 1890s for a life devoted to the Middle East. She traveled throughout Iraq, Arabia, and Persia learning Farsi, Arabic, and local dialects. She worked for the British intelligence in Cairo during the First World War before becoming director of antiquities in Baghdad after the war and the creation of the nation.

In addition to approving applications for archaeologists to dig at sites, she visited them on their sites and was especially credited for keeping the finds in Iraq instead of leaving the country.

The museum now had twenty public galleries, arranged chronologically from the prehistoric through the Sumerian, Babylonian, Assyrian, and Islamic periods, displaying clay tablets, cylinder seals, ivories, jewelry, and statues. The most impressive gallery contained the Assyrian antiquities. Gigantic carvings covered its walls and giant human-headed winged bulls stood on pedestals. The museum's most prized possession was the Sacred Vase of Warka. Over five thousand years old, it was the oldest known carved stone ritual vessel.

Objects spanning more than ten thousand years of civilization were on display in the museum, but the displayed pieces represented only about 3 percent of its holdings, making it the world's greatest holder of cultural treasures. In total, the museum housed almost two hundred thousand artifacts.

Abdullah had learned to read and write and was knowledgeable about the antiquities of the museum, but unlike the other curators, he had limited formal education. Most of the curators had advanced degrees in archaeology, art, and other similar areas of study. He made up for a lack of formal education with hard work, enthusiasm, and dedication.

Abdullah's devotion propelled him now out of a sickbed to the museum.

The world of antiquities had not changed greatly since the day his

❖

father was murdered for protecting a museum piece. At thousands of sites all over the nation, people—some poor and desperate, some just avaricious—still stole and sold pieces of the nation's history. But now was a time of special concern: For the second time in just over a decade, foreign armies were pounding Baghdad.

In 1991, Saddam Hussein invaded Kuwait and grabbed its oil, bringing the wrath of Western allies on him and the nation. After twelve contentious years of containment and defiance, the foreigners had returned, only this time the American, British, and other forces had crushed Saddam's armies, pushing all the way to Baghdad.

News of allied forces entering the city and fighting near the museum had gotten Abdullah out of his sickbed.

That Saddam, his brutal sons, and the hated Ba'th political party should be driven from power was right and just. "Allah Akbar!" God is Great! But the museum was too important to become a casualty of the war between Saddam and the West.

A decision was made to lock up the museum and send the employees home for their protection. The museum director advised the staff that the museum would not be harmed in the coming battle, that under the international conventions of war museums could not be targeted.

When the lockup occurred, Abdullah was suffering from a recurring problem with malaria attacks and had been bedridden for three days. Suffering fever and chills, he forced himself out of bed and onto the street when he got news from a friend that a unit of Saddam's elite Republican Guard was using the museum as a defensive position and that American troops were approaching. That made the treasure-house of culture a battlefield.

As Abdullah came around the corner to a side entrance of the museum he uttered an exclamation of grief and distress: "Ya ellahe!"

Both Iraqi and American military vehicles were parked near the side door. Two Iraqi Republican Guard soldiers were standing by the trucks smoking cigarettes.

They're fighting inside! was the first thought that ran through Abdullah's mind.

He didn't know what to do. If he barged in, one side or the other would shoot him. He needed to find the Americans inside and tell them

❖

they must leave the museum and wait for the Iraqis to surrender. Everyone knew Saddam had fled the city and resistance was useless.

Abdullah's command of English was good because over the years he had assisted British, Canadian, American, and Australian archaeologists who had come to the museum to study the antiquities of Mesopotamia. He would reason with the soldiers, make both sides understand that what would be destroyed was not the weapons of war but the irreplaceable heritage of an entire nation.

He went to the other side of the building and used his key to enter through a door restricted to employee use only. Making his way down a deserted corridor, he was relieved not to hear gunfire.

Maybe the fighting was over, he thought.

He came into the front exhibition room and stared in astonishment. American and Iraqi uniformed soldiers were not fighting but were busy at work, concentrating on what they were doing—boxing museum antiquities!

He wasn't a fool. He realized instantly that they weren't preserving the pieces—they were robbing the museum.

Stunned and speechless, he watched soldiers who were supposed to be fighting and killing each other stealing the most important cultural relics of the nation. Statues too large or heavy to move easily were having their most valuable part—the heads—cut off.

He gasped at the sight of a soldier using an electric saw to cut the head from a white marble statue of Poseidon recovered from the Hatra site. Another Hatra relic, a marble money box, was being bubble-wrapped. An ivory plaque of a lion killing a Nubian, an Assyrian piece from Nimrud, and the copper head of the Goddess of Victory were being carried out the door.

He staggered into the room, his mouth agape, his mind swirling.

"Stop! In the name of God. Stop!"

The men in the room suddenly noticed him.

"Abdullah! You fool! What are you doing here?"

The man who had spoken was one of Abdullah's superiors. Everyone knew the man was a member of Saddam's Ba'th Party and would be discharged as soon as a new government was formed. But he had been Abdullah's friend for over twenty years. Now he was helping the foreigners and Iraqi soldiers loot the museum.

❖

An American soldier wearing a cap with the word "SEAL" on it stepped in front of Abdullah and drew his pistol.

"Please," Abdullah's superior pleaded, "he's just a sick old man."

Abdullah's head exploded with pain as someone struck him from behind with the butt of a rifle.

6

❖

Jamaica Plains, New York City, the present

Abdullah's daughter, Asima, held her head in her hands to try to suppress a growing headache. She was tired of listening to her father rant. For the last hour he had been directing his diatribe at the TV set in her fifth-floor walk-up flat located in a low-rent district in Queens, one of the five boroughs of New York City.

She had been in the United States for twenty years now, having emigrated with her late husband. When her father suffered a serious head injury during the U.S. occupation of Iraq, she had him brought to the States, first on a hardship medical visa and then seeking asylum on the grounds that he would be prosecuted for political crimes if he returned to Iraq. The new administration had accused him of dereliction of duty in his failure to preserve and protect the property of the Iraqi museum from looters.

The looters were identified as a mob of Iraqis who had entered the museum after law and order had broken down in the city.

Asima was a dispatcher for a taxi company whose owner had come from Iraq. After spending many hours teaching Abdullah the street system of the city, she had arranged a taxi-driving job for him. Because of

❖

headaches from his injury and bouts of malaria, her father frequently missed work. But that was the easy part for her to deal with. His great passion . . . no, his great obsession was the identification and recovery of antiquities stolen from the museum.

"Thieves! Murderers!" he ranted at the television.

Thousands of antiquities were missing from the museum. After a passage of years, he was certain that many of them were slowly coming out of the woodwork and making their way into the public eye in museums and galleries.

Her father spent every spare moment casing museum and art shows for the items. When he found antiquities that he believed belonged to the collection, he sent a fax to the Iraqi consulate. Nearly ten thousand pieces were expressly missing, but that was from the museum itself. How many thousands more were dug out of the ground by tomb robbers and sold to be smuggled out of the country was impossible to estimate.

"It's the Mask of Sammu-ramat," he told her.

The news story on television that set him off an hour earlier was about the $55 million auction sale for a Mask of Semiramis.

"They call it Semiramis," she said. She had heard his ravings a hundred times about antiquities, especially the one that he felt a personal connection with.

He was so excited he bounced on the edge of the worn, stuffed couch. "That's the Greek name, but she is Sammu-ramat to our people. It is the mask that was stolen from the museum."

"How can you prove it?"

That was her immediate response each time he told her he had found a piece taken in the looting of the museum. Officially, the Iraqi government claimed that the museum was looted by a mob. Abdullah's contention that it had been an organized conspiracy involving Iraqi and American troops had been the reason his daughter and sympathetic friends in Baghdad had helped him get out of the country. The claim had not found favor in Baghdad at a time when the government desperately needed American help.

"Only one Mask of Sammu-ramat was in the museum," he said, turning to face Asima. "A mask that is no stranger to me. Your grandfather died for it."

She closed her eyes and sighed. Life was hard. She had two small children to support, a husband who had died too soon, and a father who reminded her of the famous Spanish knight-errant who had jousted with windmills.

Abdullah constantly made the rounds of galleries and museums and had made many claims of looted Iraqi antiquities being held by public and private collections. All the accusations had been ignored.

This time he was accusing a private museum of buying stolen property. She had heard the name Piedmont and recognized it as the name of one of the rich families of the world.

Asima and her father were simple people who were barely able to maintain basic subsistence. Much of what they earned went to the attorney who was handling her father's claim of political asylum. She worried that he would set powerful forces into motion that would harm them.

"Didn't you tell me that Sammu-ramat brings bad luck?"

He waved away her concerns without looking at her, his attention drawn to a news story about the sale at auction being repeated. A reporter was interviewing the Piedmont Museum curator, Madison Dupre, and Abdullah wanted to hear it.

"You said she brought bad luck."

"Shhh. A tale to frighten children."

"I don't think so. Your father was murdered after he possessed it. The museum he gave it to was looted. You were nearly killed and forced to flee. You told me that Sammu-ramat killed her own husband and lovers. I wonder, Father," a look of concern in her eyes now, "whether you should continue—"

He slapped his hands and jumped up and down on the edge of the couch.

"Aha! I have them; I have them. This time I have them for certain. The mask they call Semiramis is the mask that was stolen from the museum." He stood and beamed at his daughter. "I have the proof."

Asima didn't respond. Her attention was drawn to the mask being shown on the news program. She had expected the mask to have the features of a beautiful woman. But the facial features went beyond beauty, conveying instead something darker and more sinister.

"Allah be merciful! She's evil!"

EMERGENCY RED LIST OF IRAQI ANTIQUITIES AT RISK

The International Council of Museums (ICOM) announces the official publication of its Emergency Red List of Iraqi Antiquities at Risk, describing types of objects especially at risk or likely to have been stolen from Iraq. . . .

Cultural heritage in Iraq has suffered seriously as a result of war. Many objects have been looted and stolen from museums and archaeological sites and risk appearing on the market through illicit trafficking.

Although the Iraq museum in Baghdad is not the only place that has suffered, it is certainly by far the most important institution. The museum has been looted and is missing a great part of its former collection.

The Iraq museum is a national archaeological museum that serves as the repository for all artifacts from excavations in Iraq. It contains hundreds of thousands of objects covering 10,000 years of human civilization, representing many different cultures and styles.

The bulk of the collection dates between 8000 B.C. and A.D. 1800, and comprises objects made of clay, stone, pottery, metal, bone, ivory, cloth, paper, glass, and wood.

7

❖

Manhattan

After I completed the arrangements for delivery of the Semiramis, I made my way to Neal's office. I wasn't interested in the other lots still left to be auctioned. I already had what I wanted. I knew Neal was going to mingle a bit after the auction before he returned to his office. He would still be on a high from nervous energy.

I was on my own high. I had finally managed to find the centerpiece for the museum. Hiram was thrilled, even though he was out $55 million. A drop in the bucket to him. The ultrarich didn't worry about spending an outrageous sum of money for something they had to have.

Hiram would give me a nice bonus. I certainly deserved it. But I had to check whether white crocodiles were an endangered species. And the balance on my black American Express card. If I wasn't careful, I'd miss a payment and my card would become an endangered species.

Aaak! I took deep breaths and paced the office, ready to soar up to the sixteen-foot ceiling with nervous energy. I could scream for joy. *My God, I've done it.*

I thought about the past year that I had been working at the Piedmont Museum. I had worked hard and put in long hours to bring in the

❖

right pieces for the museum. The pressure was intense at times, but I was determined not to go out that "revolving door" like the other curators.

A tough business, but I had kicked ass! You had to be one step ahead of the game because other people were looking for the same things, and the more money you had to spend, the more control you had. Of course it helped to know the right people who would help you acquire what you wanted. Like Neal. That's how I looked at it. Maybe it was unscrupulous, but it was a fact of life in the art world.

In the end all that mattered was getting something no one else had.

I had soared so high, my brain felt breathless. I collapsed in the leather chair in front of Neal's desk and leaned back my head.

Driven, that's what I had been, what had brought me to this moment. You went after *it* no matter what the cost. I suppose indirectly it was something I had picked up from my parents. Their mistake was not going after what they wanted in life but just dreaming about it. They weren't really unhappy. I just think secretly they wished things had turned out differently.

I didn't want that to happen to me.

My mother dreamed of being a dancer and ended up being a home-maker and librarian. Most women would think that's great. My father ended up as an instructor in art history at a small community college in Ohio and never completed his education to get his Ph.D. Teaching community college, like being a librarian, was an occupation that transcended merely working for a living because it had elements of the arts and public service attached.

Sadly, for him, what my father really wanted was to be Indiana Jones and do archaeological digs in places like Egypt, Hellenistic Turkey, and Angkor Wat in Cambodia. Wouldn't we all like to be Indie? But a bad leg barely allowed my father to hobble around Native American sites. His lone claim to fame was mentioned in a *National Enquirer* story when he "investigated" the New Mexico Roswell site for alien presence. I was a freshman in high school at the time, and kids were merciless with their jokes.

My parents were the epitome of Henry David Thoreau's contention that "the mass of men lead lives of quiet desperation." Quiet desperation. Providing for a family when you'd rather be onstage or on a dig. They

❖

were killed in a car accident soon after I graduated from college. I miss them both.

They nurtured me and loved me, but I always sensed in them a little disappointment about the road they took in life. I heard a song on an oldies radio station that reminded me of my parents' attitudes: In Peggy Lee's "Is That All There Is?" each time the narrator experienced something new in life and when she had her first love affair she expressed her disappointment by asking if that was all there was to it, concluding, "If that's all there is, my friends, then let's keep dancing."

The message I drew from the song was that the woman saw life fatalistically—that she had no control over the world. Instead, her role in the world around her was predestined by fate. And that was my parents' attitudes: They wanted something different but took what the gods doled out . . . and ending up wishing they had taken a different path.

A driving force that I recognized in myself was a reaction to my parents' fatalistic sense of defeat . . . a fear of ending up with a wish list on my deathbed. And that I had inherited the fear as a genetic defect.

That's why I just kept dancing.

I WASN'T SURE WHAT time it was when I felt Neal's lips nuzzling at my neck. His breath smelled of alcohol. He had a bottle of champagne and two glasses with him.

"Hey, wake up, sleepyhead."

"I guess I dozed off. What time is it?"

"Late. Sorry. I saw an opportunity to drum up some business for the auction house and I couldn't pass on it. Ben Raygun, the cable billionaire, died, you know. I was talking to the widow. She needs to unload some things. You know how it is. Forgive me?"

His job entailed not only bringing down the gavel at the auction house but also bringing in business. Finding ways to bring in collections for the auction house was always a challenge. It always came down to knowing the right people at the right time, both when they were alive . . . and especially when they died. Nothing warmed the cockles of an auctioneer's heart more than a big estate sale of art to pay death taxes.

"Sure, I understand. Business first, pleasure later."

❖

"Let's have a toast." Neal filled our glasses with champagne. "Here's to finding your masterpiece . . . and my making millions . . . so to speak."

Neal downed his drink quickly.

"You looked pretty calm up there tonight," I said.

"I actually felt good. It's not easy looking cool and calm when you have to make the company's payroll for the next few months in just a few minutes. Hey—for a moment there, I thought your friend Hamad was going to outbid you."

"He's not my friend," I said with a testy voice.

"Oh, a little touchy, are we?"

"I don't like that man."

"He's superrich."

"Not interested."

"Handsome."

"Not interested. He confuses women with camels. What I am interested in is eating. Let's go and talk about your making millions."

I started to get up, but Neal put his hand over my breast. "How about a quick fuck before we eat? I'm horny as hell. Feel me." He took my hand and put it on his hard crotch.

I wasn't in the mood for a session of heavy sex, either. "I can fix that real quick."

"That's what I like about you. You know how to please a man."

I unzipped his pants and started massaging his penis in a steady rhythm while I French-kissed him. It didn't take him long to explode in my hands.

"Okay, let's go now. I'm starving."

8

❖

Hiram had planned a social gathering for the following evening to celebrate his newest addition to the museum. After passing through ground-floor security that a president would have felt safe having, I took the elevator up to Hiram's penthouse. A private elevator, of course. Hiram had the top three floors of a thirty-two-story building.

This was the first time I had been invited to the penthouse. I considered it a signal that I had arrived, transcending from a mere employee—a member of the great unwashed masses—to part of the executive inner circle. Like getting the proverbial key to the executives' washroom.

I smothered an excited giggle at the thought.

According to Neal, the penthouse was ritzy. I figured it would be something out of *Architectural Digest*. What Hiram lacked in taste he made up for in money to buy the best. If I had his big bucks, I'd probably surround myself with luxurious things, too. Being superrich was never going to happen to me, not unless I married it, but I was curious about how the anointed ones lived.

I stepped off the elevator into the reception area and into the arms of two more security guards. Only these two were in tuxedos. The foyer was capacious, with walls of pale green Italian marble and an enormous rug portraying the cosmic sea called Varu-Karta from ancient Persian cosmography. Eric told me the rug once belonged to the Shah of Iran.

I identified myself, and a security guard relayed news of my presence to another person standing at the double doors to the penthouse.

"Good evening, Ms. Dupre," the greeter said, opening the door for me. I noticed a mike on his lapel. My name was being transmitted inside.

An image of servants shouting the entrance of a guest into a great hall in Shakespearean times popped into my head and I almost giggled again. Actually, I was so excited when I was getting dressed for this evening that I had opened a bottle of champagne and sipped a glass as I soaked in my spa-tub. I might have had more than one glass, because I was feeling a little light-headed.

I stepped through the double doors into the living space and was welcomed by Hiram's wife.

"Madison, darling, come in, I'm so glad you're here; this is as much your night as the rest of us."

She gave me a friendly cheek-to-cheek greeting on each cheek, Hollywood style.

I wanted to ask her who "the rest of us" were who deserved credit, other than Hiram for spending thirty seconds writing a check, but I just smiled and told her how beautiful she looked. Rich bitch that she was, her outfit was gorgeous. "I love your outfit."

She wore a couture beaded white evening dress that complemented her golden tanned skin. Around her neck was an elaborate twenty-four-stone drop emerald necklace and matching earrings. No doubt worth millions, I quickly calculated in my head. I couldn't help but notice her sparkling diamond ring on her left hand that almost blinded me when I approached.

I hadn't seen her in a couple of months and she looked like she had taken off years. . . . I was sure a surgeon's knife had a lot to do with it. The perfectly white teeth she flashed were also the best smile money could buy.

Yes, I was petty and spiteful when it came to Hiram's wife. Besides being abundantly endowed with the beauty, grace, and charm that I had been so meagerly rationed with, she had married billions. And not once did she have to use her teeny-weenie little brain for anything.

❖

Prior to being Mrs. Hiram Piedmont III, she was Angela St. John, a not-too-famous actress in Hollywood.

Hiram had met her in Beverly Hills buying a pair of Jimmy Choo shoes, and it had been love at first sight as soon as Angela found out he was a billionaire.

That was nearly five years ago, when Angela was an actress pushing forty, a sin in Hollywood, where the only admired feminine attribute over forty was a bustline. She had been mostly a pretty showpiece in movies, often cast as the Other Woman, and that fit her personality nicely. She had a bitchy quality about her, part of that unique substance called charisma that movie stars must possess.

Her acting was not uncommonly described as unintentionally funny.

Okay, that wasn't really true, but I still didn't like the woman, though sometimes I wondered if I was being unjust. Maybe it was harder than I thought to be rich and beautiful and brainless.

Neal said there was a five-year qualifier in Angela's prenup with Hiram: If they stayed married five years and a day, she would get full spousal rights as opposed to what she would get from the prenuptial contract. They were fast approaching that magic date, and bets were being placed as to whether Hiram would file for divorce because she would get a bigger piece of him if he didn't.

I had my money on Angela. She was an attractive woman and no matter what I personally thought of her—in my old-fashioned, small-town mentality, a woman who married for money was a high-class whore—there was no denying that she was an appealing woman.

Once she found out I wasn't after her husband, she tolerated me well. Fortunately, antiquities and museums and anything else that required thinking bored her, except when it brought camera crews.

While I found Hiram the Third uninteresting, I had to admit it wouldn't be above me to take my turn on a casting-room couch for a chance to catch a billionaire. I know what that makes me, but as long as I was an expensive one, it didn't bother my conscience at all. Simply marrying for money was a sin, but God would be forgiving if you married a whole lot of money.

Besides, I was curious about what it would be like to have a disposable marriage where one simply trashed it and moved on. . . .

❖

Hiram, of course, had no difficulty attracting beautiful women. He was on his third marriage and probably had at least one more in him. And I'm sure he didn't fool himself into thinking that women were attracted to anything but his money.

Angela touched the emerald earring on her right ear and excused herself. "Eric's been looking for you. Some business matter, he said. Go get yourself a drink first," she said, as if reading my mind.

The earring obviously hid the receiver signaling an arriving guest.

She flew off, leaving a whiff of perfume in her wake. I recognized the scent. Chanel No. 5. It had a distinctive smell that was hard to describe, a scent that had been around for decades, since the 1920s, in fact, and still retained its classy appeal. Personally, I preferred a more earthy, musky scent.

I spotted Eric as I made my way across the wide-open room. The cavernous space was too big, bare, and open for a living room. Its only purpose was for parties, so I supposed it was the modern penthouse version of a stately old mansion's ballroom.

Eric was at the bar getting a drink. Even though the room was filled with people, it didn't feel at all crowded. But like the auction house, the place smelled of money . . . magazine-quality interior design and furnishings and deep-pocket guests.

Marble was everywhere—walls, floors, and pillars—along with an intricately coffered ceiling. Splattered around the room were old master paintings and sculptures that contrasted with a modern high-gloss black grand piano. Nothing hanging on the walls was worth less than a million.

I shouldn't have been surprised that the art style lent itself toward European paintings rather than antiquities. Hiram had no interest in either style, leaving the penthouse art collection up to his personal art curator and the museum's Mesopotamian character in the hands of hired help like me.

I walked by floor-to-ceiling windows that gave a stunning view outside. Neal mentioned the master bedroom level at the top of the building was surrounded by a terrace that captured a 360-degree view of the city.

An eclectic mix of people was in the room. As I moved by the guests, I acknowledged those I knew. Along with Hiram's superrich friends were the cream of the nation's art scene, gallery owners and superrich collectors.

❖

Most of the people in the room were there to tell Hiram what a terrific addition he had made to the museum. In other words, to admire him. Only a couple of museum curators were there. Hiram obviously preferred to rub shoulders with money rather than knowledge.

Even though I knew I looked good, I still felt underdressed in my simple but elegant dress compared to the haute couture–dressed people in the room. Should I have worn something more ostentatious? A line from the movie *Working Girl* suddenly popped into my mind, something about if a woman wore cheap clothes, people noticed the clothes, but if she wore expensive clothes, they noticed the woman.

I wondered if people were staring at my clothes . . . or me. Why should I care anyway? That was my father's practical voice. But the truth was, I guess a part of me did care.

On my way over to the bar, I talked briefly to a couple of gallery owners whom I knew. Eric's back was to me, so he hadn't seen me yet.

"Miss Dupre?"

I turned around and stared at a spitting image of Dolly Parton, big breasts and all. Only this one was younger, very much younger. She was perfect for the role I had cast her in for the night.

"I'm Chastity. The agency said I should speak to you." She had a slight southern accent.

I gave her a big smile. "Okay, just give me a few minutes. There's someone I need to speak to first." I wanted to be sure the arrangement was still on before I made a commitment to her.

My reason for being at the party was more than just social. Eric wanted me to take care of a business matter for him. The girl from the agency was the reason Eric wanted to talk to me. I smothered another champagne laugh when I thought about the girl's name.

"Hi, Eric," I said to his back.

"Maddy, what took you so long?"

"Traffic," I lied. It had been champagne, bubble bath, and mellowing out after the stress of the auction the day before. I ordered an apple martini instead of champagne for a change.

"The Huntzbergers are here. Have you made the arrangements with them?" he asked.

"No, I just got here, but I've met Chastity. She looks perfect for the job." I nodded in her direction.

❖

"She does, doesn't she." He drooled like a horny college kid when he looked at her. "I certainly wouldn't mind getting some southern comfort from her."

"I'm sure you wouldn't," I said. I almost added that his wife might object to it, though.

"She comes highly recommended," he added, as if that qualified his reason for desiring her.

"I'll bet she does."

What was it about a girl with blond hair, big boobs, and a short skirt that made men go all gaga? I didn't get it.

"So where are the Huntzbergers?" I asked.

He pointed to a couple in the opposite corner of the room. They appeared to be fiftyish. Even though they were dressed in designer clothes, they looked a bit stuffy to me, but one could never tell from outward appearances what lurks underneath. This PG-rated Midwest couple wanted X-rated excitement.

"These people are very wealthy, Maddy. They want to loan a valuable collection to the museum. It'll turn into a donation if we play our cards right."

People who donated pieces to museums and galleries nowadays often wanted something else besides a tax break and a little recognition. The perks were increasing. I wasn't sure what else Eric had promised, but sex seemed to be high on the list for this couple. And they wanted more bang for their buck than a simple fuck: I was told to get someone they both would enjoy.

Pimping wasn't supposed to be part of my job description, but somewhere along the line since the sexual revolution of the sixties depravity had become more and more acceptable in social and business arrangements.

I had arranged sex for other people before. Eric didn't want to do the dirty work himself and made me make the arrangements. I hated it. Now that I had arrived career-wise, so to speak, I planned to tell Eric to have his assistant, a woman I detested, do his pimping in the future. The job required a call to an escort service and a coded conversation in which you explained what you wanted . . . without really revealing what you wanted: "I have friends coming in from out of town . . . husband and wife . . . they are lonely and would both enjoy the company of a young woman with stimulating conversation . . . wholesome looks would be nice. . . ."

In other words, I needed a prostitute with pigtails who would go down on both of them.

I smiled at Eric. *Asshole.* "I know. I'll take care of it."

"I know you will."

I took one sip of my drink and set it back on the bar. "Don't let any-one touch this. I'll be back to finish it," I told the bartender.

"You got it." He winked.

Cute guy, I thought. Drinking champagne always makes me horny. I've always blamed it on the bubbles but had no scientific proof. As I went by Chastity, I said, "When you see me looking at you, come over."

I navigated my way to the lucky couple.

"Good evening," I said to the Huntzbergers. "I'm Madison Dupre."

They both smiled slightly as their eyes traveled salaciously over my body. "I'm the Piedmont's curator, not their—" Shit, I almost said, *Not their whore.* "I'm the curator of the Piedmont Museum," I repeated.

"Oh, nice to meet you, Miss Dupre," Mr. Huntzberger said. His wife nodded in agreement. "I told Eric we're considering loaning our collec-tion of Mesopotamian vases to your museum."

"Yes, that's what I understand. We're all very excited. It would make a very impressive display. In fact, there's someone here tonight, an in-tern who's studying in that particular area, that's very anxious to learn all about your collection." I caught Chastity's eye and gave her a nod. "I hope you don't mind explaining the history of the pieces in your collec-tion. I'm afraid our educational system has left Chastity with virgin ears when it comes to Mesopotamian art."

I could have added that her ears were the only orifices she had left that hadn't been poked and stroked many times.

The two middle-aged perverts left with the Dolly Parton look-alike, literally cooing all the way out the double doors. I was sure Chastity wouldn't let them down. She was getting paid very good money.

I waved to Eric and gave him a thumbs-up, signaling everything was arranged. He was chatting with Hiram and gave me a wide smile. An-other job well done. Jesus, what a couple of hypocritical pricks.

❖

As far as I was concerned, Eric had degraded me once too often. He was dead meat. History. As far as being the museum's curator, as of now I had a been-there, done-that attitude. Now I wanted weasel Eric's job. I had to keep dancing.

When I went back to the bar to get my drink, I didn't see my glass. "Hey, what happened to my drink?"

"Oops! Someone must have taken it." He leaned closer to me. "You know, you just can't trust these rich people, can you?"

"How do you know I'm not one of these untrustworthy rich people?"

"Well, after what I just saw, I figured you for a working girl. Or at the very least, their madam."

I started laughing. He was cute and funny. I considered it a compliment that he'd think I was good enough to sell my body. "You are so right. Okay, I'll take another apple martini, please."

"Coming right up."

"So tell me, since you're so smart, what other things do rich people do besides steal drinks?"

"Let me tell you about the very rich. They're different from you and me."

That was so stupid, it got me laughing again. Those champagne bubbles still had control of my mind. "Tell me something I don't know."

"I was just kidding about the working girl stuff—and you being rich."

"Why don't you think I'm rich? It's my clothes, isn't it? The movie was right."

"Huh?"

"Was it the clothes or me you noticed?'"

"Oh, I noticed what's inside the clothes, all right." He smiled. "It's your eyes. The windows to the soul. That's the tip-off."

"My eyes?"

"They're not greedy."

He moved away to fill two glasses of champagne. He came back and said, "Your clothes are great. And unlike everyone else in the room, you're not in a uniform. You're different."

"What do you mean different?"

"No Winston, Bvlgari, Gucci, Armani, Piguet, Cartier. They're all wearing designer labels, designer diamonds and watches, smoking aged

❖

Gurkha cigars, driving Jaguars and Bentleys. They look like they all came off the same assembly line. The only thing that distinguishes them from each other is the size of their back accounts."

I didn't want to disappoint him and tell him that I owned a Jaguar and had some of those designer clothes, though not the most expensive ones, and I lived in a penthouse. A small one.

"You know what this one bottle's worth?" He brought up a bottle from underneath the bar.

"Haven't got a clue."

"About six grand. A Scotch whiskey aged in sherry barrels for over fifty years. Designer liquor."

"Must be nice.

"Check out this. Designer ice cubes."

"Designer ice cubes?"

"Hand-cut, so they don't melt as fast."

He wasn't kidding. I started laughing. "Do you ever envy them, the rich, I mean?"

"No," he said, putting away glasses in the holder above the bar. "They're too goddamn greedy. You know that old saying 'money is the root of evil.' Well, it's true."

I didn't buy his philosophy. If I had a choice, I'd rather be rich than poor. "But money can buy you things."

"I'm not saying you don't need money. I just don't care for the filthy rich. And there're a lot of them around here. Money can't buy you happiness."

But it sure helped warding off the blues.

I liked his honesty, liked him, and especially liked his fine-toned body. I set aside the apple martini and told him to get me a glass of champagne. My sexual appetite was rising and needed to be lubricated. I didn't get any satisfaction from Neal in the sex department, which was fine with me. I didn't love Neal and we had no commitments with each other. We both saw other people.

I stared at the bartender over the rim of my glass. "What time do you finish tonight? Do you want to get together afterward?"

Okay, so I was a horny thirtysomething sexual predator and he was probably a college kid—who else would quote F. Scott Fitzgerald? But that didn't put me into the category of female schoolteachers sleeping with their young students. I was more the older sister type, rather than a cradle robber.

"Sure. I'm only filling in for another bartender. A last-minute emergency. Someone else is taking over in a couple hours."

"Well, I guess I'll go mingle with the filthy rich for a while. My name is Maddy by the way."

"Jeffrey."

I wrote down my address and apartment number for him. He whistled when he saw the address.

"I'll tell my doorman to let you in."

I took the glass of champagne and left him staring at my address.

I spoke to Hiram briefly. He told me again how pleased he was with the auction and informed me he was going to be generous in his bonuses this year, which meant Eric was also going to get an even bigger check.

Not only do the rich get richer, but also people like Eric get more than their share of the droppings.

Neal was busy chatting up people around the room, probably trying to strum up more business for Rutgers. At one point I saw him talking to Hiram's wife. They seemed pretty chummy with each other. Was Neal poking her? A sure bet. But it was none of my business. I had my own plans for tonight.

9

❖

I took a cab back to my apartment at a few minutes past midnight. The champagne had made me giddy. Even though it juiced up my sexual drive, it also made me sleepy if I drank too much.

I told my doorman that I was expecting someone named Jeffrey and to send him up when he arrived. One thing about Manhattan doormen—they never showed surprise. The ability to always respond with a blank look and nod was a prerequisite for the job.

My doorbell buzzed thirty minutes later.

"Your knight in shining armor has arrived," he said, "and I bring gifts." He held up a bottle.

"Great. More champagne."

He came inside, nodding his head in approval as he walked around the living room. "Nice place. Great neighborhood, too."

"I don't have any complaints."

"So you are part of the rich and famous people."

"Not by a long shot."

"What exactly do you do?"

"I'm the curator for the Piedmont Museum."

"Ah, so you're Madison Dupre. You never gave me your last name at

❖

the party. I overheard pieces of conversation about you. Made some big purchase at Rutgers for Piedmont. So you work for the rich and famous."

I nodded my head. "Are you going to hold that against me?"

"No."

"Okay, now that we've got that settled, you can open the champagne while I start the water." Another glass wasn't going to hurt me.

"Start the water?"

"I feel like soaking in the tub. Want to join me?"

I caught the look of surprise on his face.

"Okay. Sounds good to me."

I came back dressed only in my bra and panties. I still had my heels on because there was something sexy about wearing high heels with underwear.

His eyes went up and down my body. "You know, I like you without your dress on." His lazy gaze over my body made me tremble with excitement.

We were practically strangers and here I was almost naked in front of this guy. I didn't care. My body was horny for some sexual satisfaction. I wanted to play with him a little, but I wasn't sure how much longer I could wait.

"You might like this even more."

Unashamedly, I slipped out of my panties and bra. I stood there totally naked in front of him, with heels on.

He stared, still as a statue, at my body.

"This is getting better and better. You're giving me a hard-on, you know."

A tremor went down my body. "I'll give you more than that. Bring the champagne and glasses."

I turned and walked to the tub. I shook off my heels and stepped into the perfumed bubble bath. The water was soft and warm. I let the bubbles soak up my body.

Jeff had stripped out of his clothes on the way to the bedroom. I almost laughed when I saw him in the doorway. He had the champagne in one hand and two glasses in the other and his penis was sticking straight up.

"What are you waiting for?"

He stood in the doorway for a minute. "Just admiring the view."

❖

"You can admire it in here."

The bathtub was big enough for three people. He slipped down in the warm water, then poured the champagne. He also poured some in the tub.

"Ah, almost like the rich and famous," he said. He leaned back and closed his eyes.

"You have a thing about rich people, don't you?"

"I find them fascinating to watch."

I thought the same thing about him right now.

He was younger than anyone I'd ever dated, much younger. I stared at his smooth toned body as I sipped my drink. He had no body hair. Male movie stars who went through painful body waxing would be damn envious of it.

An innocence about him was stimulating. Now I understood why the Huntzbergers wanted someone like Chastity—the exotic thrill of making love to a younger person. Unlike teenagers, who lacked the maturity in mind and body to be sexually interesting, young people in their twenties were fully developed yet treated the body as an exploration of passion and sexual mystery.

I poured the rest of my drink in the tub and did the same with his.

I spread my legs apart slowly and moved his fingers over my swollen button. My clitoris was already throbbing.

"Massage it," I said, as I leaned back and closed my eyes. I was ready to come any second.

"Feel good?" He started rubbing it slowly.

"Yes," I moaned. "Do it harder. It's coming."

I gave in to the orgasm as it coursed through my body, writhing in the warm water with sexual ecstasy.

Sweat broke out on my face. I opened my eyes. "Wow, that felt so good." My body felt like gelatin.

"Yeah, me, too. I jerked off just watching you." He smiled.

We both didn't say anything for a couple of minutes.

"I'm not finished yet. Just pretend that I'm your older sister," I said. "I can do things to you that you've never had done before."

"Go ahead and rock my world, Sister."

"Follow me."

I got out of the tub and dried off lightly before I went to the bed.

❖

His body reminded me of a marble statue, like Michelangelo's *David*. Pubic hair was left off statues because it wasn't sexy.

I put his slender penis in my mouth. Still flaccid, it fit nicely in my mouth. I didn't enjoy giving Neal head. I had to fake everything with him.

This Adonis I sucked with pleasure. He was starting to grow in my mouth and I sucked his brains out. He whimpered like a puppy. Before the night was over, I had come three times and he had come twice.

I lay in bed and watched him dress. "That was the best sex I've ever had." I smiled at him.

"Good. Then it was worth five hundred."

"What?"

"Five hundred. That's what I get for doing older women."

I gaped at him. "You motherfucker."

He raised his eyebrows. "Sisterfucker?"

10

❖

The following morning an interview was scheduled for me to talk about the Semiramis on a popular morning TV talky-news show: *Mornin' with Cassie and Dane* had a gossipy, latest-Hollywood-celebrity-sex-triangle format. The fact that Hiram was on the board of directors of the network made it a shoo-in for our publicity people to arrange my appearance.

Cassie Martin was a talking head, a "news" person with collagen lips so puffed a wit had dubbed her the Goodyear Blimp Girl. A natural blonde, she was vulnerable to being the subject of blonde jokes. When I saw her, I started to hum in my mind the country western song sung by Toby Keith where he asks, "Do blondes really have more fun or are they easier to spot in the dark?"

In a strange way, I realized that Cassie got her job for reasons other than being a pretty face. The world was full of pretty faces, but Cassie had charisma, at least for people who thrive on celebrity gossip. However, Cassie pushed the envelope when she ventured into news commentary about world events. I felt much more confidence about news of the world listening to Paula Zahn and Katie Couric. Frankly, Cassie reminded me of a life-size blow-up doll, a sex object lonely men take to bed for unconditional love.

❖

Her morning news-talk partner, Dane Evers, was also for display purposes only. His role was to purse his lips and appear grave and concerned when Cassie revealed the intimate details of celebrities. He was also blond but definitely the bottle variety.

Buff, with skintight short-sleeve shirts exposing thousands of dollars' worth of personal trainer–created physique, he wore horned-rim glasses to look intelligent and frequently commented on the T & A of women in order to appear masculine and cool. But underneath the thin veneer of macho man was a sensitive countenance and soulful eyes that no heterosexual male since Adam has possessed. The only way I could imagine being in bed with Dane Evers was if I were breast-feeding him.

As soon as I sat down in front of the cameras, Cassie asked, "So tell us, Madison, about the fascinating history of murder and madness surrounding the museum piece you just bought for fifty-five million dollars."

She gave me a toothy smile of perfect caps, bright enough to give me a sunburn.

It didn't surprise me that the main interest would be in a tabloid element. I had a problem with history of murder and madness because I wasn't sure how much it was a product of the imagination of Sir Henri Lipton, the London art dealer who had arranged the auction of the piece. But I returned her smile—much less dazzling—and gave it my best.

"Well, the mask has been possessed by some famous people in history, all of whom it seemed to bring bad luck to. Semiramis was a Babylonian queen who became a heroine of legendary proportions—"

"She wasn't real?"

That from the show intellectual, Dane. But actually, it was a good question.

"As you know, some legends are about real people and some fall more under myth. Semiramis was a real person, but like many historical greats, stories came down over the millenniums that may be exaggerated or even invented. Semiramis was a Babylonian queen, believed to be the mother of Nebuchadnezzar who built the Hanging Gardens of Babylon. She murdered her own husband, and arranged for the murder of a stepson who had a better claim to the throne than her own son."

The smile on Cassie's face was slowly turning into a frown.

I went on. "Her death mask was given to her son, who subsequently went mad. It's said that he ran through the Hanging Gardens, screaming that the ghost of his mother was chasing him."

"My God! What a horrible thing!" Cassie said, scrunching her face and shoulders in horror.

Actually, I wondered about the story. It was awfully similar to King Herod being chased around the palace by the ghost of his wife Mariamne after he put her to death.

"After Alexander the Great conquered his way to the Himalayas, he turned around and came back to Babylon, the most magnificent city in the world. He moved into Nebuchadnezzar's palace and was given the Mask of Semiramis. He died shortly thereafter, quickly and mysteriously, at the age of thirty-three.

"Afterward, of course, the mask eventually passed down to Hārūn al-Rashīd, the Caliph of Baghdad whose royal court was the basis for the story of *Arabian Nights, the Thousand and One Nights.*"

Cassie clapped her hands. "Aladdin! I loved the movie." The brilliant smile glowed.

"Yes, well, as you know, it's the story of the caliph discovering that his wife has been sleeping with harem guards. He has her head chopped off and thereafter marries a different young woman every night. In the morning, the new bride has her head chopped off."

Cassie had a ghastly look on her face.

"What a waste of beauty," Dane, the intellectual, said.

I forced a smile. *What a waste of a brain!* "Anyway, even the most recent owner, a man in Beirut, was murdered."

"Now, Madison, isn't there a controversy about how museums and rich people are grabbing up the national heritage of poorer countries?"

I was impressed. Dane's question was actually newsworthy.

"We think of it as preserving endangered antiquities so they can be enjoyed by the entire world. I'm sure you know that in many third-world countries antiquities are—"

Cassie clapped her hands again. "Sinbad!" she blurted out.

Dane and I stared at her for a few seconds, not believing what had just come out of her mouth. I found my voice first. "Sinbad?"

"He was in *Arabian Nights.* I liked that movie, too. Tell us some more about the lust and disgust your statue has caused."

❖

I didn't correct her by reminding her it was a mask. She was getting into it now.

Apparently I had underestimated Cassie's repertoire of film and literature. She was well versed, at least in the Disney-type movies.

"The Hope Diamond," she said.

I didn't follow her train of thought. "The Hope Diamond?"

"You know, the one with the mummy's curse."

Dane said, "I think Cassie is referring to the gem's curse."

I cleared my throat. "Actually, Cassie, I think the mummy's curse was King Tut's revenge. . . ."

It went on like this for fifteen minutes. Luckily it was a short interview. I don't think I would've survived any longer.

11

❖

A week later I stepped out of a limo in front of the museum. My heart was fluttering. I lived only a few blocks away, but rather than walk or take a proletarian taxi, I ordered up a limo as if it were Academy Award time.

This is going to be my night.

A reception would introduce Queen Semiramis to an even larger art world audience, some of the world's crème de la crème of the antiquities trade, along with some politicians and billionaires, but most important to the news media.

No doubt Hiram thought it was going to be his night, too, but his contribution to Semiramis and the museum itself was in the form of writing checks. Having a billion-dollar checking account was very convenient, but it didn't make him a hero. As far as I was concerned, I was the star of the show.

The world of priceless art was a playground for billionaires, a rarified atmosphere even more privileged and snooty—and cutthroat—than that of owning a Kentucky Derby champion or a sports team. Or having a movie star or supermodel wife.

The Piedmont Museum was Hiram's "trophy," his ego trip—an

accomplishment he could buy with his inherited money, as opposed to working for a living. But I had to give Hiram credit. He was ruthless about acquiring pieces for the museum. He wasn't alone. J. Paul Getty treated acquisitions of art with the same Art of War mentality with which he ran the oil companies that made him the richest man in the world during his lifetime.

But unlike J. Paul Getty, Hiram never personally earned a dime from his sweat, although I didn't give old man Getty too much slack, either—most of America's successful billionaires who hadn't made their fortunes with computer and Internet technology had had wealthy parents who gave them a multimillion-dollar head start. Getty's father had been an oil millionaire a hundred years ago, a time when a million dollars stretched a long ways.

The Piedmont family made its first fortune in wine. Hiram I, the founder of the family fortune, brought his family to New York in the 1890s from the Asti winegrowing region of Piedmont in northern Italy. A cousin who had a small business importing wines had already preceded Hiram I. He took over the cousin's business and built it into a major importer.

Around the turn of the century the company started distributing Asti Spumante, a sparkling wine that became a popular alcoholic beverage.

During World War I, while Getty was getting rich from the hunger for oil to drive the war effort, Hiram heard a lot of talk about a growing temperance moment that advocated a "prohibition" on selling alcoholic beverages. He looked around and decided that the manufacturing plants for war vehicles were going to turn into an enormous boom for cars for ordinary people. Deciding nobody was going to outlaw cars, he sold his wine-importing business and invested his money in the stock of a new, risky business called General Motors. It wouldn't be long before the car company was the largest manufacturing company in the world.

The next in line, Hiram II, added AT&T and IBM to the family's stock portfolio.

By the time the family fortune came to the current Hiram, he was already far too rich to acquire more money. He also inherited one of the grand houses on the Upper East Side that his grandfather Hiram I had built for his wife, Sophia.

The huge mansion was built for her at a time when the Upper East

Side along Central Park was known as Millionaire's Row instead of Museum Mile.

Sophia was a fanatic about roses. She developed several varieties of hybrid tea roses—including the prizewinning Piedmont and Asti varieties. Unfortunately, she carried her love for roses not only into the garden but also to her home.

Surrounding the outside of the mansion were rose gardens and fountains and statues with rose motifs. At enormous expense, Sofia had "old-world craftsmen" in Europe create a large Gothic "rose window," a round stained-glass window with rose floral designs.

The general consensus was that the rose window, which was in the front of the house and considered the focal point, would have looked much better in a cathedral.

Naturally, the house was called the Rose House . . . although people in the neighboring mansions called it a gaudy eyesore.

The word was that Hiram III wasn't displeased when the place burned down ten years ago. What he constructed in its stead was not a home but a museum.

The Piedmont Museum was designed to look like a box—or, more accurately, a series of square boxes. From the outside it was all straight lines. Hiram's theory was that if you made it in the shape of a box, you wouldn't be restricted in how you filled the interiors. He was right. He wanted a "theme museum," and the boxed shape permitted him to design the interior without posing any restrictions from the exterior.

The neighbors were unanimous in their opinion again that the new house was worse than the old—at least the old one had Sophia's exuberant bad taste going for it.

In discussing acquisitions for the museum with Hiram, I soon found out that his taste in art was not much better than his grandmother's taste in decorating. His most serious interest in the art he acquired was in having his picture taken next to the pieces. His wife's attitude was exactly the same.

When I first came to work at the Piedmont it had been a traditional museum—visitors walked by enclosed glass cases and roped-off exhibits. In other words, it was very boring. Pieces were rarely displayed as anything but individual works.

My own feeling was that works of art could be best appreciated if they were presented with a story.

When I first proposed the concept to Eric, he instantly disliked it.

"This is a museum," he said. "Each and every piece has its own unique history, sometimes a thousand years apart from the piece next to it. We can't tell a story by combining a Babylonian chariot wheel, a Persian helmet a millennium younger, and a Roman spear from hundreds of years after that."

I disagreed. "Every one of those civilizations battled each other. You could have an exciting story about war and conquest."

Hiram had been intrigued with the idea.

Considering all the Mesopotamian art that we had, it was easy for me to come up with a theme.

"Babylon," I told them, "and specifically, Nebuchadnezzar's Babylon. He was the greatest king in the world during his time, and Babylon was the most fabulous city. Everybody has heard of the Tower of Babel and the Babylonian Captivity of the Jews. Both are themes taught in Sunday school. And of one of the Seven Wonders of the Ancient World: the Hanging Gardens of Babylon."

I was right, of course. With so much colorful history and architecture, a Babylonian theme was perfect for the museum.

"We can make a visit to the museum an experience," I told Hiram and Eric. "People wouldn't walk by lifeless objects on stands and in display cases but pieces that combine with scenery to tell them a story. Periodically we can change the theme, reusing some of the pieces and adding those we have in storage."

"What sort of themes?" Hiram asked.

"Universal ones—love, war, and money, the three building blocks of civilization. The public is more interested in how Cleopatra seduced Caesar and Mark Antony and ended up taking the bite of a snake than they are in how many countries the Romans conquered."

I called it "world building," taking a concept from science fiction writers who create futuristic and alien worlds from scratch with their imaginations.

The world I set out to build was Babylon when it was the Queen of the World . . . well, that was what I told Hiram and Eric, but knowing that sex was more important than culture, what I really set out to re-create was the Whore of Babylon.

As the entrance to the exhibit gallery, I chose the Ishtar Gate, the most famous entry of the city.

"Ishtar was the Babylonian Venus, the Goddess of Love," I pointed out, showing them pictures of the enormous re-created gate that the Iraqis had built at the modern entrance to the ancient ruins. I didn't add that she was also a shady lady, the protectress of prostitutes and ale-houses.

The gate, blue with gold and white trim, resembled the entrance to a medieval castle. As with the original design, metallic images of dragons and young bulls were embedded in the walls.

Once you came through the gate, the Hanging Gardens, ziggurat terraces with sloping sides covered with carpets of magnificent flowers and vines, flowed down on both sides of the aisle. We called the pathway Processional Way, naming it after the ancient thoroughfare.

At the far end was the Tower of Babel, the "Gate of God."

According to the Bible, the Babylonians wanted to build a tower that reached the heavens. But God disrupted the work by so confusing the languages of the workers that they could no longer understand one another.

Along the path, I placed exhibits—a fierce Assyrian in a Babylonian war chariot, statues, vases, a ninth century A.D. reproduction of the Code of Hammurabi, perhaps the oldest promulgation of laws in human history, and other artifacts of the era. Each museum piece was placed in a scene that recounted the story of Babylon.

The only thing missing was a centerpiece.

Then I found it.

When the auction hammer fell on my bid for the Mask of Semiramis, I had my showpiece—and my place in museum lore.

Both Hiram and Eric basked in the publicity light that the Babylonian theme generated . . . and ignored the fact that I was the one who came up with the idea of making the Piedmont a theme museum.

I arrived inside the museum just as the public announcement came on to remind people that the museum was closing in ten minutes. Although we had hired a professional event planner to supervise the event,

❖

I double-checked everything, on the theory that if anything could go wrong, it would.

The museum was closing earlier than normal because of the private reception at six o'clock. The professional caterers needed three hours to set everything up and I figured an extra hour on top of that in case of an unexpected surprise. I instructed the planner to furnish the food tables with platters of fancy hors d'oeuvre, as well as expensive wine and champagne. Nothing but the best. Two chocolate waterfalls, one milk and one dark, made from premier chocolate, surrounded by mounds of fruit and cookies for dipping, made up the dessert table. Who didn't love chocolate?

The extra guards I had hired to make a show of security for Semiramis were already on duty.

As I walked through the museum, I noticed a man suddenly reach out to touch a marble nude statue on display. The security sensor immediately sounded. One of the guards quickly approached him and guided him out. Although we had signs posted throughout the museum that prohibited touching, for some reason people always had an urge to touch the nude statue. The same went for religious art. I never understood why.

12

❖

Abdullah waited anxiously on the sidewalk outside the Piedmont Museum for the Iraqi UN delegation to arrive, including its ambassador. He planned to accompany the delegation when they entered the museum.

"The diplomats are invited to a blasphemy and a sacrilege," Abdullah had told his daughter when he left the house. "They will stand by the looted treasures of our country and smile as their pictures are taken. But will one of them raise their voice and say that Iraqi culture belongs in Iraq? Will even one of them ask how Americans would feel if the Statue of Liberty was dismantled and shipped to Baghdad?"

His long-suffering daughter refused to answer. But as he was going down the stairs, she had told him, "Don't call me if you are arrested. I will tell them I don't know you."

She was right, of course. What he was doing was foolish, even stupid, and even he realized it. He was going to storm the museum and expose the fraud. To attempt that in Iraq when Saddam was in power, or even today, would get him shot. Here in America, he would be arrested and released after appearing before a judge, with a promise to come back to court on another day.

❖

Not so bad, he thought. The only real leverage they had over him was the threat of deportation.

He had come to the United States because his life was in danger in his own country, and he was grateful that he was here. His complaints were not against the Americans in general but against the rich and powerful people who used their status to steal the cultural treasures of his nation.

He had stopped trying to defend his actions with his daughter. He was doing something foolish. "What if you are deported back to Iraq for your actions?" she asked many times. That would be a death sentence. For a moment he wavered, ready to abandon his mission, but then he thought of his father, who had died for the mask, and it encouraged him.

A fine mist had now turned into a light drizzle. Abdullah was eager to get inside where it was dry and warm, even though he stood under an awning to avoid the rain. He cursed himself for not bringing his umbrella.

When the six-party delegation finally arrived in a stretch limo, he quickly fell in behind them and entered the museum with them.

13

❖

Hiram's store-bought wife, Angela, was again serving as official hostess tonight. A position I should have held. Antiquities and museums bored her . . . except when the cameras were on her.

"Madison, darling."

"Angela. You look dazzling." *And she did, dammit.*

We gave each other superficial pecks on the cheek.

My next obstacle was Eric's assistant, Monica Spencer. I called her Nurse Ratched, from the book and the movie *One Flew over the Cuckoo's Nest,* starring Jack Nicholson and produced by Michael Douglas. Louise Fletcher got an Oscar for playing Ratched, the bitch nurse who took great delight in tormenting patients in the mental institution Ken Kesey had created.

Frankly, I hated Monica. She was the type of person who would take serious delight if she heard someone had gotten fired for having doctor appointments for Stage 4 cancer.

"Monica," I said, showing no warmth in my voice.

I went out of my way to treat Monica neutrally. I didn't show my disrespect or kiss up to her. She'd take disrespect as a challenge—and ass kissing as a victory. My own tactic amounted to barely tolerating her, a response that left her confused.

I was spared further conversation with her because Neal grabbed me and gave me a big hug. "Congratulations, Madison. This is your night." He acted like he hadn't seen me in ages. He whispered in my ear, "Let's get together afterward."

I smiled and nodded. *Great, another night of passionate abandon with him . . . and a faked orgasm. And Angela thought she was a good actress.*

As the room filled with distinguished guests, I found myself wishing my parents were here. I missed them a lot. I had no man in my life, no really close friends. People I'd meet would try to socialize with me—guys asking me out for dates, women wanting to get together with me for girl talk—but after I turned them down repeatedly, they would veer off and stop asking. It suddenly dawned on me that I hadn't been invited to a Halloween party or New Year's bash for years. Being a workaholic didn't leave much time for friends.

I wandered over to look at my crowning achievement. The Mask of Semiramis needed a body, and we gave her one. I had an elegant feminine figure created from clay shipped in from the Babylonian site.

Baked clay was symbolic of the Middle East: The ingredient of pottery that played a large role in the daily lives of people there for thousands of years, it was used for cooking, serving, and storing foods, as the "canvas" for works of art, the "pages" of the first "books" and accounting tablets the laws of the land were printed on. It even became the building blocks of palaces and walls.

The clay Semiramis wore her mask as she sat on her golden throne. I had other clay figures with similar masks around her. It was a death scene in which Semiramis was having the heir to the throne murdered because he stood in the way of her own son having the position.

"Too Hollywoodish," Eric scoffed when I told him my plan.

"Exactly," I said. "People love to be entertained."

He also objected to the expense of importing clay from near the Babylon site in Iraq. "Use Silly Putty instead. Much cheaper."

Unimaginative little shit. If he had his way, the mask would be sitting in a typical glass case with a little white identification card next to it.

When everyone we counted as mandatory had arrived, I took my place next to Hiram and Eric and glowed as Hiram made a speech about the history of Queen Semiramis and the mask that had been passed down over the centuries to kings, queens, and conquerors. He didn't exactly say he had acquired it because of his own kingly status, but he certainly implied it.

A significant player in the Semiramis acquisition wasn't present. Sir Henri Lipton, the London art dealer who had guided the piece to auction, wasn't able to attend. We were preempted by a garden party for the queen, his assistant said.

A man standing with the Iraqi delegation caught my attention. He frowned at me, almost angrily. I didn't recognize him, so I assumed he wasn't someone I had personally offended.

He still wore his raincoat, and his hair had dried in tangles from the rain outside. Rather odd, since most of the people in the room had arrived by car and checked their coats after entering.

My inclination was that he was a lower-ranking member of the Iraqi UN delegation, maybe even someone recently arrived who hadn't shaken off hometown dust yet.

He suddenly stepped forward and shouted, *"It's stolen!"*

Hiram stopped in midsentence and stared at him.

We all did. I gaped, wide-eyed.

He pounded the air with his fist. "Sammu-ramat was looted from the Iraqi museum as American troops entered Baghdad." He turned to the audience and touched his head. "I was there. I was attacked and almost murdered when I tried to stop the looting."

All eyes and cameras were on him as he demanded that the mask be returned to the people of Iraq.

Hiram and Eric both shouted for security.

"It's not true! We have the provenance!" I yelled.

"American and Iraqi soldiers looted it from the museum!"

My God—this is insane! I ran toward him waving my arms, flapping them like a seagull running on the beach, as I tried to attract the cameras off of him and onto me. I acted instinctively, a drowning rat clutching for a life raft that keeps slipping away.

Before security hustled him out of the room, he tossed out handouts with a faded picture of the Semiramis, along with his name and address. I grabbed one of the handouts.

❖

"Ladies and Gentlemen," Hiram said, calling the room back to order, "I apologize for the intrusion. The man is obviously a lunatic. As you all know, there have been a number of incidents around the world where crazies have attacked great works of art. Remember the attack on Michelangelo's *David*. . . ."

As Hiram rambled on, I left the stage and quickly ran down the corridor for the front doors.

The handout said his name was Abdullah ibn Hussein and had a Jamaica Plains address in Queens. He was no doubt a nutcase, some whacked-out Iraqi who wanted everything that came out of the country in the last ten thousand years returned, but I had to make sure myself. I saw all my hard work—*my career*—being mauled by this crazy old man.

What had caused my sudden bolt from the room had been the grainy black-and-white picture of the Semiramis in his handout. Printed from an old photograph, it was a bit fuzzy, but one thing shouted to me: The mask was on a worktable.

That didn't say much unless you had spent your life around a museum and knew what a restoration workbench looked like.

14

❖

The rain had picked up from what it had been when I came in earlier. Naturally, I rushed out of the building without a hat or coat. I spotted the intruder a hundred feet up the street and I yelled to him.

"Mr. ibn Hussein—wait!"

He waited for me, a forlorn little skinny man with wet hair who needed a haircut and new shoes.

"I have to talk to you about the mask."

"It was stolen. It belongs to my people."

"That's not true. I have a provenance, the paperwork."

"Your paperwork is a lie."

"Who are you to say such a thing? We've had experts—"

"I was a curator at the Iraqi National Museum. I know the piece; it came to the museum over fifty years ago after the people of my village discovered it. It belongs to the Iraqi museum. It's part of our cultural history."

"We investigated the history of the piece. It was never at the museum."

"Look at my papers. Look at the picture."

"The picture could have been taken anywhere—and of an imitation of the mask. You can't tell me that a piece as famous and valuable as this was at the museum. It's not cataloged; it's not on the list of items stolen—"

"Over fifteen thousand pieces were taken, most of them not cataloged. The catalog for those that were inventoried was also stolen. Valuable pieces were deliberately kept out of catalogs to keep Saddam and the tyrants before him from stealing them." He grabbed my arm. "Listen to me. I spent most of my life at the museum. I was there because my father had died protecting Sammu-ramat, and the duty became mine. It was stolen by American soldiers—"

"Miss Dupre!"

Nurse Ratched had come up behind me with an umbrella. "Mr. Piedmont wants you back in the museum immediately. The police will take care of this intruder."

He backed away, frightened. "You're all the same. Thieves and robbers." He spit and spun around, walking away.

"Wait!" I yelled.

He quickened his pace and didn't turn around. He came from a country where the word "police" meant so much more.

Ratched confronted me. "You shouldn't get yourself involved with—"

"Shut the fuck up."

It was the first time I had seen her speechless. I ran for cover back into the building and headed for the bathroom to check my outfit and fix my wet hair.

I leaned on a washbasin and closed my eyes, shutting them tight. How could this be happening to me?

Could there be two masks? Duplicates? Not likely, unless we had paid over $50 million for a fake.

What devastated me besides the accusation and the picture in the handout was a feeling that I had heard the simple truth from Abdullah. His claim that the mask had been looted left me breathless.

Neal was standing nearby when I came out. We spoke in a confidential tone.

"What'd that guy say?" Neal asked.

"That the piece was looted."

"I heard that. What else? What's his proof?"

"He says he was the guardian of it."

"What do you mean?"

"I don't know; Christ, he said his father was murdered protecting it, then it passed down to him—"

"The Keeper of the Flame. He's a wacko."

Abdullah did sound like a crazy when I explained him.

"Don't worry; you have the provenance."

"Yes, I have a provenance."

A tiny voice of doubt crept in. I was certain we had a good provenance, I had had it examined for fraud, but right at the moment my whole life depended on a piece of paper.

"Crazy or not," I said, "he's ruined the reception. My God, we're going to be trashed in the news. I'd better go see Hiram and Eric."

As I came in, Angela intercepted me.

"Put a smile on your face and keep it there. When newspeople ask you if the mask was stolen, look them straight in the eye and tell them that the poor man needs medical assistance."

Sound advice. I suppose movie stars spend a lot of time denying accusations.

"I'm the one in need of medical assistance."

I dodged a reporter and made it to Eric. Hiram was busy with a group of collectors.

I gave Eric a quick summary of what the man had said.

"Get together the paperwork," Eric said. "Get me a copy of the entire file. We'll get it to our lawyers. They can get a restraining order against this madman."

I had started to walk away when Eric's voice caused me to stop.

"This is bad, very bad, a black eye for the museum. Hiram will not be happy tomorrow. You'd better hope the documentation is as good as you represented to us."

I almost reminded him that he had been taking credit for the Semiramis a moment ago but remembered my father's advice about bosses. Besides, Eric was right—the mask was my project. And I would sink or swim with it.

Right at the moment I needed a life vest.

"Don't answer any questions from anyone, not the newspeople nor the Iraqi delegation. We'll talk tomorrow. Go out and mingle. Just pretend nothing's happened."

Easy for him to say. The crowd was buzzing about the accusation.

I put on a happy face and floated around the room, chatting up potential donors, jealous curators, and glad-handing politicians, acting as if

❖

nothing had happened, waving away the incident as just some crazy publicity stunt. What I really felt like doing was rushing home and hiding my head under the covers.

The Piedmonts and Eric departed early. The artificial smiles they gave me as they left didn't leave me with any warm feelings. It didn't take much imagination to realize I was in deep trouble.

Hiram's parting words to me were that he wanted an explanation of what had happened. I told him I would get back to him in the morning with an answer. After I found out myself.

15

❖

Abdullah trembled as he hurried away from the two women in front of the museum. He wished he were home in bed. His knees were weak and his stomach in knots. Now his chest was tightening and he felt a stabbing pressure between his shoulder blades.

He was a simple man, and appearing before "notables" and members of the news media had frightened him. His daughter had warned him . . . begged him not to do it. "Write a letter to the newspapers," she pleaded.

But like his own father, he had great moral courage that kept him from surrendering to his fears. "They won't listen if they read about it. I have to shout the truth to be heard," he told her.

When he had left the apartment earlier he felt tense and fearful—fearing the unknown—as he moved his feet doggedly from the apartment and propelled himself toward the Piedmont.

The violent image of his father confronting tomb robbers was embedded in his mind.

Tomb robbers. That was how he thought of the people at the rich and powerful museum. Murderous thieves who stole his country's heritage to put on display halfway around the world.

Why didn't they put their own heritage on display? Why his? Just as

❖

they would be devastated if he dismantled the Statue of Liberty and shipped it to Iraq, how would these Americans feel if he dug up George Washington and took him back to Baghdad to be displayed as a dried skeleton in an open coffin? Or put the Declaration of Independence and Constitution in a glass case for Iraqi children to see as their teachers took them to the Baghdad museum?

After Abdullah had blurted out his accusations and been escorted out of the museum by security, away from the excited questions of the news media, he walked swiftly down the street, blindly, more from nervous energy than anything else. He wasn't sure where he was going.

The rain had now turned into a cloudburst, as his America-wise daughter called it. He lacked a hat, and the rain ran down his head and face and soaked his collar. He felt a chill and worried that his malaria was acting up again.

He slowed down his pace, realizing he was lost. He wasn't familiar with the area and wasn't sure which street would take him back to the underground station that he had exited earlier on his way to the museum.

There were no taxis on the street; there never were when it rained, a phenomenon he heard others complain about but that he never understood. Where did the taxis all disappear to?

The street he walked on was dark and quiet. A car had just turned on the same street and was moving slowly, almost as if it was looking for something or someone.

Adrenaline kicked in. There were bad people everywhere, even in nice neighborhoods. Maybe the people in the car were going to rob him and beat him. Maybe kill him.

He suddenly heard the car speed up. Abdullah started to run. It was a gut impulse. He almost knocked down a person as he rounded the corner.

The car was almost beside him. He tried not to look at it, keeping his feet in motion and his focus in front of him, planning his next move.

A familiar voice shouted out from the passenger side window, "Father! Stop! We've been trying to find you!"

16

❖

As soon as the last guests left, I rushed to review the provenance for the mask. Neal had already split earlier, which was fine with me, after I told him I was too bummed out to have sex with him. I'm sure he found somebody else to satisfy him. From looks I saw pass between him and Angela before, I wouldn't be surprised if they had something going.

I took another look at the man's handout as I made my way to the museum's executive suite. Just as he had told me, it stated he was a former curator for the Iraqi museum. The title had different meanings in different places, from someone in charge of the collections, as I was at the Piedmont, down to someone who swept the floors.

Studying the fuzzy, grainy picture again, I didn't see anything that clearly identified the location of the mask when it was photographed. It sat on a workbench, for sure. But I didn't see anything that identified where the bench was.

The fact the picture didn't clearly infer that the location was the Iraqi museum was critical. Worse than artifacts that were freshly dug up by tomb robbers—pieces with actual dirt on them—were ones stolen from other museums and collectors. Those weren't dirty metaphorically;

they had stripes on them—*prison stripes*—because they usually could be identified and traced back to the rightful owner.

Everyone in the art world was familiar with the looting of Iraqi antiquities following the American invasion in 2003. Many thousands of museum pieces had been stolen. No one knew the exact amount, although I've seen a figure of 15,000 or more mentioned. In addition, when the police restraints came off and the country turned to chaos as sectarian violence erupted and law and order broke down, thousands of antiquity sites had been invaded by tomb robbers who often inadvertently destroyed as much as they stole.

At the same time the museum was being looted, priceless and irreplaceable books and manuscripts were being destroyed at the Iraqi National Library as flames devoured thousands of rare pieces.

The devastation of knowledge and the cultural heritage of both the museum and the library had been compared to the burning of the great Library of Alexandria that came about as a result of the intrigues of Caesar and Cleopatra. By today's standards, it would be like the destruction of both the Louvre and the Vatican Library.

As would be expected, the availability of Middle Eastern artifacts shot up after the debacle.

Certainly I bought some pieces; in fact, the best pieces in the Piedmont collection were acquired by me during the past year, but I always made sure to check the Art Loss Register first. Not that that act alone would fly about missing Iraqi museum pieces. Like everyone else in the business, because of the nature of the losses and the inadequacy of the record keeping at the museum I was well aware that not all of the losses were actually listed in the Register.

But I wouldn't have bought a piece that I definitely knew was contraband. I wasn't that stupid. *Not fifty-five million dollars stupid.*

I knew the provenance of the mask by heart, but I wanted the comfort level again of seeing the written history that spelled out that the private ownership of the Semiramis went back over a hundred years, into the late nineteenth century. A critical time period, because most of the national laws prohibiting the exporting of antiquities from their countries of origin dated from the twentieth century. Anything in private ownership before 1900 was generally open game.

❖

All vital documents concerning the collection were kept in the "Panic Room" in the executive office area. Officially, it was called the Document Storage Room. I gave it the nickname after seeing the Jodie Foster movie because it reminded me of the sealed, fireproof, vaultlike room she holed up in during a robbery.

"Good evening, Ms. Dupre." The greeting came from hidden speakers as I walked through an exhibit area.

"Hi, Carlos," I replied, waving my hand in the air.

My presence, picked up by hidden cameras, had been displayed on a monitor in the security center—which was also hidden.

"Hidden" was the key word for museum security. Prominent security measures didn't seem to discourage people from stealing. Now everything from cameras to laser beams and radio transmission tags on individual items was being concealed.

I retrieved the file folder from the Panic Room and took it back to my assistant's desk to review and copy it. Besides a copy for Hiram, Eric, and the lawyers, I wanted my own copy of it . . . more security blanket mentality.

The provenance report, made by a Swiss art appraiser named Viktor Milan, was the top document in the file.

The provenance said that the Semiramis had been acquired by a man named Rashid Kalb in 1883 in a marketplace in Beirut, Lebanon. No paperwork accompanied the sale, which was typical of both the time and the place. In those days Lebanon was a region under the rule of the Sultan of the Ottoman Empire. Istanbul, Turkey, was the capital. The empire collapsed after World War I.

No one would expect a receipt from a "marketplace" purchase, either. But again, that wasn't unusual for the time or place. Credible oral histories could support a chain of ownership.

Various members of the Kalb family owned it until the last member died out in 1934. It was sold shortly before the death of Rana Kalb, the last surviving member of the family—who apparently was murdered for reasons that were not revealed—to a Panamanian company, which held it for fifty-five years. They sold it three years ago to Milan. He in turn sold it a few months ago to Henri Lipton, the London art dealer who had arranged the auction in New York.

❖

Although I had never met Viktor Milan, I recalled seeing his name on the provenances of other pieces I'd bought from Lipton. Lipton I knew reasonably well, having met with him several times in New York and at his London gallery.

The fact that a priceless artifact had turned up in a Lebanese marketplace over 120 years ago was not unusual. Even today, antiquities were sold in third-world countries for a tiny fraction of their value. In the nineteenth century, the laws protecting antiquities in the region probably didn't exist—and if they were on the books were easily avoided, as they were today.

A solid history of personal ownership going back an eon would have been nice, but that was the exception, not the rule, with antiquities. Records of sales get lost or destroyed or never were prepared. In this case, the most important document was the bill of sale from Rana Kalb to the Panamanian company in 1934. Two versions were present: one written in Arabic scrawl, the other typed in English. The document included a sworn narration of the original marketplace purchase of the piece decades before.

It wasn't the most perfect provenance I had seen, but this was how art pieces were frequently sold back then—and even now. Little formality was involved in the transfer of pieces worth millions. Sometimes there was no formality at all, other than a thorough inspection of the piece by an expert—and often that was not even done.

I sighed with relief. The provenance was "acceptable," which was what I said in my memo to Eric and Hiram at the time.

After reading my memo, I quickly skimmed through some correspondence from Neal at the auction house and appraisals by two experts I had hired to give me an opinion on the piece's value and authenticity.

I came across a report prepared by Charles Bensky, a professional document examiner, an expert whom I had retained to scrutinize the paperwork supporting the provenance. His job was to determine whether the documents were genuine. I recalled speaking to him over the phone when he had given me the all clear on the paperwork supporting the provenance, but I didn't remember seeing his report before.

I started to skim over the report and stopped dead when I got to the Summary of Conclusion in the middle of the first page:

❖

THE LOOTERS

*The purported bill of sale of the Semiramis from Rana Kalb
to the Panamanian corporation is suspicious because the
document was prepared later than the 1934 date it bears.*

I stared at the statement, but my brain refused to further process
the information. I read it again—and again, staring at the words, trying
to make them say something other than what I saw in black-and-white.

Stripped of its verbosity, it said the bill of sale was a phony.

The provenance was invalid.

❖

17

❖

I jumped out of the chair and backed away from the report as if it were a snake.

"It can't be," I said out loud. Not possible. No way in hell could the provenance be a fraud.

Grabbing the report, I reread the statement: *suspicious . . . prepared later than the 1934 date.*

How could he say that? My heart banged against the wall of my chest. I couldn't get enough air.

"This can't be true."

I had hired Bensky to examine the documents supporting the provenance. Basically, that came down to the bills of sale from the last surviving member of the Lebanese family to the Panamanian corporation, the sale from the Panamanian corporation to Viktor Milan, and the sale from Milan to the London dealer. There were also birth and death certificates of the members of the Lebanese family to prove their existence.

I didn't order a document examination on every purchase, not even high-end ones. In buying art and antiquities, you rely more on *who* you are doing business with, since documents might be forged. In this case I ordered it because the Semiramis was such a huge investment and none of the people in the Lebanese and Panamanian connections were still alive. Even though I was dealing with Henri Lipton, an icon in the world of art whom I had dealt with many times in the past, the Semiramis was too big a purchase not to double-check the provenance documents.

The report in the file was dated two days *after* I spoke to Bensky. How it got past me and into the file was baffling.

Almost anyone from Eric and Hiram down to the clerical staff, even security guards, had access to the Panic Room. It wasn't even locked, because it was intended to protect against fire, not thieves—only records were kept in it. And there was no security surveillance anywhere in the executive suite.

I forced myself to continue reading the full report. In my frazzled state, I had to read it twice.

Bensky stated the problem was with the font and spacing of individual letters of the alphabet:

Two problems are noted with the Times New Roman font. The bill of sale dated January 1934 states it was prepared in Panama City, Panama, and transmitted to Lebanon for signature. The document is written in the English language. The typewriter font, Times New Roman, was first used by the Times newspaper of London in October 1932.

Bensky claimed that a manual typewriter being used in Panama with the same font just fifteen months later was "highly improbable, though possible."

More suspicious was the second problem with the font:

The individual letters of the alphabet typed on the bill of sale had proportional spacing rather than monospacing. Proportional spacing for the font was not available at that time period for ordinary manual typewriters, but a forger might not have realized that.

He gave an explanation about the two types of spacing:

Prior to the 1960s, each letter, number, and punctuation mark in a typewriter occupied a "typing bar." When a key was pressed, the typing bar for that letter flew forward, struck the inked ribbon, and made an impression on the paper. Most office typewriters had about forty typing bars to accommodate upper-/lowercase letters, numbers, and punctuation marks.

To keep the bars from jamming, *the bars had to be all the same width.* Even though the letter *I* occupied less space on paper than the letter *M,* the widths of the bars were the same. So on paper an *I* had more space around it than an *M.*

This was called *monospacing.*

A more advanced form of spacing is *proportional spacing,* in which the space between letters is proportioned so that the letter *I* does not have more space before and after it than the letter *M.*

Proportional spacing came into home and office typewriters in the early 1960s with IBM's introduction of the typing ball in Selectric typewriters: A single golf ball–size typing head replaced the dozens of typing bars.

Bensky's report said that the introduction of computers also enhanced the profession of forgery because computers were so versatile. They could be used to create an "ancient document" with almost any type of font or other characteristic. But they could also lead to mistakes by the forger:

> *This forger erred in not knowing the history of typesetting. He assumed that since the Times New Roman font dated back to 1932 and the document was dated in 1934, it was safe to use that font. I suspect the forger may have used a scanner and computer to duplicate the font from a 1934 newspaper. What the forger did not realize was that the newspaper font in that era was set with an electric typesetting machine that could do proportional spacing with the Times New Roman font. Ordinary home and office typewriters were not capable of proportional spacing at that time, which came with the widespread use of computers.*

If I had read this report, I never would have recommended going through with the purchase.

I lost my breath again. Mother of God. Hiram would go berserk when he saw Bensky's report.

❖

Questions flew through my head, ricocheting around my skull, banging against one another. How could this happen to me? Why would the examiner call and tell me nothing was wrong—and then send a report two days later saying the provenance was suspicious? It made no sense. Did he find something suspicious after he spoke to me?

I found the answer to that question at the bottom of his report:

Ms. Dupre, I told you during our telephone conversation that when I first observed the documents I found nothing suspicious. However, it wasn't until I reexamined them that I caught the discrepancy. Sorry if I caused you any inconvenience.

No, you bastard, you didn't cause me any inconvenience. You just cost me my fucking job! My life.

I closed my eyes and told myself this was just a nightmare, that I had wandered into a John Farris tale of horror.

"Why didn't you call me when you found something suspicious?" I asked Bensky. Rhetorically, of course, since he wasn't present. But it was a very good question. A $55 million question.

My survival financially and emotionally—and a big chunk of Hiram's money—was riding on it. Of course, Bensky didn't know that. Not as far as I knew. I never disclosed how valuable the piece was that we were planning to bid on. He probably did examinations for individuals who were more worried about $55,000 purchases than what we paid for the Semiramis.

But even if he didn't know the purchase price, no one with any business sense would have sent a written report that directly conflicted with his verbal report without picking up the phone and explaining it. It just didn't make sense. Bensky was a professional; he couldn't be that stupid. But as I thought about it, I realized with a growing sense of horror that he might have called.

I had left for an art sale in London soon after talking on the phone to him. Went there at Lipton's invitation, as a matter of fact. Bensky may have called, found out I was out of town, and simply sent over his report. I may have even mentioned to him that I would be leaving town shortly. Jesus. I did tell him that. I'm sure of it.

I also realized now how the report could have gotten filed without my seeing it.

Before I left for London, I had dictated a memo to Hiram and Eric telling them that the document examiner had validated the provenance. My secretary, Rita, would have typed and distributed it the day I flew out. Bensky's report was faxed over late that same afternoon. Rita could have decided that I had already seen the report and filed it. She was no rocket scientist, which was why I was happy when she left suddenly a week ago to return to care for her sick mother in Puerto Rico.

The Iraqi curator was right.

The fuckin' mask had been stolen when the museum was looted.

Holy shit.

I held my head in my hands.

My penthouse. My Jag. My designer clothes. My bloody career.

Hiram was not just going to fire me; he was going to have me burned at the stake.

I squeezed my head, breathless, ready to vomit, when I realized that everything was even worse than I had imagined.

Besides losing everything I had worked for and being hounded out of the trade, I would be facing an accusation of buying stolen property . . . and sitting on a report that proved my guilt.

I didn't know much about the law, but I knew that buying stolen artifacts was a serious crime.

My brains were scrambled. Not knowing which way to turn, I made four copies of the provenance: a copy for Hiram, one for Eric, one to keep at my desk, and another to carry with me. I didn't bother copying Bensky's report. I stuck that in my pocket. I wasn't sure yet how to deal with it.

I returned to my office to make a phone call. I didn't have Rita's number in Puerto Rico. She might have given it to Nurse Ratched and I could get it in the morning, but the last thing I would do was ask that woman for it, out of fear she'd instinctively sense my panic and use it against me.

Rita would never admit to filing a report without showing it to me, anyway. At the moment, I was reasonably certain that I was the only one who knew the contents of the report.

❖

I had to talk to Bensky to find out if there was any other interpretation than the one he had stated. I needed to get across to him that the report got filed without my seeing it. Get him behind me before the police or anyone else got to him.

I looked at my watch. Two o'clock in the morning. Bensky lived in Pelham, about an hour north of the city. I knew he worked out of his house. I hoped I would wake him up from a deep sleep, when he was most susceptible to the power of suggestion.

After six rings, his telephone recorder came on. "Out of town, leave a message; I check frequently."

Trying to keep the stress out of my voice, I said that I needed to talk to him immediately. I left my cell number.

My next call went to Neal. He was cranky and groggy when he answered.

"The provenance is a fraud."

"What provenance?" It took a minute for the statement to sink into his head.

"The Semiramis."

"What? Are you kidding me?" He was wide awake now.

I told him about the report.

"Font? You mean the type style is wrong?"

"That's what Bensky said. The font and the space between letters."

"He told you on the phone that nothing looked suspicious and then sent you a report trashing it? Is he a fuckin' idiot?"

"No, I am the idiot—and fucked."

"I don't believe this. You got an adverse document examination report and simply filed it?" he said accusingly.

My grip tightened on the phone. "My secretary filed it without showing it to me." I was getting irritated.

"It doesn't make any difference. Do you think anyone will believe that?"

"Don't you think I already thought of that? The question is, What do we do now?"

I knew the "we" would cause him to freeze.

"Maddy . . ."

"Neal . . . you convinced me to bid on the goddamned piece. And it wasn't the only piece I bought because of you. You acted as the middle-man in treaty sales between Lipton and me. Do I have to tell you who the provenance agent was on those sales?"

No answer from his end.

"The same Viktor Milan who prepared the provenances on everything you sold me. What do you think the chances are that some of those won't pass muster when Hiram has everything he ever bought examined?"

More silence.

"Who is this Milan anyway?" I asked. "How long have you been deal-ing with him?"

"I don't deal with him. I've never even met him. Lipton knows him."

"Lipton, Lipton, Lipton. Jesus, his name's been popping up tonight. I'm beginning to get an ugly suspicion that he dumped stuff on us when he knew better."

"Did you get provenances for other pieces examined by Bensky?"

"No, the Semiramis was the only piece expensive enough to justify it. Besides, I know Lipton. I didn't think there would be a problem." I didn't keep the anger out of my voice. Lipton's reputation wasn't that he was an angel, but that he had a corner on the lion's share of Middle East antiq-uities. I'd never heard of him pushing a phony provenance.

"Are you going to have those provenances checked?" Neal asked.

I thought for a moment. "Should I?"

"Only if you want to tighten the rope around your neck."

"Are you saying they're frauds?"

"I'm not saying anything. I know nothing about them. Like you, be-cause I have a long history of dealing with Lipton, his word is gold with me. But if you start going through your collection looking for dirt, you're liable to find some."

I shook my head, trying to clear it. "I don't know what to do."

"There's one thing you should do . . . absolutely nothing. Don't do a thing. Let the world turn without you."

"Hide my head. What good will that do?"

"Not hide your head, just keep your mouth shut. This isn't over. If it was a small piece, like the others you bought, it would blow over. Muse-ums return pieces to other countries all the time . . . after haggling about it for a dozen years. But the Semiramis is too important. You're liable to get the Iraqi government involved. The news media will hit

❖

the accusation of U.S. military involvement hard. Maybe the police will be—"

"The police? Why the police?" It was a stupid question. I already knew the answer. "If the pieces were stolen . . ."

"Exactly. It's a crime."

"What do I do?"

"I just told you. Nothing. Keep your mouth shut. *Deny, deny, deny.* That's how it works. You admit to anything, even something innocent, and they use it against you. You volunteer nothing and deny everything."

"But Bensky's report. They'll see—"

"What report?"

"The report I just told you—"

"*What report?*"

Jesus. I finally got it. He was telling me to hide the report.

"Neal, Bensky knows about the report."

"Did Bensky personally deliver the report to your office and place it in your hands?"

"Of course not; he faxed it."

"Then how does anyone prove you've ever seen the report?"

"This is getting complicated."

"No, it's really simple. If the report isn't in the file, no one will know about it. If word gets out from Bensky or otherwise that there was a report, hell, you were out of town when the report was faxed over. You never saw it—"

"That's the real truth."

"Bensky may not have heard about the accusation—you said he's out of town. And even if he did, once you let him know he's part of a fifty-five-million-dollar problem, you can bet your ass he won't be out to make an enemy of you. You have to get to him and neutralize him."

"What about Milan?"

"I'll see what I can find out. Maddy, I know a lawyer, a guy who buys art; he knows the trade. I'll call him tomorrow."

"I don't need a lawyer."

"Just in case."

I squeezed my eyes shut. Was I stupid or what? Of course I needed a lawyer. What kind of rotten karma did I have? I've gone from the woman of the hour to a woman in desperate need of a lawyer.

❖

We hung up and I stared down at the document examiner's report. A smoking gun. That's what they called it on the cop and lawyer shows on television.

In a sense, I was sitting on a museum full of smoking guns: The provenance on the Semiramis was a fraud, and I'd bought other pieces from Lipton with provenances provided by the same man.

What the hell had I gotten myself into?

FBI
Top Ten Art Crimes

The FBI Art Crime Team has identified the TEN TOP ART CRIMES. We ask your help in bringing these masterworks to light by contributing any information on the circumstances of the crime or the whereabouts of the stolen works of art. In this way we ask your help in bringing the thieves to justice.

1. 7,000–10,000 looted and stolen Iraqi artifacts, 2003

Iraqi cultural institutions and archaeological sites suffered major losses of historical artifacts. Between 7,000–10,000 remain missing from the Baghdad museum. Looting from archaeological sites continues on a massive scale.

2. 13 paintings from the Isabella Stewart Gardner Museum theft, 1990

In March 1990, the Isabella Stewart Gardner Museum, Boston, was robbed by two unidentified men. The thieves removed works of art whose value has been estimated as high as $300 million.

3. Munch's *The Scream* and *The Madonna,* the Munch Museum in Oslo, 2004

Two masked thieves entered in daylight while the museum was open and stole the two paintings. Museum-goers witnessed the thieves threaten the museum staff with guns and remove the paintings. They escaped in a black Audi. (*The Madonna* alone was worth $15 million.)

4. Benvenuto Cellini *Salt Cellar* from Vienna's Kunsthistorisches Museum, 2003

In May 2003, at 4 A.M., a thief used a workmen's scaffolding to break into the museum through a first-floor window. Smashing the unprotected glass display case, the thief stole a gold, ebony, and enamel salt cellar valued at $55 million. (A salt cellar holds salt on a dinner table. This one was made for a king.)

5. Caravaggio's *Nativity with San Lorenzo and San Francesco* from Palermo, 1969

Two thieves entered the Oratory of San Lorenzo and removed the Caravaggio *Nativity* from its frame. Experts estimate its value at $20 million.

6. Davidoff-Morini Stradivarius violin from a New York apartment, 1995

A $3 million Stradivarius violin was stolen from the New York City apartment of Erica Morini, a noted concert violinist. Made in 1727 by Antonio Stradivari, the violin is known as the Davidoff-Morini Stradivarius.

7. Two Van Gogh paintings from Amsterdam's Vincent Van Gogh Museum, 2002

Two thieves used a ladder to climb to the roof and break into the museum. They stole two Van Goghs with a combined value of $30 million.

8. Cezanne's *View of Auvers-sur-Oise* from Oxford's Ashmolean Museum, 1999

During the fireworks that accompanied the celebration of the millennium, a thief broke into the museum and stole the £3 million Cezanne landscape.

9. Da Vinci's *Madonna of the Yarnwinder* from Scotland's Drumlanrig Castle, 2003

Two men dressed as tourists taking a public tour of the castle overpowered a tour guide and stole the Da Vinci valued at $65 million. With two accomplices, the men escaped in a white VW Golf, found abandoned nearby.

10. Theft of Gertrude Vanderbilt Whitney Murals, 2002

Two oil paintings by Maxfield Parrish valued at $4 million were cut from their frames and stolen during a burglary of a gallery in West Hollywood, California.

—FBI Web site

18

❖

Brighton Beach, Brooklyn

"Na zdorovie." FBI Special Agent Rick Nunes raised a shot of chilled vodka and gave his informant Vlad the traditional Russian drinking toast. As Nunes downed the burning liquid, he wondered how long the Russian *mafiya* would let Vlad live.

The bar in Little Odessa, the Russian sector of the sprawling New York City behemoth, smelled of borscht, sex, and sweat. Beet and cabbage soup and the meat and onion turnovers called *pirozhkis* were heated up in microwaves behind the bar to Nunes's left. At the bar, two older men wearing fur hats and heavy, old-fashioned wool suits in the warm bar were arguing as they drank vodka and ate pirozhkis. Beefy men, both were built like Soviet T-34 tanks. One had thick black hair swept back, heavy eyebrows, high cheekbones, and a rock jaw, giving him the look of Brezhnev, the 1970s Soviet leader. A red and gold medal making him a Hero of the Soviet Union hung from his lapel.

"A couple former KGB apparatchiks," Vlad said, "arguing over which was the best way to break a dissenter's will during questioning."

Nunes had picked up enough Russian words and body language to understand that the two were really refighting the Cold War, but he didn't doubt they'd get around to KGB torture methods at some point.

❖

"Big trouble," Vlad said. He wasn't referring to the two old men. "That means some fish will be eaten. I don't want to be one of them." He wiped sweat from his face with a handkerchief. As he poured another shot for each of them, Nunes could see his hand shake.

Nunes had joined the Russian in tackling a bottle of Zubrówka, a yellowish vodka with a fragrance and slightly bitter undertone created by steeping the liquor in stalks of buffalo grass.

Small fish would be eaten, Nunes thought. Minnows like Vlad were what the big mafiya fish ate when things went wrong. While Nunes listened to the Russian informer, his eyes made sweeps of the bar. He didn't want to be in the line of fire if Vlad was terminated. To Nunes's right a sapped pole dancer with tired blood bumped and grinded for two construction workers drinking their lunch. She probably worked a split shift, coming in midday for the lunch crowd after working half the night.

The Brighton Beach neighborhood got its "Little Odessa" tag after it became heavily populated by émigrés from the former Soviet republics, mostly Jews fleeing discrimination. The language and storefront signs on the streets were as much in Russian as English, even though Ukrainians dominated the area. Not only did the Russian culture emigrate, but organized crime Russian style—the mafiya—came with it, bringing along violence and naked avariciousness not exercised by organized American crime since Lucky Luciano put together a national syndicate in the 1930s.

"What's got everybody kill crazy?" Nunes asked.

Vlad gave the four corners of the bar another nervous check. He was as subtle as a lamb baaing at a pack of wolves.

"Like I said, a guy came to them a couple months ago that wanted to make a big score in a deal to supply arms to an African rebel leader."

Nunes was working undercover as an art appraiser with no scruples, but there was nothing unique about a connection between art and arms in the international world of crime he operated in.

"You never told me the name of the guy selling the arms."

"I still don't know it. He's American; I know that. He has a Bulgarian deputy defense minister willing to sell him a shipload of small arms— rifles, machine guns, shoulder-launched rockets, that type of stuff. He tells our people he needs money to pay the Bulgarians and ship the stuff to Angola in Africa, where he'll have a big payday in diamonds from a rebel colonel."

Drugs ranked number one in the multibillion-dollar international trade in contraband, with military arms coming in second and art ranking third. Major drug deals were sometimes even financed by contraband art. Major art heists were pulled off to get artworks that were used as collateral to buy narcotics for resale. Because there was little formality in purchasing multimillion-dollar art pieces, traffickers could also launder drug money by buying art with cash and reselling it, collecting the money in bank transfers. It took less legal formality to buy a hundred-million-dollar painting than a hundred-dollar car.

Art's rank of third in the world of crime was not insignificant. That made the illicit trade in works of art often as murderous as that of blood diamonds.

Nunes nodded. "He sells the diamonds through Switzerland, repays the local boys, and pockets the rest."

"Right. But he needed collateral for the loan from our people. He put up antiquities to front the deal."

Vlad had already dropped the word "antiquities" on him in the phone conversation that set up the meeting. Technically, it meant artifacts produced before the Middle Ages, but to Little Odessa mobsters it could mean anything that was old and valuable. But to finance a major arms deal the collateral had to be worth millions. Many millions.

"What kind of antiquities?"

Vlad shook his head, shaking off drops of sweat that hit the table.

Definitely hot in here, Nunes thought, *but not enough to make a man break out in a sweat.* That took fear.

"I know it's Middle Eastern stuff, but I don't know exactly what or how much. They had me examine three pieces they said had been picked by random from the whole lot: a vase, a drinking cup, and a marble head. They were all Mesopotamian."

Nunes got a big jolt of interest. Mesopotamia was the site of a number of great civilizations of the ancient world. More important was its modern relationship to antiquities: The looting of the museum when American troops were entering the city of Baghdad was the greatest tragedy to a national culture since the rape of European culture by the Nazis.

❖

The thousands of stolen items still missing were on the FBI's Top Ten Art Crimes list, the art world's version of the "ten most wanted."

Nunes had been floating in and out of the Russian community for six months, investigating the trade in contraband works of art. He never understood why it took the FBI three-quarters of a century to get serious about the trade in contraband art. The racket was fueled by the trade in antiquities smuggled out of countries of origin, robberies of homes and museums, and the creation of fraudulent works.

His experience with American-style organized crime served him well in dealing with the Russian-style mob. Like its American Mafia counterparts, the mafiya had no central authority but powerful gangs that got involved in almost any action that turned an illegal buck, with the drug and sex trade and business extortion being the staples.

The Russians in many ways were more brutal than the American homegrown variety of gangster. Brighton Beach had a long history as a solid, working-class Jewish community. Over the past couple of decades, it added a criminal flavor to its dimensions as thousands of émigrés landed there after they fled the Soviet Union. Some of the new arrivals had criminal experiences back in the Old Country. And it didn't take U.S. law enforcement long to discover that criminals who had gone head-to-head with the infamous KGB thought American cops were pussycats in comparison. Getting their "rights" read to them by an American cop was a piece of cake to thugs who had survived KGB "interviews" that often began with a beating.

Nunes had become a familiar figure in Vlad's company. With Nunes's own background in art, rather than arranging clandestine meetings with Vlad and worrying about the man being followed, Nunes was brought in to "appraise" works of art. Naturally, everything he was asked to place a value on had been stolen.

He looked over at the stripper on stage. Nunes had empathy for the stripper, who danced as if she were bored to the point of screaming. He had gone through his own burnout. Working nearly three decades on organized crime, drugs, and money laundering, he was ready to flame out when he got assigned to the Bureau's newly formed Art Crime Team.

Besides twenty-nine years of service, his qualifications included a master's in art history he had picked up with a decade of night classes at NYU. Part of his motivation for the evening classes had been to stay out

❖

of the house and avoid conflict with his wife as their marriage disintegrated and they stuck it out until their youngest son left college to launch a computer game company out of his garage.

On this case, Nunes was "in drag," as he characterized it, playing the role of a down-on-the-heels art professor appraising stolen art. He worked the case using the name and ID of an actual UT–Austin professor. The real professor was sent off to work a tell in Israel just in case anyone in Little Odessa picked up the phone to check whether the professor was still in Austin.

A friend of Vlad's stopped by the table and chatted in Russian to him. After he left, Vlad said, "Our kids go to the same school, play soccer on the same team, and that bastard would have me put down if he could make a ruble out of it."

"Tell me more about the deal," Nunes said.

The Russian art dealer shrugged. "That's all I know. It's a simple business arrangement."

The scenario of buying on credit and reselling for a profit would be understood by any businessperson. Except here the return on investment was astronomical when everything went right . . . and the penalty for defaulting was death.

"What went wrong?"

Another shrug. More baaing at the wolves in the place. "I don't know. Someone defaulted. It's like paying for a car. Sometimes you don't pay and they send the collector out."

Nunes was sure he knew why the deal went south. A news report from Angola stated that a rebel leader had been killed in a plane crash. That would leave the American arms seller with a shipload of munitions or, if he had delivered the merchandise, the rebels or government troops might have the guns . . . and still have the money.

The surge of terrorist groups and rebel armies in Africa, the Middle East, and Latin America created a high demand for weapons that could only be purchased on the black market. When the Soviet bloc disintegrated, the world's largest supply of surplus military weapons was suddenly created—along with legions of generals and munition depot guards willing to sell them.

Because of their connections in the Old Country, the illegal arms trade was perfect for the Little Odessa mafiya who funneled pistols to

❖

shoulder-launched missiles and tanks out of the country on Black Sea ships sailing out of the original Odessa and former Soviet republics.

Despite Vlad's contention that the American had put together the deal, Nunes was reasonably sure that the local Russians were getting something from both ends of the Bulgarian arms purchase.

No honor among thieves was one of the principles of businesses on both sides of the law.

"What's going on between the American and the locals?" Nunes asked.

"Our people would rather have the cash electronically deposited in their accounts than a bunch of old relics. I've heard the American has a source for buying back the collateral. If he can't, they'll keep his collateral and . . ." Vlad tapped his head with a finger.

Nunes got the message: Like the legal executioners in the old Soviet Union, the Odessa mafiya used the traditional method of a single bullet to the head. The Soviets did it to save on bullets . . . the mafiya considered it an advertising gimmick.

To welsh on a deal with the mafiya was not exactly akin to failing to pay a credit card.

Who could put up millions of dollars in contraband antiquities? The archaeological sites of the world were all sources of smuggled relics that could finance a criminal arms conspiracy: Italy, Greece, Turkey, Egypt, Angkor Wat, India, Mesoamerica, and Peru were all rich sources of antiquities with dirt on them.

The largest source of all was the looting of the Iraqi museum. That pieces would start showing up in the art world was inevitable. And that they would be hard to trace was one of the curses of preserving the cultural heritage of third-world countries.

The Iraqis had not been efficient about cataloging the enormous number of items in their collection. The museum held over 150,000 items, and only a small percentage of the pieces were properly cataloged and photographed. And many of the catalog records were destroyed by the looters for the express purpose of making it difficult or impossible to track pieces.

The problem of not preserving and protecting its natural heritage wasn't unique to Iraq—it was epidemic in third-world countries, which was why so much of their cultural heritage ended up in the rich museums of Europe, the United States, and the Far East.

To make a significant recovery of the missing relics would be Olympic gold for Nunes, capping off his career with a big win.

He had to consider whether Vlad was the actual source of the Mesopotamian art to the Russian mob. He could be fencing stolen items from the museum heist for the person he was describing as the "American." Vlad was sweating a hell of a lot for a deal that went sour and his small part in it. But Nunes's gut told him that Vlad wasn't the source.

The Russian ran a small-time art galley specializing in Russian icons, religious images typically painted on wood panels in Eastern Europe. Naturally, the icons were smuggled out of Eastern Europe and former Soviet republics, but it was a business that dealt in art pieces worth hundreds and thousands of dollars, not millions. Nunes had gone after him because he figured the man's Little Odessa location would bring him into contact with other illegal art transactions.

When Vlad had been approached by a local mafioso to find an expert to appraise contraband art being offered as collateral, Vlad had come to the FBI with the information.

His motivation to cooperate with the feds didn't arise from his sense of responsibility as a citizen. Because almost everything in his shop was stolen and smuggled in, he was trying to work off about a hundred years in prison by cooperating with the FBI. After his usefulness ended, he was destined to have his disappearance orchestrated by the Witness Protection Program.

This wasn't the first time Nunes had investigated art with a Mafia—or mafiya—connection. Many of the items that had appeared on the FBI's Top Ten Art Crimes list had a connection to trafficking in drugs and arms because organized crime got involved somewhere along the line.

The Bureau's Top Ten Art Crimes list included the $300 million robbery of the Gardner Museum in Boston, a 1990 low-tech heist in which two thieves dressed as police officers conned the guards into letting them into the museum at night. The haul, which has never been recovered, included thirteen works, among them paintings by Vermeer, Manet, Degas, and Rembrandt, but the thieves, who were suspected of having Boston

❖

Mafia connections, were definitely not art connoisseurs: They took the bronzed top off a flagpole and left behind Titian's *Rape of Europa,* the most valuable piece in the museum.

None of the pieces were protected by an alarm system, and none were insured.

Like the Gardner heist, many thefts were astonishingly low-tech. Often someone simply grabbed an item off a museum wall and walked out with it.

Now the biggest theft of all was back in the news as another piece of Mesopotamia's cultural history was on the investigation table: An Iraqi taxi driver was claiming that a premier museum piece had been stolen from the Iraqi museum. Nunes had already sent his partner over to question the taxi driver.

Added to the accusation that the museum piece was part of the Iraqi loot, a hoard of Mesopotamian antiquities were used to finance an international arms deal. And there was a sudden demand for payment by the Odessa gang.

Then over $50 million was paid for a Babylonian piece that suddenly appeared on the market out of nowhere.

No coincidences here, Nunes thought.

BEFORE HE GOT UP to leave, Nunes told Vlad to stop sweating. "It makes you look guilty."

Grabbing his notebook computer bag, Nunes left the bar. The four-lane street running down Brighton Beach's several block-long business district was mostly covered by elevated subway tracks. He took a train to Coney Island where his partner, Steiner, was waiting with an unmarked Agency car.

"Did you talk to the camel jockey?" Nunes asked.

"It's not politically correct to call an immigrant taxi driver a camel jockey. The proper expression is 'towel head.' And yes, I talked to him. His name is Abdullah Hussein. Iraqi, early sixties, filed a political amnesty claim. Says he was a curator at the Iraqi museum in Baghdad. Lives with his daughter in Jamaica Plains. She has political amnesty. Her husband was a newspaperman killed by Saddam's goons."

"What's Abdullah's story?"

❖

"He considered the Semiramis his personal baby. Says his father died protecting it, that he also almost got killed when he tried to stop looters from taking it." Steiner gave Nunes a look full of meaning. "Get this. American troops were working with Saddam's boys to clean out the place."

"That's his story? Americans looted the museum?"

"American uniforms, the word 'SEAL' on the hat of a guy who almost killed him."

"SEAL. That's Navy stuff. What evidence does he have to prove the mask was stolen from the museum?"

"He claims he's getting the proof. Wouldn't tell me what, though."

"Why?"

"He's suspicious of any authority. Saddam's Iraq was a police state. The American military in Iraq have a police state. The museum looters were American." Steiner glanced at Nunes. "Funny, isn't it? This guy comes to us for asylum from the bad guys back home and thinks we're also the bad guys."

"It's a complicated world. When I was a kid, we always knew who wore the black hat. And we always knew they would get their punishment at the end. What about this Piedmont curator who bought the Semiramis, Madison Dupre?"

"No record. Small-time antiquities expert for the Met until she got the job at the Piedmont. The museum specializes in Mesopotamian art. From news archives on the Internet, she's managed to pick up a number of pieces that could have come out of the museum in Baghdad."

"'Could have,' that's as big a word as 'if' and 'maybe.'"

"Sorry, I'd be more specific if the bastards hadn't destroyed the catalog records to cover their trail. You think this Dupre woman is involved in your art-for-arms deal?"

Nunes thought over the question. "I don't know. She could have sat down with the Odessa gang and planned it out. It's more probable she's like those bank employees we bust occasionally. They spend their lives counting other people's money. One day the devil whispers in their ears and tells them that if they launder a little money, they will have some of the green stuff themselves. They have a fascination with money, it goes with the territory, but they've never had a big wad of their own."

"Temptation?"

❖

"Exactly. Dupre herself may be in it over her head or she might be just looking the other way in order to grab up pieces for her museum. Either way, she's receiving stolen property. Take me to the Piedmont Museum. I have a couple questions for the woman."

CONTRABAND AT THE MET AND GETTY

In February 2006, the Metropolitan Museum of Art, one of the world's largest and most important museums, announced it was returning 20 pieces of contraband art to Italy. The museum pieces smuggled out of Italy and sold to the Met had been found by tomb robbers.

Among the items was the 2500-year-old Euphronios Krater, one of the most beautiful pieces of ancient art ever found. Excavated at Cerveteri, near Rome, the krater (a vessel used to mix water and wine) depicts the Greek god Hermes directing Sleep and Death as they carry the son of Zeus for burial.

In November 2005, the Getty, one of the richest museums on Earth, announced that it was returning a number of contraband items to Italy, including a 2300-year-old vase. At the time of the announcement, a Getty curator and a well-known art dealer were on trial in Italy. The allegation made by the Italian government was that the two knowingly purchased stolen artifacts. The defendants denied the charges.

Italian authorities claim they have traced more than 100 artifacts looted by *tombaroli,* tomb robbers, to the Met, the Getty, and other major museums and collections in the United States and Europe.

19

❖

Manhattan

As I walked through the museum the next morning, I realized that overnight I had gone from prima donna to pariah. The Untouchables of India had nothing on me as I made my way to my office. The guards who used to smile now looked like they were wondering if they should do a body cavity search for stolen antiquities.

Okay, maybe it was only my imagination, but I wasn't feeling good about myself this morning. My mind and body roiled with attacks of guilt, doubt, confusion, and just plain fear.

A note on my desk said that Eric was meeting with Hiram that morning and would see me later. I didn't need a crystal ball to know what Hiram and Eric would be talking about, but why wasn't I invited? Had I already been tried and convicted—and sentenced?

With the museum under attack, shouldn't everyone come together to present a united front?

For sure . . . unless Hiram and Eric had decided to throw me to the wolves in the hopes that would satisfy the hungry pack of newspeople and police that will be snarling at the museum door.

If I were dealing with people of honor and courage, I wouldn't be so

❖

damn paranoid that I was going to be stabbed in the back. But both did most of their damage with weasel moves, always ready to duck out of a situation by slipping it to someone else. The only attractive thing about Hiram was his money, and Eric even lacked that.

I called Neal but couldn't reach him. I was surprised and annoyed that he hadn't called this morning to offer me comfort, since I was pretty upset when I talked to him last night.

Too early for him to be in an auction. I hit the redial button but no answer. I hoped he was busy tracking down the enigmatic Viktor Milan. I wondered how much Neal knew about document examiners. Did he work with them? With Bensky? I wasn't sure Neal ever bothered to hire one. He was on the other end of sales, the middleman. Of course, like all of us, he would have checked the Art Loss Register on anything he bought or sold. It was standard protocol. If an object wasn't on it, the auction house would close their eyes and let it pass through on the grounds that it was up to the buyer to investigate the provenance; they were just going by what the seller told them.

I tried Bensky in Pelham again. I got the answering machine.

London was five hours ahead and I had tried calling Lipton as soon as I woke up. His assistant told me he wasn't in the office. That was possible, but with a raging controversy about the Semiramis you'd think he'd have been on the phone to me immediately. I had to wonder why he was ducking me. The assistant's cool tone shot up my ire. I called again an hour later before I left my apartment. And got a brush-off again.

"I don't give a damn if he's not in; he's still on the goddamn planet and can call me back."

She hung up on me. *Bitch.*

Lipton knew what had happened last night, of course. The antiquities trade was a small, exclusive club. He probably got fifty calls since last night. But I was the one who counted.

I was tempted to call back and tell the bitch I was going to have her and her boss arrested for peddling stolen artifacts when our receptionist knocked on the door.

"Come in."

"An FBI agent is here to see you," she said, wide-eyed as she handed me his business card.

❖

Richard Nunes
Special Agent.

I stared at it. Perfect. That's all I needed. Neal's warning about keeping my mouth shut loomed big in my head.

"Are you all right, Madison?"

"Just fine; everything's perfect." *Except for my reputation, my career, and now my freedom,* I almost blurted out. "Send him in."

My voice was calmer than my nerves. Normally I would have gotten up and escorted a visitor into my office, but I needed the time to think. I had never been questioned by the FBI before. The closest I ever got to a police interrogation happened when a traffic cop wanted to know if I wanted to work off a ticket by going out with him. I said yes. Didn't get the ticket. And stood him up for the date.

What had Neal said about dealing with the police?

Deny, deny, deny.

FBI agents were typically cast on television as uptight, insensitive jerks with closed minds who tried to grab the glory from hardworking local cops, and that's what I expected.

Special Agent Nunes came through the door. He didn't look like someone I could tearfully tell my story to while I rested my head on his shoulder.

I went around my desk and shook hands. "Please have a seat."

I directed him to a chair in my conference area. I didn't have chairs for visitors in front of my desk. Instead, one corner of the office had a small couch and two chairs set around a glass-topped coffee table. Visible through the glass was a ninth-century stela, a block of stone with ancient Native American writing.

Nunes stared at the artifact after he sat down.

"My father found it in New Mexico. He was an archaeologist." Actually, he was an art historian. And had bought the piece eons ago at a flea market in Albuquerque. My explanation sounded a little lame, even to myself. Nunes probably thought I was a smuggler of pre-Columbian artwork.

"Belongs in a museum."

"Well, that's where it's at. What can I do for you, Agent Nunes?"

He locked eyes with me. My eyeballs wanted to leap out of the sockets

❖

and run. But I smiled and kept from jumping up and screaming my innocence.

"There's been an accusation that the mask called Semiramis was stolen during the looting of the Iraqi museum."

I nodded automatically. "Yes, that's true. A man who is obviously irra-tional caused a disturbance in the museum last night during a reception."

"Are you aware that thousands of items were looted from the mu-seum?"

"He snuck in."

"Excuse me?"

"The man. Abdullah. He snuck into the museum."

"Are you aware that—"

"I believe everyone in the art world is aware of the Iraqi museum prob-lem. Do you have some proof that the mask was stolen from Baghdad?"

"The matter is still under investigation. I'd like to see it, the Semi-ramis."

"What does that mean? 'Under investigation'?"

"It means we are conducting an investigation."

I smiled. "That's enlightening. Let's get down to basics. We paid fifty-five million dollars for an art object at a reputable auction. We are not thieves."

"Really. And why do you think . . . that I think . . . you are thieves?"

Shit. He had kicked my holier-than-thou platform out from under me.

"What can I do to help you, Agent Nunes?"

"Like I said, I'd like to see the mask."

"Of course."

"A crime scene tech will also need to examine it. Take some pictures. We'll let you know after the visual examination if more definitive tests will be necessary."

"You'll have to make those arrangements with my boss, Eric Vander-hof. He's the director of the museum. He'll be in later. I'll have him call you." *If he has any sense, he'll make you get a warrant,* I thought.

"Okay. I also need to see your provenance on the Semiramis. I'll need a copy of it."

"As it happens, I have a copy right here." I handed him the copy I'd left in my top drawer. Another copy was in my purse, along with the examiner's report. My knees were shaking. "The provenance was commissioned by the owner of the piece, a London art dealer, one of the premier dealers in the world. We relied upon it, of course."

As Nunes read the history, my mind convulsed with ideas and impulses. I wanted to leap up, show him Bensky's damning report, and shout, *I'm being framed!*

I didn't dare open my mouth. How could I prove that I had never seen the document examiner's report? It was in my file. If I showed Nunes the report, he would arrest me on the spot. He would have to. My word against a written report was a noose around my neck. I still needed to talk to Bensky and make sure he'd be on my side.

Nunes read the ownership information and then looked up from the papers. "Interesting."

I didn't know what he found interesting. It was a standard provenance, boring to anyone not involved in a sale of the item. What was really interesting was the document examiner's report I didn't show Nunes.

I asked him what he found interesting.

"I always find Lebanon an interesting point of origin for Middle Eastern antiquities. For centuries, it was part of an empire that no longer exists and left behind no records. For the past three or four decades, it's been a war zone, not a country. The most powerful force in the place is terrorists who hate America's guts. That makes it impossible for American police agencies to check out fraudulent provenances."

I tried to look sympathetic. "That's all very true, and the same holds true for most of the countries in the Middle East. I'm sure you realize that the most significant factor about dealing with Middle Eastern antiquities is that at some point most of the provenances will originate in . . . a Middle Eastern country. Last time I heard, Americans were not loved anywhere in the region . . . and I'm sure none would put out a welcome mat for the FBI."

"I understand it was the most violent civil war in modern history."

He was referring to the civil war in Lebanon. I guess he was pretending that he didn't hear me. Or maybe what I said just didn't count.

He studied the report again before looking up. "It appears the family that allegedly owned the mask died out more than seventy years ago. That, of course, adds to the difficulty of checking out the provenance. Dead people can't confirm it, can they?"

❖

He was intimating that someone had deliberately chosen a family that wouldn't have someone around to remember the past. Even I realized it wasn't a difficult task. Death records could be checked for the selected time period in Beirut to see who died with no next of kin.

"Families die out," I responded. "Even kings end up with no heirs. In the ownership history of the mask, it appears the last member was murdered. As you said, over seventy years ago."

That was lame, but I wanted to make sure he understood that I wasn't even born when the man was murdered.

"Interesting about the marketplace purchase, too. The transaction can't be traced. And the nineteenth-century date gets us beyond most patrimony laws."

"I see." Yes, I saw very well. All of that had occurred to me, too. The inability to check out the statements in the provenance was something that made it attractive to me in the first place.

"The marketplace purchase, of course, is a favorite tool of tomb robbers and smugglers because it makes it impossible to track down exactly who actually possessed it. No receipts, no tax records, nothing to check out."

"I'm sure many items were sold in marketplaces in third-world countries. To you it's suspicious; to people who work in the trade it's how business was done."

"And then there's the Panama ownership," he said.

"Yes, it was purchased by a Panamanian company. That's not unusual. Some companies like to use Panama as their, uh, national headquarters. Some sort of tax thing, I think."

He nodded and pursed his lips, staring beyond me. "Panama is another place that makes it difficult for the police to do their job. It doesn't take much to register a company in Panama today. Little information other than a rented mailbox is needed for an address." He smiled a shark's grin. "You can only imagine how little information was required to do business and how few records exist of companies formed there in the 1930s. My partner made a call to our FBI resident at the embassy in Panama City this morning. The resident howled with laughter when my partner asked him about tracing a 1930s Panamanian corporate registry."

"Why is that?" I smothered a cough. A death rattle.

He kept nodding, his head rocking back and forth as if it were on a swivel. "The dead Lebanese from the marketplace sold it to the invisible Panamanians in the jungle. Making it very, very difficult to track."

"Aah." I tried to make it sound like he had given me an eye-opening revelation. Every word out of his mouth came across as an inference of my guilt. I wanted to run screaming from my office.

"And there's the Swiss middleman."

I cleared my throat. "The Swiss are significant players in the world art scene."

Agent Nunes's head rocked up and down again. "Correct . . . along with storing Nazi gold and laundering African blood diamonds, they're noted for being middlemen for contraband art."

"Excuse me, but it hasn't been proven that the Semiramis is contraband."

"It's getting there. From a policeman's standpoint, the problem with Switzerland as an entry point for an item into Europe is that it has very loose import laws and very restrictive ones protecting the privacy of business dealings." He shook his head, proving it also swiveled sideways. "It seems like the provenance of your artifact hits all the hot spots for an investigator."

My blood temperature and fears had gone up several notches. "If you come into this controversy with that attitude, we're not going to get anywhere. You can't look at the origins of ancient artifacts with tunnel vision. Some of the pieces have been floating around for thousands of years, from person to person, country to country, without leaving paper trails. Pieces changed hands during rape and pillage over the millennia, with none of the thieves signing contracts. We're not dealing with cars that require a bill of sale and registration."

He appeared singularly unimpressed with my outburst. "The question about the Semiramis isn't whether the provenance goes back to Genghis Khan's rape of Baghdad a thousand years ago but whether the mask was stolen from the Iraqi National Museum a few years ago."

"Baghdad wasn't taken by Genghis Khan; his grandson Hülegü sacked the city." I smiled sweetly. "Before the U.S. Army did."

Nunes leaned forward, locking eyes with me again. My heart thumped. I was innocent but was glad that I wasn't on a lie detector machine at that moment, because my panic would have sent the ink needle screeching up and down the graph paper.

❖

"I'm not here to play games with you, Ms. Dupre. The provenance smells. You have a serious problem with it."

"I relied upon—"

"Getting a piece of paper from a thief doesn't let a buyer off the hook if the buyer knew the item was hot. You've gotten most of your acquisitions from the same auction house. The seller in every case was a London art dealer, who got them from a dealer in Switzerland. An interesting pattern, don't you think? I got that with just a quick Internet search. What do you think the chances are that we'll come up with more interesting information when we start examining the underlying documents and pieces?"

"The dealer and auction house had the items we wanted. The sellers provided documentation. End of story."

"Why did they have such a supply of antiquities? Artifacts were looted from the Baghdad museum. After a couple years, the market has a sudden influx of artifacts from the region. It doesn't take a rocket scientist to make a connection. We both know that there's a worldwide network of smugglers, dealers, and buyers for contraband antiquities. It's a dirty business that attracts not only collectors but major museums."

That did it. I jumped to my feet. "How dare you come in here and insinuate that our museum has been involved in illegal purchases." I went to the door and jerked it open. "If you want to see the Semiramis or anything else in the museum, contact Eric Vanderhof, the director."

"I'll do that. Thanks for your time."

I shut the door behind him and leaned against it, my head swirling. *My God . . . how could this be happening?*

I phoned Neal again. No answer on his cell phone. I tried his office.

"I'm sorry, Ms. Dupre," his assistant told me. "I'm not sure where Neal is right at the moment."

Yeah, like the Secret Service doesn't know where the president is at any given moment. Eric wasn't back from his meeting with Piedmont, either.

The people who got me into this mess were keeping their heads down while I was the target in a shooting gallery.

On top of being involved in a sensational purchase of a Middle Eastern antiquity at a time when such transactions were under the microscopes of

❖

agencies around the world, I had the bad luck of drawing a hard-ass FBI agent. And unfortunately he knew something about art.

I touched the pocket where I had the examiner's report.

Too nervous to sit at my desk, I grabbed my purse and coat. It was time I confronted my accuser.

❖

20

❖

I took a taxi to the address on Abdullah's handout. To make sure he was home, I called the number on his handout and hung up when I heard his voice. He lived in Jamaica Plains, a neighborhood on western Long Island in the borough of Queens, the largest of the five boroughs of New York City. Queens was mostly residential, with some manufacturing in Long Island City and shipping facilities along the East River. The JFK and LaGuardia airports were in Queens.

The clapboard five-story apartment building in a depressed neighborhood looked like a fire waiting to happen. Next door was a Middle Eastern grocery store. The pungent aroma of spices filled the air outside the doorway. Two women with black head scarves—a symbol of female servitude for a billion Muslims—stood chatting at the bottom of the short flight of stairs to the apartment building's entrance. They stopped and stared at me. Probably the only businesswomen they saw were child welfare workers.

I found the man's last name written in pencil on the registry for the fifth floor. The door to the building was already ajar. The rusted lock looked as if it had been busted for some time.

❖

I stepped inside a worn and dirty entryway and faced four flights of stairs, not relishing the thought of walking up. I didn't expect to see an elevator and got my expects. The old building was a building inspector's wet dream.

At the bottom of the stairway a little girl was playing with a home-made doll. When I said hello to her, she smiled shyly and stared up with large almond eyes.

I heard Middle Eastern music as I made my way up the stairs. I hated the sound of it. It grated on my nerves worse than rap. A loud tele-vision was blaring a soap opera through the walls. The farther I climbed, the more I smelled stagnant odors of lamb and butter in the corridors.

Abdullah's apartment was closest to the stairway.

I knocked on the door.

He must have been eating, because when he opened the door he was still chewing on something. He had on jogger's pants and a sleeveless white undershirt. Surprised to see me, he immediately stuck his head out to see who else was with me.

"I'm alone," I said. "My driver is waiting downstairs." I actually hadn't thought of having the taxi driver wait, but I felt better making Abdullah think I wasn't entirely alone.

"Come in. Sit down."

"Thanks. I apologize for not calling, but I was in the neighborhood and decided to drop by." That rang false even to my ear.

He was calmer than the last time I saw him outside the museum.

"Mr. ibn Hussein, I'm Madison Dupre, the curator—"

"I know you who are."

"Has anybody else come to see you?"

"The police have been here."

Nunes, I imagined.

"You say the Semiramis was stolen. How can you prove that?"

My career was on the line and possibly even my freedom. I wanted to see his proof that the museum piece was stolen.

He looked to the window and sighed, suddenly appearing tired and weary.

"My daughter will be here soon. She was the one who made arrange-ments for me to come to America. My health is not too good. I lost my job

❖

as curator for the Iraqi museum. They wouldn't listen to me when I told them that Iraqi traitors worked with the foreigners to take away our treasures."

"You said you saw them."

"I was there. I tried to stop them, but one of the foreigners hit me on my head, an American. I came to America to avoid being killed for saying that Americans looted the museum. Strange, I know. But it wasn't America that looted the museum, just some of its soldiers. Unfortunately, that's the way solders are everywhere. Saddam's Republican Guard helped them take the best pieces and then came back themselves to loot thousands more of our nation's treasures."

"Are you sure they were Americans?"

"I speak English very well. I know the difference between the way the British and Americans sound. Besides, their uniforms and caps were American military. I saw the word." He tapped an imaginary cap on his head. "I stood as close to them as I am to you."

He stood silent for a moment and stared into the past. "My father also tried to preserve our heritage. The Semiramis was found by men in our village when I was a boy. My father stopped them from selling it on the black market. They murdered him for protecting it."

"I'm sorry."

"The museum had over one hundred and fifty thousand items in its collection. Only a fraction of those were displayed for public view and had been cataloged. It takes time and patience for such a task, and for years we did not have the resources to do that. We were slowly making progress. We had to lock away our precious antiquities to prevent further thefts."

"And the Semiramis?"

He gave me a sly look. "The Semiramis and some of the other best pieces were only cataloged here," he said, tapping his head.

"Why?"

"Because Iraq has seen one dictator after another during most of my lifetime. When the dictator or his family wasn't stealing from the people, his underlings were. If they knew how valuable some of the artifacts at the museum were, they would have taken them for their palaces. Or sent them to be sold in Europe and the money put in their Swiss bank accounts."

"Mr. ibn Hussein, I've seen paperwork that says the Semiramis was in private hands in Lebanon over a hundred years ago, not in the Baghdad museum."

"Let me show you something."

He took a picture out of a dresser drawer and handed it to me. The photo was a faded Polaroid of the mask that was reproduced on his handout. The background was no clearer in the original.

"This doesn't show—"

"I have proof. The mask has the imprint of a cylinder seal on the bottom of it."

A cylinder seal was a sign of ownership used in ancient Babylon, often made of hard clay or, more commonly, stone. Many were about the size of a short cigar. Property owners often used these seals to leave an impression on their possessions. The process involved using wet clay on the item and the seal rolled over it. The carving on the seal was intaglio, so that it left an impression that could be read or viewed. Many were elaborate. Some had names; others had motifs of various designs representing people and animals, a hieroglyphic-type scene that could tell a story about its owner.

I knew from news accounts that a U.S. soldier serving in Iraq had purchased cylinder seals from a street vendor selling trinkets. When the soldier returned to the States, he discovered they were valuable antiquities and turned them over to the FBI.

"I know about the seal. It's mentioned in the auction catalog and in the provenance documents," I said. "But having a seal is to be expected. How do you connect it up to the museum? You need a picture and description in a museum catalog. Your picture doesn't show the bottom where the seal is imprinted."

He suddenly grinned triumphantly. "There is one document the thieves did not know about."

My heart skipped a beat.

"In 1958, after my father was murdered for protecting the Sammuramat, King Faisal sent a commendation to the village, praising my father as a hero of Iraq. Faisal was overthrown later in July of that year. The commendation contains a drawing of the piece and the cylinder imprint."

Shit.

❖

"The commendation hangs in my father's house that now belongs to my sister, who lives in it. I have asked her to send it to me."

"When do you expect to receive it?"

"My daughter has tracked the package delivery on the global express Web site. I should get the commendation tomorrow."

I let everything he said sink into my brain. I felt cold and vulnerable. The look on my face must have exposed my agony.

He said softly, "I'm sorry I have caused you trouble. You are not the one who stole it."

"No, but I'm going to be the one who pays for it in blood."

"Your life is at risk?"

"No, I meant—I don't mean that kind of blood. It's just that we never suspected it was stolen. I'll lose my job."

I was losing more than that. My career would be history.

"I'm sorry if the Semiramis has caused you grief. It took my father's life. It cost my job, too. Like you I was a museum curator. Now," shrugging his shoulders, "I drive a taxi in a city I hardly know. It truly carries a curse with it. But it's also a national treasure of my country. If you were in my place wouldn't you do the same?"

I didn't answer.

I suppose I would protect our cultural treasures just as much as he wanted to protect his. But I wasn't in his position. I was on the other end. Right now I was thinking more about how to save my career from spiraling downward.

The smell of spices in the room was making me nauseous. I had to get some fresh air.

"Would you, uh, give me a call, so I can see the commendation when it comes in?"

He nodded. "Yes, but after I get it, I must also call the policeman who was here, an FBI agent."

Wonderful. We could have a party in the apartment and Special Agent Nunes could bring handcuffs.

I left in a hurry.

As I came out the front door, a woman was coming up the steps. She stared at me with surprise and looked toward the window of the apartment five stories up.

"You've seen my father."

❖

It wasn't a question but a concerned statement.

"Your father . . ." I took a deep breath. "Perhaps your father should consider a reward for—"

She recoiled down a step. I might as well have slapped her.

"My grandfather died to save the Semiramis. It almost cost my father his own life. We don't want your money."

"I'm sorry." Horribly embarrassed, I rushed by her and hurried down the street.

I had just offered her a bribe to shut him up. I felt dirty and ashamed. I lived in a penthouse that cost me more money for the building maintenance fee every month than the rent they paid here in a year. And Abdullah's daughter, who probably waited on tables or clerked in a store, had showed more integrity than me. I guess money wasn't the answer to everything.

I wanted to get away from the smells of the neighborhood as quickly as I could. And from the humiliation of being less honest and dedicated than these courageous people who gave everything—money, comfortable lives, and real blood—to protect a principle.

Abdullah's question roiled in my head.

Would I be that dedicated to my country?

I wanted to think so, but I wasn't sure.

❖

21

❖

When I got back to the office, I tried Neal's private number again. This time he answered. I told him about the interview with Nunes and what the Iraqi curator said. Neal's reaction to the commendation Abdullah was expecting from Iraq was the same as mine.

"Sonofabitch."

"Neal, I'm worried."

"I told you not to worry."

"It's time to worry. Nunes has implied that since so many of my pieces came from Lipton—through your recommendation, I might add—and Viktor Milan, it's some sort of conspiracy."

"I'm nothing but a middleman. It's not up to me to establish the provenance. If you hadn't been negligent, neither one of us would be in this jam."

Whoa. The rat was abandoning the ship. I kept my cool and tried not to panic. "I need to talk to Milan."

"I don't know how to reach him. I told you, I know nothing about the guy. Lipton hasn't returned my calls."

"Lipton won't answer my calls, either."

"He could be out of town. He travels constantly—"

❖

"He doesn't check phone messages at his office? He doesn't know the sky is falling? He's avoiding me. And you. If I don't get a response from him soon, I'm going to encourage that FBI agent who's breathing down my neck to have Lipton investigated. You know, Nunes asked a good question. How did a number of fine museum pieces suddenly come on the market with great provenances after the Iraqi museum was looted?"

As I asked the question, I realized how suspicious it sounded. And that I would never be able to say with a straight face that I haven't looked the other way when buying antiques. Everyone in the business knew better than to examine provenances too carefully.

"Maddy, I can't talk now. I don't know why I answered the phone. I have a meeting starting. Let's get together later."

We set a time to meet at his office. I wanted to ask him the name of the lawyer he mentioned previously, but he hung up before I could.

I pulled out the document report and went over it again, thinking about the characters involved. Sir Henri Lipton was big-time, the most prestigious dealer in the world of Mediterranean antiquities. He was a gay Englishman with a cute young boyfriend. The boyfriend was nice, but I found Lipton an insufferable snob and intellectual bully.

Before my father passed away a couple of years ago, he gave me a golden piece of advice when I told him about an antiquities dealer who tried to screw me and how I planned to tell him off: "Antiquities are a cottage industry. Get out of the business if you plan to make enemies."

He was right. The antiquities business was a small world with a finite number of people involved. If I started alienating everyone who offended me, I might as well get another career, because I would soon be out of this one.

So I smiled and tolerated Sir Henri and sent him cases of Louis Roederer Champagne when I would've rather kicked him in the tush. And I hadn't found him any more unscrupulous than the rest of the people in this cutthroat business driven by ego and greed. It might be that he was relying on Milan, the man of mystery.

For sure, Lipton had sold me several pieces that I was surprised had come on the market. Why had he offered them to me?

I assumed at the time that I had an inside track because Neal handled the sales and I was so good at faking my orgasms with him. I was now beginning to wonder if my attraction might not have been that I was an eager new curator full of unrealized ambitions . . . a combination that old-timers in the trade would read as someone who would buy first and ask questions afterward.

Dammit, it was true, but that was the nature of the trade. There were only a small number of good pieces. You had to—

I shook off trying to alibi. Neal was right. I had to keep myself in a good mind frame. If I started thinking I was guilty, I would signal it to others.

I did an Internet search on Viktor Milan. His Web site said that he specialized in antiquities . . . that was it. Not whether he bought or sold or appraised them. Nothing about eastern Mediterranean and Middle East antiquities or pieces from China, Angkor Wat, or other Far East venues . . . just antiquities.

The guy's a real storehouse of information.

Besides the vagueness about what role he played in the antiquities market, he offered an address in Zurich, Switzerland . . . and no phone or fax number. That made it a bit hard to contact him.

I knew he prepared provenances; he put the documentation together for the Semiramis and other pieces. But there was no mention of it. Nor was there any offer to buy, sell, or trade anything.

The most interesting thing about the Web site was its lack of information.

My intercom buzzed. Eric's voice was brisk and businesslike: "See me in my office."

He looked grim when I walked in.

"Hiram is very upset."

"I don't blame him. I'm not exactly cheerful myself."

"He says you got us into a fine mess. It means we'll be under a microscope. The authorities will be looking over everything we ever bought."

"Wait a minute. I went over every piece with both of you before making the buys. Why is it all my fault?"

"I relied upon you to verify the provenances."

My blood boiled. I know I must have turned several shades of purple, because I could see all the blame being thrown my way.

He lifted his hands in a gesture of frustration. "It comes down to this. Hiram made some phone calls to his political connections and got a picture of what we can expect. The U.S. Attorney has political ambitions.

❖

He'd like nothing better than to get an indictment and bring out evidence of U.S. troop involvement in the looting of the antiquities in Iraq. It would give him enormous publicity."

Another nail in my coffin. First there's an FBI agent with a mentality of a robotic pit bull. Now it's a U.S. Attorney who wants to run for president or something by trampling my life.

"Naturally, the museum can't be faulted if one of its employees fails to properly authenticate the origins of the item. It relies upon the honesty of its employees."

"What? Excuse me—what do you mean by 'honesty'? We're talking about whether a mistake was made. How did my integrity suddenly get questioned?"

"Hiram has been told that there'll be an investigation by the FBI of every Mesopotamian piece that we've acquired since the Iraqi museum was looted. Those are our finest . . . and most expensive pieces. Purchased by you."

"With the encouragement of you and Hiram."

"The FBI is focusing on the fact that your purchases all involved two foreigners, one in London and the other in Switzerland."

"What bullshit. Since when is Sir Henri Lipton considered a foreign enemy? He's the biggest antiquities dealer in the world. You bought museum pieces through him before I even came on board. So have half the other museums in the country."

"I'm sorry, but I have to put you on a leave of absence. As of now."

It took a moment to get my voice. I spoke calmly because I was hurt. "I see. The museum plans on abandoning me. After all I've done for it."

"Piedmont's orders. My hands are tied. I'm sorry."

He got up and walked out.

He left me sitting in his office. I heard him whisper to Nurse Ratched to get my electronic card key before I left. Naturally, the electronic code would be changed. I wouldn't be allowed to remove anything except for some personal items.

I returned to my office. My whole world was unraveling. I picked up my few personal things and left after dropping my card key on Nurse Ratched's desk. She smirked, but I didn't say a word to her.

❖

UNESCO [United Nations Educational, Scientific and Cultural Organization] International Code of Ethics for Dealers in Cultural Properties

ARTICLE 1 Professional traders in cultural property will not import, export or transfer the ownership of this property when they have reasonable cause to believe it has been stolen, illegally alienated, clandestinely excavated or illegally exported.

The effect of the phrase "reasonable cause to believe" . . . *is to be read as requiring traders to investigate the provenance of the material they handle.*

It is not sufficient to trade in material without questions and consider that the clause only comes into effect when somehow evidence of the illegality is fortuitously acquired.

—UNESCO Web site

22

❖

I woke up in the middle of the night with my head feeling as if it were encased in a cobweb. Not a buzz on from booze, recreational drugs, or even a pleasure-producing prescription pill. I didn't know how to describe it. It just wasn't a pleasant feeling—as if my brain was dehydrated.

I had taken two over-the-counter sleeping aids that were in my medicine cabinet for eons, along with two glasses of wine. The combination put me into a deep sleep for about four hours, but my head was clogged and fuzzy when I woke up.

The word "roadkill" kept popping into my head, as if my life had been stretched out on the Cross Bronx Expressway at commute time. I wouldn't be surprised if my next opportunity assignment was giving blow jobs to prison guards for extra privileges. The thought scared the hell out of me. I imagined being in a prison cell, smelling smoke, seeing fire. I tend to be claustrophobic anyway. I started shaking in bed and couldn't keep the tears from coming. Finally, I got my nerves calmed and lay awake thinking.

Waking up during the night wasn't unusual for me. I did some of my best thinking lying awake in bed at three or four in the morning. For

❖

some reason, it was at these times that answers to questions came to me and my revelations about mistakes and omissions occurred.

Tonight the only clarity was that life had me on the run and the focus of my energies had to be to keep myself out of jail.

In terms of continuing to live in my current lifestyle . . . well, the penthouse and the Jaguar in the underground garage were going to be part of my past history. I did enjoy having my very own private parking spot—in Manhattan that was as rare as having a private swimming pool. I knew I would never be able to keep the penthouse and the car without the salary that Hiram paid me. And my black American Express card . . .

Welcome back to the real world.

I picked up the phone and dialed Bensky's number.

Nunes would no doubt ask Eric or Hiram if the provenance had been examined by a document expert and a lightbulb would go off in the head of one of them as they remembered Bensky . . . and couldn't find the report.

After four rings, the answering machine came on.

CHARLES BENSKY WATCHED HIS answering machine as Madison Dupre's voice was broadcast in his home office: "Mr. Bensky, this is Madison Dupre. I need to speak to you. It's urgent. Please call me when you get this message." He was too preoccupied with his own fears to recognize the stress in her voice.

His throat was dry. Earlier, he had been visibly trembling. Now he sat very still and held his knees with his hands as he stared at the man standing next to his bookcase. The man had his back to Bensky and was idly leafing through a book. When he returned from a fishing trip, Bensky entered his home and found the man waiting for him.

At first he thought the man was an intruder he had the bad luck to interrupt burglarizing the house.

When the man turned around, Bensky again noted the cap with a Navy SEAL emblem. He had served a hitch in the Navy out of high school forty years ago. In those days they referred to sailors in that branch of the Navy as frogmen.

The gun was still in his hand, pointed at Bensky.

❖

"I was Navy, too," Bensky said. "Did four years. Most of it on a carrier."

The man with the cap said nothing.

Bensky earlier told him to take whatever he wanted, even offered him his credit cards and ATM card, but the man was not interested in money. He just wanted one document.

"What are you going to do to me?" Bensky asked.

Unfortunately for Bensky, the information was also in his head.

❖

23

❖

I stayed in bed refusing to face the world until midmorning.

Desperate, I tried to call Bensky again. This time instead of a recording I heard a strange garbled noise on the line. Through a telephonic miracle, I managed to actually get a real operator who told me it sounded like the line was out of order or the phone was off the hook. Or maybe Bensky just didn't want to talk to me, a conclusion I came to all by myself.

Whatever the reason, it meant I was going to have to confront him in person. I got dressed and grabbed my car keys.

New York had two Pelhams. Bensky lived in the small upscale one in Westchester. I input the address into my GPS and followed the instructions, taking the FDR to the Triborough Bridge and onto the Bruckner Expressway. It felt good to get out of the city. Felt good driving a car more expensive than I could afford. Not that New York was an expensive-car town. Expensive clothes, apartment, jewelry, for sure, but owning a car that cost more than you could afford was more a West Coast thing, mostly L.A., where you never went to a restaurant unless it had valet service to make sure your car didn't get parking lot rash—or stolen.

❖

I opened the windows to let in air. Maybe some of my trouble would blow away.

Pelham was a small, quaint Americana town but with convenient train service that transported you back and forth to the big city. That made it pretty much a bedroom suburb for executive types.

Watching my GPS screen when I made the turn onto Bensky's street, I almost ran into a police car parked in the middle of the road. The street was blocked. Fire trucks and more police cars were ahead.

I pulled alongside a woman who was pushing a baby stroller away from the scene and asked her out the window, "What's going on?"

"There's been a fire."

"Do you know which house?"

"My neighbor, Chuck Bensky."

I had already guessed it, but it still gave me a jolt.

"Was he home?"

"They didn't find anybody inside."

Lucky for him, I thought. "Do you know if he's been out of town?"

"Probably. He does a lot of fishing."

I thanked her and pulled away. My scaredy-cat left knee shook.

No chance in hell it was just a coincidence that Bensky's house burned down. Coincidences like that, flukes, accidents, twists of fate, the luck of the draw, just didn't happen when the FBI was investigating a case. As my father would have put it, there wasn't a snowball's chance in hell that the fire wasn't connected to the accusation of theft surrounding a museum piece worth over $50 million.

I didn't wish Bensky any ill will. I'd never actually met him. No reason for it. I remembered now, Lipton had recommended him, said he had used Bensky before. To me, he'd been a voice over the phone and someone on the other side of a fax machine. I had a mental image of a skinny middle-aged man with thick glasses.

At least he wasn't home and asleep in bed when his house burned. Now he'd return to find his place burned to the ground.

My mind was working overtime. Bensky's house was also his office. Maybe somebody wanted to destroy any evidence of the Semiramis report. Somebody dangerous or murderously desperate. If Bensky had been in the house when it burned, it would have been murder.

❖

I wasn't willing to accept any other explanation.

Somebody was ready to commit murder to protect the provenance.

I had a sick feeling in my stomach. Lipton might know about the report, since he had a connection with the man. For certain, the only person I had told about the devastating report was Neal.

24

❖

I was supposed to get together with Neal later in the evening, but I deliberately cold-called him, catching him by surprise.

I sat down in one of the leather chairs in front of his desk and told him about the fire at Bensky's house.

He shrugged it off. "So."

"It wasn't a coincidence."

"You're going overboard, Maddy. The pressure has gotten to you. Now you're seeing murder. Houses do burn down by accident, you know."

"Not when they're part of a criminal investigation."

"Great. Keep it up. Why don't you call your FBI pal and tell him someone's out burning down houses to destroy evidence."

"Neal—"

"Wise up, Maddy. I don't think I'd run around shouting that someone burned Bensky's house because they wanted to destroy evidence of a report. As far as I know, you're the only person who has a motive."

That thought kept coming back at me and I kept slapping it away. Other than knowing I wasn't guilty, I didn't know who was. Neal knew of my predicament, but he wasn't the one with the smoking gun.

"Come on. Tell me," he said.

❖

"What?" My mind was a million miles away.

"Your mind is working overtime. And you're staring at me like I just crawled out of an Egyptian tomb wrapped in rags."

"I told you about Bensky's report."

"And?"

"His house got burned down."

His eyebrows went up. "You think I burned down his house to protect you?"

"Of course not."

"Then what are you saying?"

"I don't know."

He held out his hand. "Let me see that report."

I pulled Bensky's report out of my pocket and gave it to him. I rubbed my forehead. I had a king-size headache. I got up to get some water out of his fountain and took three aspirin.

Nothing made sense. I certainly didn't sleepwalk to Bensky's house last night and torch it. And I didn't think I was the only person with a motive. If there was proof that the Semiramis was part of the looted pieces, the fallout would hit everyone in the chain. I was just the weakest link.

Neal's document shredder went on and I jerked around.

"What are you doing?"

"Assuming your theory is correct that Bensky's house got torched to destroy the report, you had the last copy. Now there are no other copies."

"That's illegal."

He gaped at me. "Illegal? For sure. Immoral and reprehensible, too, no doubt. But someone is obviously out to get rid of that report and I don't think you want to be the last person waving it around."

"You've destroyed evidence."

"I did it for you. Besides, it's only *evidence* if the police find it. Now they can't."

"Neal . . . you shouldn't have done it. What if there's another copy?"

"Where? Who else would have a copy?"

"Bensky. I don't know, maybe his house burned by accident; maybe he has a copy on his laptop or his fishing reel—"

"The man can say what he likes. No one can prove you ever had a copy. And if that fire did destroy Bensky's copy, you can bet he'll keep his

❖

mouth shut, too. He was negligent in how he got the report to you. Besides, now you don't have a motive."

"A motive for what?"

"For burning Bensky's house. As long as you had the report, it gave you a motive for destroying other copies."

I sat back down. Drained. I was way out of my league when it came to chicanery. Working with cutthroat gallery owners and fanatical collectors was a piece of cake compared to engaging in this kind of deception.

Neal sat on the arm of the chair and ran his hand through my hair. "You have to understand, this thing is big. Fifty-five million to Piedmont is chump change, but to Viktor Milan it's everything. He can't afford to lose. And people like you and me can't afford to be in his way."

"Who *is* this man?"

"He's been around for years, but Lipton's the only one I know who's met him."

"What does Lipton say about him?"

"He's scared of him; that much I know."

"Why?"

"I don't know. He calls him 'the Swiss' and I remember he said the guy's a loose cannon. Milan also has a vault collection."

That meant he kept his pieces out of the public eye, not showing them to other collectors or loaning them to museums. Some collections were kept secret because they were contraband.

"Milan seems to be the one behind this whole thing," I told Neal. "He passes illegal antiquities with forged provenances. I don't understand how someone like Lipton could get involved."

"I know nothing. And neither do you. And keep it that way. The enemies in this matter aren't in the art world but on the political side."

"What do you mean?"

"What's this Iraqi cabdriver claiming? That the museum in Baghdad was looted. And that American troops were involved. Maybe they burned Bensky's house. Maybe they even snatched him."

"Who are they?"

"The FBI, NSA, CIA, hell, any one of those spook agencies with initials that get us into wars and are constantly screwing up and blaming it on everyone else."

My head felt like it was going to explode. The aspirin hadn't kicked in yet. "Neal—that's crazy."

"Maybe. But it wouldn't be the first time those spy agencies covered up their messes."

"God, I don't know what to do. I'm so scared."

"You're panicking for nothing."

"Nothing? What planet have you been on? I've already been fired from my job. I'm probably going to be arrested any minute."

"Not true. First, you're on a leave; you haven't been fired. Second, you've only been interviewed by the FBI. They haven't indicted you. And won't. You know what it would take for them to really check out the provenance? The agent told you it made it hell for them. He's right. They'd never put it together. You should lay low, keep your head down."

"That's easy for you to say. My life is spinning out of control. I've tried to call Lipton, but I can't get him on the phone. I can't get Bensky. When the FBI agent comes knocking at my door again, I need to emphasize they need to check out Milan. He's the devil behind this mess."

Another worrisome thought hit me. "What if the FBI has its own document examiner look at the provenance?"

"So what? If it takes an expert to tell it's a fraud, you're clear. Now." He jerked his head at the shredder.

My life had come down to shredding evidence.

I felt like Joan of Arc being burned at the stake.

25

❖

Pelham, New York

Nunes drove to the small Westchester village of Pelham after he got the call from a fire investigator that the house of Charles Bensky had burned down. Bensky had been on the FBI's watch list distributed to local, state, and federal agencies in the region.

Bob Rees, the head of the county's arson investigations, met Nunes in front of the charred remains of the three-bedroom suburban house.

"I saw the name Charles Bensky on your heads-up alert," Rees told him. "But he didn't come up in the computer on a wanted status."

"He's not. Bensky's a document examiner, a potential witness in a case where there's suspicious chain of ownership on an expensive item."

They entered the backyard through a side gate as they talked.

"No sign of a body," Rees said. "The next-door neighbor says he's been away on a fishing trip. Bensky's a widower, lives alone; it's not unusual for him to take off for a week at a time, not letting anyone know where he's at. Only close relative is a daughter stationed in Germany, a career U.S. Air Force officer. I called her and she hasn't heard from her father in a month but says that's normal. One neighbor thinks Bensky went to a Maine lake to camp out and fish but doesn't know which one. He's got a

❖

cell phone, but the phone company says it's not turned on and doesn't have a GPS chip."

"I'll need that cell number, the contact numbers for the daughter and neighbors, and anything else before I leave. What have you got on the fire?"

"Still preliminary, but my gut reaction is that it was done by someone who knew what he was doing."

"A pro?"

Rees shrugged. "There's so much information available on the Internet, anyone can be a pro at burning down houses or building an atomic bomb."

The fire investigator led Nunes to the back of the house.

"This was Bensky's home office." He glanced at Nunes. "You do any fire investigations for the Bureau?"

"Nope. You have to hold my hand."

"From the damage pattern to this room and the way the fire spread, it makes this wall a good candidate for the point of origin. A normal burn pattern is for a fire to spread upward and outward in a V shape. We have heaviest damage to the wall and ceiling here."

"You look to see where the wood is the most charred?"

"That helps, but it can also lead to a false conclusion because burn patterns can be created more than one way. A few years ago a guy got executed in Texas for killing his three kids in a home fire. He claimed he was innocent right up to the lethal injection. I worked with a team of arson investigators who reviewed the evidence. We concluded that the burn patterns weren't necessarily created by gasoline. Since we did the review postmortem for the poor bastard, I'm real cautious now about conclusions."

"But you think this one's arson?"

"That's my preliminary conclusion, yes. The bottom line to any fire is that you need a fuel supply to burn—wood, cloth, gas, whatever. And a heat source to start the fire—an electrical short, a match, or even lightning. I've eliminated natural causes like lightning and I haven't seen any evidence of an accidental cause, but we're still examining the electrical."

Rees pointed at a fire-damaged object by the wall. "That was an electric heater. Funny thing about it, the heater was turned against the wall."

"Causing it to catch on fire?"

Rees shook his head. "It was the heat source, but it didn't ignite the wood and drywall. About halfway up that burned wall I found a thumbtack. My bet is that thumbtack held up a coffee filter."

"A coffee filter?"

"A large paper one, cone type probably, the ones that look like pastry bags."

"Filled with a combustible."

"Right. Tack it on the wall near a flame, fill it with gas or a highly flammable solvent, and let it drip down slowly. While it's dripping, the arsonist puts miles between him and the house. The dripping combustible builds up a gas vapor near the heater. If that heater wasn't turned toward the wall, I probably wouldn't have found the tack.

"Looks like the arsonist also piled crumbled paperwork under curtains in the office just to give the fire extra kick. The office is at the back of the house. As you can see, there's a tall fence, so the fire wouldn't become noticeable until it had a good head on it."

"Have you recovered any paperwork from the house?"

"Found some in a couple drawers of a metal filing cabinet that was pretty well fried, but the files are still intact in layers." Rees grinned. "I suppose if we had an FBI forensic lab, an unlimited budget, and it was a matter of great national concern, the burned sheets could be read."

Nunes gave the sarcasm a headshake. "Probably not worth the investment. Yet. If the arsonist was after paperwork, he would have either taken it with him or used it as the ignition source. But we need to keep that cabinet as evidence until we find out what's happened to Bensky. How about a computer?"

"No computer. Not now, at least. We found accessories for both a desktop and a laptop but haven't seen either in the debris. The fact that there should have been computers in the room and they were removed before the fire began also tends to back an arson theory. But they might be out for repair."

"Not likely both computers would be out for repair at the same time."

"True, but the desktop could be in a repair shop and he could have the laptop with him. Anyway, we're checking every company in town that does computer repairs."

"Any backup computer equipment he saved files to? Disks, removable drives—"

"Nothing. If he had any, they're gone now."

"Did he have a fax machine?"

Rees checked his crime scene inventory. "Yes, there's one in the debris."

"I'll need the number." Nunes made a note about the fax and to check for an Internet provider. He couldn't get Bensky's phone records yet because there wasn't enough evidence that he was missing and a victim of a violent crime for a judge to issue a search warrant. Bensky probably had Internet service. It seemed unlikely the man would be in the business of researching artworks with international connections without using history's greatest research tool. Some people did almost all of their communicating over the Internet. But Nunes would need a search warrant for detailed information from that source, too.

"Exactly what kind of case are you investigating?" Rees asked.

The fire investigator was not on a need-to-know basis for the whole case, but Nunes figured he needed to give the man enough information to recognize significant evidence . . . and ensure his cooperation. Not all local agencies made a serious effort to cooperate with the feds. And Nunes knew that the Bureau had a reputation for not letting the locals in on investigative results.

"Bensky's a document examiner. He has a background also in art history. He's used by some art dealers to examine the provenance of art items."

"Provenance?"

They walked the perimeter as they talked.

"The ownership history of a piece of art. Bills of sale, letters, wills, probate documents, old catalogs of dealers and museums, pictures, news stories, anything on paper that establishes the chain of ownership."

"So he did a report on a case you're investigating?"

"Exactly. So far it appears he did only a verbal call to the client, a museum curator. I've discovered the curator sent an inner office memo saying that Bensky found nothing suspicious about the provenance he examined."

"You don't buy that?"

"If all she got was a phone call, it would be the first time in history that an expert didn't back up an opinion in writing."

"That's not quite true. It's done all the time."

❖

Nunes stopped and stared at the arson investigator. "What'd you mean?"

"We see it all the time in the courts. Lawyers hire an expert and tell the expert not to issue a written report but to do it verbally. That way the expert's opinion isn't engraved in stone. When everything's nailed down, they tell the expert to write a report."

"I don't think that's the case here. If the report was positive, the curator would want it in writing in order to document her file. It was a big transaction."

"And if the report was negative?"

"If she knew the museum piece being purchased had been stolen, she could have destroyed the negative report, claimed she was told it was a go, and let the sale happen."

"And then she or her co-conspirators burn down the house and destroy any remaining copies of the report?"

Nunes nodded. "But they still have one copy to get rid of."

Rees tapped his head. "The one Bensky carries around."

"Which means I need to get agents out scouring that lake for Bensky. And we'll have to stake the house out, too. In case he comes back."

Fat chance of getting agents out, Nunes thought. In the Age of Terrorism and Weapons of Mass Destruction, contraband art investigations were low on the totem pole.

Nunes gave the arson investigator his fax number and went back to his car. He had a meeting set up for that afternoon with his partner and the Assistant U.S. Attorney he worked with. The discussion would center around the art-for-arms connection and how the Semiramis might fit into the scenario.

He decided he needed to talk in person to the Iraqi curator before the meeting.

❖

26

❖

Jamaica Plains

I decided to pay a visit to Abdullah, again. I had questions to ask him. No longer did I think of my troubles as having started when I waved the paddle to buy the mask. Abdullah made a connection that went straight back to the looting of the museum. I wanted to know more about what he saw that day when Baghdad fell to the allied forces. And more about the evidence he said he was getting to prove the mask had been a museum piece.

After a restless night tossing and turning and thinking about my conversation with Neal, I had come to the conclusion that I had to take care of my own interests. Two things drove this home: Neal was shallow enough to throw a woman he slept with to the wolves, and I couldn't play innocent with Agent Nunes because he knew I was lying. I had to give him someone else to chew on.

The one name that kept dominating my thoughts was Viktor Milan. He had come to signify an evil force in my mind, a Svengali who stayed behind the scenes and manipulated others to do his bidding. Even his name sounded sinister.

More than anything, I needed someone to fill in the blanks about Milan. Neal claimed ignorance, and Lipton was ducking my calls.

❖

It occurred to me that Abdullah might recognize Milan's name or know something about him. Or perhaps he had come across other items that Milan had been behind besides the ones I had bought.

If Abdullah knew of other pieces that exchanged hands in the city, I could track down the gallery owner or auctioneer who had handled the sale and find out what they knew about Milan.

THE MAN WEARING THE SEAL cap sat in the car and stared up at the fifth floor across the street. He watched as Abdullah opened the window and peered down to the street. A package delivery truck driver had rung the apartment and Abdullah had stuck his head out the window to see who it was.

The Iraqi didn't notice the man in the car observing him. Nor would Abdullah have recognized the muscular individual whose features were half-concealed under a cap and aviator-style sunglasses. Had Abdullah seen the cap, he would have immediately recognized it. And been terrified because the last time he saw the man wearing it was in the Baghdad museum when the man was about to shoot him.

The man knew the approximate time the global delivery truck had been expected to arrive. He had called the company before he began his stakeout.

He checked his watch. The delivery truck was on time. He had smiled when he saw the truck make its way up the street and double-park in front of Abdullah's building.

He waited until the driver made the delivery and had driven away before he got out of the car.

BACK IN HIS APARTMENT, Abdullah opened the package and unwrapped the commendation. He swelled with pride, and tears ran down his cheeks as he held the elaborate scroll. His father would have been proud of the award from the king of Iraq.

A handsome document, not just a sheet of paper but a scroll written on parchment made from worked goat's skin and emblazoned with the flag of Iraq and the signature of King Faisal II. The monarchy fell in 1958 and Abdullah wondered if this had been the last commendation

❖

signed by the young king. The twenty-three-year-old king and other members of the royal family were murdered by revolting military officers in July of 1958. A year later, Army officers, a young Saddam Hussein among them, attempted to assassinate the officer who had organized the overthrow of the king and assumed a virtual dictatorship. That attempt failed, but the man was murdered four years later. Blood continued to flow in Iraq for decades afterward.

The commendation stated that Abdullah's father had given his life to safeguard the Mask of Sammu-ramat, a national treasure. Beneath a drawing of the mask that the Americans called Semiramis, the artist had sketched the imprint of the cylinder. Like the brand on a farm animal or the license on a car, the inscription identified the owner of the piece of antiquity.

Abdullah kissed the commendation.

Now no one would be able to deny the origin of the mask purchased by the Piedmont Museum.

He got up to answer a knock on his door, believing it to be the deliveryman again returning for some reason.

He opened the door to a man who had on a baseball-type cap and dark glasses.

"Yes—" Abdul caught his breath as he stared at the cap and recognized the letters on it. "You!"

The man stepped forward and with one swift thrust stabbed Abdullah in the stomach with a long-bladed knife.

Abdullah stared at him wide-eyed.

The man twisted the blade deeper inside as Abdullah collapsed against him.

27

❖

A taxi let me off in front of Abdullah's building. The little girl with the large almond eyes who had stared at me on my last visit wasn't in sight.

I sighed as I began the climb, remembering the days when I had a fifth-floor studio walk-up on the Lower East Side. The entire studio was no larger than my bath and dressing room in my penthouse. I didn't miss those days when it felt as if I were hiking up the Empire State Building every night when I came home.

When I reached the fourth-floor landing I heard someone groan above. I paused and listened. Nothing. I started up again. I was on the last leg when I heard a choking, gagging sound coming from the landing above.

I tensed. Something was wrong.

"Hello . . . anyone there," I said cautiously.

Oprah talking about another child lost by the Florida Department of Children and Families blared from a television.

The stomach-churning pounding of Middle Eastern music was absent.

"Hello," I said again.

The hell with it. I ran up the last steps.

Oh my God. Abdullah was lying full length on his back. His shirt was bloody.

❖

I knelt beside him. "Mr. ibn Hussein."

He stared at me. His mouth opened and closed, but no sound came out. He lifted his hand toward his head, but his arm fell back.

A great sigh escaped from his mouth.

The door to another apartment opened and a woman stepped out. I stared at her and she stared at me. She screamed first, then shouted in Arabic.

I didn't know what she was spewing, but the look on her face implied I was a murderer and I was sure she was alerting the whole world to her opinion.

I ran down the steps, rushing by another woman who stepped out on the third floor. I hit the ground floor at a run, stumbling, almost falling as I burst out the door.

I flew headlong into Special Agent Nunes.

He was as surprised as I was as he caught me.

28

❖

"You're getting subway treatment," Kimmie, my fellow prisoner, told me. She'd been busted for jabbing a john with the toe of her shoe.

"Broke off the tip of a kitchen knife and pushed it into the toe of the shoe, point out," she told me earlier. "Honey, you'd be surprised how often you need a little sharp persuasion to get some bastard to back off." She demonstrated how she'd kick an aggressive john in the shin with the knife tip.

I refused to be the first to cast a stone at the whore. Who was I to say that she was wrong in protecting herself? Buying sex didn't give a man the right to batter the provider. The bastard had knocked her around. Now he needed surgery to repair his shin and she would do the time.

I listened to her grievance that she was the one who got busted instead of the john. "There's no justice in this fuckin' world."

"Amen," I said. "What's subway treatment?"

"This is the third station you've been booked in tonight, right, honey? They're moving you from station to station to keep your lawyer from catching up. That way they can keep questioning you until your lawyer finds out where they're holding you and springs you."

❖

"You don't have to talk to the cops," I said. I knew that from television.

She howled and leaned back on the cot, kicking her legs in the air before she came back up. "Buuullshiiit. You clam up and demand to see your lawyer and they just keep fuckin' with you. Better to talk and just keep denying it, honey. They'll get tired of fuckin' with you."

This woman must have gotten her legal tactics from Neal, I thought.

I talked to Neal briefly on the phone at the first station where they booked me. Just enough to tell him I'd been arrested for murder and needed a lawyer. After that, I got on the "subway."

Fifteen minutes later I was taken out of the holding tank and put into a room with Nunes and an NYPD homicide detective named Elena Rodriguez.

I was glad Nunes was there—Rodriguez looked mean enough to break my thumbs for jaywalking. The woman just sat there and stared at me as if she'd like nothing better than to turn off the secret camera and give me an attitude adjustment. Someone at a cocktail party claimed female cops were meaner and more vicious than male ones. He gave me a list of reasons, none of which I remembered as I kept Detective Rodriguez in the corner of my eye and worried that she was going to beat the shit out of me.

"This is an NYPD case," Nunes said. "It hasn't gone federal yet. Detective Rodriguez is permitting me to participate because it's likely this case will overlap with my investigation."

"I didn't harm that poor man."

"We know you didn't kill him. You didn't have a weapon on you. We found nothing in the building. He was stabbed in the apartment and had bled for a minute or two before you found him on the landing."

"Then why am I here?"

"The victim said the fifty-five-million-dollar mask you bought for the museum was part of the Baghdad museum loot."

"I didn't have anything to do with hurting him."

"We already established that."

"So why are you holding me?"

"Because you're mixed up in what got him killed. You've been buying Mesopotamian art engineered by the same auction house, the same

London dealer, and the same Swiss provenance agent, culminating in a piece worth a king's ransom. In fact, every major piece of art you acquired fits that scenario. Where did you deposit your cut?"

"My cut? I'm a curator, not a salesperson. I get paid a salary, not a commission."

"You're saying you weren't paid to steer Piedmont into purchases that totaled nearly seventy million dollars in about a year?"

"I only got my salary."

"If you have an account somewhere, Switzerland, the Grand Caymans, Luxembourg, we'll find it. When we do, we'll nail you for murder."

"I didn't—"

"You're not getting it, Dupre." That from Detective Rodriquez. "You don't have to pull the trigger, shove the knife, or throw the match to get charged with murder. If the group you're involved with is killing people to cover their tracks, you're as guilty as they are."

"I don't know why people are getting hurt."

"People?" Nunes's eyes shot up. "Who else besides the Iraqi has been killed?"

"I don't know. I didn't mean that." I meant Bensky, but I was probably a bit premature about claims he was dead.

Nunes leaned forward, drilling me with his beady eyes. "Then why'd you say it? We've only been talking about Abdullah. Do you know about another body?"

"No, I don't know anything."

"You hired a man named Bensky to examine the provenance. Bensky's house was burned down. Were you aware of that?"

"No. Yes."

"How do you know?"

"I went out to see him because he didn't answer my phone calls. I saw police there. Some woman said his house had been burned."

"Why did you want to talk to him?"

"He examined the provenance on the mask for me." I knew I was going deeper and deeper.

Nunes stood up and glared down on me. Righteous. An avenging angel about to swoop down on a sinner.

"We know Bensky's house was torched, obviously to cover up evidence.

❖

He's missing. At this point, I'm pretty sure he won't be found anytime soon. That leaves two conclusions."

I didn't want to hear either of them.

"Either Bensky was in on the scam with you and your pals and cut and run or he had evidence against you and had to be gotten rid of."

"I don't know anything about his disappearance."

My voice had dropped almost to a whisper. Earlier, when I was arrested, I was in a state of shock. Later I wanted to cry. Now I was so tired and drained I just wanted to lie down and sleep.

"Why did you lie about Bensky's report?"

"I-I-I don't know what you're talking about." Jesus, my stammering was a dead giveaway.

Rodriguez suddenly was at my side, staring down at me. Another avenging angel. "It will go easier on you if you tell us the truth. What did you do with the report from Bensky?"

I was about to fess up, but something in her tone and Nunes's body language caused me to keep quiet.

I realized they were asking me because they didn't know. They suspected a report but wanted me to confirm it. Once I did, I'd never see the light of day until I was in a prison yard.

"I want to see my lawyer."

THEY LET ME STAY in the holding tank most of the night with drunks, drugged-out party girls, and agitated whores cursing the world's injustices.

The lawyer Neal sent finally got me out and walked me down the steps of the jail. Dawn was breaking.

I was so tired, I could have curled upon the steps and gone to sleep. The holding tank didn't have enough room to lie down even on the floor, not to mention there were no beds—and no seat on the toilet.

"I spoke to the homicide detective handling the case. She wants to get rid of it fast. She figures the feds will make her do all the footwork and then take over the case and get the glory when it's filed. She's willing to cut you a deal if you roll over."

"Roll over?"

"Tell them about your accomplices."

❖

"Accomplices?" I heard what he said, but none of it was making sense right now.

"Ms. Dupre, the police believe you've been buying stolen art as part of a ring. They say they know of three other people involved. If you testify against them, the police will recommend a lighter sentence."

I stopped and stared at him, trying to see whether he was really on my side. "Mr. Spellman. Listen to me. I have no accomplices. I have done nothing wrong. And I certainly haven't killed anyone. I'm innocent. Completely, totally innocent."

He checked his watch. "I have to get home, get ready for the office, and drop my kid at day care pretty soon. I came out as a favor to Neal. He said he'd get me a deal on a piece, but I'm not a criminal lawyer. I'll get you one later today. I know enough about the law to advise you to give some thought to the idea of turning state's evidence. You could be arrested again at any moment."

"But they just released me."

"They're still working on this Bensky thing. If they have evidence to connect you up to the arson or his disappearance, they'll bring you in. Rodriguez says the locals out in Westchester have film taken by a TV news chopper. Nunes is going to examine it, see if you're on it."

"They filmed the fire being set?"

"Of course not. Arson investigators believe a firebug loves to come back and gawk at the flames. It's a sexual thing."

"I just told you I'm innocent." But even as I said it, I knew they'd spot me on that tape, even though the place was probably cool to lukewarm by the time I got there.

"Lawyers have a different definition of guilt than laypeople. We're not concerned with whether you actually committed a crime or not. We have to deal strictly with the evidence. If they can prove you're guilty, believing you're innocent . . . even being innocent . . . doesn't mean you won't get convicted."

"I don't get it."

"You know that DNA can get people out of prison who were wrongfully convicted? They were innocent, too, but they were still convicted because the *evidence* made them appear guilty. If the police can link you to the market in looted antiquities and people connected to the transactions start dying . . . if you look guilty, a jury will find you guilty."

❖

I shook my head. "This is insane. I've done nothing."

"The other thing lawyers know is that nobody ever admits to being guilty, even if they are. Better think about cutting a deal. You might get eight or ten years. If you go to trial and you're found guilty, you could be looking at life or even the death penalty."

❖

29

❖

I barricaded my apartment door and crawled under the covers. I slept three hours and woke up feeling anxious and scared. And angry. Fury snapped me out of depression. I jumped into the shower, washing the stench of jail off.

I felt betrayal and abandonment from Hiram and that worm Eric. Even from Neal. He had given me advice and referral to a lawyer, but I no longer trusted him.

My father always said there were people in this world who were money oriented and people who weren't: "If you took all the money in the world and passed it around evenly, in five years the same people would have what they had before."

I didn't know how true that was, but Hiram, Eric, and Neal were much better at the money game than me. They had carefully avoided getting their hands dirty. It was beginning to dawn on me that Bensky's document actually worked in their favor: They had a patsy for the police to go after if everything went to hell.

Neal wasn't on my side, even though he acted like it. He certainly wouldn't risk anything for me. Sure, he'd called a lawyer for me, but where was Neal now? He was too fluid for me. He seemed to be able to pour in and fill any need I had . . . before he pulled the plug. I kept thinking about how he had shredded Bensky's report. He said he did it for me. But did he really do it for himself?

Rolling over on my co-conspirators was a joke: *I didn't know enough to throw anyone to the police.*

I had to trace the Semiramis back to the source—do my own "provenance" and follow the chain of custody of the mask from the time it was taken from the Iraqi museum to Rutgers's auction table.

What I needed was information on the dirty work of Viktor Milan, Lipton, and whoever else was involved to feed to the FBI so they would get off my back.

The only way I could prove my innocence was by finding out who was guilty.

Sir Henri Lipton, the world's foremost dealer in antiquities, had sent some dirt my way. He was the man with the answers.

London was where I needed to go.

I made an airline reservation for the next flight, leaving in three hours. That gave me just enough time to get to the airport, clear security, and get to the gate.

And hope it threw the feds off my trail.

AGENT STEINER PULLED IN behind the taxi that picked up Madison in front of her apartment building. As soon as he saw the carry-on, he knew she was headed for the airport.

As he followed the taxi, he called Nunes, knowing he would still be asleep after the long session with Dupre and an NYPD homicide detective that lasted into the wee hours of the morning.

"You're right again, partner," Steiner told Nunes. "She's headed for the airport. What else do you have in your crystal ball?"

"I'll give you ten-to-one her destination is London."

"Why London?"

"Mr. Big. Sir Henri Lipton. A mega-buck art dealer. He's the source for her purchases. I looked at her cell phone records. She's been trying to call him and he hasn't answered her calls."

"Why do you think Lipton's not returning her calls?"

"No honor among thieves."

❖

"You're sure she's involved in this?"

"You want odds?"

"Nah, you know what I want? A ten percent finder's fee for the fifty-five-million-dollar mask when it goes back to Iraq. That's five and a half mil."

"Don't be so sure it's going back to Iraq. Unless we find that commendation the Iraqi curator got killed for, it's going to be tough to prove the mask was part of the loot. And you know how finder's fees work: Thieves steal a famous painting, they can't do anything with it because it's too well-known, so an 'innocent' person steps forward and arranges its return for a finder's fee."

"Which goes to the thieves."

"You know how many banks you have to rob before it adds up to a million bucks? Probably a hundred."

The taxi that Steiner was following turned onto the Van Wick Expressway. "Okay, she's definitely flying out of JFK."

"When you get there, confirm the London trip. It's a six- or seven-hour flight. The art theft detail at Scotland Yard is already watching Lipton. I'll give a heads-up to our embassy people there. They can add her to the watch list."

"Why are we letting her have a get-out-of-jail-free card?"

"She's going to lead us to her accomplices, Lipton and Milan. And, more important, to the rest of the pieces. When she does, we'll have the British police and Interpol grab them."

30

❖

London

A gray, cold, liquid day greeted my flight from New York. London drizzle and chill, perfect for the way I felt. The Lanesborough hotel usually sent a car and driver to meet me, but this time I took a taxi from the airport to a smaller, cheaper place that I used to stay at before my job as a curator.

I took a quick shower, hoping it would ease the weariness of travel, then crashed in bed, falling into a deep sleep to make up for the last few days of troubled sleep.

The following morning, after a breakfast of coffee and toast, I took a taxi to Sir Henri Lipton's gallery to cold-call him. I hadn't phoned ahead because I wasn't sure what kind of reception was waiting for me. Maybe Scotland Yard. I had no idea what trouble I had left behind in New York or how much of it had followed me across the Atlantic. Or even if anyone knew I had gone.

I tried to keep the image of Abdullah out of my mind, but his blood and anguished features kept creeping into my thoughts. His daughter right now must be going through pure hell. First her grandfather had died to protect the museum piece, and now it had taken her father's life. Not to mention she'd lost a country sometime in between.

The reputation of the Semiramis as a harbinger of bad luck was well

❖

deserved. I wished I had never heard of the piece. Better yet . . . I wished I could rewind my life for the past week and do it all over again, this time not pitching the mask as the centerpiece of the museum. I wished . . . what do they say? Wish in one hand and . . . oh well, I had to move forward.

LIPTON HAD CONVERTED A brick warehouse into an art gallery. The building was in London's Lambeth Borough not far from one of Europe's great cultural centers, the South Bank Centre arts complex, twenty-seven acres along the Thames with theaters, halls, and museums. Waterloo Station, an enormous train facility, was nearby. Across the river was Big Ben and Parliament.

Sir Henri got the august title before his name by making a major contribution to the British art world—back in the days when his name was spelled "Henry." Some considered him the world's biggest art pirate. He wasn't always particular about how art made its way to his gallery. He came to prominence in an era when third-world countries were more tolerant—and corrupt—about the theft of their national heritage.

I was aware of Lipton's reputation in the art world. But I was also aware that there were limited works of antiquity on the market. If you wanted to build a collection, you bought what was available from whoever was offering it. You grabbed the opportunity when it presented itself.

I rang the doorbell and waited a minute. I rang it again. Lipton's assistant, Mrs. Drumball, answered the door. I called her the Gate Keeper. She was a stern-faced woman who seemed to hate everything and everyone and always had a chip on her shoulder. No doubt the only thing that made her smile was shutting the door in the faces of people who dared to enter the world's most prestigious and private art gallery without an appointment. Her spiritual twin was Nurse Ratched.

Mrs. Drumball recognized me but gave no sign of it. I felt like reminding her that I—and my checkbook—had been welcomed many times before.

"Can I help you?"

"You know who I am, Mrs. Drumball," I said through the outer iron-gated door.

The Gate Keeper kept her hair and personality in a tight bun. She must have smelled the desperation in my body language.

"Of course. Wait here a moment." She closed the door before I could say anything else.

A minute later the door opened again. But not the iron grating.

"Sir Henri is unavailable. You need to make an appointment."

She shut the door in my face.

She was lying, of course. Normally Lipton would have rushed down to greet me if he knew I had turned up at his door, even without an appointment. The Piedmont Museum was one of his substantial clients.

A chauffeur-driven vintage Rolls-Royce Phantom pulled up to the curb just as I turned around to leave.

Lipton's "significant other" was seated in the back. His timing couldn't have been more perfect.

Albert was very handsome and had the delicacy of a refined young woman, slender in size. He wore Ninja black pajamas, making him look like he had just stepped off of a Hong Kong martial arts movie set. Most women would have killed for the pearl choker and the large ruby ring on his finger. Two bags from Harrods were next to him.

I had met Albert a dozen times here at the gallery and at parties in New York and London.

"It's good to see you again, Albert."

"Maddy, darling, what a nice surprise." He smiled, greeting me with a kiss on each cheek. "Are you here to see Henri?"

"Of course. Here, let me help you with your bags."

"Oh, thank you. You're an angel. I'm absolutely drained from all this shopping."

I was sure Albert didn't know I was persona non grata, so I grabbed his bags so he could use his key to open the door. I went inside with him, chattering about the shopping at Harrods.

When Lipton had remodeled the warehouse, he gutted the entire interior. There were three levels. When you stepped inside you entered a large, round reception room that had four doors leading into showrooms. A brass cage elevator was in the center. The second level was used for storage of the pieces not on display. Lipton's office and personal quarters were on the third level. Each level had twenty-foot ceilings, making the tall glass dome on the roof as high as a six-story building. Teak paneling

❖

covered much of the interior, and each of the upper levels had a brass railing from which you could look down on the first-floor reception area.

As we stepped into the cage elevator, the Gate Keeper entered the reception room. Her jaw dropped when she saw me in the elevator with Albert. She frowned at Albert as the doors closed.

"That woman is simply dreadful." He spoke in a stage whisper and shivered theatrically. "I don't know why Henri has her around. She gives me the chills." He raised his eyebrows. "Bedding her would be fucking a cold fish, one that's dead and packed in ice."

I started laughing. I couldn't have agreed with him more. It felt good to laugh for a change.

He started laughing, too. Then his face turned serious. "I hear there's a bit of trouble with one of the pieces Henri sold."

"That's an understatement."

It came out of me in a gush as the cage moved up. "There's a dead man who claimed the piece was stolen, the provenance examiner is missing, probably dead, there's been arson, I've been in jail, and I have the FBI after me."

He gaped. "My goodness, you have been having fun, haven't you?"

"Oh, it's been a blast."

"It's that damn Swiss man. Henri's been cursing him for days. I told Henri we should go see him and straighten it out. It's the place to be this time of year, you know. Sun, sea, and the beach."

Viktor Milan obviously wasn't in Switzerland. I started to ask where he was when the elevator shuddered to a stop and I saw Lipton waiting for us.

Lipton's face was red and he was not in a happy mood.

"Go to your room," he snapped at Albert.

"*Well!*" Albert's handsome Chinese features twisted in an expression of mock resignation. "*Excuse me!*"

He muttered, "Bastard," under his breath loud enough for both of us to hear as he grabbed the bags from me and paraded off.

Lipton turned around and went to his office.

I followed.

He got behind his desk and glared at me. His goatee, thin mustache, silver hair that came to a point above his rounded features, and significant belly reminded me of a well-fed, pudgy Satan.

❖

"You don't have an appointment," he said tersely.

"An appointment? I came here to talk about murder. You can talk to me or to the police."

He scoffed. "The police are outside. They're taking a picture of everyone coming and going."

Shit. If that was true, it wouldn't be long before the FBI knew I was in London.

"They're trying to scare me. I've dealt with police agencies on three continents that make London art theft bobbies look like country parsons in comparison."

"You may be experienced, but it just so happens *my* dealings with the police started with you."

"What do you want me to do about it? It's not my fault."

"Then whose fault is it?"

He shrugged his shoulders. "We were all fooled."

"Who prepared the phony provenance?"

"Viktor Milan. You know that. His name is on it."

"Do you know where he is?"

"His office is in Zurich. The address is on the provenance."

"Do you have a phone number?"

"No. You can't contact him. I hear he went south to get some sunshine."

"Does he check his messages?"

"I don't know."

"I think you do know. You have too many deals going with Milan not to know how to contact him."

"Look, I don't know where he is. If you have any sense, you don't want to know, either. I suspect that Iraqi curator in New York isn't the first man that Milan has murdered—and probably won't be the last."

"Jesus. You've really got us into a fine mess."

His eyebrows shot up. "And you're completely innocent? An incredibly valuable antiquity suddenly is on the market with a very questionable history. Did you properly investigate it? Or just close your eyes and thank heaven for the opportunity to acquire it."

"I didn't know it was looted from another museum. Or that a poor man trying to get it back would be murdered. How did it get from the Iraqi museum to the auction house?"

❖

"You saw the provenance; it was—"

"Fabricated."

"Tell that to the police. It should get you no more than a dozen years in prison, if you're not also held responsible for a murder."

"You crooked bastard," I yelled. "You knew all the time that the provenance was phony. You set me up!"

"I must tell you that getting hysterical is not going to help you in this situation. You seem intent on proving the provenance is a fraud. That's a foolish position."

"And you need to know that the police won't have a problem proving it's a fraud. The typing font is wrong for that period of time, or did you forget that little minor detail?"

His eyebrows shot up again. "What? Good God! It certainly fooled me. I acted in good faith, without knowing that. I know nothing about typewriters and their markings. But I'm getting the impression that you were not duped by the fraud."

A laugh erupted from me that came out as a choke. "That's your line—that I duped you into auctioning off a stolen piece? Duped you into getting fifty-five million dollars for it? Very clever of me."

He shook his head, disgusted. "I got nothing for it. Piedmont managed to stop payment. Right now he's sitting on the piece and the money. Rather convenient for the two of you, I would say. I imagine he gave you quite a bonus for taking advantage of an old man. And murdering another."

I closed my eyes. This wasn't going well at all.

I came to drag the truth out of him and he was getting target practice burying me with lies and innuendos. I wanted to take the Roman statue on his desk that he used as a paperweight and pound him with it.

"Go home," he said.

"I can't. I'll get arrested."

"Better than being dead. Your coming here puts both of us in danger. Not just with the police. He's running crazy."

"You mean Milan?"

"Yes. He's out the money and he wants blood. He'll be here soon. If he sees you, he'll think we're conspiring against him."

"I need answers."

A buzzer sounded at his desk.

"He's here," the Gate Keeper said.

❖

"I'll be down in a moment." Lipton took my arm. "There's a stairway that leads downstairs." He threw a switch under a wood panel. "The fire door is unarmed. Go out the back way."

If the man downstairs was Milan, there was no way I was going without confronting him.

Lipton led me out of his office and whispered, "Hurry. There's a door on the other side."

I had quietly walked to the other side when I heard Lipton's startled shout, "No! For God's sake!"

I looked over the banister. A man stood in the round reception room, holding a shoulder-mounted rocket launcher, similar to what I'd seen terrorists and soldiers on television use. He pulled the trigger. There was a flash and then a fiery explosion as the rocket hit the level I was on.

The explosion knocked me off my feet. The world went dim. I couldn't hear. My eardrums hurt. Smoke and fire roared. I managed to crawl toward the door. It was blown open. I used the railing for support as I made my way down the staircase that was filled with smoke.

At the bottom landing the steel security door was already ajar. I pushed through it and gasped for air. People in the alley ran to me.

I think I heard a man ask, "Are you all right?"

I coughed and gasped for air.

"What happened?" the man asked.

I could only shake my head. It sounded like the man was talking at me through a tunnel.

More people had gathered around. I heard voices talking all at once and then everyone was moving farther away. I was swept away with them. Another explosion sounded. I looked back at the building. It was fully engulfed.

"No one could survive that," someone yelled.

My God. It suddenly hit me. Everyone was dead inside. I just barely escaped getting killed.

I heard the words "gas explosion" and "terrorist attack."

Sirens blared on the main street.

I had to get away. As I walked down the street, cold chills racked me. My ears still rang. My mind was amazingly clear, so I knew I wasn't in shock. A near-death experience had made me more lucid than I had been in days.

❖

Someone, I wasn't sure it was Viktor Milan, had just committed mass murder. I didn't know how many people were in the building, but I knew of at least three: Lipton, Albert, and the Gate Keeper. Three more people dead now, in addition to the Iraqi curator in New York. And where was Bensky? Probably dead, too.

Nothing made sense.

How does someone enter a building with a rocket launcher and open fire in the middle of London? Where were the police Lipton said were watching the building?

It dawned on me that the shooter probably escaped out the back way and into the alley as I had done.

I looked around, wondering if I was followed.

❖

31

❖

I kept on walking until I found myself in front of a tube station that sold English Channel tunnel train tickets to Calais. I stared stupidly at the sign. I could be in France in less than two hours. My carry-on was back at the hotel. But I had my money, credit cards, and passport with me. I was certain I'd be arrested, if not killed, if I didn't leave London. I bought a ticket and boarded the train.

They say that severe trauma can cause your emotions to retreat. Mine had curled up into a tight ball. I couldn't face what had happened at Lipton's. So I didn't. I simply sat on the train that would take me under the Channel to France and stared straight ahead.

I was no longer scared. Fear had fled, along with my emotions.

A killer who knew no mercy had taken four lives, possibly five. I was on the list. It had come down to a simple equation in my mind: I had to hunt him down and turn him over to the police. Or kill him myself, if it came to that.

The thought of killing Viktor Milan wasn't repulsive to me. I had never committed a violent act in my life. But then I had stared down into the face of a rocket launcher, and people of flesh and blood had been consumed in the explosion and fire.

❖

I imagined ways a woman could kill a man: a knife . . . running him down with a car . . . pushing him off a ledge . . . poison.

The bastard could rot in hell for all I cared. Killing the mad dog didn't bother my conscience either.

I leaned back and closed my eyes, trying to get my focus.

My destination was Zurich, the home of the mysterious Swiss. Viktor Milan. His name gave no real clue as to its national origin. "Viktor" sounded like a German or Eastern European spelling of "Victor". Milan was a city in Italy. Switzerland, of course, had a mixture of people with German, French, and Italian heritages.

I planned on renting a car in Calais instead of continuing on to Paris by rail. Keeping track of me when I had the freedom of a car would be much harder.

I knew I wouldn't find Milan in Zurich. He was somewhere with sun and sea. I now believed that Milan wasn't the man with the rocket launcher. A man who dealt in $55 million art pieces would hire someone to do his dirty work. But Zurich would be a starting point. And that was where the provenance led.

Despite my murder fantasies, I wondered what I would do if I came face-to-face with him. Calling the police would be my first instinct.

But it was the last thing I wanted to do now. Lipton and the others had been killed with the police parked outside. Abdullah had been murdered in New York after talking to the FBI. The least that would happen to me if I went to the police was that I would be jailed . . . perhaps forever.

The other alternative was that I would be murdered.

32

❖

London

Nunes took a red-eye flight into Heathrow the evening following the attack on Lipton's gallery. Red-eyed himself from little sleep on the plane, he took a taxi to Scotland Yard's Arts & Antiques Unit soon after checking into his hotel and grabbing a quick breakfast.

The specialized police group was based not far from New Scotland Yard's modern twenty-story building. The location was on the other side of the Thames from Lipton's art gallery.

Nunes envied the British resolve when it came to fighting theft of cultural items. Unlike the bare-bones FBI art theft unit, the well-staffed British unit worked closely with police agencies around the world to combat the illicit trade in stolen art and cultural property.

The FBI's own "Most Wanted" artworks list was inspired by the unit's SLAD, Stolen London Art Database, which stored details and images of over fifty thousand stolen items.

"Like you Americans," Neil Tanner, an Arts & Antiquities Unit detective, told Nunes, "we take a special interest in the tragic looting of Iraq's cultural heritage. We have an alert out to the art trade advising them to take a good look at the provenance of items from the region. Not that those in the trade are unaware of the need to investigate chains of ownership claims. Our reminders are just to nudge them a little closer to the letter of the law."

Seated in a conference room, Nunes waited patiently while Tanner set up equipment for a slide show of digital images taken of the Lipton gallery around the time of the attack. Kaye Burl, an FBI agent from the U.S. Embassy in London, was also at the table. The FBI maintained an office in most major nations in order to coordinate international investigations and check out leads for domestic investigations.

"We've had an eye on Sir Henri ever since I've been with the unit," Tanner said. "He's the world's top dealer in antiquities, and it's a position that would be damn hard to maintain if you gave every provenance a good look, now wouldn't it. We upped our surveillance of him since the looting of the Iraqi museum, expecting we'd see a big increase in sales of Mesopotamian antiquities, but the Semiramis was the first patently suspicious piece we've seen."

Nunes nodded. "That's because he's been releasing the stuff very slowly through New York. He waited several years to even begin the process and didn't really go whole hog until about a year ago. Dupre has literally stocked her museum through Lipton. But the Semiramis was the first sit-up-and-take-notice piece. I'm surprised he put it through a public auction rather than a private sale."

"He probably tried a treaty sale first and the owner of the piece wasn't satisfied with the price. There's nothing comparable to the mask to help gauge a selling price, so it all came down to how much someone was willing to pay."

Tanner got his slide show going. A series of pictures showing Madison entering Lipton's gallery before the explosion and fire came on the screen.

"We've had an around-the-clock surveillance on Lipton's gallery for weeks. We set it up when we found out he was going to auction the Semiramis. Our immediate suspicion was that it was part of the Iraqi loot. A museum piece like the mask couldn't have been in a private collection for over a century without news of it leaking out, now would it?"

Nunes wished the FBI had the same vigilance toward contraband art. He heard about the Semiramis from the news media.

"This is the shooter," Tanner said.

Not much of the man was exposed. He appeared bundled for the cold,

❖

wearing a full-length overcoat, with a hood and scarf. The clothing was too heavy for the weather, but in London that didn't make the clothing stand out. Nothing was seen of his face. The form was identified as a male only because of his size. He was a large man, but not enough was exposed to determine how much of it was blubber.

He carried a long, narrow bag. Tanner used a laser pointer to emphasize the object.

"The bag's similar to airline check-in luggage for a golf bag. In fact, we think that's exactly what it is. Our people assumed it contained a piece of contraband artwork. It held something a helluva lot more lethal—a Soviet RPG-7. A portable shoulder-held rocket grenade launcher."

The shooter rang the doorbell and was admitted by a woman.

"Lipton's assistant. She was obviously expecting the visitor."

"She's dead?"

"We're certain she's one of the charred bodies. A fireman who went in looking for bodies found the weapon. The shooter simply dropped it on the floor after he used it. The firing tube is only about three feet long. Fully loaded, it weighs about twenty pounds. It's small, lightweight, and cheap. They're very popular with guerrillas and terrorists around the world. IRA probably has a car train load of them."

"And they're readily available in the international trade in contraband arms," Nunes added. "The rocket launchers are an IRA item, a Russian mafiya weapon, a favorite of Middle Eastern terrorists and any other number of other users."

Nunes watched the fiery holocaust engulf the gallery after the initial explosion. *A mass killer,* Nunes thought. The shooter had to know people would be in the building. The count was four. Only Madison Dupre walked away. And the shooter.

"Your curator came out the back way," Tanner said. "Unfortunately, we had the surveillance only set up for the front."

"Why?"

"We have limited resources and couldn't cover everything. Besides, we set up the surveillance to shake up Lipton. We let him know we were out there. The idea was to get him scared enough to come in and make a deal. Or starve him out by scaring off his business clientele.

"We had to move cautiously . . . the man's been an institution in the world of art for decades. Most of the power players in the country have bought art from him, including royals. We were watching for sellers and buyers of artworks and expected them to come through the front door. Unfortunately, we got a shooter who walked in the front and left by the back."

"Along with the Dupre woman," Nunes said. "Rather convenient."

"We have witness statements about her. She appeared harried, distraught, and scared. In other words, someone genuinely caught by surprise. We haven't found anyone who saw the shooter. He apparently went out the back and melted into the crowd that gathered. But the woman stood out because she was obviously shocked and frightened."

"Was the shooter observed in any vehicle?"

"Dropped off in front by a taxi. We've spoken to the driver. Said he picked up the bloke three blocks back. We think he parked his car and grabbed a passing taxi."

"Any description from him?"

"None helpful. The shooter had a scarf covering his mouth and nose. Told the driver he had a cold. Voice was muffled."

"Do you have *anything* on the shooter?" Nunes asked.

"What you've seen is what we have. A big man in an overcoat carrying a golf bag. We don't have anything else. Lipton made quite a few enemies, it's that kind of trade, and we're checking alibis."

"No candidates?"

"None that would use a terrorist weapon like a rocket launcher. That implies a professional. Ex-military. From what I've seen of the art crowd, Lipton's known enemies would be more likely to put poisoned sweetener in his cappuccino. Do you people have any ideas?"

Nunes shook his head. "I've heard of Lipton, of course, but he hasn't been the focus of any of our investigations. Like you, I find the choice of weapons interesting. Either someone's hired a military man—"

"Or they're military themselves," Agent Burl said.

Tanner cleared his throat. "You know, there were those rumors about U.S. troops participating in the looting. . . ."

Nunes and Burl gave him stone-cold expressions.

"Rumors of war," Agent Burl said. "You know how it goes . . . rumors about U.S. troops, rumors about British troops . . ."

Everyone understood one another.

The notion that the shooter could be someone involved in the Baghdad heist had been roiling in Nunes's head ever since he heard about the rocket launcher. The choice of weapon coming on the heels of the fallout over the Semiramis lent itself to an Iraqi connection. Shoulder-mounted rocket launchers were a mainstay in the violent world of Middle East wars and terrorism. But he didn't have a clue as to whether the shooter was Iraqi or American.

Nunes said to Tanner, "I need everything you can give me on Lipton. And a copy of all the surveillance reports. I'll see if any of it correlates to what we already have."

"Do you have anything on the Dupre woman? Other than propinquity to Lipton?"

Nunes shook his head. "The only thing we have is that she managed to put together a Mesopotamian collection in a short time, most of it through Lipton. Frankly, if that Iraqi curator hadn't crashed a museum event and made a claim with cameras rolling we wouldn't be investigating Dupre or her connections. I know she's involved, but how deep . . . I'm not sure yet. I'm trying to get up enough probable cause to get warrants so we can examine the provenances of all the pieces she bought that came through Lipton."

"Any progress on the murder of the curator?"

"Well, we know Dupre didn't actually kill him. But I don't know if she stumbled in by accident or went there to retrieve evidence she knew the curator had. The killer obviously took it."

"Evidence?"

"A commendation made to the father of the curator. It would prove that the Semiramis had come from the museum."

"What's the legal status of the Semiramis?"

"About the same as you have with Greek claims for the Elgin marbles. Unless the proof materializes, the Iraqis will still be making a demand for return of the Semiramis a hundred years from now, because there's no solid proof it came out of the museum."

"What's your next step?" Tanner asked.

"Probably the same as yours—try to find Madison Dupre. Like you, I'd like to know what she saw in those moments before the gallery was destroyed. And besides the murder of the curator, there's another body I want to talk to her about."

He told Tanner about the arson fire at Bensky's.

❖

"We found his body. Someone weighted down Bensky's body and dropped it in Long Island Sound. By sheer luck, a fisherman pulling up a trap brought it up with his catch."

"Dupre ran from New York," Tanner said. "We suspect she's run from London . . . if she's still alive. She didn't return to her hotel after the explosion. Her luggage is still there. That leads us to believe she's either too scared . . . or dead. It may be that the shooter caught up with her. But then again, it's not that hard to leave our little island. Dozens of airlines, the Channel tunnel, several ferries across to France, Belgium, and Ireland . . . it'll take time to check them all."

"If she's running," Agent Burl said, "that certainly makes her look guilty."

"One thing's for certain: She knows something. Something that somebody wants her dead for . . . or something she thinks she can use." Nunes pursed his lips. "My take is that she's in over her head. She's made herself a moving target in the hope that she'll be harder to hit. But she's no match for a man who uses a missile to make a hit in the middle of London."

33

❖

Calais, France

I decided to rent an economical car when I arrived in Calais. I picked the Citroën because it was relatively inexpensive and also popular. That made it a low-profile car in my mind. I also purchased a Michelin road map for Western Europe.

By the time I got on the road, it was nearly seven o'clock in the evening. I didn't want to travel all night to Zurich or even take the most direct route in the daytime. Instead, I headed for Brugge in Belgium and stayed at a roadside inn.

I chose a route that took me by Brussels, Luxembourg, Strasbourg, and Basel, in the hope that hitting four countries in one day would confuse whoever was after me.

I calculated that it would take me about eight hours to reach Zurich, so I planned an early start for the next morning.

I had been in Zurich once before when I was in college and young enough for a cheap stay in a youth hostel. It was an expensive city then as well as now.

Zurich wasn't just an important Swiss city; it had the rich little country's Wall Street and Rodeo Drive. I understood why Milan would choose Zurich and a Paradeplatz—Parade Square—address; the city

❖

and the location were a financial center of Europe and connoted money and straitlaced Swiss respectability. Major banks, flagships of the notoriously secretive Swiss banking system, were headquartered there.

I'd heard there was more gold under the Paradeplatz than in Fort Knox. Put there by Saudi oil princes, dot-com billionaires, and dead Nazis.

Hasbro's game of Monopoly is sold in many countries and has real estate names that reflect the locale. The most valuable property in the American set is Boardwalk. In the Swiss version, it's Paradeplatz.

I made my way to Zurich through Strasbourg and Basel. As I crossed the border from France to Switzerland, I was reminded of the country's beautiful, picture-postcard perfect scenery. I once accused a Swiss friend of living in a country where lakes were dyed bright blue, meadows dyed bright green, and snow hauled to the top of the Alps to make them snow-capped in the summer.

Zurich was quaint, a city with clock faces on medieval spires. Ordinarily I would have paused along the way to enjoy the beauty, but I was on a mission and running scared. At the moment the geography of the city was more important than its charm, because I needed to find my way around in a short time. And I didn't know if I would be leaving in a hurry.

Old Town Zurich, like Paris, had a Left and Right Bank, divided by the Limmat River. The Left Bank included the Paradeplatz, ritzy shopping on Bahnhofstrasse, and Viktor Milan's office. I chose the Right Bank to stay, with its artsy atmosphere, red-light district, and gay scene, because it was so culturally diverse, no one stood out.

The area was famous for its connection to a famous revolutionary and one of the deciding moments in modern history: Vladimir Ilyich Ulyanov, better known as Lenin, was living in the Niederdorf section when he got the call to return to Russia when the revolution broke out during World War I. Hoping he would disrupt the Russian war effort, the Germans transported Lenin to Russia in a sealed train.

The Right Bank was also the medieval heart of the city. Niederdorfstrasse and its tributaries were a maze of narrow, cobbled thoroughfares and alleys occasionally opening into quaint squares with small stores, galleries, and antique shops. As one drew closer to the rail station, the area became seedier, hosting fast-food joints and strip joints.

I found a room at a pensione that appeared reasonably respectable

❖

and clean. I lay down to rest and unwind my nerves. Since it was late afternoon, I didn't want to approach Milan's business in an unfamiliar neighborhood in the dark. I also needed to build up my courage.

After a nap, I took a walk to stretch my legs and get something to eat. The Kunsthaus, an art museum, was open, and I went inside.

Though not a very large museum, the Kunsthaus had important works by van Gogh, Picasso, Matisse, and others. I had seen van Gogh's painting called *Strohdächer bei Auvers* years ago, and I wanted another look at it. I'd always been fascinated with his life and work. He was the quintessential tortured artist, desperately poor, wandering in and out of sanity. Of the fifteen hundred works of art he created, he had sold only one in his lifetime . . . today some of his works went for *a hundred million dollars.*

One of his last paintings before he killed himself, it was a study of two children, one of whom has been interpreted as being van Gogh himself. The children appear to be trapped in a hopeless situation.

The painting reflected how I felt myself.

Curious as to whether the curator knew Viktor Milan, I didn't want to blatantly ask. A risk of being recognized by a curator also existed. For all I knew, my face was being broadcast around the world as a Most Wanted.

Instead of asking the question face-to-face, I had the desk clerk at the pensione get me the name of the museum curator. Under the pretense that I was trying to locate Milan, I phoned the curator and asked if he knew Milan. His response that he had never met the man didn't surprise me—the Kunsthaus specialized in European art, and Milan was involved in antiquities.

The following morning I made my way slowly down Bahnhofstrasse, a wide street closed to everything but foot traffic and electric trams. The street crossed Paradeplatz and was Zurich's Rodeo Drive.

Milan's business address was on a side street near the square. The address turned out to be a small, expensive hotel.

Gathering my courage, I went inside.

I quickly learned that Milan didn't have an office in the hotel but used it as a mail drop. No one there appeared to have actually met him or know what he looked like, nor would they give me Milan's current forwarding address.

❖

To mull the situation over, I headed over to Sprungli's, a 150-year-old confectionery shop and café on Bahnhofstrasse overlooking Paradeplatz, and enjoyed some coffee and mocha-favored *Luxemburgerli,* the small, airy, cream-filled macaroons that were a local specialty there.

Albert's words were swirling in my mind: "Sun, sea, and the beach." That's where I would find Milan.

The nearest places that came to mind for winter vacations were the French Riviera, Positano in the south of Italy, and the Greek isles.

I looked out the window and saw a package delivery truck across the street. An idea struck me.

I went back to the Kunsthaus and bought a large print in their museum shop. I had them package it in a long tube-shaped mailer with a sticker that said: *DRINGEND* for "urgent." I also asked the woman to scribble a note on their museum letterhead instructing the hotel to forward the item to Viktor Milan immediately.

I gave the package to a taxi driver to deliver to the hotel.

I returned to the business district where Milan's hotel "office" was located and hung around, window-shopping, eating lunch, and just trying to hang out inconspicuously. A delivery truck arrived at the little boutique hotel. When the driver came out with the tube-shaped package, I acted like I had just come out of the hotel and was looking for my keys in my handbag.

"Is that the package for Viktor? He was expecting one, but he's not here, you know," I said, smiling at him, trying to sound like I knew Milan.

He smiled back. "They gave me the forwarding address."

"Did they give you the right one? Because he owns several places," I said. "Let me see." I quickly glanced at Milan's address. "That's the right one. Have a good day."

Milan was at a small town near Málaga, Spain. I hadn't thought about sun, sea, and the beach at the Costa del Sol, the "Sun Coast" on the Mediterranean at the southern end of Spain.

❖

34

❖

That evening I had dinner at a small German restaurant recommended by my hotel. I ordered Wiener schnitzel, mashed potatoes, creamed spinach, and fresh-baked bread. The veal cutlet was delicious, as was the homemade bread. I usually avoided meat, but I decided it might give me energy.

Warm and cozy, the restaurant had a fire blazing in the stone fireplace.

During dinner, one of the waiters brought out his accordion and played it while his waitress wife sang "Edelweiss." I recognized the song from the movie *The Sound of Music* and remembered reading somewhere that the song wasn't really German but written by Rodgers and Hammerstein.

Despite the cozy atmosphere, I couldn't relax, not even with two glasses of red wine. The wine gave me a little buzz, but I was still tense.

My game plan was to head out next morning for Málaga. I didn't know what else to do. I had set out on a mission and now I had to finish it. I still hadn't figured out exactly what I would do when I met face-to-face with the enigmatic Viktor Milan.

My father's old expression that he had learned from his Austrian grandmother reminded me of my own circumstances: "The situation is hopeless but not serious."

Sometime during the evening a nice man in his fifties came over and asked me in German if he could join me. I knew enough German to say, "Nein, vielen Dank."

He was attractive, but I wasn't in a good enough mood for small talk, especially if it involved overcoming language difficulties by playing charades.

I left the restaurant to walk back to my hotel. The restaurant had been on the main street, but I took a less noisy and more peaceful way back to my hotel.

I had walked two blocks when a man grabbed me from behind and shoved me toward the open side door of a van. A second man was waiting inside the van to pull me in. I let out a yell for help and tried to break free. The second man had stepped out to grab me when another man appeared and hit the assailant holding me. The blow caught the man on the side of the head. He grunted and turned me loose.

"Police!" my rescuer yelled.

The two men scrambled back into the van when they heard the word "police" and sped off.

I didn't move for a second.

"Are you okay?" my rescuer asked.

"Yes."

Without another word, I started walking fast, almost jogging, in the direction of my hotel. He caught up with me.

"We should call the police," he said.

"No, I'd rather not." Afraid he'd see the patent fear on my face, I avoided looking at him.

"Are you sure?"

Oh, Jesus. I hadn't even thanked him. I stopped and grabbed his arm, shaking my head. "Forgive me. You risked your own life to save me. I'm really grateful."

He grinned and shrugged. "All in a day's work for a knight-errant."

That made me smile. A knight-errant wandered in search of princesses to rescue and dragons to fight. I could use a knight in shining armor right about now.

"Are you okay?" he asked.

❖

"I'm fine, thanks to you. How about you? Are you okay?"

"Sure. Look, let me walk you to your hotel. Just in case they decide to come back."

I told him where I was staying.

"Hey, I'm staying there, too."

"Really?" What luck.

He raised his eyebrows as we walked. "I guess they were purse snatchers?"

In a pig's eye. They weren't after my purse but my body—for battering, not sex. And it wasn't hard to figure out why. Viktor Milan knew I was in town looking for him. He must have gotten a call from the hotel telling him a woman was asking about him. From my description, it wouldn't be hard for him to figure out who I was. Another phone call from him and his thug friends are sent after me. What would they have done? Beaten me to get answers? Killed me?

"Probably a purse snatching," I agreed.

"Strange, though. Not the sort of thing that happens in Zurich or anywhere else in Switzerland. The country's not exactly a high-crime zone."

"Can happen anywhere," I murmured. "Oh my gosh. I just realized—you're an American."

"Guilty." He grinned. "Although I sometimes try to pass for Canadian. Not as many people in the world hate Canadians as they do Americans."

"Good idea."

"Let me buy you a drink in the tavern by the pensione," he said. "You look like you could use one."

"Yeah, I could, actually." I was still shaken from the incident. I wanted to blurt out the truth about my predicament, but I kept my mouth shut.

"Coby Lewis," he said, offering a handshake.

"Madison Dupre." I squeezed his hand. I had to use my real name because the hotel was holding my passport.

I ordered a Chianti Classico; he had dark beer. We chitchatted for a while, mostly my questioning him about his reason for being in Europe.

"Just doing some sightseeing stuff," he said, "before I head back to the States. What about you? Here on business?"

"Playing tourist. You were on business?"

"I did a short hitch as a personal trainer and bodyguard to the daughter of an oil-rich Dubai sheikh. He thought I got a little too friendly with her and gave me the boot."

"Did you?"

"Nope." He held up his hand with fingers folded in a Boy Scout sign. "She was a party girl; I just took the heat."

"So what's back in the States for you?" I asked him. I wondered if he was married. No ring, but many men didn't wear them.

"Heading out to Hollywood. I have a buddy who does stunt work for action movies. I'd thought I'd give it a try."

"You look like you shouldn't have any problem."

"Yeah, I try to keep in pretty good shape."

He certainly looked like he put time in at the gym. He wasn't bulging with muscles like some guys who overpumped but had a nice definition to his body.

I was immediately attracted to him, his toned body, and the fact that he was big and strong and apparently didn't frighten easily.

"So enough about me. Why didn't you want to call the police? Did you know these guys?"

"No. I never saw them before."

"They could have hurt you. A lot of crazy fucking people in this world."

I hesitated, wondering how much I should tell this guy. I didn't know him from Adam, but he had an honest face and seemed to be really concerned about me. And he had just saved my life.

"I don't know who attacked me, not the actual names at least, but I think I know why." Maybe it was the liquor talking. I had already had wine earlier and was hitting it again. Or maybe it was just desperation.

"You don't know who, but you know why?" He gave me a puzzled look. "Care to explain?"

"I'm involved in a business deal that went sour."

"What kind of business deal would involve you getting kidnapped off the street? Sounds like you have something that someone else wants. Drugs, maybe?"

I needed a lie and reached for one. The drug connection was a good lead-in to something that he would believe about a businesswoman.

"I inadvertently got involved in a money-laundering scheme. I have to find the person who got me involved and turn him over to the police in order to clear myself."

❖

"The guy's in Zurich?"

"I thought so at first, but now he's moved on. I think he arranged long-distance for the men to grab me here."

"Where do you think he is?"

"I traced him to an address in Málaga. Spain. I was planning to go there." I perked up as if I suddenly had a brilliant idea, but the notion had been buzzing in my head just before we stepped into the bar. "Why don't you come with me? I don't expect you to get involved in anything dangerous. I'll pay you, of course."

"Sounds like just being around you is dangerous."

He was right on that point.

"You're right. I appreciate what you did tonight. If you hadn't come along . . . well . . . I don't want to put you in any more danger. Thanks for saving my life."

I started to get up to leave.

"How much?"

"What?"

"Money. To accompany you. What are you offering?"

I didn't know what to say.

He squirmed a little, embarrassed. "Look, if you told me your ex-boyfriend was abusive and on your ass, or anything that provokes sympathy, but getting involved in money laundering . . . that's a little too mercenary to rouse the Sir Galahad in me."

"Well, I figure about five days . . . five hundred a day . . . plus expenses."

"Make it a thousand and you've got yourself a deal."

A thousand was more than I wanted to pay, but I really wanted him to come with me.

"Okay, a thousand it is."

"I've always wanted to see the south of Spain. When do we start?"

"Tomorrow."

"How long is it by plane, maybe three or four hours?"

"We're driving," I said.

"Driving? To southern Spain? It must be a couple thousand miles."

"About twelve hundred." I had already looked it up. "If we took turns at the wheel, we could probably do it in twenty-four hours."

"Okay. You're the boss. I'm at your command."

As we were walking through the reception area of the pensione, pictures of Lipton's burned gallery were being shown on the television. The news program was in German.

"Did you hear about that?" Coby asked. "Three people dead; terrorist or some other kind of nut took out the place with a rocket launcher."

Seeing the pictures made me sick.

I LAY IN BED that night, exhausted from nerves. I was glad that Coby had agreed to go with me. I told him I wanted to get a very early start in the morning. I hoped the men who'd tried to kidnap me would still be asleep.

I thought about Coby. He had a great physique. Sexy but not overpowering. If I met him at a party and he asked to see me again, I'd definitely go out with him. But there was something else about him that conveyed he had more talent than just physical strength. A man who knew what he wanted and did damn well as he pleased.

I realized I knew zero about him and that I was reaching out from desperation. I also didn't want him to get killed trying to help me. Still, I felt this edge of guilt. I wanted to tell him the truth, but I was afraid to reveal too much.

One question I was going to ask him tomorrow was about his cap. I'd seen the word and emblem before. Some sort of military thing.

Navy SEAL.

❖

35

❖

Coby was already waiting for me downstairs in the reception area when I came down in the morning. We both carried light luggage. Mine was little more than a large backpack, and his was a small carry-on.

"You don't look like you got much sleep," he said.

"I didn't."

"I don't blame you. It's not every day you narrowly miss getting kidnapped."

"Just an average day for me." I grinned with false courage.

"I can drive the first leg if you want to get some sleep."

"No, I'm too nervous to sleep. I need to drive to get my mind off my problems."

In the back of my mind I thought about what I was doing. *Was I really on my way to Spain to confront a killer? To risk my life and someone else's? I must be crazy.*

Guilt and worries kept pecking at me as I drove. We were on the outskirts of Zurich when I suddenly pulled over to the curb.

"Change your mind? Want me to drive?"

"No. I want you to get out."

He looked at me like I'd slapped him in the face.

"There's a bus stop over there. I'll pay you for today." I started rummaging in my purse.

"Whoa, wait a minute. What's the matter? Did I do something wrong?"

"No, it's me. I can't let you get blindly involved into my troubles. I have to go it alone."

"All right then. Do you want to tell me what's going on?"

"I can't."

"Look, I need the money. You need the help. If you've done something really criminal, I'll get out. But you don't look like that type. If it's just a couple of guys who are pissed about a drug—"

"It's not a couple of guys." Dammit. I was starting to get tension in my neck. "That art gallery you saw on TV last night, the one blown up in London, I was in it when it was attacked. If I hadn't been superlucky, I would be dead now, too."

"No shit!"

"No shit."

"What the hell's going on?"

It gushed out of me. I told him about the $55 million Semiramis, Neal Nathan, the fraudulent provenance, the dead Iraqi curator, the Swiss man named Viktor Milan who wasn't in Zurich and might not even live or work there, my going to London to confront Henri Lipton . . .

"Did you see the guy who fired the rocket launcher?"

"I looked over the railing and saw a dark figure, a man, good sized, wearing a coat, hood. I didn't see much of his face, not enough to recognize him."

After I was through telling him everything, I leaned back and closed my eyes. I was exhausted but also relieved to get it all out in the open.

"Madison . . ."

I felt a tremor of excitement as he brushed my arm.

"Yes?"

He leaned closer to me. "You'd better let me take the first leg. You're too wasted to drive right now."

"You still want to come with me?"

"I don't have to do anything I don't want to . . . and haven't since I was about eighteen, except when I had to obey orders in the Navy. And this isn't charity; my price has gone up. It's now two thousand dollars a day, five-day guarantee."

❖

"I don't have that much cash." I didn't have that much money, period, but . . . *how much was my life worth?* I'd get it somehow. I wondered if my black American Express card was still good. I only assumed the company had pulled the plug on it. Maybe—

"I'll trust you. Now get out. We have a lot of miles to cover and I'm driving."

I liked his take-charge attitude. What a relief it was to let someone take over directing my life. I certainly hadn't done a terrific job of it lately.

I closed my eyes. I'd worry later about where to get the money to pay him.

WHEN I AWOKE A couple hours later, we were near the French border. We stopped at a roadside café and got coffee and rolls. As we set out again, I was too fuzzy to drive. I still hadn't woken up.

"What exactly is a Navy SEAL?" I asked.

"You've probably heard them called frogmen in old movies. They started out as commandos who blew up ships and coastal defenses. Now SEALs do missions on land, too. 'SEAL' stands for sea, air, and land. You have to go to jump school and qualify as a paratrooper." He shot me a quick grin. "Fly like a bird, swim like a fish, and crawl like a snake, that's what it takes."

I remembered where I saw the name before. "Weren't there some Navy SEALs killed during the Afghanistan conflict a few years ago?"

"Yeah. I wasn't in Afghanistan. I did some time in Iraq and the Persian Gulf."

I stiffened at the mention of Iraq. I looked out the side window so I wouldn't let my expression expose my sudden fear.

"Did you see any action in Baghdad?"

"No, I was in the first Iraqi conflict, back in 1991. We never got closer than hundreds of miles before Baghdad. Stopped way down south, by Basra."

He was right. I remembered that the United States and its allies had pushed Saddam out of Kuwait but never pushed on to Baghdad. Some of the tension left me.

He glanced over. "By the way, the next time you rent a car to flee the police and these killers, get something a little faster."

"Next time I'm fleeing the police and killers, I'll rent an Army tank."

We drove in silence for a moment before I noticed he was pursing his lips, deep in thought.

"What are you thinking about?" I asked.

"About what kind of lunatic would use a rocket launcher."

"Someone who wants to kill a lot of people."

"But not very subtle. A pro would use a pistol with a silencer, maybe even a .22 like the Mafia does, a weapon that has a high velocity but doesn't make a lot of noise."

"I still say he's kill crazy."

"No, I think it's more basic than that . . . he's destroying evidence."

"The evidence of his crime?"

"No, the evidence of his dealings with your pal the art dealer. There's nothing like a raging fire to cover your tracks. From the sounds of it, he used an incendiary explosive. That would be the way to go. You kill all the living evidence and wipe out the paper trail at the same time."

"You sound almost like you admire him."

He shrugged it off. "No, I don't admire the guy. But I have to give him credit. He set out to do a job and he did it right."

"Hmmm. That's certainly a plus in his favor. But I hope he's a little less competent when he comes after me."

36

❖

Barcelona

We drove all day across France, taking turns behind the wheel, stopping only briefly for food and gas. Looking at a map, I figured we could take turns driving all the way to Málaga and make it in about twenty-four hours. It could be done, but I had overestimated my energy level. After days of no solid sleep, I was ready to fold.

When we were crossing the Pyrenees, I told Coby, "I've changed my mind about driving straight through."

"Okay. Tired?"

"I'm beat. I've also been thinking about the two men back at Zurich. I'd rather not be on the road at night."

"Sounds good to me. I'd rather sleep in a nice comfortable bed tonight than in a car."

Barcelona was a jewel on a continent that had so many beautiful cities. Spread out before us to the Mediterranean, the city was a perfect romantic spot. Of course, the fact that I was running from killers and the police took away some of the mystique . . .

We ended up eating at the hotel instead of venturing out. Neither of us felt like doing any more driving into the city center to find a place to eat.

❖

Since dinner wasn't usually served until after nine in the evening, we ate a "late lunch" at the bar in the hotel. The main meal in Barcelona was lunch, eaten between 2:00 and 4:00 P.M. Although the bar was still offering their *ménu del día,* a set-price meal usually comprising three courses with a beverage thrown in, we ended up just ordering a plate of their *entremesos,* which was a platter of hors d'oeuvres consisting of potato salad, olives, asparagus, a selection of cold cuts, cheese, and some rolls—a meal in itself. We finished with coffee and a local specialty, *crema Catalana,* a cold custard with a crispy caramel coating.

Happy that I had company, I was still quiet as we ate. I didn't feel like talking about my problems. I noticed he wore a unique wristwatch.

"What's that on your watch? It looks like a coin."

"It's an old silver coin from the days of real pirates of the Caribbean, what the Spanish called a piece of eight. Cleverly done so the value of the coin isn't destroyed."

"Very nice."

"Yeah, I like it because it's the real thing, so I didn't mess it up putting it to use."

"Where did you get it?"

"Found it scuba diving off the coast of Florida."

I had been idly poking at food on my plate as I spoke. I looked up and into his soulful eyes.

"Searching for sunken treasure?"

"No, just dumb luck."

"Why are you looking at me like that?"

"Like what? I'm just admiring a good-looking woman."

"You're making me uncomfortable."

"And you need to relax." He took my hands and lazily stroked them with his masculine fingers. "You're tense."

The touch of his hands sent tiny shivers through me again.

"I know exactly what you need," he said in a slow, sensuous voice.

"A good lawyer? And a gun?"

"A good man in your life."

I looked down at his tanned hands, then studied his face.

Damn! He was right. Was it that obvious? Could he see the loneliness and unhappiness that occupied my life? I hardly knew this guy, yet I felt safe with him.

❖

I didn't answer him. Right now I had to take care of a more pressing problem. Love would have to wait.

He seemed to have read my thoughts. "When you're ready, let me know." He let go of my hands. "Any idea as to how you'll find this Milan guy?"

I shook my head. "I don't know. How would a real detective do it?"

"Phone book?"

"Doubtful. Probably there on vacation."

"Property tax records?"

"Same thing. On vacation."

"Check with rental agencies?"

"That'll take time, a cover story, and knowledge of locales. Sounds like I should hire a Málaga detective. But there's another possibility."

"Which is?"

"There's an archaeology museum in Málaga. It's housed in the Alcaz-abar, an old fortress and palace of Moorish kings. It's on a hillside below Castillo de Gibralfaro, another Moorish citadel. They might know him there."

"Maybe. But you said you tried that in Zurich and no one knew him."

"I tried one person at an art museum. Milan deals in antiquities, especially Middle Eastern ones. Better chance to find them in Spain than Switzerland."

"So you think he'd be more at home hanging around a museum of Moorish antiquities than a Swiss one?"

"Not just hanging around. People who deal in art are like the ones who collect Avon bottles or Coca-Cola memorabilia. They never stop looking. They die and go to heaven when they bump into another collector. He wouldn't be in Málaga long without checking out the antiquities scene at the museum and galleries. I guarantee you."

"Why?"

"Spain has seen the rise and fall of great civilizations for thousands of years—the Phoenicians three thousand years ago, not to mention the Greeks, Carthaginians, and Celts. It was a major Roman province. They're still finding Roman ruins all over the country. Then you had the Visigoths, and finally, for about eight hundred years after the Muslims burst out of Mecca, the Moors dominated the peninsula. Ferdinand and Isabella managed to drive them out and unite Spain. In fact, the last great battle that took place was the siege of Málaga in 1487." I stopped and took a breath before going on.

"Did you know the Moors, whom the Spanish finally defeated and drove out five hundred years ago, were a mixture of North African Arab, Berber, and Iberian culture?"

"No."

"Most Americans probably think of places like Morocco, Libya, and Egypt as Middle Eastern rather than African for a good reason—their religion, language, and much of their culture came from the Middle East. Toward the end of the Islamic presence on the peninsula, Málaga was a Moorish kingdom ruled by an emir who called it a terrestrial paradise."

"Sounds like I'm in a history class. You know a lot about Málaga."

I opened my bag and held up my tour book. "The source of genius. I bought it at the last gas station."

He shook his head. "And I thought you were just plain smart. ¿Habla español?"

"Sí, senor. I'm a little rusty, but I can get along. I took it in high school and spent a month studying the Chichen Itza site in the Yucatán during graduate school. ¿Habla usted español?"

"Muy poco. With mucho malo grammar. I spent two years at the Navy base in San Diego and all my off-duty time in Tijuana. The beer was cheap, and there were plenty of women to go around. I guess I picked up some of the language by osmosis. How big does your guidebook say Málaga is?"

"Half a million in town, twice that many in the metro area."

"That's manageable. I'd say hire a detective and have him and his pals start calling rental agencies. I can check out that while you pay a visit to the museum."

"Sounds like a plan to me," I said. "The book says there's one more thing you should know about Málaga."

"What?"

"Two famous people were born there. Picasso and Antonio Banderas."

"Just tell me about bars and beer." He grinned. "Just kidding. I'm really an intellectual scholar under all this macho veneer. What does your book tell you about Barcelona?"

"Hans Christian Andersen called it the Paris of Spain."

"You know what the people of Barcelona say?"

"Paris is the Barcelona of France?"

"How the hell did a smart woman like you get mixed up in something so stupid?"

I lowered my eyes and just stared at my hands. Everything had been going fine up to that point, but then my emotions took over. I didn't have an answer for him. Tears suddenly welled in my eyes and I left the table and went to my room. I shut the door and locked it. I wanted to be alone to wallow in self-pity.

Coby knocked on my door a few minutes later.

Damn! I wiped my eyes and opened the door.

"Okay, I'm not very diplomatic. That was stupid."

"No, that was accurate."

"I didn't mean to attack your intelligence."

"Smart people don't do stupid things."

"Yeah, sometimes they do. Hey, let's go back to the bar and I'll buy you a nightcap."

"Thanks, but I'll take a rain check. I'm tired."

"Okay, if you want to talk, just knock on my door . . . or if you want to do anything else," he smiled at me, "that's fine with me, too."

I broke out in a grin. "Good night, Coby."

"See you tomorrow."

I walked to the window and stared at the lights of the city below. I suddenly realized why I had insisted we stop before proceeding on to Málaga.

I was scared.

37

❖

Málaga

We arrived on the outskirts of Málaga late the following evening and checked into a hotel. A sense of dread had been gathering inside me. Was I foolish to find Milan and confront him? My logical mind was saying yes, but my instincts said no. I had to clear my name and he was the key. And I couldn't rely on the police—not when I was the chief suspect.

"Too late to start inquiries about Milan," I told Coby. "I want daylight and to be surrounded by a million people when I face this madman."

"You may not have that option. Your pal doesn't sound like the kind of guy who's going to like crowds."

"What about a bulletproof vest?"

"Won't stop a shoulder-launched rocket. There's only one sure way to deal with this guy . . . go home."

The logical answer.

"Thanks. But I'm afraid Viktor Milan's seen to it that I'd take up residence in a jail cell if I went home without giving the police the bastard—and the evidence to hang him."

I had dragged my heels leaving Barcelona and slowed our pace. We could have arrived a couple hours earlier, but it still would have been too late to start a search. At least, that's what I told myself.

❖

The hotel we checked into was off the N331. For dinner I chose a tapas bar where we got a table in a dark corner. I wasn't in a mood to display myself in the middle of a restaurant. It soon became obvious that confronting a savage killer didn't affect Coby's appetite. But by now we had become experts at ordering à la carte. He ordered vino tinto, a red table wine, and half a dozen tapas. I picked at mushrooms in garlic sauce and octopus in paprika sauce and wished I had a hamburger and fries . . . and to be a long ways from Spain's Sun Coast.

Oh, how the mighty have fallen. Not very long ago, I wouldn't think of being at sun, sea, and the beach without a tanned hunk with me. True, I had a tanned hunk with me, but . . .

"I'm getting cold feet about tackling a maniac who kills people with rockets."

"You should be," Coby said. "Try the lamb brochettes and the fried fish called pescaito frito. They're both very good."

"I'm happy that the fact I may be murdered tomorrow hasn't ruined your appetite."

He took a swig of wine, wiped his mouth, and grinned at me. "You'll be murdered only over my dead body."

I grabbed his hand. "Don't talk like that."

"Just hang tight. We're going to get this guy for you."

"Coby . . . all the courage and resolve when I ran to Zurich has drained out of me as I got closer to Málaga. I think it's because I knew he wasn't in Zurich, that I was there just to find out where he was. But I know he's here. And I'm pretty sure he knows I'm here."

"It's a big city. You're not going to run into him on the street. We're going to hire a detective like you said, track him down."

"What do we do then? Ask him to sign a confession? Or offer to buy him a ticket back to New York so he can turn himself in to the FBI?"

"Let's see what he's doing here. If he's into anything dirty, we can get the Spanish police to bust him. You said he has a connection to the killings in London and a murder in New York. That's probably enough for the locals to hold him until Scotland Yard and the FBI can question him."

Was it that easy? Just see the guy and call the police? "But what if they arrest me instead?"

"Call from a pay phone on your way out of town."

❖

I stared into his penetrating eyes. "I like talking to you, Coby. You have simple answers to complicated questions. You should have been a psychologist. The kind that tells you to take five minutes and get your life into order."

"Tell me your life story and I'll tell you where you went wrong."

"Tell me your life story first."

He shrugged. "Did the surfing scene in California and Hawaii when I should have been hitting textbooks. Malibu women, margaritas, and thick, juicy waves. It was a great life until a shark took a bite out of my board and a small chunk of my thigh. But I had webfeet, so I became a SEAL."

"Why didn't you stick with it? Twenty years, pension check."

"I loved being a SEAL. It was a blast. What I hated was all the rules and regulations that went with it. I couldn't take the regimentation, so I jumped ship. I've been knocking around ever since."

"Tell me the truth. Did you knock up the Dubai sheikh's daughter?"

"Naw, she wasn't stupid; she'd been down the road before. Many times. She told me she and her girlfriends fuck around all they like because they're sent off to Switzerland to have their hymens reconstructed."

I laughed and choked on my wine. "Hiram's wife did that."

"Angela St. John? She couldn't pass for a virgin if she had her taco sewed shut."

"She's just tightening up to make herself more sexy. Certainly not for her husband. I think his main interest in sex was having a sexy wife."

"All right, I told you my life story. It's your turn."

"Small-town girl. Poor but honest. Wanted to experience the big city. Wanted everything I'd seen in the movies. I learned many good things from my parents, especially one they taught me unconsciously. I thought my parents were big successes, but they weren't. My mother and father held it against themselves because they never went for broke and they weren't lucky enough to have their dreams realized through sheer luck or buying a lottery ticket. They went to their graves with a lot of 'I wish I hads.' So that's my bottom-line objective in life. I don't want to be on my deathbed, lying there lamenting, 'Oh, shit, I wish I'd done that.'"

"So you go for broke. My analysis is that you're too damn hard on your parents. We all have dreams and no one gets them all. I'm sure even

❖

Bill Gates has an I-wish-I'd-done-that or two. It's okay if you just take it one day at a time and don't fall into too many manholes."

I saluted him with my glass. "There you go again, a brilliantly simple solution to all the problems in my life. You're so right . . . it all comes down to staying away from manhole covers. I *was* proud of my parents. And I loved them very much. I wish they were here now. I'd be with them, crying my eyes out. They were the ones who had the hang-ups about who and what they were."

The wine gave me a buzz. It also caused me to talk too much and to alibi about talking too much. "There's a Latin phrase, *in vino veritas.* Means something like there's truth in wine. Do you think I talk too much when I drink? That I'm spilling the beans? That liquor releases our inhibitions and brings out the truth?"

"Naw. Booze just makes honest people more honest."

"Tell me what you're thinking right now."

"How beautiful, intelligent, and brave you are."

"Liar. I can see your bedroom eyes. Right now they're saying you want to have sex with me."

"Well, I can't deny that. I want that, too."

"You're just like the rest of them."

"I know," he said, rolling his eyes. "We think with our dicks, not our brains."

"This may surprise you—"

"Nothing would surprise me about you anymore."

"I used to arrange for sex in my business." I leaned forward. "My boss made me do it."

"You did it with your boss?"

"No, of course not. He was a swine. I did it for other people."

"Did what?"

"Arranged sex."

"You were a pimp?"

"Jesus, that's an awful thing to say."

"What else would you call someone who arranged sex for men—"

"And women."

He raised an eyebrow. "Okay, what would you call it? A bi-pimp?"

"It's called the art and antiquities trade. And it's not for the faint of heart. If you look too close at a provenance, or if someone who's willing to pay millions of dollars for a piece for your museum wants his ego or whatever else stroked, you do whatever it takes. Those are things they don't teach you in an art history course."

"Pimp or perish."

"Right." I toasted him with my wineglass, splashing a little on the table. "Oops, sorry. That's how it's done in the Art School of Hard Knocks."

"And you're a graduate of the School of Hard Knocks."

"Damn right. I worked my ass off . . . I worked harder, faster, and smarter than the rest of them . . . and look where it's gotten me. The police on two continents are searching for me, and a lunatic with a rocket launcher wants to blow me up."

"Maybe you tried too hard."

"Maybe you're right. And maybe I stepped into a manhole. I want to go. I'm tried of confessing my sins to you," I said, annoyed at him.

I tried to get my wallet to pay the bill, but I was having a hard time getting it out of my handbag.

"Hey, you're the one that wanted the truth." He threw some money on the table. "I'll get this one."

"Whatever." I was too drunk to care who paid. I took a deep breath of air and pride and walked determinedly out of the bar without swaying. I think.

When we got back to the hotel, I stood outside the door to my room and faced him, full of remorse. "I'm feeling sorry for myself again. I keep thinking about Abdullah and Albert. Two innocent people dying because of something I was involved in. Lipton and his snotty Gate Keeper didn't deserve to die, either. But it's the faces of the first two that haunt me. I guess because I liked both of them. Sometimes you run into people who are unique. In a homogenized world, the idealistic Iraqi and the gay young artist were unique. They were priceless."

"You didn't cause their deaths."

"Yes, I did. My boss, Neal, Lipton, all the dealers and curators and collectors in the world . . . we're all whores of Babylon, willing to do anything to get what we want."

"You can't stop all the crazies in this world. Shit happens. You just gotta deal with it."

He made it sound so simple. But it wasn't. I had pushed too hard. And looked the other way too often. Now look at the mess I was in.

❖

I gazed into his eyes, searching for an answer. I thought about the comment he made that I needed a good man in my life. He was right. I did. The words came out without any hesitation. "Do you want to fuck me?"

I suddenly needed to be held in a man's arms and loved, really loved.

He put my hand on the bulge between his legs. He was getting a hard-on. It pulsated against my palm.

"I cannot tell a lie."

"You men are pricks. Sex is always on your minds. We poor women have to satisfy your cravings." I pulled him into my room. "Go ahead, you bastard; take advantage of me."

I didn't want to think about my troubles. I just wanted my brains fucked out so I could get a good night's sleep.

I AWOKE SOMETIME DURING the night and snuggled up against his back. He turned and took me in his arms.

This time our sex wasn't fast and desperate but slow and deliberate. We caressed each other, building up the sexual excitement, climbing higher and higher, until we both couldn't stand it anymore. I felt something different that evening with Coby.

For the first time I didn't feel alone in my life.

❖

38

❖

We both slept late. I climbed into a hot bath and soaked for an hour while Coby got dressed and eager to get going.

"I'm tried of looking for this Milan guy and I haven't even started. I'll get you a detective to find this bastard," he told me before he left. "Then I'm going to rip the bastard to pieces so you can shove the pieces into a bag and drop him off at a police station."

I liked the way Coby talked.

He kept it up as he went out the door. "We'll get people on the phone calling every hotel and rental outfit in the area. Going door-to-door looking for him. By dinnertime, this Milan dude will be begging you to turn him over to the police."

I was looking forward to that.

I leaned back in the tub and prayed that the nightmare would be over. I promised God I would do something good if He helped me out of the mess. I know it wasn't right . . . I hadn't been in church since Sunday school a million years ago. I had my parents' attitude toward religion, a vague belief that this incredible universe couldn't have been an accident . . . and that I didn't need to find God in a man-made church.

❖

Still, this was the first time I had asked for divine help even though I felt like a hypocrite. But I still asked.

Coby and I had agreed to meet back here at two o'clock. In the meantime, I pulled myself out of the tub and got dressed. My job was to hit the local antiquities museum, the Alcazabar, and the galleries to see if I could get a lead on Milan.

The Alcazabar was a fifteenth-century Moorish fort converted into an archaeological museum. I got a taxi in front of the hotel and told the driver to take me to the museum. He drove for a moment before he examined me in the rearview mirror and turned around in the driver's seat.

"Señorita, do you realize that the museum is closed for siesta?"

I forgot. Businesses were closed during midday and wouldn't reopen until four o'clock.

"What about art galleries?"

"Open after siesta," he said. "Restaurants are open. I can take you to a good one."

I wasn't hungry. I kicked myself for being so stupid. Lunch is the big meal, then back to work until around seven, then a light dinner after nine or ten o'clock.

"Why don't you just drive me around," I said. "I need to get orientated to the city."

I sat back and relaxed. Maybe it was better that I didn't go to the museum. This way at least I'd have a chance to scope out my surroundings.

We drove around for fifteen minutes before I saw the van with the Swiss license plate.

"Go back around and come down the street again," I told the driver.

Could it be a different van? I wasn't sure. But the same color and Swiss plates gave me a chill and sent my heart pumping.

When we came back around, I couldn't believe my eyes.

I saw Coby going into a bodega, a wine bar, with two men. The same two men who had grabbed me on the street in Zurich.

I SAT ALONE IN the taxi and kept an eye on the front door of the wine bar. I had given the driver a wad of euros and sent him to get himself something to eat and told him to stay nearby. I was going to need him as soon as Coby came out so I could follow him.

Not much of a plan, but sitting frozen in the cab with thoughts roiling through my mind was the best I could do.

Actually, my mind was amazingly clear for someone who just had the rug of love and trust pulled out from under her. Obviously, I had been duped. Coby was a fraud. The attempt to kidnap me was staged. But why? I chuckled without humor. He said he wanted to get into the movies. That meet-the-girl-by-saving-her was as old as Hollywood flicks. But it was a particularly dirty trick because I had needed the help so badly.

Emotion welled up in me and I fought back tears. *That bastard!* I had given him my heart and my trust.

Who the hell are you?

The obvious answer was that he was an enforcer for Viktor Milan. He fit the mode perfectly . . . muscular, athletic . . . a hired "gun" for me, literally. Why not for Milan?

The more I thought about it, the more I wondered . . . could he be Viktor Milan himself? Why not? I had no idea what the man looked like. And Coby—if that was his name—had two links to antiquities: the antique Spanish coin on his watch and the Iraq military tour he did. He said he served in the first Gulf War. Maybe it was the second one instead. That would fit perfectly with the looting of the museum.

But if he was Milan, why hadn't he just killed me?

I thought I knew the answer: If he killed me, he wouldn't know how much I knew. And he and his cohorts couldn't continue to use me as a fall guy. I'd been at the scene shortly after Abdullah was murdered and in the London gallery when the place was torched. He knew the police thought I was involved.

He tried to kill me at the London gallery. Might even have been waiting to kill me at the top of Abdullah's stairs, but I had run too fast.

I wondered what the third act would be. Leaving me dead clutching an incriminating suicide note that took responsibility for the other murders?

Abdullah had seen the men who robbed the museum. He told me the uniforms and caps were American.

❖

I kicked myself for not asking Abdullah more questions.

From what I'd seen on the news, the battle dress of most countries was similar.

A cap—Abdullah had pointed to his head. He probably recognized the thieves as Americans from their caps. Why? What did he see?

I scrolled through previously called numbers on my cell phone, found Abdullah's, and hit the call button. I had Western European service in my plan.

Ten rings later a sleepy feminine voice answered. The time difference hadn't occurred to me. New York would be six or seven hours earlier.

I spoke fast. "Don't hang up. This is Madison Dupre. I'm calling from halfway around the world. I'm trying to find out who killed your father and who destroyed my career."

I stopped and let Abdullah's daughter digest my plea.

Silence. Some static.

"Are you there?"

I thought I could hear breathing. "Please. I'm trying to track down the killer. You must have heard about that Lipton gallery being blown up in London. I was in it when the killer struck. I believe it's the same man who killed your father."

Silence again. Did I lose her?

"What do you want?" a tearful voice finally said.

I smothered a sob. "I'm so sorry about your father. I really am." I couldn't suppress it anymore. I started crying. "Hold on," I gasped. I took deep breaths. "Your father was a brave and honest man. You should be very proud of him. He was right; the Semiramis was stolen."

"I'm going to call the police."

"It won't do you any good; I'm thousands of miles away."

"Why did you call? Why are you doing this?"

"I'm following a man I think is involved in the museum robbery and your father's murder. I have a question that I was hoping you would answer. Did your father ever describe any of the men he saw?" What I really wanted to know was whether one was a blond-haired, muscular, athletic-looking guy, about in his midthirties?

Silence.

"Anything?"

❖

"He didn't describe the men. He just said they were Americans."

"How did he know they were Americans?"

"Their uniforms."

"But the British and other countries had similar-looking battle uni-forms. Did he see the American flag or—"

"He recognized something on a hat."

"A word, a picture?"

"He'd seen it on news programs about American commandos."

"What did he see?"

"Four letters."

"Four letters?"

"*S . . . E . . . A . . . L. . . .*"

❖

39

❖

My impatient driver stood outside and smoked a cigarette as I made another call. To Special Agent Nunes.

His voice mail came on. I left my message after I heard the beep.

"This is Madison Dupre. I'm in Málaga," I said. "Spain. You probably know that I was in London when Henri Lipton was killed. I was almost killed. I went there to confront him about selling me the Semiramis. He got it from Viktor Milan."

I said I'd traced Viktor Milan to Zurich and then Málaga and that I was with a man who wore a SEAL cap and I believed to be Milan. I also told him that Abdullah's daughter said her father saw a SEAL hat on a soldier robbing the museum.

"Two men tried to grab me in Zurich and this guy pretending not to be Milan saved me. Now I know it's all a crock." My voice faltered. My throat went dry. I ran out of steam. I didn't know what else to say.

I pressed the end button. My heart was beating a mile a minute. My underarms were wet.

One more thing I had to tell Nunes.

I pressed the send button again and his number was redialed. After his voice mail came on, I left another message.

❖

"If I'm murdered, Viktor Milan is the one you should be after. He's the killer. I didn't do anything. I'm innocent." Before I hung up I added, "And scared."

The last words came out as a gasp.

I squeezed my eyes tightly shut and leaned back in the seat trying to fight back panic. *Don't lose it, Madison.* Not now.

When I opened my eyes the driver was coming back to the taxi, squinting at me. "It's okay," I said. I used English, but he understood. "Okay" was universal.

Coby and the two men from Zurich came out of the wine bar. I frantically motioned the driver to get back in the cab.

As the trio paused by the van to talk, my driver turned in the seat to me. "You will have to get another taxi. My shift is over."

That's what he thought. He didn't know about the plan I'd just thought up.

"It's my husband," I said. "He's cheating on me."

I knew that would strike home to any red-blooded Spaniard, a culture where machismo protection of women—and love affairs—were perfected.

He looked at the three men and back to me. I cleared up his puzzlement.

"Those men are his lovers," I told the driver, trying to sound convincing.

"Bastardo!"

My sentiments exactly.

Coby shook hands with both of his pals and grabbed a taxi.

"Follow him."

My driver muttered something derogatory about modern men and pulled out into the street. From the distance he kept behind Coby's taxi, I could see that my driver had gotten into the spirit of things.

"Where will he lead us?" he asked me.

"To his love nest. Where's he's hiding my children's money."

God, what a golden tongue I suddenly had. Trembling in my boots one moment, playing the wronged woman the next. I wasn't really getting into the role, but the calls to Abdullah's daughter and the FBI had gotten my nerves' energy racing.

At least now I knew that if I was killed, the murderer would be tracked down.

❖

Coby's taxi took us to a road that ran near the coast and along the Mediterranean to a small beach town west of the central Málaga metro. I recognized it as the city address that the hotel in Zurich put on the phony package to Milan.

We followed the taxi off the main road and down a dirt path that went by a seaside villa. I noted the address on a bronze plaque as my cab drove past it with me crouching down in the backseat.

Again, I wasn't surprised that it was the house address written on the package for Milan in Zurich.

40

❖

"Please wait for me." I paid the driver twice what he asked for.

Fifty feet down the road, I turned and watched him drive away. Great. That was smart of me. He seemed like a decent guy, too. I should have held the extra money to make sure he waited.

Strutting down the long, tree-lined driveway straight to the villa didn't seem advisable, so I went back down the main road until I found a trail that led to the beach. I took it and turned right when I reached the sand. As one came up the beach, the villa was atop the hill, surrounded by a large wall.

I stood behind an outcropping from the small hills that rolled down to the beach, and studied the villa. Only the second floor and red tile roof were visible because of the wall. Not the abode of the superrich, at least not an ostentatious one, I decided. On the Jersey shore I'd call it a beach house. But this was Europe and it did have a Mediterranean ambiance.

A stone stairway led down from the villa to a boathouse on the water. A sleek powerboat, long and narrow with a big engine and small cockpit, was moored next to the boathouse.

Coby came out of the boathouse and I ducked down to avoid being seen.

Sneaking a peek from behind the outcrop, I watched him disappear

❖

through the gate. I hurried across to the boathouse. He wouldn't be able to see me unless he went to the second floor. I risked it because I needed a peek in the window of the boathouse. The fact that he had immediately gone down to it was a sure sign something important was in it. My instincts were chiming, *Iraqi loot, Iraqi loot.*

As I ran down the beach and got close enough to the boathouse, I could see that the windows on my side were covered. Coby had come out of a door at the back, and I headed for that, hoping he had left it unlocked. My adrenaline was pumping full-time. Where I got the courage—and the stupidity—to do these things was beyond me. *I must be out of my mind,* I told myself. But I had come this far and I needed a roomful of stolen Iraqi museum pieces to get the police on my side.

As I was going by the boat, my foot hit a raised board on the dock and I stumbled and almost fell. Terrified I was being observed from the villa, I quickly got around the backside and out of sight. I stood with my back to the wall, panting. *Unbelievably stupid.* That's what I was.

A window next to the door was also covered, but the dark curtains had a narrow slit. The window was fouled with sand and saltwater residue from wind and waves. I cleared a spot that would let me see through the split in the curtains and peered in closer. Using my hands to block out light, I strained to see something but only saw darkness. The lights were not on inside.

Damn.

I stared mindlessly at the door. Rational thought had long since stopped. I was operating off of adrenaline, terror, and anticipation.

A padlock was hanging from the hasp. I stared at it. It wasn't snapped shut. It lay there open and easy to remove. I took the lock off and pushed open the door. Stepping in, not bothering to look for a light switch out of fear someone at the house would see the light go on, I closed the door most of the way behind me. I left it open just a crack to take the edge off the darkness.

The immediate odor of dried salt water and stale seaweed hit me. The smell of things that had been in the sea for a long time.

From a stream of sunlight coming through the open doorway I made out a small bronze cannon layered and tarnished from sitting at the bottom of the sea for an eon. Old, perhaps centuries old, but certainly not an antiquity from the Iraqi museum.

❖

As I looked closer I made out a sea-encrusted metal chest. An anchor from an old Spanish galleon or other ship of the era.

Like the piece of eight Coby claimed was a lucky find off Florida, the boathouse had the stuff of Blackbeard's treasure trove, not Mesopotamian antiquities.

A shadow fell across my stream of light from the doorway. Someone kicked the door open.

I turned—and screamed.

"I left it unlocked for you." Coby grinned.

I ran, bursting by him. He grabbed me by the shirt and jerked me back. I spun around swinging my fists and he grabbed both my wrists and held me.

"Stop it!" he yelled.

My hands were gripped in vises.

"And don't kick me."

He had read my mind. Again.

"Just stop. If I wanted to hurt you, I had plenty of time alone to do it. So relax. I won't hurt you."

"You bastard," I spit out.

"True. But you're going to learn to love me. If you haven't already."

"Not likely. I'm going to have you thrown in prison. I've already called the police." That was technically true. I had left a message for Agent Nunes.

He stared at me. "What number did you dial for the police? Nine-one-one won't do it."

"I . . . I . . . had the hotel call."

"You're lying. You didn't see me until you were in the taxi."

"You knew I was following you?"

"Hell, you did everything but send off flares." He let go of my wrists. "Just calm down. I told you I left the door open for you. I wasn't lying. I wanted you to see that I wasn't hoarding pieces from Baghdad."

I gestured around. "What are you hoarding?"

"What does it look like to you?"

He turned on the light. More chests and cannons, wine bottles, olive oil jars, old rigging, tools, and other implements were stacked around the room.

"It looks like you've found a galleon," I said. I shot a glance out the

❖

door at the bay. "Spain had an empire the sun never set on before the British, and they also brought home the riches. There must be dozens of sunken galleons off this part of the coast alone."

"Hundreds, probably. Over five thousand Spanish ships went down around the world. We found one of them."

I knew enough about the laws of the sea to realize that treasure hunting—robbing antiquities from sunken ships—was generally illegal. But it wasn't the right time or place for me to be tempting fate with more threats I couldn't back up.

"Let's get some air," he said. "This place stinks."

"Are you Viktor Milan?" I blurted out. I wanted him to confirm it.

"Yeah. I'm Viktor Milan."

41

❖

I didn't know what to think as we walked along the beach together. He never pointed a gun at me or threatened me. He acted as if he had arranged the meeting. And at this point, I wasn't sure that he hadn't.

Nothing made sense to me, especially walking on a romantic beach with a good-looking blond, tanned, slightly aging surfer type, an L.A. Venice Beach golden sun god in his youth . . . wondering whether I was going to be murdered.

"I guess I should call you Viktor, though I admit, you don't look like a Viktor," I said.

"Call me Coby."

"But you just said you're Viktor."

"What's in a name?"

"Are you going to murder me?"

He shot me a look. "Should I?"

"You've already tried it once. Maybe twice. Maybe three times if you count grabbing me in Zurich."

"Give me a break. That was obviously set up to meet you."

"You're a military guy. You know how to use weapons."

❖

He raised his eyebrows. "You think that was me behind the rocket launcher?"

I wasn't sure, but I couldn't hold my tongue. "You also murdered that poor man in New York. He saw your SEAL cap. And you killed Mr. Bensky to cover your tracks."

I was strangely calm. I had absolutely no control over anything. I not only didn't have any answers, I didn't know the questions to ask.

"You are one gutsy woman. Do you always tell murderers that they're murderers, right to their faces?"

"I'm insane." And revved up.

He nodded. "That, too."

"Why did you kill those people? Is the money really worth it?"

He sighed. "Okay, let's clear this up right now. Look me in the eye. Do I really strike you as someone who could kill people?"

I looked into his probing eyes. "I think so. You look like you can be a bastard when you want to be."

"I forgot eyes are mirrors to the soul. So let me rephrase the question. Do I look like I'm crazy enough to blow up a building with unarmed people in it with a rocket launcher?"

I had to think about that one. I didn't want to believe he was a killer, but I couldn't be sure of anything anymore. Things weren't making any sense.

"Who exactly is Viktor Milan? Besides a liar and bastard."

"Is that any way to talk to someone you made passionate love to?"

"You're avoiding my questions?"

"I am an enigma."

"You are a shit."

"Okay." He nodded and pursed his lips. "You earned the right to know. Viktor Milan is . . . I guess he's what lawyers call a legal fiction. It's a made-up name. Like Microsoft or IBM or General Motors. It's like if your name is John Blow and you want to start a company named Jack Shit, you have to get a legal paper that says you're John Blow doing business as Jack Shit."

I nodded like a bobbing doll. "Is that lecture supposed to explain anything? We're talking murder and thievery, not Business 101. Why don't you try plain English?"

❖

"That answer was supposed to point out that there are millions of people operating companies under names besides their own. Viktor Milan was created so we could do business under a prestigious international-sounding name in one of the world's financial capitals."

"Wasn't it also created so you could forge provenances without getting caught?"

He tried to smother a smirk, but it didn't work. "That, too."

"So you're the crooked bastard that created the fraudulent provenance that ruined my life and got people killed. If I had a gun, you sonofabitch, I'd shoot you, really shoot you where it hurts."

That didn't make much sense to me, either, but I was seething.

"I haven't killed anyone. Yet. But I'm working up to it."

"If you didn't kill Lipton and the others, who did?"

"That's a good question. The only thing I can tell you is that it wasn't me."

"You're lying, of course, lying, lying, lying." I shook an accusatory finger at him. "Does not compute. If you didn't do it, you know who did. The killings all go back to your phony provenances and the looting of the Iraqi museum."

He made a noncommittal listening response, then said, "Since you know so much, why don't you tell me."

"All right, I don't believe you blew up Lipton's gallery. Not personally, at least, though you might have arranged for it. But I have proof that you murdered Abdullah, the Iraqi curator."

He acted like I had just slapped him in the face.

Steering me with a grip on my arm, he turned us around and started back toward the boathouse. My heart started beating faster. Had I said too much?

"Has it occurred to you, Miss Know-It-All, that if I was a cold-blooded killer, you would be digging a hole for yourself right now?"

The thought had occurred to me, but my life was in ruins and I couldn't keep my mouth shut. I was so frustrated, I could have thrown myself at him and beaten him with my fists. I felt tears coming, but I fought them back. "I want the truth from you."

"One thing I've learned in life is that there is more than one version of the truth in most situations. But let's take it one a step at a time. I

❖

didn't kill Abdullah. In fact, I saved his life once. I didn't kill Lipton and the others. I also wasn't aware they were going to be killed and the place torched."

"Tell me about Abdullah."

"He was a stupid old man." He shook his head. "No, that's unfair. He should have just kept his mouth shut. He was too . . ."

"Idealistic?"

"Yeah, a real romantic in a world without pity. He didn't understand that no one cared about what he was willing to give his life for, not even the people in his own country. Yeah, I saved his life, but getting his head whacked didn't teach him to keep his mouth shut. Ultimately it got him killed."

I stared at his SEAL cap. "How did you save his life?"

"We'll go into that in a moment."

He led me up to the boathouse and the speedboat tied up at the pier. The boat was nosed toward the bay.

"I want you to meet some friends," he said.

Cold fear gripped me. It must have shown on my face. I was ready to make a run for it. He took my arm firmly and led me to the boat.

"They're out there," he said.

A large fishing boat sat in the distance.

"Over the sunken galleon?" I asked. "Is that how you're bringing up the treasure?"

"Your mother apparently never told you that curiosity killed the cat. So does having a big mouth."

He led me aboard the speedboat.

"Things have gotten a little more high-tech than sending down a lone diver in a diving suit. We use a million-dollar robot with cameras for eyes that probes the wreck. And we have a high-powered suction tube that can bring small items to the surface. Before we get to the point of finding treasure, we need to find the sunken vessel.

"It used to just take a pirate's treasure map, some quill scratches on a piece of leather by Long John Silver. Things have changed. Now we start with a vague historic record of the region where a ship went down, preferably a Spanish galleon with a bellyful of Inca and Aztec gold and silver. Almost always the history record is full of holes because where the ship went down is a matter of conjecture."

❖

As he talked, he pulled in the plastic bumpers that kept the boat from rubbing against the dock.

"Using all the clues we get from records and rumors of the day, we refine the ship's location with GPS tracking and imaging. Once we pin down a manageable area in which to make a focused search, we use sonar, sound waves, and ground-penetrating radar to map the ocean floor for forms that fit a ship's contours."

"That makes you nothing more than a high-tech thief."

He pretended to wince at the accusation as he started the engine. "I consider myself a savior and custodian of antiquities."

I screeched. "My God—you're delusional."

He grabbed a beer out of a cold box in the cockpit and asked, "Beer? Soda with a little arsenic chaser?"

"No, thanks."

He steered the boat toward the larger vessel in the distance. He kept the throttle low, with the boat barely making headway in the water. Obviously he wanted to talk before we reached the bigger boat.

He peered at me again over a swig of beer. "You realize that everything I say is my word against yours."

I made a zipping motion across my lips. "My lips are sealed."

I didn't volunteer that I'd already used his name in vain in a voice-mail message to an FBI agent.

"You're lying again," he said, "but after falling in love with you, I find myself completely at your mercy."

"You're confusing lust with love. And I'm sorry I made love with a thief and a murderer." *Good girl, Madison; that should help your present hopeless situation.*

"All right, let's deal with your uninformed prejudices. There's a ship out in the bay, at the bottom. It went down around three hundred years ago with a rich cargo. No one cares about it. It sits at the bottom of the bay, covered by sand. Lost, ignored, abandoned, no one to love it."

"You love it. At least the rich cargo."

"My motives are not important. My job is to find the sunken galleon. After I find it, to recover the treasure—"

"Treasure to you, precious cultural relics to the people of Spain."

He raised his eyebrows. "Okay, let's deal with that theory. You think of me as a thief. I see myself as another Lord Elgin."

I burst out laughing. I howled. "You *are* delusional."

"Lord Elgin was the British ambassador to the Ottoman Empire in the early 1800s. At the time, the vast Turkish empire, ruled by a sultan in Istanbul, included Greece, along with much of the rest of the Balkans."

"I'm familiar with the Elgin tale. And historical geography."

"I should have thought of that myself, you being a . . . what did you call yourself? A pimp?"

"Bastard."

"Let me refresh your memory. While he was visiting Athens, Elgin saw the Parthenon and other irreplaceable relics of Western civilization deteriorating and even being deliberately damaged. He watched soldiers use marble sculptures thousands of years old as target practice for their muskets. At an earlier time, when Venice was fighting the Ottoman Empire, the Parthenon was used as a powder magazine by the Turks. It blew up, destroying the center of the building."

I finished it for him. "So Elgin grabbed everything he could and shipped it off to Britain."

"Shipped it off where it is safe and sound today in the British Museum, rather than being damaged and destroyed by war, theft, and neglect. The world can appreciate irreplaceable works done thousands of years ago because Lord Elgin saved them. The marble reliefs are there, along with a lot of other priceless antiquities like the Rosetta Stone, which provided the key to reading ancient Egyptian hieroglyphs."

"Are you aware there are a few million Greeks who believe that those antiquities belong back in Greece? Not to mention that I'm sure the Rosetta Stone is just one of a long list of antiquities the Egyptians would like to see returned."

"Sure, like the Semiramis and the dozens of other artifacts you have at the Piedmont."

"Those were bought legitimately. Not stolen from the people of the Middle East."

He scoffed. "Where were those millions of people when their country was being destroyed by war, looting, and neglect?"

I raised my eyebrows. "Helpless? Hungry?"

"Exactly, but that's not an excuse. You know that probably fifteen thousand artifacts were looted from the Iraqi museum."

❖

I nodded. "While the literary heritage of the nation burned in the national library."

"My recollection was that Saddam's boys trashed the library to hide evidence against him and them. Apparently modern history of his atrocities was stored there, too. But let's get back to the fifteen thousand museum artifacts. Let's assume that some dudes did rip off—"

"You're one of the dudes."

"—a few items, even some very valuable ones. That left about fourteen thousand, nine hundred for the local mob to steal and/or destroy."

We were still only halfway to the fishing vessel. My paranoia was growing. What was he going to do once we got there? He and his modern-day pirates could murder me and feed me to the sharks. No body, no proof of a crime.

"Is this going to be one of those no corpus delicti things?" I asked.

42

❖

"A what?"

"Are you going to murder me and dump my body in the sea so I'll never be found? If you're not, would you please mind telling me what's going on?"

He took another swig of beer. "Okay. Here's the bottom line. As you can see from my cap, I was once a Navy SEAL. So were my partners, all except Gwyn, but she was also Navy and is half-fish. You're going to meet them shortly." He waved the beer bottle at the fishing boat. "There were five of us SEALs, all part of the same unit. I told you what a SEAL is."

"Some kind of frogman. Only you fight everywhere." I wondered if Gwyn was his girlfriend.

"Yeah, that's about it. To wear the trident, the insignia of a SEAL, means you've survived the toughest military training in the world."

"I guess they train you to kill in more ways than any other soldiers. That should make you very proud."

"Yeah, it does, especially when some wiseass civilian who I've protected from foreign enemies wants to get sarcastic."

"What foreign enemies have you and your pals protected me from?"

"That big bad wolf Saddam. We were in Desert Storm and Desert

❖

Sabre, the first Gulf War." He grinned. "We got into a little trouble during that one."

"Uh-huh. A little trouble as in . . . ?"

"You have to understand. It's hard to be part of the sea, to have salt water in your blood, and not have a fascination for sunken treasure. It goes with the territory. When we were in the Persian Gulf, we heard stories about ships that had gone down over the centuries carrying treasure. The Gulf was once famous for its pearls. Gwyn, who was a Navy communications officer, did some research and found the record of a shipment of pearls that were being sent from a potentate in Baghdad to an Indian raja as a wedding gift. We located the wreck and recovered the pearls."

I shrugged and shook my head. "That doesn't sound too bad. I thought you were going to tell me you stole Saddam's gold or something."

"We didn't think it was so bad, but the Navy got its nose bent out of shape because we used Navy time and equipment to locate the wreck and recover the pearls."

"Oh, I see. You did it illegally. While other people were fighting a war, you were out diving for treasure with assets that the military needed." I thought using the word "assets" gave a nice touch to my sarcasm. I'd heard talking-head generals on TV use the word.

"Something like that, though it wasn't much of a war. The brass were more annoyed because we wouldn't turn over the pearls."

"So you got a court-martial."

"No, that would have given the SEALs a black eye. We parted company with the Navy with general discharges. There was too much pirate and adventure in us, anyway. The regimentation in the military is a killer, especially with a war that turned out to be all show but no go.

"But because of the salt water in our blood, we had to keep our feet wet. We learned a lot about deep-sea diving and recovery while in the Navy, tech stuff that civilians would only learn at a world-class oceanography institute like Cousteau or Woods Hole. It would have been a shame to let all that knowledge go to waste. And we also borrowed some equipment before we left."

I nodded at the fishing boat we were slowly approaching. "And you used the stolen equipment to find sunken treasure. Illegally."

"That's an interesting word. It doesn't always mean the same thing

❖

wherever you go. You can say something in New York that gets you a laugh, whereas in North Korea they shoot you. The Spanish consider what we're doing illegal. We don't."

"You decide what laws you'll obey."

"We decide what laws are reasonable. Do you know anything about the laws of the sea concerning salvaging sunken treasure?"

I shook my head. "Not really."

"For the eight or ten or how many thousands of years we've had ships on the sea, the law has been real simple—finder's keepers. If you can find it and recover it off the bottom of the ocean, it's yours. Then some political genius decided that if the wreck was in the three-mile, or twelve-mile, or whatever limit they said their nation's boundaries extended out to sea, they still had jurisdiction over it. Ever hear of Spanish ships called *Juno* and *La Galga*?"

I pleaded ignorance again.

"They both went down off the coast of Virginia, one in 1750, the other in 1802. We're talking about wood galleons that have been on the bottom of the sea for two hundred to two hundred and fifty years. When salvagers located them, the Spanish government sued in a U.S. court, claiming the ships still belonged to them."

"Who won?"

"The Spanish. The scenario even gets crazier. About one hundred and fifty years ago, a paddle wheel steamer went down in deep water a couple hundred miles out to sea. It was carrying an enormous amount of gold from the California gold rush. It took about twenty years of clever thought, planning, raising millions of dollars, and raw courage to find the wreck in water eight thousand feet deep. When they brought up the gold, thirty-nine insurance companies were waiting to put claims on it."

He shook his head. "The bottom line is that there are too many governments making too many rules. All individual initiative is suppressed. We once had people who trekked pathless jungles, climbed the highest mountains; now most people are couch potatoes who watch TV reality shows about people lost on deserted islands—beachcombers who are followed around by a camera crew, of course. Look at the guys who sailed around the world in a balloon for the first time. Instead of cheering them, there were threats from some countries that they would be shot down if they flew over."

❖

"You are a common thief of uncommon things. Just another tomb raider."

"So what's an archaeologist but a tomb raider? You think King Tut's mummy likes it any better because the guy who violated his tomb had a college degree? What's a museum curator but just one more link in the chain of antiquities that have been ripped out of tombs with and without government permission? And this crap about not touching any ship that has gone down anywhere anytime in history. Hell, most of the countries that sent out those ships a thousand or two thousand years ago aren't even in existence anymore. And the ones that are just let the stuff sit there rotting until someone with guts brings it up."

I said, "There are billions of people in this world. If we don't have rules, we'll have to live by the laws of the jungle. That's fine . . . if you happen to be a muscle-bound ex–surfing bum."

"Ouch! Anyway, I'm not objecting to rules; it's the chains I don't like."

"So looting the Iraqi museum was an expression of your individual right to do what you wanted regardless of the law."

"We didn't *loot* the museum. We went there and saved and preserved priceless artifacts."

My jaw dropped. "What? You broke into a museum in a foreign country, armed and dressed as American soldiers, took antiquities to sell . . . and you don't consider that looting?"

"Yeah, and how about the sex you used to pass around to get deals on antiquities? You don't consider that whoring and pimping?"

"I'm not proud of what I did, but at least it didn't get people killed. What did Lipton have to do with all this?"

"Your pal Lipton, and I emphasize the fact he was *your pal,* came to us with a museum deal. But he didn't come to us and say, 'Hey, fellas, let's go and rob a museum.' He was one of the group of Anglo-American art experts who went to the White House and Whitehall to plead for protection of the Baghdad museum and library when the U.S. and its allies were gearing up for war. He saw that the politicians and generals were more interested in oil and military engagements where they could test their latest high-tech weapons than they were in antiquities.

"So he came to us with a plan to remove the most valuable pieces so they wouldn't be looted or damaged by a mob. Which is what happened to ninety-nine percent of the missing fifteen thousand artifacts."

❖

I rubbed my head with my hands. "I . . . you must think I'm very stu-pid or very naïve. Do you think me or anyone else will believe that you robbed the museum to save the antiquities for the world? Do I look like I just fell off a lettuce truck?"

"Turnips. People fall off of turnip trucks. I'm not telling you our mo-tivation was to save the antiquities for Iraq. I told you we didn't simply set out to rob the museum. Taking abandoned treasure off the ocean floor is our thing. We consider it open season because it really belongs to no one. And we're not into robbing museums. Lipton told us that if we didn't get the antiquities out, they would be taken by mobs and Iraqi criminal elements. Hell, Saddam's government was one big criminal el-ement."

"Did he also tell you that this humanitarian deed would bring you tens of millions of dollars when the artifacts were sold?"

"We were too low on the food chain for those tens of millions." He grinned. "But we were in the single-digit category. The deal was money up front for expenses and ten percent of what the artifacts brought when they were sold."

"So there was never an intent by Lipton or you and your gang of forty thieves to preserve the antiquities for the Iraqi people. Right from the beginning they were to be sold to rich collectors and museums."

"You're beginning to sound more like a prosecuting attorney than an accomplice."

"A what?"

"Keep your pants on and listen up. Let's go back to motivation. I keep telling you, I never said the idea was to preserve the pieces for the Iraqi people. For every guy like the Iraqi curator who got murdered trying to protect his country's cultural heritage there were a dozen Saddam cronies who were waiting for law and order to break down to grab trea-sure. We saved the antiquities for the world—"

"I have a hard time buying your high moral position—"

"I didn't say I had a high moral position. You keep making me a mer-ciless devil and saying I'm trying to act like I'm a saint. What we did we did for money . . . but we didn't do it to harm the antiquities. Lipton was a big-time art dealer; I imagine he cut a few corners—and probably wasn't the only one in the business who did. . . ." He gave me a penetrat-ing stare.

❖

"Why don't you just call me a pimp and whore again? A good offense is always a good defense, isn't it?"

"Look, Maddy, I'm no angel and neither was Lipton. I like to think that most of what I do is for adventure, but maybe I do have a little larceny in my heart, a little Blackbeard the Pirate. But I don't destroy antiquities. Not even when I use an old coin on a watch."

He waved his wrist at me.

"Lipton was the same way. Regardless of his profit motives or the corners he cut to get pieces, he was a lover of art. He really wanted to save the antiquities from looters. And if he made a buck doing it, that was all the better. So he hired us to grab some of the best pieces before the doors got knocked down and the mob burst in. We would have taken the whole museum if we'd had transportation for it. As it was, we took forty good items. The Semiramis was the cream of the lot. It wasn't even on public display out of fear Saddam or one of his cronies would grab it."

"You took the best and left the rest for looters. What happened to Abdullah?"

"Like I told you, he was a real romantic in a cold-ass world, too idealistic." He grinned again. "He wasn't willing to compromise his ideals like you and me, eh?"

Bastard. "What did you mean when you said you saved his life?"

"We were in the museum, protecting the antiquities of Mesopotamia from common looters. Arrangements had been made with an Iraqi general, one of Saddam's elite guard, to give us access. A money arrangement, of course. He even provided an honor guard—included in the price, but I think they were also there to grab what they could as soon as we drove away.

"Abdullah came barging in when we were loading stuff. Suddenly came in from nowhere, shouting like a maniac that we were thieves."

"Which you were."

"I hit him over the head and knocked him out to keep him from taking a bullet from someone else."

"You should be very proud of yourself."

He leaned forward, staring at me. "Did you hear what I said? He came stumbling in when we were loading up, raising a stink. He was about to get wasted when I hit him. Hey—I saved the guy's life."

❖

"He was about to get wasted, as you put it, because he walked into a criminal scheme you helped create."

"And what would've happened to him if he had walked in a few minutes later when the mob was looting the place? You never seem to get the big picture."

"Oh, I get it. You saved him in Baghdad. And killed him in New York."

❖

LEAVING THE GHOSTS OF THE SEA IN DAVY JONES'S LOCKER

In a landmark case, salvagers who spent enormous amounts of time and money finding the lost wrecks of two Spanish ships, *La Galga* (sunk in 1802) and *Juno* (lost in 1750), off the coast of Virginia, were barred from recovering the contents of the vessels. Despite the fact that the ships went down nearly 200 and 250 years ago, respectively, a federal court decided that the ships still belonged to Spain.

In supporting Spain, the United States seeks to insure that its sunken vessels and lost crews are treated as sovereign ships and honored graves, and are not subject to exploration, or exploitation, by private parties seeking treasures of the sea.

—*Sea Hunt, Inc., v. Unidentified Shipwrecked Vessels, Kingdom of Spain, et al.,* U. S. Court of Appeals, Fourth Circuit (June 21, 2000)

43

❖

I couldn't believe I was accusing him of murder again.

He threw his hands up at the sky and beseeched the heavens, "Lord, keep me from cutting this woman up for fish bait and throwing the pieces to the sharks."

We were still a hundred yards from the fishing boat. He cut the engine. We sat basking in the sun while I digested what he'd said.

"Why are you telling me all this?" I finally asked.

"My associates aren't going to be very happy if I bring you aboard babbling like a harpy how you're going to put all of us in prison. And I'm doing it to help you get your thinking straight. You are on the run from the police because you're part of the same daisy chain as Lipton, me, and—"

"That's nonsense; I had nothing to do with the robbery."

"If there wasn't a market for the loot, we wouldn't have stolen it. It's called receiving stolen property. Lipton told us that he already had a person who would buy the pieces."

The statement hit home so hard that I was speechless. "It wasn't me. The robbery took place years before I became curator."

"He didn't give a name; maybe you were just handy when it came

❖

time to start pushing the stuff. We all agreed that he'd hold back several years before a single piece even hit the market. But you're the one who he unloaded on finally."

"That wasn't my fault. I knew nothing about the looting."

My defense came out as a whisper and sounded false even to me. True, I didn't know for sure that the pieces were from the museum. But I didn't look too hard, either.

Coby leaned over and patted me on the knee. "Look, I told you, me and my buddies figure that what's been under the sea for hundreds or thousand of years is up for grabs for the people who have the guts and know-how to recover it. We made an exception for the Iraqi museum heist because we figured it wasn't just stealing. It would keep the stuff out of the hands of people worse than us. I'm not telling you we're angels, but we aren't into murder."

"I'm glad to hear that."

"Not yet, anyway."

"And what is that supposed to mean?"

"It means that we aren't ready to spend the rest of our lives in prison because someone rolled over on us."

I thought about the call I had made to Agent Nunes, but I kept a straight face. "I can be trusted—"

He held up his hand. "Please. Nobody can be trusted when the cops put the squeeze on. But that's a bridge we can cross later. Right now we have to make sure we're all operating on the same page. Let's go meet the rest of the team."

"Must I?"

He goosed the engine and directed us toward the larger boat. I was still in the dark as to what he had in mind—and why he was telling me so much. At least I hadn't been murdered . . . yet.

"Tell me about the ship you're salvaging."

"The *Ronda* was a galleon that sailed from the New World with a bellyful of Inca gold back in the 1600s. It was headed for Cádiz, but the port was under attack by the British when it got there. It kept going, through the Straits, on a course for Málaga. It sank in a storm before it reached the port."

He nodded down at the water. "It's a grave of sailors and passengers besides being a treasure trove. We do honor to the bodies, holding a service

❖

before we start opening up the galleon to look for treasure. Nothing is removed from a skeleton. If there's a valuable ring on a bony finger, it stays there. We're sailors, too."

"That should get you some leniency when the Spanish send you to prison for looting the ship."

He sighed and shook his head. "You know, Madison, you're really a good fuck, but you have a sharp tongue."

A sharp tongue that can get me in trouble.

44

❖

We finally reached the larger boat and I went aboard to meet the band of pirates, smugglers, and thieves.

Three men, former SEALs who served with Coby, and the woman he said was half fish, Gwyn, a former Navy officer, made up the gang. The men were all chips off the old block of Coby . . . short hair, big pecks, firm abs, tight butts. Gwyn was an all-American tall, farm-fed blonde, with a butt that was going south. She had a wide smile, impish blue eyes, and a bottle of cold beer in her hand.

"Wow, underwater looting really has gone high-tech, hasn't it," I said, as I stared at the computers and monitors that served as tools of their nefarious trade.

"Let's feed her to the sharks," Gwyn said.

"I'm considering it," Coby said. "Meet Moby Dick."

He pointed at a monitor showing a remote operating vehicle inside the hole of the sunken ship. The ROV looked like it had been made with an Erector set. The steel creature's electronic eyes—cameras—and arms and hands were the only humanoid features.

"Moby has a gentle touch. We use it because we don't want to destroy what we recover."

❖

"I can understand that. You won't be able to sell loot that's broken."

He gave me a thin smile. "We are concerned with preserving what we recover. Moby can pick up an egg."

"Scrambled?" I asked.

From the looks on their faces, I wasn't making any friends, but I was too disgusted—and too stupid—to stroke these people. Frankly, none of them looked ready to murder me. Yet.

"Here," Coby said, "try it yourself. Then tell me that Moby isn't gentle enough to pick up a baby."

I sat down and he showed me how to work the controls. It really was harder than it looked . . . like rubbing your tummy and patting your head at the same time. Gwyn took a picture of me working the controls. She either was softening toward me or wanted a souvenir to keep after I was eaten by denizens of the deep.

Next they showed me some pieces of eight—Spanish silver coins— that had been brought up. I examined them closely. They were corroded from their centuries on the seafloor but could be easily cleaned. Gwyn snapped more pictures. I grinned and held up a coin so she would get a good shot.

"This is all very interesting, but what does this prove other than the fact that you people are really good at stealing antiquities off the bottom of the sea? And that you're probably going to spend your best years in a small, low-tech prison cell. Why exactly did you want to put on a dog and pony show for me? Do you think I'd be a character witness at your trials?"

Coby smiled and gestured at his co-conspirators. "We wanted you to see that we're human. And pretty nice people."

"Wonderful. And what's to keep me from going to the police and telling them what I saw today?"

"That's easy. We work for you."

"You what?"

"You and Lipton and your pal Viktor Milan hired us. That will be our story. What's yours?

I chortled. "That's stupid. Who would believe that?"

"Everyone who sees the pictures."

"What pictures?"

"You using the robot to pick up contraband treasure off the bottom. You handling pieces of eight."

❖

Gwyn held up the camera and gave me a grin as she pretended to snap my picture.

"You dirty bastards. That's blackmail."

Coby failed to smother a grin. "I prefer to think of it as a negotiating point. The other alternative is that corpus delicti scenario you mentioned."

If he knew I'd already called the FBI, I'd be fish bait.

I SAID GOOD-BYE TO my new co-conspirators and got back into the speed-boat for the trip back to the villa. Pissed.

"Don't look so angry," Coby said. "You could do worse for partners in crime."

"Oh, I'm beyond that. I'm not angry at you; you're only protecting yourself. I'm mad at myself. You were right when you said I was part of the looting of the Iraqi museum all along. I was. Not in body but soul. Without people like me who turn their heads at suspicious provenances, there wouldn't be a market in contraband antiquities."

"And most of the antiquities would be destroyed by the indigenous people who should be preserving them."

I shook my head. "No, the fact that there are bad people willing to sell their cultural heritage to foreigners doesn't justify what we do. If there weren't willing buyers for the stolen artifacts, you wouldn't have tomb robbers and museum looters even at the local level."

"We can go on and on. Like so much in life, it's a circle, a chicken or the egg scenario. You're being too introspective and intellectual. This is the real world. Don't forget that 99.9 percent of the items looted from the museum were taken by Iraqis themselves. And it was Iraqis hiding the atrocities of Saddam's regime that destroyed the Iraqi library. These people have to take some responsibility for their own lawless society. We turned Iraq into chaos only because we removed Saddam and the big gun he held that kept everyone in line."

We drove for a moment before I asked, "What do you think I should do now?" I almost broke out in a laugh. Was I really asking a modern-day pirate for advice?

"There are two things you have to deal with. The police are the easiest. They have zero against you. The provenance on the Semiramis is suspicious—but it takes more than suspicion to convict you of receiving stolen property. It takes proof. And that will be impossible for the police to obtain. Even if Lebanon turned into a haven for the FBI tomorrow, they wouldn't be able to find evidence that rebuts what the provenance says was a handshake deal in a marketplace over a century ago. If you keep your mouth shut, the police will make a lot of noise but will eventually go away because they don't have the evidence to charge you."

"I hate to burst your bubble." I told him about the document examiner's report. I told him about the Times New Roman font, about the proportional spacing between letters.

"Who has the report?"

"Neal destroyed my copy. I suppose he destroyed his."

"Lipton would have destroyed his. If not, it went up with the gallery."

"That leaves Bensky."

"Bensky's dead. Gwyn saw it on the Internet. Pulled out of the river."

"Jesus. The poor man."

"Before you have too much sympathy for him, you should know he was in on framing you."

"What do you mean?"

"It wasn't any accident that the report got into your file without you knowing it. Lipton and your pal Neal needed someone to take a fall if everything went to hell. They paid Bensky to give you an all clear with a phone call, and then your pal had your assistant bury the report." He grinned. "I got that heads-up from Lipton. I actually wrote the provenance and prepared the backup documents. They were intended to be good, but it would take more talent and time than I had to make them perfect enough to pass the world's greatest experts. It had to get by only one expert—and he was getting paid to look the other way."

Nothing surprised me any longer. But it didn't quite jive. "But Neal destroyed the copy I had."

"By that time, Bensky was probably murdered and his copies burned. There was too much coming down to put it all at your door. It was one thing to set you up to take a fall on buying the mask if they needed a fall guy for the police to go after, but when bodies started showing up . . . well, I talked to Lipton before his place got hit. He was in a panic. He said the police were outside. I'm sure he had the shredder going full blast."

My head swirled. "This is so crazy."

❖

"No, it's not. You're talking about fifty-five million dollars. People do a lot more for a hell of a lot less. The person who made out like a bandit in the deal was your boss Piedmont. He stopped payment on the mask. And still has it. How many years do you think it will take the Iraqi government to recover it?"

"They'll never recover it. With Abdullah's evidence gone, they'll never be able to prove it was stolen."

Incredible. The rich get richer. Buying the mask had turned my life into a nightmare . . . and Hiram had the piece and the money.

WE ARRIVED AT THE dock and tied the boat up. I reached another conclusion by the time I walked by the boat shed filled with the contraband from the *Ronda.*

"One thing doesn't make any sense to me. I can't imagine Neal behind the London bombing. And murdering Abdullah and Bensky."

"He's not. The killer is the second thing you have to worry about."

As we came around the boat shed I saw a man standing by a car at the road about two hundred feet away. He had something that looked familiar on his shoulder. It was pointed at us. I stared stupidly again as he fired.

Coby yelled and knocked me to the ground. A deafening explosion erupted. I felt the hot flaming wind of a blast and thousands of tiny pieces of debris.

Coby was up instantly, pulling me along with him. I moved mindlessly, with pure nervous energy, like a snake with its head cut off.

He pulled me around the corner of the shed. "Get back in the boat."

We ran down the dock and jumped onto the speedboat. The "second thing" I had to worry about had just arrived.

❖

45

We roared off just seconds before a rocket hit the boathouse.

"Hold on," Coby yelled.

He steered the boat on a zigzag course. I looked back and saw the man with the rocket launcher heading off the beach. The boathouse was damaged but still standing.

"Who is this man who wants to murder me?" I yelled.

Coby's speedboat had the gravity compression feel of my XK Jag as we raced away from land. He phoned his fellow treasure hunters to lift anchor and follow suit, getting out of Spanish territorial waters . . . and out of rocket range.

"His name is Ernest Stocker. He was once part of the team."

"A SEAL?"

"Right."

"Is he the one who was going to kill Abdullah?"

"Yeah, he was going to blow him away. It's Stocker's cap that Abdullah saw. He probably saw it again that day you showed up and found Abdullah gutted. Stocker always said he'd rather kill with a knife than a gun. More feeling on both sides of the blade."

"So he also killed Lipton, Albert, the receptionist . . . Bensky. God knows how many others. And this is one of your buddies?"

I suddenly felt sick. I leaned over the side and threw up.

Coby took a beer from the cold box, opened it, and handed it to me. I pushed it away.

"Rinse your mouth with it. You'll feel better."

I drank the beer and dropped the bottle over the side. I'd just seen a boathouse full of centuries-old pieces get hit by a modern weapon. I wasn't in any mood to worry about the ecology.

For the first time since I'd met Coby he appeared contrite. He avoided me, which was fine, because I stared straight ahead and saw nothing. My world was spinning out of control again.

I saw the coast of North Africa before Coby spoke.

"I owe you an explanation about Stocker."

"You sure as hell do."

"We were all in the same unit in Iraq. It's hard to explain, but the ballsy guy who can use a rocket launcher in downtown London isn't a bad guy to be backing you up on a commando mission."

"Ballsy guy? What courage does it take to kill people with a rocket launcher? Have you been so out of touch with—"

"You're right; you're right. I said it wrong. I *am* wrong. I guess my point is, he was just another gung-ho SEAL. He got crazy afterward. Or maybe it was always there and it just burst out one day. One day he was a poor kid from Georgia enlisting in the U.S. Navy as the best he could do, and the next he was sitting on tens of millions of dollars in contraband art."

"Did you hit any other museums besides the Baghdad one?"

"No. The only thing we've done is search for sunken treasure. I told you, the Iraq job was an exception. Ninety percent of the thrill was planning it and seeing that we could pull it off."

He pointed at a coastline south of us. "North Africa."

"I guessed that. Where are we going?" I asked.

"Ever been to the Casbah?"

"The Casbah? You mean the marketplace in Tangiers?"

"It's not far from Casablanca. We can drop in and see Bogie and Bacall."

❖

"Bogie and Bergman. Bogie and Bacall had it all in *Key Largo,* not *Casablanca.* Tell me why this homicidal maniac wants me dead."

"I'm sure it's not personal. Stocker hates a lot of people, including me and the team. He's a loose cannon."

"That's an understatement."

"I told you we got in trouble over some Persian Gulf pearls. We—"

"I know; you were cashiered out for being AWOL and off on a treasure hunt when real men and women were fighting a war."

"We launched a project recovering antiquities, first in the Caribbean, then did some stuff off Indonesia."

"You stole antiquities in violation of the laws of all civilized nations."

"Do you want to tell this story?"

"Can you talk about your crimes and misdemeanors without making it look like you were out saving the world instead of being a damn thief?"

"Okay, Ms. Pimp, we were a gang of thieves. Does that sound better to you? We started out in the eastern Mediterranean and Aegean Islands off the coast of Greece and Turkey. We pulled up antiquities, occasionally coming onto land at night, and picking up something being smuggled out for Lipton."

He stopped and eyed me intently. "You don't have a man in your life, do you?"

"What do you mean?"

"It's obvious, you're too damn critical. I can see that most guys would jump in for some good sex and then run. You'd constantly walk on his heels, yapping that he drinks too much, eats the wrong stuff, drives too fast—"

"I don't need a lecture from a career criminal. You are a damaged person. Let's stay on Stocker."

"Like I said, we left the Navy and got involved in a project locating and recovering artifacts from the Aegean. The Hellenistic world of the Greek islands and coast of Anatolia are loaded with antiquities. Stocker was still part of the team, then." He paused for a moment and narrowed his eyes. "And what did you mean when you called me a damaged person?"

"Some people go through life all screwed up. Maybe you got dropped on your head too often as a kid." He had a weird expression on his face, almost comical. "Go on; you were drooling like a kid in a candy store about all the antiquities you stole in the Aegean."

He chuckled without humor, then leaned over and brushed my cheek with his lips and whispered, "One of these days, you and me . . ."

I steered him back to the subject at hand. "You were talking about Stocker."

"Before Lipton, we dealt with a French art dealer who ended up dying of natural causes. Really. We needed another outlet for the artifacts. Through a smuggler in Istanbul, we learned that Henri Lipton was a guy who wouldn't look too close at a provenance. We connected up with him and did good business for quite a while. Like I told you before, he came to us with the Iraqi museum heist."

"What went wrong with your partnership with Lipton?"

"Nothing, at least from the five of us you've met. We were happy with the ten percent deal and happy to have the money flow in slowly so a bunch of the stuff didn't raise suspicion by getting dumped on the market. We all thought of it as a retirement fund, you know. That was the deal . . . Lipton would sell the stuff off very, very slowly, over a period of years, and do it with private sales that didn't generate publicity or talk in the trade."

"Instead the Semiramis went onto the auction block," I said.

He shook his head. "That dumb bastard Stocker pushed Lipton into selling the Semiramis. That piece was supposed to go last, in the distant future, because it was worth ten times more than anything else and would cause worldwide attention in the art market. I spoke to Lipton after I found out it was going to be auctioned. He said Stocker was running crazy. Lipton was scared of him, and I didn't blame him."

"Stocker just suddenly went off the deep end?"

"The insanity was probably there all the time; it just took a while for us to see it. While the rest of us were satisfied with preserving antiquities for the world, sort of the Robin Hoods of artifacts . . ."

He paused to let me make a caustic comment, but I kept a straight face and my mouth shut.

"Stocker veered off and got into a different kind of smuggling. Small arms, things like automatic weapons, machine guns—"

"Rocket launchers."

❖

"Definitely rocket launchers. The guy loves things that kill, he really does, like some of us love women. This guy literally took his rifle and bayonet to bed at night. When the rest of us were kibitzing, lying about the beer we'd drunk and the women we'd poked—"

"Now that's a romantic image. Drunken sailors grunting and humping. Spare me the details."

"Stocker would pet his gun and talk about range and velocity. Not being an art lover like the rest of us, he's perfect for gunrunning. There are civil wars and terrorist activities on every continent, so there's a huge market for the stuff. And there's a big supply of it, mostly in the old Iron Curtain countries.

"Stocker said he wanted more excitement. The gunrunning is a dirty, dangerous, bloody trade. I think some Bulgarian babe he met in Istanbul got him started. We were just glad to get rid of him. None of us were comfortable around him. Anyway, he made some money off of a couple small deals and then went for a killing."

"What kind of killing?"

"One that took a lot more money up front than he had. He got Lipton involved. I don't know how he did it. Lipton told me he was just plain scared. Maybe that was true, but I think it was more than that. I think Lipton actually bought into a gun deal with Stocker because he was having financial problems from the breakup of a partnership and some deals that went south. He was sitting on all those Iraqi museum pieces that weren't bringing in any money. Using them to finance a big gun deal, he could get money out of the pieces by putting them up for collateral and get them back when the gun deal went down. All done under the table. No publicity, period."

"I can see Lipton doing that. There were all kinds of rumors in the art world that he had financial problems. And no one would have accused Lipton of having too much integrity. No question, he loved art. But everyone knew he was willing to look the other way."

Coby gave me a simpering smile.

"Wipe that smirk off your face. The difference between me and you is that you knew for sure Lipton was a crook because you were one, too. I never bought anything that I knew was actual contraband. What happened with the Iraqi pieces and the arms deal?"

"I'm not sure. Stocker came to us first and wanted us to back him

❖

when he went to Lipton with the proposal. We wouldn't do it. Lipton bought in without telling us."

"So why didn't you want to get involved?"

"It was too much like work. Besides, there's no glory in supplying arms that kill people. No one wanted to get involved with Stocker again, either. He was always a problem. Anyway, come to find out, Stocker bought the arms on credit, using the Iraqi museum pieces as security. When the arms deal fell through, he forced Lipton into selling the Semiramis to bail them both out.

"The people he bought the arms from were no one to screw with. Some kind of mafia types. Mean enough to scare Stocker. Lipton had to buy back the pieces, and he used the money from the Semiramis to do it.

"That wasn't good enough for Stocker apparently. He wanted more. In fact, he wanted it all. He found out where Lipton had the rest of the artifacts hidden. We knew Lipton had transferred them to New York, but even we didn't know the exact location. I don't know how Stocker found out, but he stole them and has covered his trail by killing Lipton."

"Jesus. What tangled webs we weave. So he wants to kill you so you don't come after him."

"And he wants to kill you because you know too much."

"I do now. I didn't before."

"Stocker doesn't know that. We were told the Semiramis sale was greased."

"What do you mean?"

"The sale was set to go through even before it was auctioned."

"No, that's not possible. It was a public auction. There was no guarantee that we were going to buy the piece. We could have been outbid. I don't know why he said it was greased."

I thought about the players: Lipton, Neal, Hiram. Lipton and Neal could have positioned Hiram to make the buy by revealing to him the reserve price. That way they would have been assured of having a buyer . . . and Hiram would have been best prepared to make the buy.

I thought I had manipulated Hiram into paying fifty mil plus. It was looking more like I was a minor player.

"What's next?" I asked.

Coby shrugged. "Stocker has the merchandise. He'll sell the stuff and

❖

get very rich. Probably kill us off as he goes along. Will eventually get arrested because he's crazy."

"That's encouraging—that he'll eventually get caught for killing me. But it's not that simple. You can't get rid of a warehouseful of stolen antiquities with a yard sale. Stocker will have to work with someone in New York's art world to sell the artifacts."

We were both quiet for a long moment. Neal would be the obvious choice to market the contraband. But there were plenty of others in the trade who would look the other way and agent the stuff. Not to mention that I couldn't see Neal getting involved with that crazy.

Finally, Coby nudged me with his foot. "Well, Captain, what do you think we should do now?"

I sighed. "We have a murderer on our backs. As soon as the Spanish police discover the remains of the treasure trove you had and that I had been there, they'll believe we were both in on it. And killed Lipton to boot. So we're probably wanted by the police on two continents. All trails lead to New York. That's where the artifacts are and where Stocker has to sell them, especially now that he's burned his bridges in London, in a manner of speaking. If we can find out who his connection is in New York, it would lead us to Stocker and the hoard."

Coby nodded. "Yeah, sounds good."

"Once we locate Stocker and the artifacts, we can turn him over to the FBI. And make sure the museum pieces get back to Baghdad."

Coby nodded again, but this time his expression was blank. I didn't like the look on his face, an expression that meant he was just pacifying me. When you think about it, what would clear me wouldn't necessarily clear him.

We didn't have the same motives, either.

I was sure now that I knew how the mind of this self-proclaimed "savior of the world's cultural heritage" worked.

Even Robin Hood got paid for his work.

❖

United Nations Outlaws Treasure Hunting

Treasure hunters will be barred from historic shipwrecks and sunken cities pursuant to an international convention adopted by UNESCO in 2001.

The UN agency claims that the prohibition is necessary because new technologies have made the looting of deep-water wrecks easier.

The UN estimates that there are as many as 3 million shipwrecks scattered on the world's ocean floors, with 65,000 off of North America.

Whole cities and remains of ancient monuments that have sunk beneath the seas, such as Port Royal in Jamaica and locations in the Greek isles, are also covered.

Treasure hunters and auction companies have made hundreds of millions of dollars from artifacts found on the ocean floors.

46

❖

Málaga

Special Agent Rick Nunes stood by the charred boathouse and stared up at the remains of the Málaga villa. Another FBI agent, Homer Clyde, and a Málaga police captain, Antonio Ramirez, stood nearby.

The villa and boathouse had been destroyed a week ago. By a man with a shoulder-mounted rocket launcher.

Noting the similarity of the crime to the destruction of Lipton's gallery-mansion, the FBI's Madrid office had sent a heads-up to the London office.

Nunes had already returned back to New York when the London agent advised him about the incident. After convincing his superior that he should investigate the Spanish crime scene personally, Nunes flew to Madrid. The following morning he arrived in Málaga in the company of Homer Clyde, a Spanish-speaking FBI agent from the Madrid embassy.

"No human remains were found in the debris?" Nunes asked.

The question was intended for the Málaga police captain but was addressed in English to Clyde, who translated it.

"He says no. Also, the police haven't been able to get a make on who had been occupying the villa before it was attacked. It was rented three months ago through a leasing agency by a Panamanian corporation.

❖

There's still a chance that some prints will be found, but none of the neighbors knew the occupants. A woman walking on the beach saw the man who fired the rocket launcher, but other than 'a big man in dark clothes' she gave no description of him. She ran when she saw the explosion."

"Smart woman. So what we have here," Nunes muttered, more to himself, "is the same type of weapon used in London, another building burned, no one can ID the perp, another connection to antiquities—"

"Yes, the local police are excited about the hoard found in the boathouse. A little scorched, but intact. They believe it came from an illegal treasure hunt in the bay, a sunken galleon from the days when Spain ruled the seven seas. A fishing boat had been observed off the coast here for the last couple of weeks. The police think the boat brought up the antiquities. They suspect there was a quarrel over dividing up the contraband. What do you think?"

Nunes walked along, pursing his lips before he answered. "It's more complicated than that. This wasn't a squabble over what was in the boathouse. The stuff had been abandoned. Hell, it barely survived the attack. Obviously, the shooter didn't even want the items. Killing was more important to him than the antiquities. Nothing was taken from the gallery in London, either."

"What's the motive?"

"The two incidents are hits, pure and simple. He was after people. The antiquities were just a coincidence when the shooting started. At this point, we know who some of the targeted people were. Other than the Dupre woman and whoever was present for the fireworks here, they're dead. But we still don't know who's pulling the trigger, why, or who's next."

"That leaves a couple universal motives: greed and/or revenge."

Captain Ramirez asked a question, which Clyde translated. "He wants to know if you're certain that this crime and the one in London are connected."

"Absolutely. You not only have the same weapon and modus operandi with a connection to antiquities, but the clincher is the woman."

Earlier when the Spanish officer mentioned that a taxi driver had dropped off an English or American woman in the area hours before the attack, Nunes asked the police to check all nearby hotels. Not only had an American woman and man stayed at a local hotel, but their rental car, picked up in Calais, France, and their luggage were still at the hotel also. The man couldn't be identified, but the car had been rented under the name of Madison Dupre.

"The fact that Dupre never returned to her hotel again to get her things raises several possibilities. She may have been kidnapped by the shooter, be on the run from him, or, worst-case scenario, she's dead and we just haven't found the body yet."

"What about the possibility of her being in bed with the shooter?" Clyde asked.

"Possible, but unlikely. We know she went into Lipton's gallery before the shooter did and left barely escaping an inferno. I don't think she would have voluntarily put herself into that much risk. It's more likely that the shooter has the typical motive—money or revenge. Dupre got in the way, maybe as a former accomplice. She scrambled out of London without going back to her hotel. I suspect she dodged the bullet and did the same here."

When Nunes told him about the woman's cryptic voice-mail message, Clyde said, "Doesn't sound like a real call for help to me. If she was completely innocent, she could've gone to the local police."

"She avoided the Spanish police, just like she did in London. And New York."

"So what is it with this woman? Sounds like she went from mild-mannered art curator to being involved in international murder in short order."

"I don't know. It just keeps getting more and more complicated."

Nunes stuck his head in the boathouse to get a look at the antiquities being examined by museum personnel and stepped back again shaking his head. "It started with a Babylonian queen who had a reputation for stirring up murder. Sounds like Dupre is following the same path."

❖

47

❖

New York

Something big that had changed since I had returned to Manhattan was my mode of transportation.

The subway had always been the most convenient way to get around the island and across to the other boroughs but not the snootiest. I had walked on clouds when I acquired the privilege of calling for a driver in a Town Car whenever I needed to get around the city. When I got bumped up from a Town Car and rode around in one of those big black Cadillac SUVs . . . well, as the Mafia said, I was a made woman.

Kiss that luxury good-bye.

Now I sat in a subway car rubbing shoulders with the great unwashed masses at five o'clock commute time. Although subways are damn convenient, commute time was hot (any time of year), crowded (any time of year), and stinky (any time of year).

Taxis were still an option, but the subway was faster and more anonymous, not to mention cheaper.

My New York Yankee hat, sunglasses, sloppy pullover, blue jeans, and running shoes put me in disguise mode.

Coby and I had been back in the city for three days now after flying into Boston's Logan Airport, then taking Amtrak's high-speed Acela

❖

express train to Penn Station. We set up camp in an eighty-foot tri-level luxury yacht called the *Luv Mate,* which belonged to Coby's old Navy pal who had left the service and made millions with a Web site that specialized in hooking up military people with other military people.

I spent most of the day making my way around the city picking up art publications and gallery and auction house catalogs. Since Stocker needed to sell antiquities to pay off his mob creditors, I was sure he'd seek private sales, with an art dealer brokering the deals. The word had to be circulated someway. I hoped one of the catalogs or art magazines I picked up would have a clue. I made sure to check out Rutgers in case Neal was involved. I came up with zero from their catalogs.

When I got back to the yacht Coby was in a soft chair with his bare feet propped up on a railing, a cold beer in hand, tortilla chips and a bowl of guacamole at his side.

"Don't we look comfortable," I said, annoyed that he was laid-back and relaxed when my mind and body were hyperventilating.

"My mind is working every waking and sleeping moment to analyze the mission."

I wanted to slap him across his smug mouth. He was one of those people who seemed to get away with everything I never got away with in life. I knew better than to try to reform him. Some men—and women—can't be housebroken. He simply wasn't pliable. But he was hard where a woman wanted a man to be hard.

I just shook my head and sat down and started going through the thick stack of materials I had gathered. His crunching slowly got on my nerves.

"Would you mind closing your mouth when you chew?"

"Already found it," he said, crunching some more chips as he spoke.

I looked up. "Excuse me?"

"You wanted a lead on Stocker selling something. I found it."

I pressed my lips together and looked at him, stupefied. I had just spent five hours hopping in and out of subway cars, up and down steep stairs, in and out of subway stations, pounding concrete sidewalks and dodging taxis as I ran across streets to pick up a shopping bag full of written material while he sat here filling his gut with Corona and chips.

"You know, you really are a bastard."

"What did I do?"

❖

He crunched more chips and I kept myself from grabbing one of his beer bottles and giving him a good old-fashioned attitude adjustment across the side of his head.

"Well, are you going to tell me?"

"It's over there." He gestured at a laptop computer on the seat to my right, which had a stack of printed pages on it. The computer had a *Luv Mate* decal on it.

"I got on the Internet and typed in the key words for ancient Middle Eastern art, 'Mesopotamian,' 'Babylonian,' 'Akkadian,' that sort of thing."

"And you came up with something?" I grabbed the papers off the laptop.

"A lot came up, but the stuff in your hands is the most intriguing."

The first piece of paper was a gossip column article. It said that Paula Golding, who had a messy divorce going with Carter Golding, had filed a restraining order to keep him from disposing of or hiding valuable pieces of his art collection, including a Babylonian piece acquired within the last week for $3 million.

Coby shook his head. "There's just no privacy left in this world. It cost me all of seven dollars to access the court records and print out the wife's restraining-order request. Look at the page I have folded over."

The art piece was described as the marble head of Marduk, chief god of the Babylonian pantheon.

"There was a head of Marduk in the looted items, wasn't there?" I asked him. If anyone knew the answer to that question, he did.

He nodded. "Yeah, we took one. Which tells me that Stocker found out where Lipton kept the goods before he killed him. That's why Lipton became expendable. And why all the rest of us are. Course, there's the chance this may be a piece we didn't take. Any more of these around?"

"None that I know of, and for sure not one that has appeared openly on the market. He paid three million for it. That's suspicious in and of itself."

"Why?"

"Because it's worth two or three times that. I would have paid seven or eight million had it gone on the auction block. And there would have been plenty of competition bidding against me." I was so excited, I got up and paced. "No, you're right; this has to be one of the looted items. It's too important a piece not to have created a buzz if it had been offered for sale publicly. Someone didn't want the world to know it was being of-fered, so it was sold privately—at a fire-sale price. And Golding is the perfect candidate for it. He's not too scrupulous and he has enough money so he won't miss a meal if the deal turned sour and a legitimate owner showed up and claimed the piece."

"You sound like you know this guy."

"I've bumped into him a number of times at gallery showings. He's well-known in the art world. Very rich and very secretive about his col-lection. Most collectors like to beat their chest about what they own, but Golding isn't that type. He's a hoarder. He owns to possess and doesn't want to share his darlings with anyone. And he has a reputation about not being too particular about the provenances of what he buys. That works well if your transactions are kept confidential."

"He'd buy a stolen piece?"

I thought about the question. "If you mean would he buy a piece that was known to have been stolen, I'd say no. He wouldn't buy it because it would come with prison stripes on it, but there are many levels of scrutiny. He's definitely not the type to look too hard at the provenance if he really wants something. I once passed on a piece from Petra in Jordan and—"

I suddenly stopped as I realized how Golding would have gotten con-nected to the Marduk piece: Neal. I had suspicion before. Now I was sure.

"What's the matter?"

"I just got a revelation. I told you Stocker couldn't do it alone. He'd have to run newspaper ads and probably have the police on him."

"You said he needed an art pro."

"Neal."

"Your auctioneer pal?"

"He's the chief auctioneer for Rutgers. A few months ago, he offered me the Petra piece, a second century B.C. vase. The piece had significant damage and the provenance was really suspect. While I was considering it, an American archaeologist, a university professor studying the Petra site, was arrested for smuggling another piece out of Jordan. He'd put a removable ceramic coating around the vase to make it look like a cheap tourist item. A sharp-eyed customs inspector at JFK got suspicious when the professor looked tense while the inspector asked how much he paid for it. The piece Neal offered me came from the same dig as the vase. I

❖

wouldn't touch it. Neal later bragged to me that he'd sold it to Golding despite the suspect provenance."

I didn't add that Neal's boast was made in bed during one of those nights he was bragging about his deals and I was faking an orgasm.

"So you think he sold Golding the Marduk? Were you fucking your pal Neal?"

How rude. I ignored him. I was no longer surprised that Neal got involved with Stocker—Neal obviously had been connected with Lipton, and assisting Stocker may have been just a matter of survival. Though, knowing Neal, he'd figure out a way of making a profit even off a crazed killer.

"Would that much money get Stocker out of his debt to these mob people?" I asked.

"I doubt it. From what Lipton said, he'd have to sell most of the collection. You didn't answer my second question."

"Get back on the Internet and run a search on Neal's name. Because of his connection to a major auction house, you'll have a million hits, so narrow it down to the past week. I'm going to check the antique catalogs and ads."

An hour later, neither of us had anything. And I still hadn't answered his question.

"I have one more idea," I said.

I called the telephone number listed in the court papers for Paula Golding's attorney. I got past the attorney's assistant by telling her that I had information for the attorney about Mr. Golding's art collection. After I waited on hold for an intolerable time, a woman got on the line. I identified myself as an art dealer but refused to give my name. After verbally fencing for a moment, I got down to the bottom line.

"I know Golding and I don't like him. He once promised to buy a piece if I could get it for him. When I got it, he didn't go through with the deal. I may have information about another recent deal, but I need to know who sold him the Marduk head."

She gave me the name of the dealer and I told her I'd call her back— and I hung up. I stared at Coby, the wheels turning in my head.

"Gilgamesh," I said. "Gilgamesh Gallery."

"You know the outfit?"

"It doesn't exist. Look, the New York art world is a small cottage industry with a finite number of rich and superrich players. Everyone knows everyone else. If there was a Gilgamesh Gallery doing multimillion-dollar deals, I'd know about it."

The name struck a chord with me. "Gilgamesh is the hero in a heroic poem about a Mesopotamian warrior-king. It was written back around 2000 B.C. It's the Mesopotamian version of Homer's Greek epics." I stared at Coby, pursing my lips. "Neal has a fascination with the Gilgamesh tales. He even owns a piece of clay tablet with some lines of the poem on it. It's his most expensive personal piece."

"It sounds like Stocker and your pal Neal that you've been fucking are made for each other. Neal has all the connections in the world of Middle Eastern art and Stocker's sitting on the biggest stash of Middle Eastern art to hit the market since Genghis Khan looted Babylon."

He wanted a reaction from me about Neal and I passed on it again. "You seem to be having senior moments at an early age. I told you he didn't take Babylon."

"You did?"

Maybe it was Nunes I told. Anyway, a string of thoughts went off in my head like a string of firecrackers. "Jesus, he's been behind everything."

"Genghis Khan?"

"Neal, you moron. He's been more than just a way for Lipton to auction the mask. I think he's in it up to his neck. He's the one who steered me into the Mesopotamian pieces coming onto the market, not to mention the mask itself. I told him I was going to Bensky's. Bensky's house gets burned down and he goes missing. I told him Abdullah was getting proof that the mask had been stolen. The poor man is murdered. I told him I was going to London. Ditto for Lipton."

The more I thought about it, the angrier I got. *My God—he's turned that homicidal bastard Stocker on to me, too.* I had lain in bed with Neal and shared my body with him . . . and he turns a homicidal killer on to me. *What a prick!* Stocker had timed his attack in London to get me, too. And in Málaga. Worse, Neal cost me my job and framed me with the police.

How could I be so stupid!

At least I had no emotional ties with him. Sex with him had just been pure business fucking. I felt that it was on a higher plane because there had been no passion in it.

❖

"I'm glad I faked my orgasms with him, that bastard," I blurted out.

"So you did fuck him."

"Well, you wanted to know. There's your answer. That make you horny? Are you the kind of guy who likes to watch a woman fuck another man? I could—"

I got out of the way of a flying jalapeño pepper. He grabbed me and pulled me to him. I tried to struggle out of his arms, but I couldn't. He had one of my hands pinned behind my back.

"Ouch, you're hurting me."

"You know what I like; you're a cock teaser." He kissed me hard on the lips.

I felt the throbbing bulge getting hard against me. I got aroused as he kissed me. He slowly released his hold on me.

I pressed my body closer. "You're making me horny now."

"Good. That's the way I want it."

We retreated to the bedroom below and fucked our brains out like there was no tomorrow. When our sexual needs were satiated, we came back to the matter at hand even though we were still lying naked on top of the bed.

"Is Neal rich?"

"He's well-off, but if you exclude people who actually earn a living from the definition of rich, no, he's not. He earns a salary at Rutgers, a good one, but he's still just an employee. He's always bitching about how much he brings in and how little of it he sees himself. He makes up for it by putting buyers and sellers together in private deals. There was always talk about some of the stuff Neal peddled on the side, but the talk was never very loud, because it's an industry in which few of us have clean hands."

He grinned. "Most of the hands in my business are dirty, too."

"We're not outright thieves."

"As my grandmother would say, that's the pot calling the kettle black."

His grandmother was probably Ma Barker.

"I have a plan," he said.

"What's your plan?"

"We kill Stocker and Neal and get back the museum pieces."

"Hmmm." I nodded. "Not bad, but I have a better one. We catch

❖

Stocker and Neal red-handed and turn them over to the FBI along with the artifacts so I can go back to my life and start rebuilding my career."

"Good idea. We'll go with your plan. Okay, now that we've solved that problem, I have another plan."

He grabbed me and pulled me on top of him.

"You're a horny bastard."

"You're a horny bitch."

"You're lucky I really like you."

"Why?"

"I don't have to fake my orgasms."

I really did like Coby. But I also didn't totally trust him. I had a feeling that his acquiescence to my plan was about as real as my moans of ecstasy with Neal.

As I spread my legs and Coby entered me, sending a sensation of pure delight, it occurred to me that I had to watch my back with him.

48

❖

"Okay, first on our agenda is to find Stocker," Coby told me forty-eight hours later when I joined the other five members in a powerboat and headed for Neal's weekend beach house on Fire Island. The sand barrier island was off Long Island.

Up to now, the SEALs had huddled together debating tactics and gathering weapons equipment that they had stowed in a rented storeroom.

"Had them stored there just in case," Coby told me.

I never got a straight answer out of him as to what "just in case" meant or even where the hoard was stored.

I had spent many weekends with Neal at the Fire Island beach house. We confirmed he was there by having Gwyn call and speak to his housekeeper at his Manhattan apartment, pretending she was with the auction house.

Although there were small year-round communities on the narrow, thirty-two-mile-long sand pit, Fire Island was comprised mostly of state and federal parks and seashore. The only vehicle traffic was in parking lots at the end of the two bridges that came over from Long Island.

"It'll be easier to get to his place and away again by boat," Coby told me. "Besides, we're creatures of the sea. That's why they call us frog-men."

I had a few other names for the band of underwater pirates, but I re-served them for a time when I had time and distance between us.

The plan was to hit the beach after dark, with GPS guiding us to the right house. We towed a rubber boat behind us that Coby and I would use to land on the beach. Two other SEALs would swim ashore in their wet suits . . . and pull the rubber boat I was on ashore if Coby needed help, so I didn't get my feet wet. That was my idea.

"Why don't they just ride with us?" I asked Coby.

"Recon. They're going ashore first to make sure the way is clear."

"That's a good plan. Neal might be lying in wait to attack us with his laptop and cell phone."

"Or his pal Stocker might be waiting with a rocket launcher."

"Good thinking." I smiled in defeat. "I guess that's why they call you frogmen."

COBY DROVE THE BOAT in fast enough for it to belly onto the sand. He quickly leaped out in water lower than his boots and pulled the boat onto dry land so I could step out without getting wet.

Fernando, one of the two men who preceded us, appeared out of the darkness. "All clear. I got a look at the guy through a window. I'm certain he's alone."

"Okay," Coby said to me, "let's go visit your friend."

"He's not my friend anymore," I said.

We went around to the front and I knocked on Neal's door. Fernando had disappeared and his partner was no doubt somewhere playing look-out.

Coby stood a couple feet off to the side so he wouldn't be seen when Neal looked through the door's peephole to see who was knocking at his door. In the city, you'd have to get by the 24/7 door staff and surveillance cameras. On Fire Island, the weather was more of a threat.

I wondered what Neal's reaction would be when he looked in the peephole and saw me. I found out quick enough. The door flew open.

"What are you doing here?"

I smiled. "Good evening, you lying fucking bastard."

The minute Coby stepped into sight, Neal tried to slam the door, but Coby muscled his way into the house with me behind him. Fernando suddenly appeared through the doorway and closed it behind him.

"I'm calling the police."

"I don't think so, pal." Coby pulled a lethal-looking black semiautomatic pistol from inside his jacket and stuck it in Neal's face.

Neal stared at the gun in pure terror.

"Do you want him dead?" Coby asked me.

Coby's question caught me by surprise. I wasn't sure he was acting. "Not yet," I croaked.

I had never seen Neal when he wasn't calm and collected, even when he was up at the podium doing multimillion-dollar deals. Or coming in bed. Now he was clearly terrified. I guess I would be, too, if I had a gun pointed at me.

Neal gaped at me. "Why are you doing this?"

"No, the question is why did you frame me and get all those people killed?" I looked at Coby. "Why don't we just start by hurting him."

He kicked Neal in the balls.

I winced. My former business lover went down on his knees gasping with pain. I wanted him to suffer a little after what he'd put me through, but I couldn't handle watching someone actually getting beaten.

When Coby looked at me, silently asking if he should really give Neal a beating, I shook my head. *Jesus, what a wimp I am. Neal has people murdered and I can't stand to see him get knocked around.*

Coby and Fernando picked Neal up by his arms and legs and slammed him onto the couch. Each man pulled out a roll of duct tape. In seconds, they had Neal bound hand and foot.

Coby sat down on the arm of the couch and looked down at him. "We need to know where Stocker and the museum pieces are. And we don't have much time. You can avoid further pain . . . and permanent disfigurements . . . by telling us right now. Or . . . show him, Fernando."

Fernando pulled out a wicked-looking knife.

"Tell him what you do with that knife."

Fernando sat down next to Neal. "My old man has a cattle ranch in the Philippines. When you raise cattle on a ranch, you have to keep the young male calves from growing up to be bulls. You can only have one bull for a bunch of cows or there's trouble, you know what I mean? So you have to cut off the balls of calves, you know. We rope the calf and pull it down. Grab the sac and . . . just takes one quick slice," he made the motion in the air, "and the young bull is turned into a steer."

Coby said, "In other words, we turn you into a eunuch. A ball-less bastard, you understand, asshole?"

Neal spit in Coby's face. "Fuck you."

Wow! I was impressed. I didn't think Neal had the balls—excuse the pun. Coby wiped his face with his sleeve. He looked disgusted.

"Bitch!" Neal snarled at me. "If Stocker doesn't get you, the feds will. Either way you're fucked."

I was numb more from hurt than anger. How had I misjudged him so? Somehow the words flew out of my mouth. *"Kill the bastard."*

"You heard the lady." Coby put tape over Neal's struggling mouth.

"I-I-I didn't really mean . . . kill him."

"I think you'd better go into the other room," Coby said. He winked. "This could get pretty ugly."

I started for the dining room but stopped and looked back. Fernando was cutting open the crotch of Neal's pants.

"You're not really?" I mouthed almost soundlessly to Coby.

He got up and led me through the dining room and into the kitchen.

"You're not really going to castrate him, are you?"

"Not unless he doesn't tell us what we want to know. Don't worry; it doesn't hurt as much as you think. We stop the bleeding instantly."

"That's insane. You can't just—"

He saw the look of horror on my face. "I'm just kidding. We're going to bluff him, scratch him, and let him think it's for real. But I can't have you out there trying to stop us. Your pal has got to think we're going through with it."

"I didn't really mean kill him. Not all the way dead, at least."

"Don't worry."

He closed the door behind him.

But I did worry. I waited a few seconds until I was sure he had crossed into the living room before I opened the door and snuck across the dining room to get a peek of what they were doing to Neal.

They had Neal down on the floor. Coby was sitting on Neal's upper body while Fernando had Neal's legs pinned and was doing something I couldn't quite see because a coffee table was in the way.

❖

After a moment Fernando straightened up with a wide grin on his face. He held a bloody object in his hand. "You'll sing soprano now."

My God! They had actually done it. But wait a minute—Fernando was Filipino. Filipinos were famous for that medical trick where they pretended to pull bloody objects out of sick people's bodies to cure them. I remembered seeing a TV show about the routine, and the bloody mass they'd pulled out of someone's stomach. It looked like what Fernando was now holding.

I knew everything was okay, but I suddenly felt queasy and sat down at the dining room table. A moment later Coby was at my side.

"Did you . . . ?"

"We've got the info. Let's get outta here." He ran out before I could finish my question.

I followed them out the back of the house without looking at Neal. Fernando and the other man, Vince, joined us in the rubber boat. As we were racing back to the larger boat, I quietly asked Coby, "What happened?"

"Stocker has the pieces stashed at an old warehouse at the Brooklyn shipyards. We'll head for there tomorrow after we plan our approach."

"Are you sure he isn't lying?"

"Naw, he was so scared he was pissing his pants."

That from Fernando.

"Where did you learn to do that?"

Fernando grinned. "On my father's ranch. Turning bulls into steers. When they're calves, you rope 'em and tie 'em down and whack their nuts off. That way they don't grow up to be bulls and mess up the whole herd."

Why did I ask?

49

❖

As we made our way back to the yacht, I watched the white rooster tail wake behind the powerboat and tried not to listen to the chitchat back and forth about how they would have to deal with Stocker. They sounded like a gang of kids planning an attack on a neighboring tree house. But they weren't kids and they were talking about killing a former friend . . . or otherwise being killed by him.

Ever since I bought the Semiramis, I've been looking back on my life and wondering how I got sidetracked. Before that, everything just seemed to click as I went from one career goal to another. Like a game show contestant answering the questions right, I moved up, sometimes crawling, sometimes leaping, as I went from college, to job, to success.

I knew I had to stay focused on the dangerous curves that lay ahead and stop thinking about the past. I was barreling down a road that led straight to hell.

No longer was it possible to completely redeem myself.

You don't cut the balls off the biggest auctioneer in the business and expect to do business in this town.

❖

Every man whom I contacted about a deal would experience a queasy feeling in his groin. As they said in Oz . . . which is Hollywood-speak for Hollywood . . . I would never do lunch in this town again.

Ruined. Finished. Hung out to dry. I wondered if they still made license plates in prisons. Or was it quilts they made in women's prisons?

Even though my career was not redeemable, I had to worry about something else. It roiled in my head as we bellied over waves in the high-speed boat back to the Manhattan marina.

I had to save my soul.

I didn't know exactly what that meant. I guess it just meant that I had to make up for the evils that I'd spawned. Coby was right. I was part of a daisy chain that evolved from the looting of the Iraqi museum to the death of Abdullah in New York. Along with other deaths and now at least one mutilation.

That evil bitch Semiramis was at every flash point. Lipton, Bensky, Neal, myself, even Coby and his gang, we all had our lives altered by the queen's golden mask as if it spread a malevolent virus that ignited the avariciousness in Neal, Lipton, and Stocker, boiling their greed until it was consummated in murder. Even poor Abdullah was affected, because his stubborn pride got him killed.

And for me? My weakness was the lure of success.

It boggled my mind that Neal was playing such a dangerous game with my career, especially with my life. That was the real kicker. He made far more money than I did. How much more did he need?

I guess someone could ask me the same question about my career. How far would I go to get what I wanted? Sometimes along the way we take a wrong turn and it becomes difficult to get back on the right track. Sometimes it's easier not to get back. *Where did I fit in that equation?*

I suddenly felt sorry for Neal.

"Is he going to be all right?" I asked Coby when he took a break to get a beer.

"I wouldn't worry about him. He'll be ready to run the marathon in a few days."

"He'll call the police on us."

"Not likely," Coby said. "He'll get to a hospital for sure, but what's he going to tell them—he lost a nut because he wouldn't tell where stolen loot and his murdering partner are?"

I knew I shouldn't have been so concerned about Neal. He had set a deadly killer on my heels. But I wanted the cycle of violence to stop. Coby and the SEALs talked about how it was their "duty and a matter of honor" to "put Stocker down." It sounded like they were talking about a rabid dog they once owned.

What a strange bunch. Stocker was once a partner. Now he had murdered their business partner and stolen their share of the artifacts. And while they talked about "putting him down," there was never a moral outrage about the high crimes and misdemeanors the lot of them had been committing. I wondered how much of their feelings was duty and honor . . . and how much was just plain being pissed that their buddy had stolen from them.

For sure, they were crooks, with their own moral code and personal definition of duty, honor, and country.

The discussion and hashing over plans about how to breach the defenses at the waterfront warehouse, terminate Stocker silently and with extreme prejudice, and recover the antiquities continued after we boarded the yacht and while they ate hot dogs, tortilla chips, and salsa and drank plenty of beer.

"Stocker will be expecting us," Coby said. "He's not stupid. He knows that ultimately we'll find him. He'll have set up an electronic defense perimeter as an early warning. He knows we won't have to beach a boat, that we can swim ashore, come in underwater. Once we get our feet on land, that's when we have to watch out for detection beams and booby traps."

No one expected Neal to tell Stocker that he'd squealed on him any more than Neal would confess to the police. So they expected an element of surprise for the raid.

"Why would you go in by water if he's expecting that?" I asked.

"He'll have the land side approach covered, too."

"But it sounds like you and him are thinking the same way, reverting back to your military training. Maybe you should change your thinking," I pointed out.

He squinched his face like I'd said something disgusting. Everyone

❖

was quiet. I had crossed the line. A mere woman telling these commandos that maybe they didn't have all the answers. I could see the ire and contempt on their macho, gung-ho, military faces.

"Wait a minute; she's right," Gwyn said. "We're talking like the land approach is enemy territory. Hell, it's just Brooklyn; you can drive up to the front gate."

"Don't forget this is the good old USA." Coby grimaced. "We can't just start shooting and launching rockets. Our biggest problem will be noise. We can use silencers on pistols and machine guns, but if Stocker starts hurtling rockets, the whole damn city will know it."

"Like you said, he's not stupid," Gwyn said. "If we come by boat, we could always just back off and run for it if the cops arrive. He can't go anywhere without packing up a truckload of antiquities."

"You're assuming again that he's thinking like you," I said. "You're also assuming that he's rational. This guy used a rocket to kill people and destroy a building in London in broad daylight. There had to have been a quieter and more effective way to get the job done."

"Stocker's a nutcase, class triple A," Coby said. "I always told you guys that, but because he was on the team, we ignored it."

"I wouldn't exactly call him crazy," Gwyn said.

"I would. You could see it was getting worse. When he started using drugs, he got more schizoid."

I said, "I think we can all agree that a guy who plays with a rocket launcher like a pacifier isn't playing with a full deck. In that case, we shouldn't assume that he'll cross all the *t*'s and dot all the *i*'s. When you hit the beaches in those rubber commando boats, he's likely to start firing rockets that will make the area around the warehouse look like the Fourth of July."

Coby scratched his jaw. "Yeah, even just opening up with a handgun will probably bring the police."

"The police, hell," Gwyn said. "With everyone on edge about terror attacks, we're likely to have the Army, Navy, Air Force along with half a dozen fed and state agencies shooting at us."

The group started throwing out more ideas.

Someone proposed a gas to put Stocker to sleep—or better yet, kill him. But poisonous gas had a way of migrating. . . . Another suggestion was to drop onto the roof by helicopter while two others landed by rubber raft.

Names of weapons and their firepower flew around the room like confetti at a victory parade.

At some point I simply tuned out and went to bed. My mind was swirling. I just wasn't into the commando scene. I heard someone suggest that I ride shotgun on the chopper and watch for police vehicles approaching the warehouse. I couldn't quite see myself hanging out of a helicopter with a pair of binoculars. And I didn't ask who would fly the chopper.

What had I gotten myself into?

Another nagging question wiggled like a worm in my brain. What was going to happen to the Iraqi antiquities if this band of commandos managed to kill Stocker and recover them? Would Coby and company really return them to a grateful Iraqi government? Anonymously, of course.

When hell freezes over. That's how I felt about the chance of Coby and his band of frogmen thieves giving back millions of dollars in stolen loot they'd risked their lives for.

I waited until Coby came in later to wrestle the truth from him.

"Look me in the eyes," I told him. Once we had locked eyes, I said, "Now tell me the absolute, bottom-line, ironclad truth: When we get the stuff from Stocker, are we going to give it back to the Iraqis?"

"Didn't I say so?"

"Tell me the truth."

"We're going to recover the pieces and give them back." He held up his hand in a Boy Scout sign. "Scout's honor."

"You were never a Boy Scout." A wild guess on my part, since he didn't strike me as the type. And if he had been, he would have been thrown out for conning Girl Scouts out of their cookie drive money.

"True, but my intentions nonetheless have always been pure and honest."

He was lying, of course. His utter sincerity and lack of concern about turning over the museum pieces was the tip-off. Any thief who really intended to give them back would have moaned and groaned or at least showed real regret that millions of dollars in looted antiquities were going back to their owner.

❖

However, he was my best hope. No way would any of these other treasure-hunting frogmen return the stolen pieces back to the Iraqis. They were just kidding me along, taking me for a ride . . . whatever the expression. Once they had their hands on the merchandise, I'd be back to square one on the FBI's Most Wanted List.

You are screwed, I told myself as I made my way down the gangplank the next afternoon. I had to get away for a while. I needed air. To clear my head. To figure out what to do. An idea was buzzing around my little brain, one that could get me into a heap of trouble, even worse than the mess I was already in over my head.

I had spent the day moping around the yacht as the rest of the merry band of thieves and pirates made plans and requisitioned supplies. For reasons I didn't even attempt to fathom, there seemed to be a limitless supply of military weapons available here in New York City. *Jeez, I thought that even BB guns were outlawed in this city.*

Muttering to myself about how my newfound friends had painted me into a corner, one with prison stripes, I walked three blocks to where the "company car" was stored.

A garage attendant brought the yacht owner's BMW down to me. We had permission to use it—Coby did, at least. I reminded the attendant that I had been with Coby when we borrowed the car previously. After I got in, I automatically put my cell phone on the magnetic dashboard mount, since it was illegal in New York to hold a cell phone while driving—the last thing I wanted was to get pulled over by the police.

As I pulled out of the garage, I spotted Gwyn walking on the other side of the street. *Damn, had she followed me?* She waved. I cringed and pulled into traffic and sped away as fast as one could on a Manhattan street. She'd report back to Coby that I'd just taken the car and hightailed it.

Coby knew me well enough by now to know that I had something up my sleeve. Probably even well enough to guess what I was going to do— find the hoard and turn it over to the FBI.

First I had to locate the right warehouse. I hadn't paid attention to the exact address. I knew it was old, fronted water and was on a part of the Brooklyn docks that was no longer in service. And I remembered a landmark from the satellite picture I'd seen: a big old metal water tower with a picture of a brand of candy that I remembered eating when I was a kid.

❖

If I could find the tower, I could find the warehouse and direct the FBI to it.

Of course, there's always a snake in every paradise that seems to slither around just when you think you have a situation figured out.

In this case, that snake was a cold-blooded killer named Stocker.

50

❖

Coby stared at his partners in crime gathered on the aft deck after Gywn reported seeing Madison drive away in the car.

"Let's go down the list of alternatives." He flicked the first off his forefinger as he spoke. "One, she's just out for a joyride and will be back later."

"No way," Gwyn said almost immediately. "She looked like a criminal fleeing the scene of a crime when she saw me."

"Or two, she's running out on us. She's scared, panicked, running blind, or is leaving for parts unknown."

"Or all of the above?" Gwyn asked.

"I don't think she's running. Not blindly at least. She's too methodical, too organized. She knows she won't be able to clear herself until she can get the Iraqi pieces into the hands of the feds." He shook his head. "That means she's done absolutely the worst possible thing."

"Called the cops."

"Maybe. Rob, can we get a real-time satellite picture on the warehouse?"

The group gathered around the computer screen.

❖

"It's too far up and too vague to see a person," Gwyn said. "Cars are little bigger than a dot."

"It's not too far up to tell us that there aren't a dozen police cars at the warehouse. Can we get any closer?"

"Nope. If you were an NSA operative, they could get you close enough to read the license plate on that car."

"It's that car I'd like to see better. The speck moving on the street in front of the warehouse."

"It might be gray," Gwyn said, "just like the company car. But so are a million other cars in the city."

"But not all the others are moving back and forth in front of that warehouse. Look, that's the third time it's gone down the street."

Coby stood up. "I know what she's doing. The same thing she did in Málaga when she checked out the boathouse. She wants to make sure the stuff's in the warehouse and then call in the feds."

"Stocker's in the warehouse."

"Yeah, with cutting-edge surveillance equipment. He always was a nut on gadgets. He has to know that she's driven by several times."

"What should we do?" Gwyn asked.

"We have two choices. Abandon the millions of dollars in merchandise we risked our lives for in Baghdad . . . or hope we can pull the stuff out before the feds get there."

"And Madison?" Gwyn said. "What if it becomes a choice between the girl or the money?"

"Hell, that's a no-brainer. I can get another girlfriend."

As they broke up, Gwyn nudged Coby in the ribs. "You can sell that shit to the others, but not to me. You want to get in and save her from Stocker."

Coby grinned. "Let's just say that the money *and* the girl would be the best scenario. Let's try calling her and see if she answers."

51

❖

My cell phone rang and I leaned closer to see the incoming number.

Coby.

I ignored it as I drove by warehouses on the Brooklyn waterfront. I was tempted to answer the phone and warn Coby they ought to make a run for it because I was going to call the police as soon as I located the hoard, but I decided to ignore the call. If I didn't locate the hoard, I'd have to return to the yacht and pretend I had just gone for a ride.

Driving by several brick warehouses on Brooklyn's East River waterfront, I came across a good candidate for the storage area of the antiquities.

Caffrey Wholesale Regulator Company was barely visible on a sign arched over big metal barn doors guarding the front entrance of a wharf warehouse.

I drove by slowly, hoping to appear nonchalant as I did. Finding the water tower advertising a brand of candy from yesteryear was infinitely easier than finding the right warehouse. I'd only gotten a glance at the picture Coby had obtained over the Internet. And things looked different

❖

from ground level than from a picture taken by a satellite circling the Earth. I was certain I was in the right area, an access road along blocks of warehouses.

The Caffrey warehouse had a couple things going for it. Being abandoned topped the list. Every building on the street was waiting for a wrecker's ball and an enterprising slumlord to turn it into high-end artsy "factory" condos with twenty-foot ceilings and exposed plumbing, but only one appeared unoccupied. I got a closer look at that one because it didn't have a tall wall surrounding it.

I drove by the surmised warehouse several times, because I only had a clear view of the second story.

Decades of abuse by the elements had left the place with broken windows and rust stains on just about everything metal. The building itself appeared sturdy, built in the days when labor and materials were cheaper. All the outside trim, stairways, and doors that I could see, even the window trim, were metal. Building warehouses battleship style with brick and steel was a technique from another era. The brick was blackened from the days of coal and acid rain.

"Perfect," I said aloud. Brick and steel would be my choice for storing priceless antiquities.

Night was rapidly falling and I needed to make a decision whether to call in the FBI. Not that I planned to be around when they arrived. I'd make the call as I was leaving the city. But time was of the essence. Stocker could be moving the stuff—or already have moved it. By now he might know Neal had ratted on him.

What if the police were watching the warehouse just as they had been watching Lipton's when I walked in? I'd really be screwed—caught red-handed. Panic gripped me, taking away my breath. The only way to cover myself was to let Nunes know I was here to locate the stuff for him.

I sat in the car and stared at the cell phone mounted on the dashboard. I vacillated back and forth. *Should I or shouldn't I call Nunes?* I was sure the Caffrey warehouse was the right place.

I pushed the scroll button and hit send when Nunes's number came up. He answered on the first ring.

"This is Nunes."

❖

I started to say something, but nothing came out. I was tongue-tied.

"I recognize the number," Nunes said, breaking the silence. "Where are you, Ms. Dupre?"

Shit!

"I'm going to find the stuff that was stolen." I blurted it out and hit the disconnect key. *Sonofabitch.* I hoped I hung up before he could have traced the call, but I had no idea what kind of electronic wizardry the FBI might have up its sleeve.

Stupid. Why didn't I check out the warehouse first to make sure it was the place, then get away and call him from the freeway? Now I had to move fast to make sure I was right.

Caffrey's old warehouse pinged with me, but I had to be a hundred percent sure. My freedom—hell, my life—depended on it.

The only way I'd get a good enough look to risk calling Nunes back was to walk up to the big double gate for vehicles and look through the crack where the two barn door–size gate-doors met. A small door for walk-in entry was to the left.

After driving by the warehouse repeatedly, I decided it was time to put up or shut up. I made one more pass and then drove down a block and around the corner and parked in front of a warehouse that had been converted into self-storage units.

I got out and walked back to the warehouse. Ominous dark clouds were hurrying nightfall. I quickened my pace.

I bent over and peered through the big crack at the gates. All I saw of significance through the narrow slit was another set of rusty barn-size metal doors, these leading into the warehouse itself, and a set of rusty iron steps that led up from the side of the building.

None of the pieces from the Iraqi museum were lying about advertising themselves, but the solid old building seemed perfect for storing the stuff. An empty wooden frame on the wall was the same as the one down the street holding a For Rent sign. The place must have been rented, but I couldn't detect business activity.

Not much to bet my life on, but my gut was telling me this was the place where the pieces were stored.

I wondered if I could see more by opening the people-size door to my left. I moved over to it and tried the handle. It turned easily in my hand.

❖

THE LOOTERS

The rusty hinges squeaked as I pushed the door open. I stuck my head in and saw the movement out of the corner of my eye.

A hand grabbed my hair and jerked me inside as another hand came up to smother my scream.

❖

52

❖

Nunes called FBI technical support immediately after Madison Dupre hung up. He gave the cell number and time of call to a communications tech.

"Can you find this cell phone?"

Nunes stayed on the line while the tech checked the number with the carrier. Two common ways were used to locate a cell phone.

Many phone companies were equipping their cell phones with GPS chips. If Madison's phone had a GPS chip, the phone's exact location could be tracked by satellite.

Another method was by triangulation: tracing a signal from the phone as it registered at communications towers. When a cell phone was on, it periodically signaled its location to phone company communications towers. By measuring direction and power of the signal to towers, an approximate location of the phone could be determined.

GPS tracking was fast. Triangulation was much slower and its accuracy depended on how many towers were getting the signals and the strength and direction of the signals. Sometimes police choppers and vehicles on the ground with tracking equipment had to be employed to complete the triangulation.

❖

GPS especially was important because many 911 calls came in by cell phone, sometimes by a person held prisoner in the trunk of a moving car.

Nunes had once worked on a case where the FBI tech support helped pinpoint where a suspect was at the time of a shooting. The suspect had made a Mafia hit and almost immediately used his cell phone. Through triangulation, the techs were able to locate down to a few feet where the killer was standing when he made the call.

One famous cell phone tracking case involved a Unibomber suspect who was tracked to Nevada even though his phone service provider company was back east. Because his phone was on when he arrived in Las Vegas, the phone sent a message to Vegas communications towers that was transmitted back to the carrier.

The tech came back on the line. "She has a GPS chip. She's in Brooklyn. I've got the address."

Nunes took down the address and hung up. His instincts told him that something big was up. His partner was out interviewing a lead. Nunes grabbed another agent and got to his car.

He thought about calling Madison Dupre back but resisted the impulse. It would only bring her cell phone link to the FBI to her attention, and she might shut the phone off.

He was puzzled about what she was up to now.

At least she was still alive.

❖

53

❖

The hand that smothered my scream gripped my throat and lifted me off my feet.

"Make a sound and you're dead."

He put me back onto my feet. Still clutching a handful of my hair, he pushed the door shut.

Gripped by fear, I stared at this ferocious-looking man. He was big, bigger than Coby, football player big. Hockey player mean. A skinhead with a two-day black beard and a square jaw, thick eyebrows, and fat lips. What I really noticed was his eyes, eyes that were wild, like those of a feral animal. He had an unkempt look that reminded me of coyotes I'd seen in the Southwest.

I saw him as a vile human being, someone who got pleasure from hurting people and who would kill with no remorse or hesitation. I already knew his trail of bloody murder. "Meaner than a junkyard dog," was the old expression about people with vicious personalities. That's who had me by the hair—a big, mean man with the cruel temperament of a rabid pit bull.

He jerked my head back and I let out an involuntary yelp of pain.

❖

"Listen, you fuckin' cunt."

His breath stank of rotten meat.

"You make a fuckin' sound and I'll kill you." He jabbed the end of a pistol barrel under my throat. It hurt. "I can pump your ass full of lead and no one will hear with the silencer on."

He took the gun away from my throat and shoved me forward with the hand on my hair. "What happened to Neal?"

I shook my head. "I don't know—"

He slapped me hard with his palm. He had the gun in his right hand and hit me with his left. I saw a burst of stars and hit the ground. Grabbing a handful of my hair, he jerked me back to my feet.

"Next time you say something I don't like, I'll shoot off a kneecap. And I'll keep on shooting off pieces until you're a fuckin' quad. You understand, bitch?"

I nodded my head that I understood. My teeth ached. The side of my face burned. He was crazy and mean enough to kill me after he got answers to his questions.

"Are the police coming?"

"No."

He raised his hand to hit me.

"It's the truth. I never gave the address to anyone." That was true.

"What happened to Neal?"

"He—he was hurt by Coby and the others. They did things to make him talk."

Stocker grinned. "My pals don't take prisoners. And neither do I. Where are the others? Why'd you come alone?"

I answered honestly, because I was sure that anything that didn't ring true would set off this nut. "I was afraid they wouldn't turn the antiquities back to the Iraqis. They're probably looking for me right now. They'll figure out I came here."

His grin widened. "I hope they do. A little birdie told me they're going to come. I have a couple surprises for them. I have the whole dock booby-trapped. I'll be out of here in another hour. Then the place will go sky-high when my old buddies arrive."

He hadn't moved the antiquities. The fact that he was still around meant the pieces were still here. Why did he stay here if he knew the

❖

SEALs were coming? And then it hit me: He wanted to attract them. He needed to kill them. Why not have them come here to make it easier? Someone had tipped him off. I wondered who in the group was in on it with Stocker.

He gave me a shove. "Get your ass over there, up the stairs."

Up the stairs meant going into the warehouse, where my screams wouldn't be heard.

"Are you going to kill me?"

"Hell, no. Your pals are going to." He roared with laughter.

As I walked toward the stairs I saw the front end of a truck through the partially opened large doors into the warehouse. It looked like a rental truck. He was loading up the goods.

I also understood that now he was through with me. He had his answers. He'd either kill me or leave me as some sort of macabre bait to lure the SEALs and set off his surprise.

54

❖

Nunes leaned back in the passenger seat as he rode to the Brooklyn warehouse area in a Bureau SUV with emergency lights flashing. Special Agent Sarah Jones, his partner for the moment, was driving. He got another call from tech support.

"We've been studying satellite pictures of the location," the tech said. "We've pinned down the car we believe the phone is in. It's parked in front of a self-storage complex near the Brooklyn waterline. How would that fit into your estimation of where your suspect could be?"

"It fits perfectly. Are you certain it's the right car?"

"Satellite imaging shows the car parked in front of the storage complex. There are no other cars parked close enough to be candidates for the signal. And there are no pedestrians. It's after hours on the weekend and there's not much vehicle traffic. Factor in that the signal is not moving and neither is the car and it makes us pretty certain the phone's in the car, a late-model silver BMW."

"No pedestrians. Any imaging of people at all in the area?"

"No warm bodies, just an occasional car passing by. We haven't picked up any foot traffic at all around the storage facility."

Nunes broadcast that the mission was a "go" to other units who were

❖

converging on the location. He had a chopper standing by, but it wasn't time to call it in yet. The same went for other ground units. They would approach the area but stay a couple blocks away until Nunes gave the signal.

The fact that a storage facility might be involved made perfect sense. It was common practice for thieves and drug traffickers to rent self-storage units because of the privacy they provided.

He was excited. Putting in a call to his superior, he set the stage for issuance of a warrant. Once they secured the facility and anyone in it, they would need a piece of paper from a judge to start searching.

"Won't be long before we'll be kicking in a storeroom full of antiquities," Nunes said. He loved art. Recovering it from thieves was like rescuing babies to him.

55

❖

When we got to the bottom of the stairwell, I hesitated. A metal door at the top showing rust and ages-old residue of green paint was open a crack. Once that door closed behind me, I'd be a prisoner with no chance of escape.

He shoved me. "Get your ass moving."

I took the steps one at a time, my knees ready to fold, my heart pounding as waves of panic rose from my stomach and up my throat. If I had to die, I wanted to make him kill me in the open, where someone might hear or see it. When that door closed with just the two of us behind brick walls, God only knew what this crazy bastard would do.

I had my own weapon that was good for one long shot—the pepper spray ring that I wore on my right forefinger. I'd worn it so long, I'd forgotten about it. It looked like a ring but had a charge of highly potent defense spray. When a safety lock was released and a button pushed, the spray came out. If it hit the assailant in the eye, it was very debilitating. At least that's what the brochure claimed.

I'd have to spray him in the eyes to have any effect. If it didn't hit perfectly, he'd grab me and hang on, even if he was hurting. Or shoot me in the back before I reached the door at the top of the stairs. No way could I go back down the stairs even if I got lucky with the spray. He was too big to get by.

"Move it, bitch." He gave me another shove.

I fell forward and he grabbed me again by the back of my shirt and jerked me up. As I came erect, my right hand flew up and back. I released the safety catch on the pepper spray with my thumb and pressed the button. A spray hit him in the face, and he gave a startled cry. He released his hold on me, and my feet flew up the steps two at a time. Behind me he howled with pain and rage. I heard the pop of the pistol firing as bullets smacked the railing and building. I didn't look behind to see if he was aiming at me or firing blindly. I focused on the door that was cracked open.

"I'm going to kill you, you fuckin' whore!"

The door had been propped open by a small piece of wood. I slipped in and kicked the wood away and shut the door.

I was in total darkness except for a slit of light coming through a tiny window in the corner. It appeared to be some sort of storage room. I moved away from the metal door slowly, using my hand to guide me along the wall, feeling for any obstacles in my way.

I didn't know if his bullets would breach the door or even if the door was locked from the outside. I just assumed it would lock when shut because he had it propped open. Now he pounded on the door. I moved farther away from the door as bullets impacted it. More banging, like he was kicking it and throwing his shoulder against it with all that thug weight. The big bastard was sure to break through.

I dead-ended against a corner and felt another door frame. I found the handle. It turned. I slipped through just as Stocker smashed the other door open. Slamming the door behind me, I found myself in a mezzanine-like area. Below me was an open loading area. The rental truck I'd seen from the outside was there. Above was another floor. Like the one I was on, it wasn't a full floor. The ceiling was glass, some of it broken, all of it dirty, but letting in enough light from the full moon outside for me to run as fast as I could down the corridor.

I stepped through an open doorway and into another room. I leaned up against the wall just inside the doorway and tried to control my breathing.

"I'm coming for you, bitch. You can't hide from me."

His voice didn't sound as threatening as it had before. I hoped I had blinded the bastard and scorched his lungs. The spray was guaranteed to be powerful enough to put a man down for half an hour, but the manufacturers didn't have two-legged beasts in mind when they provided its assurance.

His footsteps were going the other direction. I was sure of it. But I still wanted to poke my head out and see. For that I had to reach deep down and grab a handful of courage.

I knelt and edged closer to the doorway. Why I thought I would be less visible if I was kneeling when I peeked around the corner was a mystery even to me.

Damn!

I had been wrong about his direction. His back was to me and he spun around the moment I stuck my head out. His face was red, his eyes puffy. His features were crazed. Really crazed. Mad dog demented.

I wasn't sure if he actually saw me or like a bloodthirsty primeval beast he just instinctively knew I was there. He immediately started jabbering and pulled the trigger on his pistol as I pulled my head back. Instead of the familiar popping of the gun, this time I heard a more mechanical sound. *Was his gun empty?*

The room I was crouching in didn't have enough light for me to see if there was another exit, so I took the only other option—I dashed into the hallway and ran for a stairway down that was only four or five steps away.

They were the longest steps of my life.

I didn't know if he was busy reloading or what. I wasn't about to look back. I just ran like hell and flew down the steps, nearly taking a headfirst tumble.

I was on the same level as the rental truck. I jumped onto the running board on the passenger side to see if the keys were in the ignition. As I looked through the open window, my heart fell. No keys. I jumped back off.

Stocker was lumbering down the steps. His face was bloodred and swollen, but I knew he could see me now because he looked in my direction. He had his gun in his hand but didn't aim at me. *He has to be out of bullets.* It didn't matter. He could rip me to pieces with his hands.

I ran for the closest open door and into a room that was lighted.

❖

Sonofabitch!

I stared in disbelief at a small room with a sleeping bag and some personal effects. *And no way out.*

Next to an open duffel bag that was beside the sleeping bag was a gun, a pistol that looked like the one that Stocker had been firing. I grabbed the gun and also swooped up a set of keys with the truck rental tag on the ring. I squeezed the keys in my left palm as I got one hand and half the key-holding hand around the gun handle.

Stocker came up to the door. I had a closer look at him now. His face was a stinking mess. It looked like he'd stuck it in a meat grinder. Half-blind, he tried to bring me into focus. He didn't have a gun in his hand. He must have discarded it, empty.

"Leave me alone!" I screamed.

I pointed the gun point-blank at his chest.

"Fucking stupid bitch. You have to turn off the safety latch."

I knew zero about guns. I stared at the gun in my hands in horror. During that second he lunged at me.

I staggered back and threw the gun at him. It bounced off his chest. As he reached down to get it, I shot by him and ran for the truck.

I heard his sobbing rage as he came out of the room.

"Die, bitch!"

The familiar shots popped again. Luckily, no bullets ripped into my back. I jumped up on the driver's side running board and didn't look back until I had grabbed the handle. The shots I heard weren't aimed at me. Stocker was crouched down and firing his pistol in the other direction.

"Throw it down; we've got you covered," I heard Coby shout.

I jerked open the truck door and climbed inside.

Stocker made a reply, but I didn't hear it. Fumbling with the keys, I finally managed to get the right key into the ignition and turn on the engine.

Shit. The truck had a stick shift. One of those old-fashioned gear-shifting things that came out of the floor. And a clutch. I hadn't driven a clutch since I ran my junior high boyfriend's VW Bug into the rear of my dad's car.

I pushed the clutch to the floor and jerked around the long gearshift

❖

stick and let out the clutch to the sound of grinding gears. The truck suddenly shot forward. *Thank God.*

A loud bang came from the passenger side. I saw the hand first and then the gun. Stocker had pulled himself up until he could stare at me through the open window. His left eye was swollen closed, and he glared insanely at me like a crazed Cyclops.

He leveled the gun at my face.

I stared in stunned awe—not at the gun but at the gates coming up. Something about my face must have triggered an automatic response by him, because instead of shooting me he turned his head and saw the big metal gates.

The truck burst through the gates with a bang I was sure could be heard all the way to Jersey. Stocker disappeared. He wasn't there after the truck swept through, smashing the gates aside.

The building across the street suddenly loomed in front of me. I twisted the wheel with both hands, turning the truck, feeling the weight shift and the truck lean as if it was going over.

My foot left the gas to hit the brake. I pressed hard on it and the truck started sputtering and jerking toward a stop. I instinctively pushed the clutch back in and hit the gas and popped the clutch. The truck lurched forward and I pushed the pedal to the floor, heading in the direction of where I had parked my car.

I glanced out the side window, wondering what had happened to the one-eyed beast.

56

❖

Special Agent Sarah Jones turned the agency sedan onto the street paralleling the wharfs. She turned off the emergency lights. Nunes, riding shotgun, had been deep in thought and humming for several minutes.

Nunes stopped humming. "I remember this area when I was a kid," he said. "My old man worked at a machine shop that made parts for subway cars. In those days they called this street the Red Brick Road. You know, after the Yellow Brick Road."

"Because of all the brick warehouses?"

"Clever deduction Watson. You should have been a detective."

"Yeah. And did you know that you always hum when you're deep in thought?"

"Did you know that you're about the hundredth person to tell me that?"

"You're thinking about the Dupre woman. Let's see, she left behind a mess in London and one in Spain. You're wondering what kind of mess we're going to run into now. She's not very lucky, is she?"

"I'm thinking about how unpredictable she is. You never know when or where she'll show up. And you're right—I have to wonder what surprise

❖

she'll have in store for us today. So far she's been batting a thousand for leaving chaos wherever she goes."

He looked at the GPS monitor on the dashboard. "We're coming up to the car with the cell phone in it. Let's just do a pass and cruise by first."

They went by the car, both of them pretending not to look but both giving it a quick once-over.

Agent Jones kept a steady speed as she passed by the car. Trying to get a sideways look at the car, she wasn't paying attention to the road in front of them. She didn't see the truck coming around the corner until it was almost upon them.

"*Whaaaa—,*" was all Nunes got out before the two vehicles met head-on and an air bag exploded in his face.

LOW-TECH MULTIMILLION-DOLLAR ART THEFTS
(Why It's Easier to Rob Museums Than Banks)

The $55 million Cellini Salt Cellar was stolen in Vienna in 2003 by a thief who broke in through a first floor window and smashed the glass display case housing the piece. The museum had over a hundred security cameras, but none were able to record at night. The thief tripped sound and motion detectors, but security guards turned off the alarm under the belief that it was a false alarm.

Klimt's *Portrait of a Woman* was stolen in Italy in 1997 by a thief who got in through a skylight, then used a fishing rod to hook and reel up the picture. The picture was valued at $20 million.

Thieves with a ladder, large piece of cloth, and rope broke into Amsterdam's Van Gogh Museum and made off with two Van Goghs that ranked with the most valuable and carefully guarded art pieces on earth. In the 2002 theft, the thieves got by cameras, alarms, motion sensors, and twenty-four-hour security guards by leaning a ladder against the back of the museum and getting in from the roof. They lifted the two small paintings off the wall, broke a side window, and scaled down the wall with a rope.

In 1999, thieves cut a hole in a skylight, dropped a smoke bomb to cloud the cameras, and took a Cézanne painting from an Oxford, England, museum.

Munch's *The Scream,* valued at over $50 million, was stolen in 1994 from the National Gallery in Oslo in less than a minute. The thieves used a ladder to break a window, stole the painting, and left. Video cameras recorded the theft. The thieves left a note thanking the museum for its poor security.

The biggest art theft in history (besides the looting of the Iraqi museum) was extremely low-tech. The $300 million robbery of the Gardner Museum in Boston in 1990 occurred when two thieves dressed as police officers came to the museum door and convinced a security guard to let them enter.

❖

57

❖

The FBI interrogation room was a step above in décor from the NYPD room where I had been questioned. The paint was fresher, the table less stained from God-knows-what, the chairs more comfortable. I'm sure the hidden cameras were even more focused. And, of course, the interrogation was no less intimidating.

Twenty-four hours had passed since I escaped from the warehouse and ran into an FBI car. Literally. I'd gotten little sleep since then and was too worn-out to be nervous. I was just plain dead tired. Beat. Mentally trashed.

Having the bigger vehicle, I survived the accident with just a powder dusting from an exploding air bag and wide-eyed fright. But FBI Special Agent Nunes was in a particularly foul mood. Not that I blamed him. He looked like he'd been punched in the face—his nose was red and swollen, his eyes black. Well . . . he *had* been punched in the face.

I was lucky that serious injuries from air bags were rare. As it was, he wasn't happy with the near-death experience. He had interrupted his questioning of me earlier to comment on the accident.

"I've shot it out with killers on the street without fear. But I saw my own death when you came around the corner in that big truck."

❖

I almost laughed at his melodramatics yet managed to keep my humor suppressed and my facial expression completely sympathetic. My father would've told me never to annoy an angry man who had a badge and a gun.

Special Agent Jones, to my surprise, had escaped unscathed. As she glared at me with sleepy eyes, I realized that she wasn't overly happy with me, either. I suppose a wrecked federal agency car entailed preparing a mountain of paperwork.

Having recovered a truckload of Iraqi museum pieces in the process had not completely endeared me to them. When I asked for some credit, Nunes said, "You've left a trail of death and destruction on two continents. The fact that I'm listed only as wounded on the casualty list is nothing short of a miracle."

I needed a miracle, too. It occurred to me that just maybe he would have been in a better mood if the FBI had recovered the hoard rather than a 125-pound—give or take a few—woman with no gun.

"Why won't you believe me when I tell you that I am completely innocent?" I asked.

"Why won't you tell the truth?"

Good question. Actually, I had told him the truth. More or less. I left out a few details . . . like standing around while Neal got castrated. Nunes never asked me about Neal, so it was a certainty that Neal never reported it, at least not to the police. That was a relief, but I wondered what Neal told the ER people about how he lost a testicle. Not that it was hard to imagine why Neal wouldn't tell the authorities that he had been tortured to reveal where his partner in crime had millions of dollars in stolen antiquities stashed. And had left a few dead bodies lying about. As Coby pointed out, that kind of candor would put Neal in a prison cell really singing soprano.

Also, I had lied about one or two other things, particularly when I told Nunes that Stocker's partner, the man I had encountered in Málaga and who had helped me track Stocker to the New York warehouse, was Viktor Milan of Zurich. That fit with what I had told Nunes on the telephone from Málaga when I'd thought that Coby really was Milan. And I claimed complete ignorance about how this mysterious Swiss knew where the antiquities were hidden.

Actually, blaming Viktor Milan flowed smoothly off my tongue because

❖

it was essentially true. I left out that Milan was an alias for a guy named Coby Lewis and some treasure-hunting ex-SEALs.

Nunes bought the Viktor Milan connection, which wasn't surprising, since the name figured in the Semiramis controversy from the get-go. And I gave Nunes an accurate description of Coby, without volunteering Coby's real name . . . if that was his real name.

The accusation that I was lying went back to Nunes's theory that I had a working criminal relationship with Lipton and Milan. Nunes wanted to link me to the looting of the Iraqi museum and knowingly purchasing the stolen items for the Piedmont. That scenario came with several murder charges, because I would be part of a criminal conspiracy.

My outrage and cries of innocence were genuine when it came to the Lipton/Milan steal-sell-murder conspiracy.

"You keep insisting I was in on the theft with Lipton and this Milan person. That simply isn't true."

"You bought a number of items off of Lipton that came from the museum in Baghdad. You stocked the Piedmont's collection with dirty pieces."

"I bought a number of items that Lipton offered for sale . . . *with provenances*. So did a lot of other collectors and museums."

I didn't know how many others there were, but it was a sure thing Nunes didn't know, either, since no one knew exactly what had been stolen from the museum. "I had authorization to pay full value for each item. I'm sure you've had a chance to check my finances to find out that not only didn't I receive kickbacks, but I was living beyond my means."

I figured my best defense would be the bankruptcy I'd have to file to keep bill collectors from yapping at my heels. My expensive apartment, hot car, designer clothes—spending way beyond my means because I was always expecting them to expand—were my vindication. Who knew my financial ineptitude would finally pay off big?

"My only connection to the stolen museum pieces was my desperate attempt to recover them because I was being falsely accused of conspiring to steal them. The truckload of pieces I risked my life to recover was obviously from the museum heist, though you have no documentation to connect them."

I felt confident that Iraqi museum curators would identify them as belonging to the museum.

❖

"You've also never established that a single piece that I bought for the Piedmont came from that theft," I said, continuing my defense. "There are thousands of legal artifacts for sale every day around the world. I was in the business of acquiring pieces in a lawful manner. If Lipton sold me a stolen piece with a phony provenance, I was duped. But you haven't any proof even that occurred."

Nunes stared at me with a blank look on his face. He still didn't believe me. Or didn't want to believe me. A confession from me would wrap up so many loose ends for the Bureau.

From his point of view, the evidence was missing because my partners in crime had destroyed it. Stocker's London attack had torched any incriminating evidence Lipton had been sitting on. And Milan was a shadow figure who possessed nothing: no office, no filing cabinets full of incriminating records, no computer disks or hard drives, no evidence of a human body. I wondered if Nunes had figured out yet that Milan was just a name on paper.

I had no clue as to what was recovered at the warehouse or in the back of the truck along with the antiquities, and Stocker didn't strike me as a record keeper who would've kept a list of what had originally been stolen from the museum.

Nunes's dilemma was understandable. He was a good cop who was absolutely certain that every piece Lipton sold me came from the heist. In retrospect, Nunes was probably right. But all he had was burning suspicion, not proof, at least not yet. And that was my salvation. I kept hammering away at his lack of proof.

The law's all about the evidence, not the truth, the lawyer told me last time I was arrested. Innocent people are found guilty every day because of the way the evidence stacked up against them. Well, thank God it worked the other way, too.

"You've asked me a million questions," I said, trying to sound sincere. "May I ask you one thing?"

He rolled his eyes. "If your question is how do you get out of this mess, you can start by telling the truth."

"Don't I get any credit at all for battling a homicidal maniac and recovering national treasures that belong to the Iraqi museum?"

A thin crease in his lips left the impression of a sneer rather than a smile. "You have three things in your favor. The first is that you called me from Málaga and told me about the Viktor Milan connection. You're not that good of an actress to have faked being so scared."

"Thank you. It was frightening out there all alone doing the work of police officers on two continents."

"Perhaps if the police officers on two continents knew what you knew about the crimes, you wouldn't have had to be all alone. Anyway, the second thing is that you called me before you went into the warehouse. It did occur to me that had you found anything at the warehouse, you would've made yourself scarce before you called it in."

I kept a straight face. "The third?"

"Bullet holes indicating someone, presumably Stocker, had shot at you, and a gate smashed in making your escape. Agent Jones," he indicated with a nod to his head, "believes you're telling the truth about your daring rescue with the antiquities, hopping aboard that truck and crashing through that gate like a stunt driver."

The other agent's features were frozen as she struggled to keep her eyes open. None of us had gotten any sleep.

"And what do you think?" I looked him square in the eye.

"You're either the world's greatest liar or the luckiest woman on earth." He leaned forward. "I don't know which. I find it unimaginable that you walked into that warehouse bare-handed and fought a mad killer who was armed to the teeth. Ballistics is checking out bullets recovered at the scene. I'm betting there was another shooter."

"I told you that another person appeared. I didn't have time to stick around and get a good look at him. Maybe it was Viktor Milan."

"You know, I find this Milan guy a bit weird. Every time you need an alibi or an excuse for something, his name pops up." He sighed and pursed his lips. "If you hadn't called me before you went into that warehouse . . ."

He sounded as if he regretted that I had called him. I guess everything added up better if I was simply an accomplice.

"I wish the hell we'd gotten your pal Stocker. Scotland Yard would like him, too."

"He isn't my pal. My friends don't try to kill me. Why are you keeping me a prisoner when I should be getting a medal?"

"Ms. Dupre, before I'm through with you, I will make sure you get everything you deserve."

What a threat that was! I leaned back and closed my eyes. God, I was tired. I could have just laid my head on the table and passed out. My mind was groggy and my adrenaline level way down, sure reasons to make mistakes at a time when I was playing hardball for my freedom.

The door opened and someone handed Nunes a piece of paper. After reading it, he said, "Fingerprints taken from the truck and warehouse ID'd Stocker as a former Navy SEAL. Discharged for a personality disorder. From what we've seen so far, it's an understatement of his mental condition. What did he tell you about his Navy career?"

I groaned with frustration and disgust. "Special Agent Nunes, that's about the tenth time you've tried to get me to tell you things about Stocker that I don't know so you can prove your theory that I did know him. *I never met the man.* Unless you count him trying to kill me a couple of times. And those were done without a formal introduction.

"I don't know if I was targeted because he was following me . . . or because I was following him. But please listen. I didn't even know a creature like that existed until he came into Lipton's gallery to murder me and everyone else. I never ever spoke to the man, not before he grabbed me when I poked my head through the doorway at the warehouse."

I was so frustrated I could scream. And I showed it. I leaned across the table and locked eyes with Nunes. "Is that clear? Never, never, ever even spoke to him before he had tried to kill me a couple times. And he barely said anything at the warehouse. If there is anything that will hinder your investigation, it's trying to get to Stocker through me."

Nunes had obviously spent decades listening to people lie to him, so it was good that I wasn't lying about the most important thing: I was not involved with Stocker, Lipton, and the others in stealing, storing, and selling the antiquities.

I could tell from Nunes's body language that he was at least half-convinced that I was telling the truth. He had been much tougher in his questioning and attitude after he had picked me up fleeing Abdullah's apartment. It was a giant leap for him to believe that I had walked into the warehouse and wrestled the antiquities away from Stocker. It had been a giant leap for me, too. But it was the truth and nothing but.

Of course, if Coby hadn't made a sudden appearance, Stocker probably would have put a bullet in my back as I was running for the truck. That was the main reason I kept Coby's name out of it. That and the fact that my own feelings about Coby bordered on the sentimental or maybe something stronger.

What had happened to Stocker—and Coby, for that matter—after I burst out the gates was a mystery. For sure, they had plenty of time to get away, because Nunes was busy recovering from the crash, taking me into custody, and checking the truck. When Nunes opened a crate in the back of the truck and saw a museum piece, he knew he'd struck pay dirt.

"Look, I know it's hard to believe. All I really intended to do was check the warehouse a little closer to make sure the stuff was there before I called you. I got lucky with that pepper spray ring when I squirted Stocker right in the face. Otherwise I'd be dead. God was watching over me. It wasn't my time to die. Now can I go?"

Nunes edged forward, just inches from my face. "You're lying to me. And it will end up getting you life without parole."

I flinched back.

"Your passport is in the personal effects folder at the property desk with your purse. I'm keeping it," he said as he stood up.

"Keeping my passport? Why are you—wait, you're letting me go?"

He raised his eyebrows. "Of course. Your public awaits you. Word has gotten out about the recovery of the antiquities. A horde of news media people are waiting to interview you." He leaned forward and sneered. "You're a celebrity. Maybe as big as a talking political head or a reality show wife swapper. That TV host Cassie claims you used a secret code during an interview to signal her that you knew where the stolen Iraqi pieces were being held."

Oh my God.

He stretched and then grinned maliciously down at me. "Stocker's still out there. When he tries to kill you again, let us know."

Agent Jones opened her eyes wide and said, "He will try again; you know that. Is there anything you'd like to tell us before he does?"

"Yes. Find him before he finds me."

As Nunes walked me to the property desk, he said, "By the way. We're not putting a tail on you."

"Really." I didn't know what to say. Why was he telling me this?

"Takes too damn many assets in Manhattan to do a round-the-clock surveillance. Narrow, crowded streets, a million cars and taxis, subways, takes dozens of agents for a twenty-four/seven watch."

❖

"Uh, is there a reason why you're telling me this?"

"Yeah." He stared at me gravely. "I just wanted to let you know we won't be around when Stocker comes back for you."

That was the second time he brought up the subject. I think he was trying to tell me something: *Fess up before Stocker gets you.*

❖

58

❖

Freedom tasted good, even if it was a gloomy, chilly, and wet New York City night. I took several deep breaths, savoring air not polluted by suspicious fed agents and legions of criminals. God, I felt like proverbial roadkill: burned-out, bummed-out, and stressed-out.

No reception committee was waiting for me. The newspeople must have gotten tired and decided to go home. It took three hours to get released even after I agreed to give up my passport and not leave the city. I would have promised my firstborn in exchange for my freedom if Nunes had asked.

He didn't need to hold my passport to keep me in the country. I couldn't have fled far. I had my purse back with three hundred dollars in cash and less than a thousand left on my last viable credit card. And that was it. By New York standards, that was a couple nights in a moderately priced hotel and a few deli meals. After that, the homeless shelter.

Oh, for the days when a black American Express card was my passport to the haunts of the rich and famous and wannabes like me.

I had two theories why the FBI agents let me go, besides the fact that Nunes was just plain hurting after getting smacked in the face during

❖

his near-death experience. He looked like a man with a brave front who needed to go home, have a stiff shot and a warm bed.

He knew I needed money was my first theory. In his mind, the place I'd go for it was where I was secretly hoarding stolen antiquities or ill-gotten gains. That theory didn't conflict with his statement that I wouldn't be watched. But not physically watching me didn't mean he wasn't going to keep an eye on my bank account, credit card, cell phone, and Internet use, along with anything else that was easy to track electronically.

Once I had an infusion of money, he'd pick me up to sweat the source out of me. But I had fooled him on that one. I was broke and would stay that way short of winning the lottery.

The second hypothesis rang even truer and was more scarier: They let me go to see if they could flush out Stocker . . . the premise being, of course, that he would finish the job of killing me. And since they didn't have a watch on me, they'd have to sift through the bloody clues left at the murder scene—mine—and witness statements to find him. Either that or Nunes expected me to wrestle the big maniac to the ground, hogtie him, and drag him up the steps to the federal detention building.

With those charming thoughts, I shivered and pulled up the collar of my light jacket. The night was cold, dark, deserted. A description of what my life looked like, with the fires of hell awaiting if Stocker found me.

The Metropolitan Correctional Center (MCC) was located in lower Manhattan, adjacent to Foley Square and across the street from the federal courthouse. I knew a city police station wasn't far from here, which didn't exactly comfort me. Police stations were notorious for being high-crime areas because of the flow of undesirables in, out, and around them.

The area bustled with people in the daytime but was deserted after hours. Right now it was way after hours, about three in the morning. Like most big cities, the safest places to be were the ones with people crowded around. I was tempted to go to the police station and ask them to call me a taxi but decided not to press my luck. I might be on a Most Wanted List with them, too.

Dragging myself down the stairs and onto the dark street, I felt like Nunes looked—beaten. I needed a taxi to take me to a hotel where I could feel safe, not that anywhere was overly safe from a man who packed a rocket launcher like some people pack a laptop.

❖

Two taxis passed, both occupied. I had started walking in the direction of the police station when a taxi pulled up to the curve. I got in and told the driver to take me to Times Square, an area that was always flowing with people day and night and also had several hotels.

I was leery of going to my apartment. That crazy Stocker was capable of pulling up in front of the building and blowing it up with his rocket launcher. Besides, it was entirely possible that I had been locked out and everything inside repossessed by my creditors. My rent had been due over a week ago. In these days when credit card companies keep close tabs on people, everything not nailed down was probably already cleaned out. I'd find out tomorrow when I went to the apartment to get some clothes and look for jewelry or anything else I could hock or sell instantly.

To satisfy my paranoia I locked both back doors of the taxi, then leaned my head against the seat and closed my eyes.

My mind was swirling. I was on a merry-go-round whirling out of control and couldn't get off. Being back in the graces of the FBI (since the only Madison Dupre being held prisoner was my passport picture) was a great relief, though I would have felt safer in jail. Then I wouldn't have to worry about a crazed killer and double-crossed Navy SEALs out for revenge.

Too many problems to deal with all at the same time. Getting to a quiet place where I felt safe and could relax and think out solutions one at a time was a necessity.

I must have dozed off for a few minutes, because I jerked awake when the taxi took a sharp turn.

My heartbeat quickened when I looked out and realized we weren't on a major street anymore but had entered an alley.

"Where are we?"

"Detour," the driver said.

I hadn't paid too much attention to him earlier, but now I could see he had dark olive skin and spoke with a thick Middle Eastern type accent.

Something was wrong. "Let me out!"

The cabbie suddenly braked, pulling to a stop at the back of a building. The door locks went up and my door was jerked open. Another man with Middle Eastern features and wearing black clothes said, "Get out."

When I didn't move fast enough, he grabbed my arm and pulled me out.

I opened my mouth to scream, but he put a knife to my throat.

❖

59

❖

"Why are you doing this?" I hummed aloud, with no one around to hear me.

I was alone in a small bathroom furnished with a toilet, a sink, and a roll of toilet paper.

I sat on the toilet and worried about my fate.

The bathroom wasn't exactly on the cutting edge of technology or maintenance. The toilet paper holder was broken, and the paper sat on top of the tank lid. No towel or soap was present. The sink and toilet both needed a good scrubbing, an indication that the place had more men around than women.

I replayed what had happened after I'd been taken out of the taxi. I was hustled into the back of a building and into the bathroom. No one spoke to me. Comments between the men who forced me into the building were in a foreign language. I assumed the language was Arabic and the men were Iraqi.

My initial guess was that I was in the back of a Middle Eastern restaurant or grocery store, since my nostrils got a whiff of aromatic and pungent scents when we entered the building. I picked out the smells of garlic, mint, cinnamon, and maybe saffron.

❖

The more I thought about it as I sat on the toilet, the more I concluded that it wasn't a restaurant. No smell of cooked lamb and chicken. More likely this was one of those mama-papa stores that specialized in ethnic foods and spices.

Why they put me here was easy enough to figure out. It made a nice jail cell. Hardly big enough for someone to stand in—I could sit on the toilet and wash my hands in the sink if I wanted to—the cubbyhole had no window and a single door. That meant I couldn't escape and my screams wouldn't be heard. *They could chop me up in little pieces and flush me down the toilet.*

I really didn't think my predicament was funny. On the contrary, I was terrified but just too tired to show it. Nothing short of the door opening and a mangled, bleeding, homicidal Stocker grinning crookedly at me would get a rise from my weary bones.

Why I had been kidnapped was a mystery. The possibilities were endless and all had unhappy endings for me. My abductors were Iraqis, for sure, and they hadn't kidnapped me to thank me for recovering national treasures. The time-honored universal motives for crime were profit and revenge. Neither objective fared well for me. Did they think I had more of the museum pieces and could be persuaded to turn them over?

Were they friends of Abdullah out to avenge his death? Certainly the folkways of Middle Easterners were more in tune with avenging murder with biblical solutions than my own Middle America mores, which were limited to calling the cops and/or a lawyer.

It occurred to me that they might be Iraqi intelligence agents who believed I was involved in the museum looting and would torture me to find out where some of the other fourteen thousand or so missing pieces were. That unpleasant thought sounded plausible because the FBI could have advised them that they were pursuing a suspect in the case.

"No, not Iraqi cops," I told the closed door.

More likely they were thieves who wanted to get their hands on the pieces for profit. Unfortunately, I didn't know the whereabouts of any other missing antiquities. How long would they torture me before they realized I knew absolutely nothing?

I needed to tell them something so they wouldn't harm me. I could say there were pieces at my penthouse. They would need me, of course, to

❖

get them past the doorman. Then I'd start screaming and running the first chance I got.

Speaking of running, I hadn't even tried the door handle to see if it was locked. The door opened outward and had a slip bolt on the inside. It probably wasn't locked. Who would lock a bathroom door from the outside? But either they had it blocked from opening or, worse, one of the thugs was waiting for me to make a run for it.

I was too scared and weary to try to shoulder it open if it was blocked. So far they hadn't hurt me, just tight grips on my arms as two men led me into the building. I didn't want to push my luck.

Once they had shut the bathroom door, I heard muffled voices, but I hadn't heard anything for the past hour.

My only option was to sit on the toilet until someone decided to tell me why I had been kidnapped. Or someone had an urgent need to use the toilet.

My recent fall from grace with the world made me wonder if I was being punished for doing something bad in a past life. Something very bad. The sort of thing for which you get reborn as a worm in a cesspool in hell.

I finally heard voices and footsteps approaching. A spike of fear-generated adrenaline gave me enough energy to sit up straight as the footsteps approached my door.

The door opened and Coby stared at me. He didn't look happy. In fact, he looked dangerously pissed.

I raised my eyebrows. "Gotta go?" I don't know why I made that cute remark. Not the right time, considering his mood.

He sucked air. Staring down at me, his face grew a deep red. Violent red. As if he had been storing up anger and seeing me had turned it loose.

"I should break your fuckin' neck."

I pushed a strand of hair off my forehead. "I did it for you," I said in a calm voice. I was hoping to diffuse his angry mood.

His face just got redder. He wasn't in any mood for jokes. I decided it was time to talk my way out of being murdered.

"I needed to get the stolen pieces back to the Iraqis, and Stocker in jail, so I could go on with my life. I didn't think Neal told you the truth about where the pieces were stored. I went to the warehouse to see if the stuff was really there. And to see if we would be walking into a trap. All that talk about Stocker booby-trapping the place, it sounded like a war was going to erupt, and that the antiquities would also end up being casualties."

He noisily sucked in a deep breath. Breathing was good. He was ready to kill me. Taking those deep breaths told me he was trying to keep the temptation under control.

"You're lying. You called the feds to meet you there."

I held up my hand. "Stop. You're completely wrong."

He leaned down closer, still beet red. "Tell me it's just a fuckin' coincidence that the FBI agent on the case was on his way to the warehouse when you were leaving it."

I stood up, showing real indignation. If there was anything I loved doing, it was telling the truth. Especially a version that could be sold.

"*I did not tell the FBI about the warehouse.* Nunes tracked me there because of my cell phone. They didn't even know about the warehouse. The phone was in the car parked around the corner in front of a self-storage facility. They thought I was in the storage facility, that the stolen antiquities were stored there. They were driving by my car when I came around the corner in the truck and hit them head-on."

That gave him pause. "What did you tell them about us?"

"Enough of the truth to satisfy Nunes that I wasn't holding out on him. But I never mentioned your name or the names of the others. I said the man I dealt with was Viktor Milan." I tapped him on the chest with my finger. "That is absolutely the truth. Viktor Milan was the only name I gave."

"What about Neal?"

"Jesus, get real. You don't think I'd tell the police I was in the house when Neal got—"

"How do I know you're telling the truth?"

I held up my hand in an imitation of the way he gave pledges. "Scout's honor."

He bit his lower lip and stared at me. "You planned all along to give the pieces back to the Iraqis."

That amounted to an accusation that I had betrayed them. Of course, there was a problem with putting the blame on me for the feds getting the stolen antiquities: We had both agreed to give the pieces back. I was just the one who actually intended going through with it.

In my current circumstance, it didn't seem advisable to remind him

❖

that he was going to welsh on the agreement and keep the antiquities. But no one had ever accused me of keeping my mouth shut.

"We agreed the pieces were going back to the Iraqis. Coby, I want us to be free, you, me, your friends. Free of crimes, free of guilt, free of the police and that murdering bastard Stocker. The only way to do it was to see that the stolen pieces went home."

From the sour expression on his face I could see that truth, honor, justice, and the American Way weren't going to fly with him.

"We went into Baghdad with a war going on and risked our lives to steal antiquities worth tens of millions of dollars—"

"Preserve," I reminded him. "You were preserving them for humanity."

"I oughta kick your ass for what you did."

He didn't want to walk away empty-handed. So I threw him a bone. A big juicy one.

"There's just one more piece that has to be liberated."

"What are you talking about?"

"The biggest one of all. A small golden mask worth fifty-five million dollars. It's worth more than everything in that warehouse put together. And we can get it."

His breathing became more even. "How? The Piedmont has it."

"I know more about the museum than anyone. Hiram Piedmont is a pussycat compared to your pal Stocker. Getting the Semiramis from the museum will be child's play for the SEALs." I kissed him sweetly on the lips. "I also know the security system at the museum. I designed it."

He was starting to relax now.

"Naturally," I said, "our objective would be to, uh, recover the Semiramis in the name of the people of Iraq and return it to them."

His lips slowly spread into a smile. "Naturally."

Of course I didn't believe him. But that didn't matter, not at the moment, though it was inevitable the SEALs and I would lock horns over the Semiramis when I insisted it go back to Baghdad. By now I was more thoroughly convinced that the mask actually carried the curse it was reputed to have. The real question was whether that evil whore of Babylon would cut me off at the knees before I was able to return her.

Considering the history of that region for the past five or six thousand years, I had to wonder whether they even wanted the mask back.

❖

60

❖

I had guessed right that the bathroom was in a store that specialized in Middle Eastern foods. The owner, who turned out to be the man who had pulled me out of the taxi, had also been involved in the Iraqi museum heist with the SEALs.

"He'd prefer not to have an introduction," Coby told me as he led me out of the bathroom and back outside to a taxi.

The taxi driver, the same man who had helped kidnap me earlier, simply raised his eyebrows and gave a "I was just following orders" shrug when I got inside the cab. He showed zero remorse for aiding and abetting my kidnapping.

"No tip for you," I said.

He gave me a smug, cocky, I-put-one-over-on-you-bitch grin in the rearview mirror. If he had kept his glee to himself I wouldn't have opened my mouth, but I couldn't help myself. I had to get even with him.

As he pulled out onto the main street, I leaned forward and spoke in a confidential stage whisper. "Drive carefully. I'm being followed by FBI agents."

He slammed on his brakes. Brakes and tires screeched behind us.

Coby and I braced ourselves for the impact behind us.

❖

It never came.

We both got our breathing back with a gasp.

"That was pretty stupid," Coby said, not amused at my little stunt.

Stupid or not, the smug taxi driver was no longer grinning.

ONLY GWYN SEEMED TOTALLY forgiving when Coby brought me to their new hideout: the home of Gwyn's parents on Staten Island.

The unsuspecting parents of the Navy officer turned tomb raider were off sunning in Florida, unaware that their daughter was using their house to plan a museum heist.

The house had some unusual furnishings.

"My parents are retired schoolteachers," she told me. "They both have a long love of magic. In fact, they met at a show at the Magic Castle in Hollywood. When they retired from teaching, they launched a second career doing magic at birthday parties for people with too much money."

Their interest in magic was obvious: The house was loaded with stage props, including a black coffin used as a coffee table.

Gwyn patted the coffin. "An old friend. I got cut in half in it when I was nine. At eleven they buried me alive."

The scary part is that I believed her.

Maybe it was better that her parents weren't home.

At the house of magic, I showered and slept for ten hours. When I came into the kitchen where the group was gathered at the table, I got a cool greeting. Only Gwyn was pleasant. Coby had earlier vacillated between forgiveness and homicidal tendencies toward me. Mostly the latter.

I was almost tempted to remind them that we had all agreed the Iraqi loot was to go back to the museum and I had accomplished the task without risking their lives . . . yet we all knew they never intended to go through with their promise. They were lying to me, and I was lying that I believed them. But I knew how to keep my mouth shut, at least most of the time. I was seriously pissed that they were the injured parties when I was the one who was nearly murdered, not to mention almost getting killed in a head-on collision, being arrested, and having my passport locked up in the federal jail.

These were the bastards who started the whole mess by robbing a museum. I deserved a little sympathy from them. Not to mention an apology for completely screwing up my life.

As I poured cream in my coffee, the more I thought about their attitude, the more aggravated I got. I said, "Isn't it wonderful that the Iraqis will be getting back their priceless cultural treasures?"

Bad move. I could see they had no sense of humor about the loss of priceless antiquities from the biggest museum heist since Genghis Khan or Attila the Hun or whoever sacked nations.

"You did it behind our backs," Rob said.

You bet, you jerk. That was the only way I could do it and walk away with the pieces and my head intact.

I kept those retorts silent and leaned against the wall as I sipped my coffee and smiled at them. I would've loved to turn the whole bunch of them in to the authorities. Except for Gwyn, who seemed to be nice to me, and Coby, whom I had mixed feelings about.

I forced a smile at the bastards who had ruined my life. "Can't trust anyone today, can you? No honor among thieves, eh?"

My humor fell flat. Again.

A dark look from Coby told me to put a lid on it. "Tell us about the security at the Piedmont," he said.

A laptop was up and running in front of him.

"Security is state-of-the-art because the museum's new. It's also not very large, so security doesn't have to be too complicated or heavily staffed. There's only one guard on at night, but that's all they need. All windows and doors are hardwired to the system. Motion detectors are in every hallway. The area that has the mask displayed is especially monitored. All significant pieces, like the mask, have RFID tags that trigger an alarm if they are moved outside a certain range, which is usually just a few feet. A hidden camera is directly above the mask, and its image is displayed on a separate monitor in the security room. Motion detectors crisscross each other all around the display."

Gwyn whistled. "Tight security."

I shook my head. "You don't display a fifty-five-million-dollar item small enough to fit into a purse without security backup. The rest of the museum is pretty well covered, too. Surveillance cameras watch every square foot of the display areas. The cameras have high-quality night resolution even though the display areas are illuminated with low light

❖

during the night. Naturally there's a backup battery system for every-thing and anti-tampering devices that go off if you mess with the alarm. You can't cut security system wires or turn off power without setting off the alarm. Breathing too hard in the museum at night would probably set off the alarms."

"But there's only one guard at night?" Coby asked.

"Only one, but he has camera and sound monitoring for the entire museum. He can have a hundred cops there in minutes. He sits in a heavy-armored, impregnable room. He doesn't have to keep an eye on every monitor because once the museum is shut down for the night a sig-nal goes off in the security room if any change occurs in the image a cam-era is on."

I was proud of the museum's sophisticated security. But right now I wished I had been a little more wishy-washy about protecting the collec-tion.

"What about the basement?"

That one threw me. I raised my eyebrows. "It's big. It covers the en-tire footprint of the museum, but there's nothing down there except stor-age shelves and a workshop for cleaning and repairing museum pieces."

"Any security devices?"

"No, it doesn't need it. There's no outside access to the basement. The only way you can get down there is from the stairway and elevator on the main floor."

"What's the security for the elevator?" Gwyn asked.

"There are two. The one that serves the public goes from the main floor to the second floor. It has a security camera and attic access only with a card key. The elevator shaft also has a security camera and a mo-tion detector that's turned on in the evening after the museum closes."

"The other elevator? Down to the basement?" Coby asked.

"Only goes between the first floor and the basement. There's no pub-lic access to it."

"And no security," Gwyn said.

"No. Like I said, there's no outside basement access. And there's nothing of value down there unless someone working on a piece has left it down there overnight. It's the safest part of the museum."

"Not if you're a mole," Coby said.

It took me a second to remember what a mole was: a little creature that burrowed in gardens. "I'm afraid your hairy little friends don't have teeth or claws sharp enough to go through concrete walls that are a foot thick."

"I wasn't talking about that kind of mole but the mechanical ones that dig tunnels."

I got his drift. "You're thinking about coming in through the basement?"

"The thought has occurred to us."

I shook my head in wonder. These people were amazing. And tech crazy. "I don't know what good it would do. Or how you would manage it. But even if you did, the Semiramis is on the first floor."

Gwyn said, "The basement elevator shaft isn't secured. That makes it a no-brainer to get to the first floor without detection. Then all we have to worry about is getting from the elevator to the Semiramis display."

"Why go upstairs for it?" Rob asked. "Let's have them bring the mask down to the basement."

I smiled tolerantly. "Ah, great idea. We can call them and tell them to take the Semiramis down to the basement so we can steal it."

"Very funny," he sneered. "You said they take things to the basement to clean or repair. Attacks on art by nutcases are getting more and more common. One of us goes in dressed as a derelict, hits the mask with some spray paint, and presto! Next thing you know the mask is in the basement, waiting for us to eat through the wall."

"Where we can get it without tripping alarms," Coby said. "Sounds like a plan to me."

"I'm still lost," I said to Coby. "How do you plan to get into the basement?"

"You probably don't realize that Manhattan and the rest of the city have thousands of miles of tunnels under them. Unless you're going down the stairs to a subway or the basement in a building, you never go below street level. But the subways and basements are just part of a big world beneath the city."

"I never even thought about that."

"Every building has water, electricity, and telephone in and sewage out. Where do you think all those pipes and wires come from? They come to you through tunnels under the city. And much of it has to be big enough so crews can go down and do repairs. Water and sewer pipes especially require a big capacity. There are water and sewer tunnels down there you can drive cars through.

"Hell, hundreds of feet down they're building a water tunnel large enough to drive a *big rig* through. It's being dug by a huge machine, a big, round cylinder with a cutter in front that cuts through rock and dirt and feeds the stuff through itself to the rear where it's hauled out. They call it the Mole and the guys who work down there are sandhogs. It's the same kind of machine that bored the tunnel under the English Channel."

"You're planning to do . . . what? Hijack this giant machine and bore your way into the museum?"

"We won't use the Mole this time; that was an idea we just played around with. This time we'll use something smaller."

"What does that mean?"

"There are boring machines that can cut a tunnel a couple feet wide. When we planned a heist of the Met, we were going to use a tunnel borer not much bigger than a torpedo. It makes a hole big enough for a man to squirm down."

I gaped. "You were going to rob the Met? The country's premier museum? Are you all completely insane? Can you imagine the worldwide manhunt that would be launched—"

Coby shook his head, grinning. "Hell no, we just played with the idea. After the Iraq museum job, we toyed with a heist of the Louvre, the Met, and the British Museum. Like playing a war game. We even worked out a method of stealing the *Mona Lisa*. It's been done before, you know."

"I know. But that was around a hundred years ago. I'm sure the French have instituted a bit more security for it since then."

The painting had been taken by Vicenzo Perugia, who claimed to be an Italian patriot. He simply took it off the wall, stuck it under his coat, and walked out. That was in 1911. Despite a giant reputation, it's actually a small painting done on wood rather than canvas. Two years later, he was caught trying to sell it in Italy.

"Don't be surprised if it's not that well protected," Gwyn said. "You'd be amazed at how low-tech the biggest museum robberies in history were."

Rob howled. "Yeah, all we did was pull a truck up to the back door and load it up in Baghdad."

"Stop your boasting," Coby said. "And Maddy, don't be surprised if

❖

that's not the real *Mona Lisa* hanging in the Louvre. There's good evidence that the thief destroyed the painting rather than let the French have it back. To keep a war from breaking out between France and Italy over the incident, the two governments had a reproduction made."

"And that's what's hanging in the Louvre? The fake?"

He gave me the Boy Scout sign. "The truth and nothing but."

Yeah, in a pig's eye. "Great conspiracy theory. Save it for when you get to Hollywood. Maybe you can connect up the JFK assassination and the murder of Marilyn Monroe."

"I'll put the sarcasm down to your ignorance. Anyway, we figured the best way to hit any of those museums was an entry underground. They all have high-tech security and human guards up the yin-yang, but it's mostly to protect against intruders at entry points. They're exposed below the surface because no one thinks of it. And when they do, they don't realize how easy it would be to get in that way."

He turned his laptop so she could see the screen. "We've downloaded the subterranean specs from all the water, sewage, and utility companies. This one is for the water system that goes by the Met and Piedmont."

"They just let you have these things?"

"They're not secret. Construction outfits need the charts when they're doing work." He grinned. "But we did pay a hacker to get them all, along with the location of every manhole in Manhattan. Do you know why manhole covers are always round?"

"Not a clue."

"So they can't fall into the hole. Square ones could slip in."

"That's very clever."

"You'd appreciate it more after you stepped into an open one." Using his pen, he pointed at a picture on the screen. "There are thousands of manholes. They usually lead down to a room below where the utilities can be accessed. This plan shows a water main called a trunk near the Piedmont. You open a manhole cover and climb down a ladder into the room where the main's located."

"A main is a big water pipe?"

"Basically. These trunk mains are two to seven feet in diameter. This one is easily big enough for us to crawl in."

"In what? Your frogman gear, wet suit?"

"Not without some work. These things are under pressure. We have

❖

to shut the flow off and release the pressure. We'd do that in the middle of the night so there aren't a hundred calls from people whose water's been shut off. We cut in with lasers and follow the pipe to where it runs along the basement of the museum. From there we cut into the basement. If it was the Met, it would be even easier, because there are so many tunnels passing next to and under the lowest level of the museum."

I was a bit skeptical about his motives for having gathered all this data. "You went through all this planning and data gathering so you guys could just *play* at a museum heist . . . like a computer game?"

"Ever since I read Victor Hugo's *Les Misérables* in high school, I was fascinated by Jean Valjean and the way he used the sewers of Paris to avoid the police."

"Why doesn't it surprise me that your favorite book hero would be an ex-convict?"

I doubted it was just an accident that this motley crew had a fascination for underground tunnels that passed under museums. Now I knew why the SEALs had a ready supply of weapons and equipment on hand. They actually had been planning a heist of the Metropolitan, one of the premier museums in the world.

Coby read my mind. "You don't think we'd be crazy enough to pull a heist on the Met, do you?"

"Of course not." The scary part was, I did. So far, he had lied about everything he ever told me and reneged on every promise he made. "Have you acquired one of those torpedo-size boring machines?"

He gave me a guilty grin. That certainly explained everything. What was next? The gold at Fort Knox?

I saw a problem with their plan to drill into the basement.

"What about all the noise when you're drilling through the solid concrete? Doesn't that stuff have lots of steel in it?"

"We're working on noise suppression."

"What if the drilling caused the building to tremble? The guard might feel it, and it might even set off motion detectors."

"We're—"

"Yeah, I know, you're working on it. I get the idea. I think I need some air."

"Don't get any crazy ideas," Coby said.

❖

"You think I'm going out to pull the heist by myself?" Good idea. But this one I needed help on.

I left them throwing ideas back and forth and went for a walk.

Boys with toys, was what I thought of the high-tech, imaginative caper that the SEALs were planning.

❖

61

❖

Staten Island is across Upper New York Bay, south of the island of Manhattan. My favorite cheap treat when I was a struggling student was to buy a ticket on the Staten Island Ferry and ride it over and back, starting at the southern tip of Manhattan and going by Ellis Island and the Statue of Liberty. As we sailed away for a quarter in those days, the most famous skyline in the world—Manhattan—would be seen from the stern of the ferry.

In a brown study, oblivious to everything but my own thoughts, I walked two blocks down to a view of the choppy gunmetal gray water of the bay.

The SEALs' plan bothered me. And failure wasn't acceptable. Our freedom and—if Stocker entered the picture—our lives were on the line. As I stared blankly out at the waters, my brain cells finally broke loose and I knew what bothered me about the plan: too high-tech. That was it. The SEALs were cooking up a robbery that required not only meticulous planning and execution but also complex machinery. That torpedo-size mole probably had ten thousand things about it that could go absolutely wrong at any moment. So did the plan.

❖

At the very least, I was reasonably certain that cutting through the steel-reinforced concrete in the basement would trigger the vibration sensors in the floors above. The sensors were put into the floors since it was impossible to cover the whole interior with motion detectors because of walls and furnishings. The floor sensors sent an alarm signal to the security room when they picked up the impact of footsteps after hours.

I also didn't like the idea of the spray paint. The mask was metal and could be cleaned quickly and returned to its display. But once the spray paint incident occurred, there would be heightened security, even to the point of calling in extra guard staff for a while.

No doubt by the time I came back they would have Moby, the thieving million-dollar robot, written into their script. It could knock down the front door of the Piedmont, walk to the display, grab the mask, and walk out, with bullets bouncing off it.

One thing about complicated plans like the one the SEALs were cooking up: If something could go wrong, it would. And the more complicated and sophisticated the plan, the more chances of something going wrong. NASA with its many failed space probes was a classic example of the fact that overcomplicating everything is a recipe for disaster.

Turning my back to the cold, cutting wind coming off the water, I walked up a street of small stores that were still surviving in an age of malls.

I certainly didn't want to end up in prison because a torpedo blew a computer chip, or whatever happened when they went haywire. I regretted the impulse that had gotten me into another situation that came with prison stripes in case of failure.

As I went past the display window of a TV store, two familiar faces appeared on one of the screens: Cassie the empty talking head was interviewing Angela St. John. I rushed inside the store to hear the interview.

"Angela, tell us this exciting news about you and the Semiramis!"

Cassie ended the sentence with a resounding verbal exclamation point.

Angela flapped her long phony sexy eyelashes in an attempt of modesty. *"I've been so busy building one of the premier museums in the world, I've ignored my career and my fans."*

Bullshit! I wanted to barf. Her contribution to the museum had been to pose for pictures that her PR firm planted in film trade magazines in the hopes of stirring interest in her career.

Cassie clapped her hands. *"So you've decided to move away from ancient culture and back into the movie culture limelight."*

"Really a combination of both. A project is in development for me to play the role of Semiramis in a period piece about old Babylon."

Cassie leaned forward with the expression children get when they're awed. *"Now tell the audience the exclusive secret you told me just moments before we went on the air."*

Give me a break. The "secret" was something probably cooked up at Angela's PR firm and approved by the show's staff before the appearance was even scheduled.

"Regression hypnosis revealed that in a past life I was actually Semiramis herself, the great warrior-queen of Babylon."

Cassie screeched out loud. The sound grated on my raw nerves like long, sharp fingernails. *"How exciting! Will you end up getting bit by a snake?"*

"That was Cleopatra, you dumb bitch," I said out loud.

"May I help you?" a salesman behind me asked.

"I'm beyond help."

I walked out of the store, steaming. The world was so damn unfair. I'd had to struggle my whole life while Angela St. John, not only born with beauty, also married great wealth and got fame thrown in. When luck was distributed in this world, some of us got shortchanged on our quota. And who made a rule of life that people like Cassie and Angela could be airheads and still get rich and famous? I just didn't get it.

I know there are all kinds of proverbs about being grateful for what you have, like the old saying "Don't complain about having no shoes when there are people who have no feet," but right at the moment I didn't give a damn. My feet were bloody stumps. I had a right to feel sorry for myself.

The thing that grated on me the most was Angela's taking credit for the Piedmont's success. She contributed nothing, and her husband's sole contribution had been inherited wealth.

And that nonsense about her playing Semiramis. Angela played bitches perfectly, but the ancient queen hadn't been one. Semiramis was a smart, dynamic woman who rose to power in a brutal world where might was right and disputes were settled by the sword.

❖

"Bullshit," I said, as I walked hurriedly down the street. That's what these people all sowed. Bullshit. They were neck-, not knee-, deep in it.

Angela's project in development meant her PR firm was putting out publicity feelers to see if anyone would be interested in doing the movie.

What a crock of— I stopped in my tracks. *Wait a minute.*

Semiramis. Movie. Publicity.

I walked slowly and stared straight ahead, an idea illuminating my brain cells as if a cartoon lightbulb had gone off in my head.

Angela was desperate to get back into the movies. She saw the publicity surrounding the Semiramis as her way to do it. Maybe it was the way for us to do our caper, too.

I wanted a low-tech heist. If the security system was too complex to deal with, a simple solution was available: Have the museum security turned off.

I giggled aloud as I thought about the reaction of Coby and the others when I told them my idea.

By this time, I was sure they had decided to hijack that big tunnel maker called the Mole to swallow the museum and carry the mask away.

THE GROUP WAS STILL gathered at the kitchen table when I got back. I quickly found out they weren't planning on hijacking the huge tunnel machine. Now they had themselves in full frogman gear swimming inside a large water sewer pipe near the museum's basement.

Disgusting. I shuddered at the thought of swimming through sewage. Even with protective gear, it would be the shits. Literally.

Only Coby acknowledged my existence as I stood there ready to make my announcement. I cleared my throat. "Gentlemen, Gwyn."

"She has something to tell us," Coby said. "Probably took a taxi over and grabbed the mask, right?"

"I wish. I have an objection to your plan. In fact, I have an objection to any plan in which we have to cut through the basement concrete. Floor sensors are sure to go off from the vibrations created by sawing, drilling, whatever you plan to do to get through the cement and the steel supports. There are multiple primary and secondary security devices that we would have to get by after we get in."

Coby held up his hand to quiet the clamor of the group. "Maddy, dear," he said, in a tone used to address a silly child, "we are not stupid. We're working on these problems. If you don't like our plan, why don't you come up with something better."

He didn't think I had a plan—so I dropped it on them without a preamble.

"I have. The best way to get the Semiramis is to have security turn off the alarms."

They all stared at me. Then looked at one another. The message from around the table wasn't hard to decipher: I was even more clueless about heists than they had imagined.

"Give me a break," Rob said.

Coby asked, "What have you been smoking?"

"I have a simple plan that will work. It revolves around Angela St. John, Hiram Piedmont's wife."

"The movie star?" Gwyn asked.

"The has-been, never-was-much, of a movie star." I couldn't help being catty about a woman who had everything. "She's desperately trying to stir up interest in a movie in which she'll play Semiramis. I saw her talking on TV about how she saw herself as the warrior-queen in a past life."

That got the appropriate hoots and howls from the guys.

"Hey, don't knock it," Gwyn said seriously. "In an age when we rewrite biblical history every week and see conspiracies and secret codes in paintings and Bible passages, there's nothing unusual about having been a queen three thousand years ago. I have a friend who swears she was at the grassy knoll the day JFK was assassinated . . . and she wasn't even born yet."

"Angela St. John playing Semiramis. Sex, violence, chariot chases, bad acting," Rob said. "Sounds like a winner."

"How does that translate into the museum turning off its security?" Coby asked.

I didn't have it all figured out yet, but at least I could them give the high points.

"A photo shoot is what I had in mind. We contact Angela, say we're with a European magazine and want to shoot her and the Semiramis together. If we tell her we've heard that she gets flashes of her past life when she puts on the queen's death mask, she'll really be revved up for a shoot with her wearing the mask."

"Hey! We can rent an office and have her bring it to us," Coby said.

I shook my head. "No way. The best way—the only way—would be a shoot at the museum."

"How would we set up a shoot?" Coby asked.

"By telephone. Follow up with fax confirmation. We'd have to call our company something. We probably won't be able to set the deal up with one phone call, so we'll have to get a telephone number that we can answer as if we're a photography company. Make it sound legit. I don't think there'd be a hitch. One of the assistants at the museum handles PR and basically acts as Angela's social secretary. She fields calls for publicity shots for the museum and the actress. And Angela is too desperate to refuse. She's got the ball rolling on this past-life thing and she'd jump at the chance for more publicity."

Silence.

I squirmed inside as they stared at me, but I kept up a brave front.

"How did you plan to get them to turn off the security system?" Coby asked.

"Not the entire system, just on the mask. It's done all the time. We're constantly moving, rearranging, cleaning, or even loaning out pieces. Magazines and commercials pay to send around a crew to photograph a piece that will go with something they're creating. They come in after hours and so would we. They'll turn off the security from the front door to where the mask is displayed."

"All the security?"

"No, they'd leave on the cameras that monitor the area we'll be working in and passing through. The important thing is that there's an RFID transmitter attached to the mask that sets off an alarm if the mask is moved. They'll have to turn it off."

"That's it? Camera, radio frequency tag?"

"Another couple of human security people to watch the camera crew as it passes by exhibits. You can bet that the guard in the security room will be watching the monitors like a hawk to make sure no one sticks something in their pocket."

"But how do we get the mask from Angela? Short of grabbing it and running?" Coby asked.

"The mask is on the mannequin. We say we need shots on the mannequin first. Then when the mask gets handed to Angela—"

❖

Gwyn jumped up from her chair, clapping her hands. "We make a switch of masks!"

"Exactly. We take the mask off the display and hand it to Angela—"

"That's when I make the switch!"

"You make the switch?" Coby asked Gwyn.

"I make the switch. Look around you. There is so much smoke and mirrors in this place, I could make an elephant disappear. I was raised by magicians and cut my teeth on a magic wand. I can do it. It's a piece of cake to make a switch."

"This is downright fuckin' insane," Coby said. "But I like it."

"You can thank me later." I grinned. Not too shabby a plan for robbing a museum . . . if I have to say so myself.

62

❖

Neal Nathan sat up in bed and sipped a twenty year-old Oenotheque Champagne from Dom Perignon. The only time he felt more miserable than he did right now was the moment of excruciating terror when one of his testicles was cut off.

He relived the feeling over and over . . . the feel of the cold knife against the warm skin of his sac. The horror as the scrotum was cut open. Unbearable pain as the testicle was removed.

A vital piece of his body was taken.

Fuckers. They would pay and pay and pay. . . .

His hand shook as he took another sip. The expensive champagne, bought at a wine auction and charged to Rutgers as an office expense, helped him wash down the pain medication and tranquilizer the doctor had prescribed for him. Neal had added a snort of cocaine to the concoction, but that was a mistake because it revved him up when he needed to sleep.

He perked up to listen as he heard a sound from another part of the house but stayed in bed. He was expecting his maid. "I'm in the bedroom," he yelled.

He leaned back down, groaning, not from physical pain but because

❖

he felt shitty. A single question kept roiling around his head. Why had he been so stupid to get involved in the Iraqi museum loot deal?

The whole mess belonged at the doorstep of that pompous bastard Lipton. May he rot in hell.

Before the Iraqi museum was looted, Neal had dealt with Lipton on a number of pieces that had dirt on them. The first several had been auctioned through Rutgers. But then Neal had wised up. Why should Rutgers get the fees? The Rutgers family knew what was going on but simply turned their heads the other way. If the police came sniffing around, the Rutgerses would throw him to the wolves.

The hell with them. He was taking the risks . . . he should get the rewards.

He had started doing treaty sales in which he brought buyer and seller together and kept Rutgers out of the loop. Quiet transactions, no publicity. A very nice profit. His Manhattan brownstone came from those dirty pieces.

Then the museum heist occurred and Lipton suddenly had an incredible inventory. No one ever had anything like it. But these had to be sold with even less conspicuity, and over a period of years, because the looting of the Baghdad museum received worldwide publicity.

A few of those deals and Neal had been able to purchase the Fire Island beach house.

He had no guilt about his secret dealings. The first Mr. Rutgers associated with the auction house started the business shortly after the Civil War when the defeated Southern plantation aristocracy was selling off their prize possessions. The last Rutgers family member to contribute to the bottom line at the firm died half a century ago on a trip to Saigon buying up prized possessions of French-Indochinese plantation aristocracy following France's military defeat at Dien Bien Phu.

When Neal joined the firm as an assistant appraiser fifteen years ago, the company was on its last leg . . . and even that was infested with powderpost beetles.

He had revitalized that arthritic old firm. His reward had been chump change compared to what he got from his secret side deals with Lipton.

Now those secret deals came back like a freight train running wild.

❖

Neal had made plenty of money. Why couldn't he stop? Stupid greed, pure and simple. The temptation of acquiring more wealth was always there. He should have quit when he was way ahead. He knew it then— and now. He blamed himself for squeezing more money out.

But he also blamed Madison. She should have just rolled over and played dead when her world came crashing down. Instead she fought back and caused nothing but trouble. She cost him his left nut, the fuckin' bitch. If he had a chance, he'd cut off her goddamn head. He didn't have to worry, though. That homicidal nutcase Stocker would kill her if he got his hands on her.

Neal washed down another tranquilizer as he thought about Stocker. What a fucking piece of work! Stocker was the one who had sent Neal's perfect world spinning out of control. A loose cannon—big-time. Scared both Neal and Lipton so bad, they had to put the Semiramis on sale. And got the police on their heels.

Deal with it, Neal told himself.

Neal knew exactly how he would handle the authorities. He was a gifted negotiator. He'd make a deal with the police. He would give them Stocker, Madison, too, though he'd have to make her more culpable than she actually had been. They could have Piedmont and his museum director, too. They all knew the pieces were dirty and turned their heads.

He had enough headline-grabbing details and people to get the police off his own back. It wouldn't be hard for him. He was a professional deal maker, and this would be the biggest deal of his life.

"Anna? Where the hell are you?" He needed another bottle of champagne and didn't want to get out of bed.

He wasn't supposed to be feeling any pain, but what the hell did doctors know? They told him he'd be able to lead a normal life . . . if nothing went wrong with his other testicle.

He thought again about the butchers who did this to him. *Fuckin' animals.* The police would have to guarantee him that they made no deals with his torturers. What he really wanted was them dead. He wondered if he could arrange that. Hell, he knew a hit man: Stocker would do the job just for the pleasure of seeing someone suffer and die. He'd have him take care of those thugs before he had the police remove Stocker from his life.

"Anna! Get in here; I need you."

"Anna can't make it," Stocker told him from the doorway.

THE BEACH HOUSE WAS on fire when Stocker launched his boat into the surf. Like the other ex-SEALs, he still thought in terms of movement on water. That worked out well for getting around some areas of the city. As the SEALs had done, he made his way to Fire Island in an inflatable rubber boat that was easily beached.

He had killed Neal and the maid without hesitation. It didn't bother Stocker. Never gave it a second thought. He was a mean bastard. He had been that way as a kid. He had a simple philosophy about violence: He beat up those he could and avoided conflict with those he couldn't. Like Mafia bosses and totalitarian dictators, he believed violence was just another way of doing business.

Stocker killed Lipton and Neal because he knew that they couldn't be trusted anymore. They shared a trait he saw in himself: the willingness to sacrifice anyone else to save himself. The police were on their tails. They would have rolled over on him. He would have done the same thing to avoid prison.

He wasn't through with the cleanup necessary in New York. He still had to kill Coby and the other SEALs. And the Dupre woman. He would especially take his time to make sure she died a particularly horrible death.

Like a pit bull, once he got his teeth into an idea he didn't let go until someone kicked him off. Killing the SEALs and killing the woman were concepts he had locked on and loaded. But he would make sure he got the biggest prize of all before he killed them.

When he was a mile from Fire Island, he used his cell phone to make a call.

"Hello, baby."

"Hi, lover boy."

Gwyn's voice came across the open waters clear and clean, not with the usual bad reception he got using his cell phone on city streets shouldered by skyscrapers.

With her help, he had almost killed the Dupre woman and Coby. After Gwyn called to tell him that Dupre had taken the SEALs' car and that she thought the woman might try to check out the warehouse, he had managed to take Dupre prisoner, intending to use her as bait to kill the SEALs. That plan had gone to hell, but the biggest prize of all was now almost in his reach.

"How are the plans for getting back the Semiramis?" he asked.

As a predator, he knew to wait and watch until it was time to leap and kill.

❖

63

❖

"I know where to get a mask for the switch," I told Gwyn.

Coby and the other SEALs had taken on the task of obtaining the necessary business address, cameras, and other equipment necessary for the appearance and front of a film crew.

Gwyn and I were in charge of costumes, including obtaining a mask that we could use for the switch.

We decided on dressing two members of the group in the robes, long curly beards, and helmets that were symbolic of the Babylonians. Naturally, since this was to be a shoot with a cinematic high-fashion look, the two ancient kings would be women—Gwyn and myself.

"That works out nicely, because you have to make the switch," I told Gwyn. "We'll stand behind Angela and you can turn around and take the mask off the display and hand it to her. You make the switch at that moment."

While she made the switch, I, in turn, would stand beside her and hope to God I wasn't recognized under the beard and robes. But being there in disguise was necessary: I had to stay center stage to keep an eye on the mask. I planned to make my own switch at some point, because I

❖

had no illusions about my fellow thieves honoring our bargain to return the mask to Iraq.

"We'll need to get you colored contact lenses," she said. "When Angela St. John and other people at the museum stare into your eyes, we want them to see the soul of a stranger."

Good point. But before we headed for a shopping mall optometrist, my cell phone went off.

Nunes ordered me to report immediately to the federal corrections building.

"He wants me to report to my personal interrogation cell," I told Gwyn.

I was scared as hell. When I got there, he informed me that Neal and his maid had been murdered.

"Both of them had their throats slit before the place was torched," Nunes said.

I sat down and the tears started. I wasn't even sure why I was crying. Certainly for poor Anna, the maid. She was innocent. I guess for Neal, too. The ugly mess that began with the looting of the national treasures of a poor country had turned into a bloody nightmare.

"We're certain it was your friend Stocker," Nunes said. "He likes to torch his crime scenes."

He claimed they had no leads on finding Stocker. Which meant I had to keep an eye on my back.

"We're on a terrorist attack alert for the subway system, and it takes the priority over art in the police world," Nunes had told me. "We don't think he'll try to kill you, because you've already talked to the police. Not unless you're hiding something he wants."

Of course, Nunes's tone inferred that I was hiding plenty.

"I'm hiding nothing but my fear."

And loathing, I wanted to add but didn't, *for a justice system that lets people like Stocker come after people like me.*

I took a series of taxis and subways for an hour to get back to the house. I was still confident that Nunes wasn't wasting his "assets" on a 24/7 surveillance of me, but I wanted to make sure.

"It was a good thing I cried," I told Gwyn later. "The fact that I didn't know they had been killed proved to Nunes that I wasn't involved."

❖

Getting masks for the switches wasn't difficult. The Piedmont Museum bookstore sold good reproductions of the Semiramis.

Wearing a head scarf and dark glasses and looking like someone in the Witness Protection Program trying to disguise herself, I waited in a taxi two blocks from the museum as Gwyn went in to buy masks.

I needed my own mask for the switch that I would be making, so I had her get several and gave her a good reason. "That way we can practice your switch without worrying about damaging a mask."

When we got back, Coby examined one of the reproductions. I assured him that it looked really good. "I was the one who had the reproductions made for sale. I insisted they look real. There's not much detail on the original, so it wasn't hard to do."

"But what about the weight?" he said. "She's probably handled the Semiramis. So have you. How does it compare in weight?"

"Close enough." The Semiramis was thin gold. The bookstore mask was stamped out of a lighter metal but a bit thicker. All in all, the outfit I commissioned, a group of artists who did repair and reproduction work for museums and galleries, had done a super job on the masks.

We bought a mannequin similar to the one at the museum display so Gwyn could practice making a switch as she took the mask off the display queen and handed it to Angela.

When the day of reckoning came, I had horrible stage fright. I stared at the blue-eyed Babylonian king in the mirror and wondered if colored contacts were how movie stars all got their blue eyes.

Besides my shocking blue eyes, I wore a tall, cone-shaped hat that resembled a beehive and covered half my head, a long, curly black Babylonian beard that came up to the hat and covered most of my face, and a floor-length robe big enough for two people. The only identifiable part of my body left uncovered was my nose. And I had never been accused of having a unique snout.

To make the disguise bulletproof, all I had to do was keep my mouth shut.

Gwyn was dressed the same but used her own eye color.

The arrangements with the PR assistant at the museum had been made, the "camera crew" had their equipment and manners down pat, and Gwyn and I were decked out like we-three-kings-of-Orient.

❖

"It's a go, Houston," I told the assembly. I smiled bravely and prayed no one saw how scared I was.

I secretly made one alteration to my costume.

I stuck the spare Semiramis mock-up mask in an inside pouch of my robe. I hadn't figured out how I would get the mask from Gwyn to make the switch. I would have to play it by ear, probably tell her I wanted to examine it.

I knew what I would do with the mask once I had it in my hand: take a taxi to the Jamaica Plains apartment of Abdullah's daughter and give it to her. Because of the sacrifices her father and grandfather made, she should have the honor of returning it.

Then I would run like hell, because there would be some awfully angry SEALs looking for me.

I THINK I WAS the only nervous person when we arrived at the Piedmont after closing time to film Angela with the mask. Gwyn and the SEALs talked and joked like they were on their way to a party. God, what nerves of steel. My nerves were stretched rubber bands ready to snap. How they could be calm was beyond my understanding. I imagined Angela taking one look at me and screaming that it was Dupre in disguise.

Was I just plain whacked-out from stress to imagine I could really fool anyone at the museum? And that we could switch the Semiramis? I knew that almost every major museum art theft was low-tech. But could Gwyn really make a switch with Eric standing by and a security guard watching the monitor of an overhead camera?

I had to be the only one with any common sense if the others didn't realize how crazy the plan was . . . and the only one with enough common sense to be scared, too. They say psychopaths don't have human feelings like fear and pity. If you have to be sane to be scared, I was the only one who wasn't crazy.

Coby read my fears. "No guts, no glory."

"You can have the glory. Just drop me off at the nearest airport so I can get a ticket to someplace where no one wants to kill me or arrest me."

Approaching the building in a van with the others, I was certain that I saw police helicopters and unmarked police cars. I half-expected Agent

❖

Nunes to be at the museum to greet me with a pair of handcuffs as I entered.

I recognized the guard who let us in and was tempted to say, *Hi, Carol*.

Carol looked at me and smiled. I kept a straight face and jaws locked and hoped she didn't see through the disguise.

Eric and Angela were waiting in front of the Semiramis display. A makeup artist was putting the finishing touches on Angela's face.

"The alarms are off," Eric told Coby, our film director. "But we have video surveillance from every angle. None of your people are to touch anything but the mask. And they must take utter care in handling it."

Eric hung around long enough to let Angela know that he was there if she needed anything and then disappeared, because he wasn't the one who was going to have his picture taken. Besides the prying eyes of the overhead cameras, one guard was posted in the room with us, but he stayed back, out of the way, and seemed to be more interested in watching movie star Angela than the rest of us.

That meant there was one less eye on the mask.

When we were ready to take our places to start filming, Coby had Angela take her place seated in front of the mannequin, Gwyn standing behind her on the right, so she could take the mask off the mannequin and hand it to Angela at the proper moment, and me standing next to Angela, on her left side.

As I started to take my place behind her, Angela stared at me. Really stared. In fact, glared at me. Jaw slack. Mouth open.

I began to melt down. Sweat poured from my underarms. My heart pounded against my chest. Had she seen through my disguise?

"Where did you get those eyes?"

I stared dumbly at her. Then stared into her eyes.

Holy shit—she is wearing the same shade of bright blue.

Coby stepped between us. "She's not going to be facing the camera. I'll have her look off to the side."

"She can look off to the side behind me. I don't want her next to me. You," she snapped at Gwyn, "change places with her."

No! I couldn't change places with Gwyn—she had to make the switch. I had a copy of the mask hidden in my robe, but it was in a pouch only accessible from the inside. Gwyn's robe had a slit on the outside to

❖

slip the mask through. And she was the sleight-of-hand artist capable of doing it with the security cameras rolling.

I didn't know what to do, so I stood frozen and did nothing.

"Are you dense?" Angela asked. "Answer me!"

"She's mute. She can't talk," Coby said.

"She can hear, can't she? Tell her to take her place behind me. And look away from the camera. Or this shoot is off."

"Take your place," Coby said. "Behind her." He didn't sound like the old, confident-even-in-a-hurricane Coby.

Oh . . . my . . . God. I couldn't do the switch. But like a mechanical doll, I automatically took up a position behind Angela. My knees shook. Sweat was streaking down the side of my face and into my long beard.

"Your beard's crooked," Gwyn whispered.

Her eyes told me she wasn't completely composed. No doubt she had imagined the door to a prison cell slamming shut when Angela reversed our roles. Gwyn stepped up in front of me and pretended to adjust my beard with one hand while she nudged me with the mock-up mask. I took the mask but didn't have anywhere to hide it. I kept it tight against my robe and hoped the folds would conceal it.

My left knee shook so bad I almost fell. Hypocrite that I am, I again silently beseeched the Good Lord for help. I hadn't been in a church since Sunday school and hadn't needed God for anything as long as I could remember, but as my father used to say, there are no atheists in the foxholes.

Maybe it wasn't such a good idea to ask for heavenly intervention to rob a museum, but I had pure motives.

When the camera crew was in position, Coby said, "First we are shooting Ms. St. John without the mask. When I signal you, remove the mask from the display and hand it to her. Never look directly at the camera."

It took a couple seconds to realize that he was talking to me. I repeated the words to myself: *Remove the mask from the display and give it to her.* And make a switch. Sure. I might as well rip off my beard and scream to be arrested. I was screwed. And for the first time, I saw something akin to worry in Coby's face: His usually calm features were locked tightly.

The fact that he and Gwyn were silently panicking didn't do much for my own confidence level.

The camera rolled.

Coby gestured at me.

I stared at him.

He grimaced and gestured again. *Give her the mask,* he silently mouthed.

Time to make the switch.

I turned and detached the mask from the gizmo that made it look as if the mannequin-queen were holding it. I fumbled it. The mask dropped to the floor at my feet.

The world stood still. Not a sound could be heard.

The sounds of silence were shattered by Angela's scream. The shrill outburst sent a jolt of pure panic juice shooting from my toes to my head.

I bent down to grab the mask. As I bent over, I switched the fake mask to my right hand and picked up the Semiramis with my free hand, keeping the real mask concealed in the folds of the baggy robe.

"Get her out of here before I kill her! Get that creature away from me!"

As Coby shot forward to grab me by the arm, I dropped the fake in Angela's lap.

Coby took me to the side. "Stand right here. Do . . . not . . . move." His eyes told me that he'd kill me if I budged an inch. He knew I had made the switch.

Coby and Gwyn calmed Angela with the medicine that worked best on her—flattery—and the shoot continued.

After Coby yelled, "Cut," like a pro, Angela replaced the mask and stormed out immediately, but not without a good-bye comment to me: "Fucking moron."

Strangely calm, I resisted the urge to taunt her with, *Ha-ha, I've got the mask; I've got the mask!* I kept it exactly where it was when I first grabbed it—pressed in a fold of the robe.

That meant I had to keep the hand holding it in an awkward position. If any guard took a good look at me, it would spell disaster.

We were heading for the door when Eric shouted Coby's name. My knees melted and I felt as if I were going to pass out.

"You forgot to give us your insurance papers," he told Coby.

Coby slapped his forehead. "Christ, sorry. They're in the van; I'll bring them back."

I just walked quickly out as Eric told Coby and the others that they also needed to film the outside of the building.

As Coby lamented that they couldn't do it now because of the lack of light, I made a run for a taxi parked outside. I told the driver, "Jamaica Plains. Hurry."

❖

64

❖

The driver pulled away from the curb and never said a word about my costume. Only in New York could a woman dressed as a Babylonian king get into a taxi without any questions being asked.

My insides were quivering gelatin. I had reacted out of pure instinct. The SEALs must have some murderous thoughts right now. And I would be the victim in all of them. God, I felt as if my feet were tangled in the webs I'd weaved and I was really to collapse.

We hadn't gone far when the cabbie suddenly pulled into an alley and slammed on the brakes. The way out was blocked by a large gasoline tanker truck parked at a gas station at the far corner.

He turned in the seat and slid open the dirty Plexiglas window that's supposed to separate drivers from robbers. He pointed a pistol at me. "Don't move."

I closed my eyes tight. Kidnapped again by an Iraqi. Same man, same taxi. *Stupid, stupid, stupid.* I was so worried about the SEALs behind me, I hadn't taken a good look at the driver.

Coby arrived in less than a minute and opened the door. He gestured for me to get out. I climbed out and tried to maintain a brave

❖

front, but I was dying inside. Caught red-handed trying to do the right thing.

"I was on my way back to the boat."

"Where did she tell you to take her?" he asked the driver, who had gotten out and was standing on the other side of the cab.

"Jamaica Plains."

Coby raised his eyebrows. "Funny. I don't remember the boat being parked there." He held out his hand. "Let me have it."

"It belongs to—"

"Me. I stole it first. Give me the mask."

"You promised to give it back to the Iraqis."

"Did you really think I would do that?"

"No."

"Then it wasn't a real promise, was it?"

"That's no—"

"Look, I'm actually going to keep my promise. The mask is going back to Iraq."

"Fine. Then let's get it to Abdullah's daughter."

"For a price."

"What do you mean?"

"I want a finder's fee."

"What? How can you get a finder's fee for something you stole in the first place?"

"Done all the time, remember. That's the main reason high-profile art is stolen. It can't be sold because it can't be displayed, so it's sold back to the owner for ten percent. In this case, we're making the finder's fee an even five mil."

"A starving country isn't going to pay millions to get back an antiquity."

He shrugged. "Hiram will if they won't."

"Bastard."

He grinned. "Thank you. I've worked hard at it. The mask?" He held out his hand.

The driver yelled something and then ran. He had yelled in Arabic and disappeared around a footpath that led between buildings.

Coby yelled, "Where you going?"

❖

I looked to the rear and gasped. A large black SUV had pulled up to block the end of the alley we had entered.

Gwyn was in the driver's seat.

The passenger door opened and Stocker got out, holding a machine gun.

❖

65

❖

"Get down!" Coby shouted as he pulled a pistol.

I wasn't about to stick around. I ran for the pathway at the back of the buildings, in the opposite direction the cabbie took. Behind me I heard the dull pops of weapons with silencers being fired from the alley. I was running as fast as I could in my disguise when my world exploded.

Knocked off my feet, I went down, stunned, lying facedown on gray brickwork pavement. I stared blankly at the brickwork. I thought I'd been hit by something, but I realized I'd been bowled over by a blast of air and noise.

I rolled over and sat up, looking back at the taxi. It was on fire. My brain was numb, but I knew immediately what had happened. Stocker's machine-gun fire had ignited the tanker truck.

I struggled to my feet and staggered back to look for Coby. A blackened human form was wedged under the back wheel of the taxi. All I could clearly make out was the soles of the shoes.

The burning taxi blew. I wasn't hit by debris, but the explosive sound caused me to spin around and keep going the other way.

My mind was swirling. I had enough sense left to know I had to get

❖

away and to take off the Babylonian robe. I held on to it as I came out of the walking path from behind the buildings.

I walked into a scene not dissimilar to the day Lipton's gallery had been blown up—excited people asking one another questions about what had happened.

I pushed through the crowd and kept walking until I came to a subway station and stumbled down the stairs like a zombie. Without thinking, I tried to get by the gate without a ticket. I fumbled in my pocket and got out a ticket with a ride still on it.

As I boarded the first train that arrived, I had no idea as to where it was headed. I just sat down and stared blankly at the opposite wall. The car was almost empty.

No one had lived through the blast in that alley; I was certain of that.

Poor Coby. Even though he had a criminal mentality, he had never really tried to hurt me. Not even when I double-crossed him twice. I grieved for him, but something inside me kept my tears back. I felt stone dead, like I had no feelings left. Just numbness from the horror I'd seen. I had fallen for Coby. Another victim of loving the wrong person.

Stocker deserved to rot in a burning sewer in hell for eternity.

I hoped to God Gwyn survived the blast because she was in the SUV. I liked her. What I didn't understand was, What was she doing with that crazy maniac bastard?

The subway had been heading downtown. I got out when it reached midtown and walked until I found myself in front of a car rental.

I needed to get distance between me and the city, to think things out. I wanted to give the mask back to Abdullah's daughter, but right now I didn't have the strength or courage to find my way to Jamaica Plains. I wanted to hide, to find some peace. Do some thinking. Figure out what I was going to do with the rest of my life. Figure out what I was going to say to Special Agent Nunes if he asked me why I had robbed a museum and blown up part of the city.

❖

Royal Lust

In *The Divine Comedy*, Dante sees Semiramis (along with Cleopatra) among the souls of the lustful in the second circle of hell.

The image was drawn from her history as a woman who loved . . . with a vengeance.

Semiramis (Sammu-ramat) first came to royal attention when she became the mistress of a King Ninus, an Assyrian general who was besotted by her beauty. The general conveniently committed "suicide" so she could marry the king.

Said to have a voracious sexual appetite, she quickened her royal husband to the grave after he discovered she was enjoying sex with palace guards.

Upon seizing the throne, she became infatuated with Ara, the handsome young King of Armenia. Spurred by his rejection, she invaded Armenia.

The young king fell in a battle against her army in the Ararat Valley of what is now Turkey.

Grieving over his death, Semiramis beseeched the gods to bring him back from the dead.

The gods sent doglike creatures down from heaven to lick Ara's wounds, bringing him back to life.

66

❖

Life had taken me from a park-view penthouse on the Upper East Side of Manhattan to a sleazy sex motel off the Jersey Turnpike.

I kept thinking about Coby. My body and mind had relaxed enough now to grieve over him. How could I have loved a man with a criminal mentality? I knew the simple but correct answer to the question: People don't pick out who they choose to love.

Anyone who thinks a man or woman chooses who they love needs a reality check. Women who have led honest, faithful lives as mothers and wives have run off with motorcycle trash or bought guns and helped scumbag felons escape from jail. Men with good business sense have trashed their marriages and careers and run off with secretaries, babysitters, or the coworker in the next cubicle.

Soul mates came together without rhyme or reason. They just happened. And they weren't always made in heaven. If they were, Gwyn's attraction to Stocker had been the work of the devil.

Her choice was nuts, but I don't believe it was voluntary. I've never blamed any of the people who get themselves into bad relationships. Love is not rational.

I'd heard the New Age word "karma" bandied about most of my life. But what exactly did it mean?

Fate? Destiny? Some sort of magnetic attraction?

Magnets have no choice in what they attract. Fate and destiny are a done deal—you are attracted to who your kismet bonds with.

Right at the moment, I didn't know and didn't care if cosmic forces were at work. I just knew that there was a vacant place in my heart now that Coby was dead. Bastard that he was, he was the bastard that I loved.

I cried myself to sleep with the john grunting and the whore faking ecstasy on the other side of the wall. And woke up from a nightmare of being in a dark room and having a man beside my bed. That much was a bad dream.

Getting a phone call from the dead was the real thing. I returned the call.

"You're supposed to be dead!"

"Would I be calling you if I was? That was Stocker's scorched body under the cab," Coby said. "As he came up to the taxi, I rolled out the other side and made a dash behind the buildings. Stocker got it as he came forward shooting from the hip."

"What about Gwyn?"

"She got away in the SUV. No doubt to put some distance between her and her partners now that we know she's been double-crossing us. That tanker truck was parked at the station for the night, almost empty. It made a hell of a bang but just blew out some windows. Stocker really took it from the gas tank in the taxi. I think his bullets started the fire and then—boom!"

"You bastard. You're really alive."

"I'm glad to hear you're overjoyed at my miraculous escape from the jaws of death. Not to mention we're clean as to the museum job. It's pretty certain your FBI pals will pin the museum heist on Stocker and that Viktor Milan guy who just keeps fading away the closer anyone gets to him. Must have been Milan that Stocker was after when he bought the farm in that alley. Hey—we're in the clear, baby."

He was right: I was bubbling with joy that he wasn't dead. But that good news was now past history by at least thirty seconds. This man had lied to me repeatedly. And now I had the upper hand: the mask.

❖

"Coby, listen carefully. You are one of those extremely rare criminals who are likeable. But you are still a criminal. And a liar."

He started to reply and I told him to shut up.

"You've lied to me and lied to me and lied to me. It's over, done with, kaput. Do you understand? No more lies."

"Scout's honor."

"Shut up, you idiot. And listen." I took a deep breath. "The mask is going back to the Iraqi museum. No arguments, no recourse. It's going back. Period."

"Maddy—"

"No, it's going back. That's a done deal. You've broken every promise you've made about the mask. This time I'm not listening to you. It's going back to where it belongs."

I heard tapping on the door. It sent my heart racing.

"Maddy—"

"Somebody's at my door."

"It's me. Open the door."

"What?"

"Open up."

I closed my eyes. It couldn't be. This couldn't be happening to me.

The knocking on the door became more insistent. I refused to believe it. It wasn't possible.

"Open the door, Maddy. I don't want to have to kick it down. Neither one of us can afford to have the cops called."

"How did you find me?"

"GPS device in the heel of your shoe."

"You sonofabitch."

"Just protecting our investment. We figured you'd never let us offer the mask back for a finder's fee."

"Of course not. It has to go back to Baghdad. I knew you were lying."

"You see? It's been a misunderstanding all the way along the line again. Now open the door before I kick it open."

I didn't fool myself with wishful thinking that the pervert at the front desk would help me if my door got kicked in. Or call the police. Not that I wanted the police called. But it would be nice if I wasn't constantly at the mercy of every predator that came along.

❖

I opened the door and faced his big grin. "You really are a bastard."

"For sure. But let's not dwell on the past. I have a couple of associates waiting that are eager to come in and break your neck. We need to get this over with before they decide they'd rather strangle you and hang than peacefully walk away with a five-million-dollar finder's fee."

"You and your buddies are the scum of the earth."

He clutched his chest. "God . . . that . . . hurt. Now give me the mask." He stepped into the room, making me give way.

"Bastard." It was the only word that kept coming to my tongue.

"Can we get beyond the personalities?"

The mask was on the dresser. I swear, the bitch was leering at us.

"Ah, the queen herself."

I shot for the dresser and Coby caught me. "You don't want my pals coming up. They blame you for Gwyn, too."

"What did I have to do with Gwyn?"

"Everything went to hell after you entered the picture. Even Stocker got crazier than he was before."

"Blame her." I pointed at the mask. "Not me."

He took the mask off the dresser. I reached for it and he put it behind his back.

"Maddy, give it up; it's not going to happen. You can't believe we robbed the museum in Baghdad while armies clashed and robbed a museum in New York while security cameras rolled just to let you give it back?"

"You don't understand what you're doing. You haven't grasped it yet. There's a curse on the mask."

"There's five million dollars on the mask."

"You'll never see the money and even if you did, you'll never live to spend it. The curse is real. Walk out of here with that mask and it'll get you."

He kissed me. Long and hard. The press of his lips against mine made me want more.

"I'll be back. With plenty of money for us."

"I don't want your blood money."

"I'm going to take you back to Europe. We'll buy a yacht and sail the Mediterranean and—"

"Rob antiquities from shipwrecks?"

❖

He patted my tush.

"Helluva idea. We'll do that, too."

I started to call him a bastard again as he left, but instead I leaned against the door frame and watched him go. Hopeless. He would never be, well . . . normal. He had gone to the dark side of art and would never come back. But my heart was still with him. And I knew that in his own mind he wasn't taking something from me. He was, as he put it, preserving an antiquity, and making a handsome profit to boot.

"Damn you," I whispered.

I gathered up my stuff. I left behind my shoes that alerted a satellite somewhere in space where I was and walked out barefoot. I was tired of leaving a trail.

Pulling out of the parking lot, I followed roads that led back to the turnpike. For the first time since I raised the paddle to place a $55 million bid, I felt at peace. My conscience had been bothering me for so long. It was finally going to be put at ease.

So much had happened since the day a taxi driver named Abdullah walked into the museum and accused me and everyone else of being less holier than thou. And he was right. He was the towel head, the camel jockey, and we were materially superior for having the cars, homes, and other economic miracle of Western society. But we were the thieves of his culture.

True, I didn't know the mask was part of the looting of his country's national museum. And most of the harm to the museum and other antiquity sites came from the Iraqis themselves. If I had known the mask was stolen, I would never have urged Piedmont to buy it. But I was also careful to look the other way.

What I didn't do expressly I did by not looking askance at something that was too good to be true. I sinned by omission.

But that was over, now.

What was that about life being a circle? All your bad deeds come back to bite you? That's why I had to return that bitch queen back to Iraq. She was truly the Whore of Babylon. And she wasn't going to let me live in peace until she was back in her own country, playing hell with those poor people.

I didn't know how that would affect Iraq, but right now I had my own skin to save from her dark curses.

❖

Once I was over the bridge and five minutes from my destination, I made a call. It was late, but it was never too late for good news.

"I have something for you," I told Abdullah's daughter. "I need you to come down to the street in front of your apartment."

What I had for her was the death mask of Semiramis.

We had entered the museum with two fake masks. Gwyn had one to make the exchange. I had one in an inside pouch of my robe, intending to use it later to make a switch for the real one.

Gwyn slipped me her fake and I gave it to Angela.

I left the museum with two masks: the real one and the fake that was inside the robe pouch.

I carried the robe into the motel room with me and put the fake mask on the dresser after I realized I still had it.

Coby took the fake mask.

Semiramis herself, or at least the real impression of her face after death, was in the glove compartment of the rental car. I had left it there when I went into the motel. Hoping I'd left bad luck behind.

She was still there, in the glove compartment. No doubt glaring at me with those shadowy empty eye sockets. Probably thinking of ways she could twist the steering wheel so my car went off the bridge.

The only way to keep out of her clutches was to dodge the bullet. That's what I was doing. Now it was going to be up to the Iraqi people.

As soon as I made the drop—and got the promise from Abdullah's daughter to swear that she had found the mask on her doorstep—I headed for my apartment. It might have been cleaned out by my creditors. I didn't know, but I wanted to see that park view one more time.

Along the way I made a phone call.

The most important thing about Coby was that I never had to fake my orgasms with him. That meant a lot to me. And it was time to let him know that he shouldn't quit his day job in expectation of getting millions.

"Coby, about that yacht you were going to buy with the finder's fee . . ."

❖

67

❖

Shifting from a buyer of antiquities to protecting the cultural treasures of the world came as a natural for me. So I set myself up in business.

My business card read: "Art Inquiries."

I thought the word "inquiries" had much more class than "investigator," which is really what I was. I liked that it sounded a bit British, too.

Anyway, the fact that the SEALs would have collected a $5 million finder's fee for returning the Semiramis had left an indelible impression on me. Million-dollar art and antiquities were pretty common on the market. A 10 percent finder's fee of $1 million was a lot of money for a girl who had fallen from grace from her park-view penthouse, Jag convertible, and black American Express card.

Hiram was suspicious that I had something to do with the loss of his prized possession but could never prove it. But his badmouthing me was enough to get me blackballed from the small, intimate world of being a museum curator.

I lost my job, but art was in my blood. Like a vampire, I had to stay around the trade to feed my bloodlust. And if I could track down and recover works of art and antiquities from thieves, preserving the cultural enrichment of the pieces, while making a living . . . why not?

❖

I just had to stay alive while I rubbed shoulders with Mafia and mafiya, IRA thugs, Middle Eastern terrorists, and Colombian drug lords, all of whom trafficked in multimillion-dollar contraband pieces. Not that I didn't have an inside track in the world of stealing and smuggling art: the SEALs.

There were no hard feelings between Coby and me. He thought it was clever that I had switched the real piece for the mock-up. His pals still wanted my hide, but after all the hell that came down over the mask, they'd decided that maybe there was something about the curse that they needed to duck.

Coby and his buddies were off searching for a Nazi submarine that went down with a load of diamonds off the coast of Africa back in WW II.

Gwyn did a disappearing act, no doubt with the help of her magician parents. The SEALs hadn't heard from her since the day she drove Stocker over to kill us.

I launched my new business by simply buying business cards. I was back in a walk-up on the cusp of SoHo, Chinatown, and Little Italy, about a hundred blocks—and an economic eon—from where I had lived when I worked at the Piedmont Museum. I was brooding about how I would pay next month's rent when I answered a knock on my door.

The Thai guy who delivered my take-out orders from a restaurant down the street stood there with a grin and a brown paper bag. He was real restaurant Thai, imported from the Old Country with a hard-to-understand accent. Sometimes I think he used pidgin English because he thought that's how I expected him to talk.

"I didn't order anything."

"You art person. Something to show you."

The name plate at the building entryway said I was in the "art business" to justify my existence in the world but hadn't gone into details. Not that I wasn't willing to pick up a bargain for resale if the right piece came along.

He put the paper bag on my coffee table and took out an object wrapped in a foreign newspaper, a slab of dark gray-green stone about the size of a car license plate.

I sucked in my breath and tried to maintain a poker face.

The carved images on the stone were *Apsarases,* angel dancers. The exotic dancers were beautiful water and forest nymphs who played music and danced for the gods.

"Found in grandmother's attic."

He spoke with a heavy Thai accent and mouthed the words as if he had memorized them from a low-budget movie.

"Uh-huh."

I didn't know if they had attics in Thailand, my image was thatched roofs and sandy beaches, but I had a pretty good idea where this Far Eastern art piece had come from: Angkor Wat, the magnificent temple ruins in the jungles of Cambodia. Archaeologists claim that the structures at Angkor are the most fabulous on earth, surpassing even those of Egypt.

Like so many other treasures of the Far East (and Near East), the magnificent ruins are prey for tomb robbers. And Bangkok was one of the routes that the antiquities traveled on their way to Japan and the West. Along with heroin.

I felt dizzy. Nothing short of greed and lust to possess this piece was gripping me. A museum in town that specialized in Oriental art would die for it. So would a horde of collectors.

I might even be able to squeeze a curator's job out of it.

Okay, grandmother's attic might not be the best provenance, but it could be true . . . couldn't it? And even if it wasn't, with a little doctoring we'd soon find out that the piece came to America two hundred years ago on a clipper ship . . . and the captain conveniently drowned a few years later, making it impossible to doubt "his" word that he had—

Oh, hell, I couldn't do it, even if Oriental art was the rage among Americans and Japanese and I was sorely in need of a break.

The piece in front of me had to be worth half a million, maybe more, even with a suspect provenance. And what kind of "finder's fee" could I get from the Cambodian government if I called Special Agent Nunes and he turned it over to them? A thank-you note on embassy stationery? Cambodia was another one of those third-world countries with problems up the yin-yang.

I sighed.

"You like?"

"Hmmm. Very nice."

❖

As much as I needed the money, I just couldn't let the cultural treasures of a small, poor country in Asia be sold by tomb robbers on the black market of stolen antiquities.

I smiled at him. "You could make a lot more money if there were more of these."

He grinned and nodded. "Many more."

As soon as I found where the "many more" were being held, I'd call Nunes.

I wondered what he'd say when he heard from me again. Last time I saw him, he had me in the federal corrections center, hammering me with questions about the theft of the Semiramis from the Piedmont. Which I had replied to by following Neal's advice of deny, deny, deny.

Later, after I turned in the Thai mafia, or whoever the tomb robbers were, and recovered cultural treasures of a small, poor country, I could worry about paying my rent and whether I would be murdered for my efforts.